PRAISE FOR

'A first-class thriller'
The Times

'*The Goldenacre* features a dense cast of vivid characters, not
least Tallis, a tortured pilgrim worthy of a Graham Greene tale
. . . an ambitious and wonderfully realized work'
Wall Street Journal

'A riveting, brutal journey into the high stakes world of legacy
art and inherited wealth'
Denise Mina

'Unusual and elegant'
Alan Massie, *The Scotsman*

'Outstanding mystery thriller . . . noir fans won't want to
miss it'
Publishers Weekly

'A literary thriller in the tradition of *The Goldfinch* . . . but
better! The suspense is real, the stakes are high, and the
mystery actually gets resolved'
Deadly Pleasures

'Beautifully written, with a brilliantly vivid sense of place and
a killer twist, *The Goldenacre* is one to savour'
Liam McIlvanney

'A gritty, propulsive and moving thriller'
Kirstin Innes

'Art, music, politics and murder, set against a backdrop of one of the most beautiful cities in the world – what's not to love?'
Lesley Kelly

'Phil Miller's Edinburgh is a city of secrets . . . imbued with the touch of supernatural shadows but also unshakeable goodness'
Jackie Copleton

'A novel about identity; what is fake and what is real; the veneer versus the reality, both of its characters and of the city itself'
Sunday Post

'Its vivid sense of location is one of this mystery's great strengths'
The Herald

A NOTE ON THE AUTHOR

Philip Miller grew up in County Durham and now lives in Edinburgh. An award-winning journalist for twenty years, he is now a civil servant. His previous novels include *The Blue Horse*, *All the Galaxies* and *The Goldenacre* (winner of the Shamus Award for Best First P.I. Novel), and his poetry has been published online and in print.

The Hollow Tree

Philip Miller

First published in 2024 by Polygon,
an imprint of Birlinn Ltd

Birlinn Ltd
West Newington House
10 Newington Road
Edinburgh
EH9 1QS

www.polygonbooks.co.uk

1

This is a work of fiction. Names, characters, businesses,
places, events and incidents are either the products of the
author's imagination or used in a fictitious manner.
Any resemblance to actual persons, living or dead,
or actual events is purely coincidental.

ISBN 978 1 84697 648 3
eBook ISBN 978 1 78885 659 1

British Library Cataloguing-in-Publication Data
A catalogue record for this book is available
on request from the British Library.

Typeset by Initial Typesetting Services, Edinburgh

For Samantha and Thomasin

In deope dalum / deora ungerim
In the deep dale / live many wild beasts
—*Durham,* anon.

hello

Shona Sandison was going to a wedding. The day would end in death.

She stood on the deck of the ferry, leaning against the metal barrier between her and the tilting sea, which stretched grey as ash to a white horizon. The world seemed huge and unfathomable, and she felt small and damaged, and unsuited to what it offered and challenged.

She was not alone. An old colleague and friend was beside her, shouting into the implacable Scottish wind. Shona looked down at her shoes, wet on the painted metal deck. Her stick was held tight in her left hand.

'Fact is, Shona, I think they're just bored of democracy, these people. They don't care for it,' Hector Stricken bellowed. 'A wee touch of fascism appeals to them. Look at them, propping up this fucking government. Seems to me, some of them prefer to be collaborators, not investigators. Cheerleaders, drunk on their access to power. They should be ashamed of themselves.'

His angry monologue had begun on the train from Glasgow to the port of Gourock. Stricken, still hanging on as an undervalued and underpaid reporter at the *Edinburgh Post*, had then raged at the front pages of the national newspapers at the ferry port's newsagent. He had picked out and bought several papers, just so he could stride across the platform to a waste basket, and bin them dramatically.

'Give it a rest,' Shona said. 'Not all of them, and not all of us. Calm down.'

Stricken went on. Shona listened, or heard. She watched the

neat rows of white houses on the headland drift past like a line of teeth. 'They're not interested in committees, reports, policy reviews, the granular workings of a rigorous democratic system. It bores them. That's why there's no council reporters any more. No court reporters. No specialist reporters. No local government reporters.'

'Really, Hec – you sound like my dad. The old Communist digging in his allotment. I need a coffee.'

'Does he still have that allotment? Good on him. Yeah, the problem is that fear, that angry nostalgia, the appeal to a mythic past, is far more attractive and easier to package than probity, reserve, compassion, moderation, compromise, subtlety.'

Shona nodded slowly. Not only had she heard this before, she had thought it before. Her body rocked gently as the ferry moved, slowly and massively, into the cold grey waters of the Firth of Clyde.

'Nuance!' he yelled. His bellow sank in the air and was lost.

'Jesus Christ. Give over, man,' Shona said, as firmly as she could without shouting. 'It might be rotten politics, but, whether you like it or not, it's good business. For those papers.'

'It's a bad business,' Stricken mumbled. 'It's the ruin of democracy.'

'Och, wheesht. I know some good reporters in those papers. And the papers you binned are at least selling – more than can be said for yours.'

The ferry chugged into thick mist. It was as if they had entered an erasure. The form and volume of the hills and the sea had been rubbed out by dreary light. The distant deep hulks of mountains were smudged and edgeless. The sky was as solid as the water below – grey, lightless, unmoving.

Winter was dying hard. It had spent its spite and drowned the land in volumes of darkness, but spring had not yet emerged. It was as if the seasons were considering whether to continue their cycle, as if they had paused.

'I tell you, though, it's not going to end well,' Stricken said. 'I think the whole country's fucked.'

'Come on, Hector – wasn't it always?' Shona said, turning to him. 'I seem to remember everything being fucked. All the time. It's just sometimes the things that are fucked are hidden or ignored. Then we all find the hidden fucked things and are astonished – wow, isn't *this* thing fucked too? Let's add that misery to the Fucked Pile. Which gets higher and higher, until it falls on fucking top of us, and then we are all well and truly fucked.'

'Well, if you put it that way.' Stricken smiled.

'Contentment is about how much you are prepared to ignore,' she said.

'Brief period, wasn't there,' he said, quieter, 'maybe in the nineties? When it seemed to me that things were on their way to being un-fucked. When we were all a wee bit younger. Then it was all wrecked again. That was probably a delusion. I think this state as a serious concern is over. No one reads the news. No one cares about anything – just shopping, sport and celebrities.'

'You're a miserable old git, Hector,' she said. 'I was wearing a school uniform in the nineties, and I don't remember too much light and hope and joy then.'

Her fingers were freezing. Her hair was wet with sea fog. As if pushed by an invisible hand, her walking stick fell to the deck, splashing in a small puddle on the green metal. 'Fuck's sake.'

Stricken picked it up and handed it to her. 'Anyway, enough about you, Reporter of the Year – how do I look?' he said, suddenly smiling, extending his arms. Despite his sudden humour, he looked miserable: his long nose was purple, his cheeks the same. Under his red anorak, he was wearing a new suit: dark blue, with thin white stripes, the tie a vivid, shiny blue. A white shirt dug into his neck. Raindrops gathered on his plastic shoulders.

Shona smiled. 'You look like the Antichrist.'

He shook his head and turned, leaned against the barrier and looked out over the sea.

'You buy that thing?' she said, pointing at his suit.

'No, rental. From that place on George Street.'

'I thought you'd go for a kilt.'

'I don't like my legs,' he muttered. 'I don't want them on display. Look, Shona – how can a man wearing a suit as fine as this look like the Antichrist?'

'You telling me Satan doesn't wear a fucking suit?' she said.

He laughed.

Shona stared into the thundering waves, which churned in coils of green and white against the hard sides of the ferry. 'When you're on a boat, do you ever look over the side and wonder what it would be like to jump?' She imagined standing on the railing, her weight tipping forward, her stick spinning in the wind, her body tumbling to the water. The sky and sea revolving about her eyes.

'What? No, Shona, I don't – do you?'

'No. Never,' she said. She peeked over the rail, down to the deck below. It would not be a clean fall to the water. There would be metal in the way, and breakage – rupturing, blood and splintering. She shivered.

'Aye, it's dreich,' Stricken said, noticing her quivering, raising his voice over the engine noise. The ferry was rocking almost imperceptibly from side to side. Enough to unsteady them.

'Who in the name of fuck gets married in winter?' Shona said, pulling her hat over her ears.

'It's spring, actually.'

'Get fucked – it's winter,' she said. 'I hate this time of year. Everything is dead. It's all chores and dread. White skies and fog. Why is Viv getting married now?'

'I dunno – because people are optimistic? It's spring, it's a time of renewal, of green shoots, of . . . you know what I mean. Optimism, anyway,' Stricken ventured, before blowing into his

4

hands. His eyes were watering now, as the ferry to Dunoon picked up pace, cutting stolidly through the waves.

Shona felt the increase of the barrelling weight of the vessel beneath her feet. The sea was opening, the firth widening between the arms of grey land. The white cloud cover split, and the sun emerged, glowing dully. The waves were now gently gilded. The metal railings glistened, the deck, the flagpoles.

They were going to a wedding. Vivienne Banks and Wayne Provan were to be married in a country hotel near Dunoon. Viv was both a friend and former colleague of Shona, and of Stricken, and of the gaggles of journalists who were huddled on and below deck. Viv had been the editorial secretary of their paper, the *Edinburgh Post*, for many years. Wayne worked for the police. Shona had met him in a pub, many months ago. He had seemed dour, unremarkable, like an undrunk cup of grey cold tea.

Viv, bright as a needle, was from the North of England and had a way with blunt observations and crude descriptions. She could be lawless and sardonic. She was also warm and, sometimes, chaotic fun. They had spent many hours and evenings together. Shona closed her eyes.

The tang and drift of the sea summoned memories. There had been one long, hot day in July when the streets of Edinburgh shimmered and the heather on Arthur's Seat seemed to fume with heat. The sky, untouched and fierce and blue. They had skived off work together and headed for the coast. They had waded, socks in hands, in the sea off the beach at Gullane, and lain together on the slowly sinking dunes, drinking from a cold long bottle and wondering how they could ever get back to the city, and if they cared. There were other memories, too. Shona shrugged them away. They were lost. She wondered if Viv remembered them.

For the wedding, Viv had asked Shona to read a poem by the nineteenth-century Scottish magician and poet Ebenezer

Mount. Shona had tried to memorise it. The folded words were in her inside pocket. She hoped she could read them without stumbling.

Like hands our fears do tether,
and once joined, disappear,
like tears that run together,
pool, and become our mirror.

She thought of Viv's dullard fiancé – and if poetry meant anything to him.

'I'm not sure what she sees in him,' Shona muttered.

'Who sees what in who?' Stricken said.

'What she sees in that guy.'

'You mean the handsome groom? And do you see anything in anyone?' he said mildly.

'Go on then, tell me more about him,' she said. 'Tell me about his hidden shallows.'

'I don't know him much.' Stricken shrugged. 'Think he's in the polis. Seen him a couple of times in the pub with Viv, seemed a pretty confident guy.'

'A knob, then.'

'Why's that?'

'I don't trust anyone who actually wants to wear a uniform.'

Stricken shook his head and looked along the deck. He saw someone he knew and waved – they nodded and waved back. 'There's a lot of hacks on this wee boat.'

'I know. Just think – if we hit a submarine and go down, consider the vast loss to Scotland,' Shona said. 'To culture.'

Stricken rubbed his eyes.

'So, what's the plan? We get off this tugboat, get to the hotel, find our rooms, get pissed?' Shona said.

'That's about it. Shall we go inside? I'm done in, and it's Baltic out here.'

'You're hungover again.'

'Yep, I drink to forget,' he said, running a hand through thinning red hair.

'Forget what?'

He smiled. 'I've forgotten. See? It worked. Let's keep it that way.'

They moved down the slippery deck to a heavy metal white door, which Stricken held open as Shona stepped unsteadily inside.

The café was busy with commuters on the short trip from Gourock to Dunoon, as well as the wedding party, laughing and chatting in groups. Loud music played, the coffee machines screeched and trays clacked in the canteen.

After some fussing, Stricken brought hot drinks, and Shona slumped onto a plastic chair fixed to the deck next to a table.

He slumped beside her, almost horizontal. 'So, how's the freelance life?'

Shona had been a freelancer for six months, working from home, still living with her elderly father in a small flat in the Lochend area of the city. She had taken a redundancy package from the *Edinburgh Post*. The money was running out, and her life had become solitary. It gnawed at her. She was missing the newsroom, with its easy chat, its joking and teasing, and its familiar faces. She spent most days on her bed or at her kitchen table, tapping at her laptop, with only an increasingly distracted Hugh Sandison as company – or her new rescue cat, MacDiarmid. Her dad had slowed down recently. He was often forgetful, tired, and he shuffled instead of walked. He kept losing his glasses.

'Fine,' she said, smoothing the froth of her coffee with a finger. 'I've got the column with the *Mercury*, and I'm on this retainer with the Buried Lede.'

'How are they?' Stricken peered. 'It's an investigation unit, right?'

'Aye. They're not bad, actually,' she said, shrugging. 'They let me get on with it. Ranald's all right – the editor. He set it up. Ranald Zawadzki. He knows how to sell our stuff to the papers.'

'Zawadzki?'

'Yeah – usual spelling.'

Stricken smiled. 'Ah, the old newsroom jokes are the best.'

She went on: 'He's a bracing guy from Shetland. We work alone or together on things and sell to the highest bidder. The Buried Lede has funding from a couple of non-profits. Ranald directs it all. He's into looking at dark money, offshore banking, that kind of thing. I do all kinds of stuff for them. Not all of it comes with a byline. There's a clutch of us on retainer. So, I'm washing my face. But not by much.'

Stricken blew out heavily. 'Sounds like hard graft. And uncertain. What you working on at the moment?'

Shona was working on nothing much. She'd spent weeks covering the trial of a disgraced Scottish minister. She had filed a column for the *Sunday Mercury* that morning. That was it. She was out of ideas.

'Oh, bits and pieces,' she said. 'Got some long-term things I'm working on.'

The ferry suddenly lurched to one side, and Stricken swore. Then he sat up, said something about creasing, took off his coat and jacket and slung them on a chair.

There was a burst of laughter, and Viv Banks and her parents staggered into the canteen, exaggerating, with staggered steps, the lurch of the boat. Viv waved and winked at Stricken and Shona. Her parents, looking nervous and seasick, smiled thinly.

A pale man in a suit came over to their low table. He took off his jacket and laid it down on a seat. His large eyes flickered. He had a shaven head and was holding something in one hand.

'Don't mind if I leave my stuff here, do you?' he said to Shona. He had a soft Northern accent. His face was open and mild.

8

Shona said not at all. His jacket was like Stricken's – blue, with thin white pinstripes.

'Thanks, pet,' he said quietly and joined Viv and her party. There was a loud cheer as the family joined the other guests. Someone hugged Viv and kissed her on the cheek. Viv beamed and wiped a tear from an eye. The pale man moved to one side and slipped behind the crowd to the bar, where he ordered a drink.

'Who is that guy?' Shona said, nudging Stricken. He did not reply. She leaned over to look at his long face, dusted with freckles and ginger stubble. He was fast asleep.

She finished her coffee, then walked to the windows. The town of Dunoon was coming into view, grey and low on the coastline, under the emerald-green opening sky.

The drone of the engines altered their pitch as the ferry approached the harbour.

More peals of laughter rolled from the wedding party. Shona looked around, and for some reason two men were lying beside each other on the floor, flapping like beached fish. People were clapping. Viv was sitting with a drink, a man with his arm around her. Her parents were looking on, smiling. The pale man was at the bar, his sleeves rolled up, drinking with no expression. He was turning something over in his hand – a pebble or a small ball. He looked drained, barely present.

The tannoy burst into life with a shudder and a squeal. The announcer said the entire crew, including the captain, wished the very best to Vivienne Banks and Wayne Provan on their imminent nuptials. People cheered. Shona grinned.

Her phone rang. It was buzzing around her inside pocket like a small animal. She took it out. The word DAD shouted at her from the screen.

'Hey,' she said. 'You all right?'

'Hi, darling,' Hugh Sandison said. There was no background noise. His voice was weak.

9

'What's up, Dad?'

'I'm not feeling too good, hen,' he said. 'I've called the doctor. How's the wedding?'

'It's not started yet – I'm on my way, remember?' she said. 'Wait a minute.'

She moved from the window and out of the café, over a bulkhead door and into the corridor. It was quieter. The ferry moved under her feet. The sky was being pulled past a porthole. Nothing seemed to be where it should be.

'What do you mean, "not feeling too good" – have you been sick?'

'No, not sick. Just a bit weak and woozy, and a wee bit of a pain. In my chest. In my arm. Doctor said come to the clinic, but I feel a bit too peely-wally for that. Someone's coming round.'

'What, an ambulance?'

'Aye, love, the ambo. I'll be fine. You have a great time. I'll call you from the Western. Took ill at the allotment. But home now.'

Shona took the phone away from her face and swore. Her heart, she noticed, was suddenly racing. She was stuck on a boat, a hundred miles from Edinburgh.

'Dad, I'll come back – I just need to get on the next ferry back to the mainland. It'll take me a while.'

'No, love, Bernie will be with me. Don't worry. I'll be fine. It's probably nothing.'

Bernadette Comfort was her father's friend from the allotments. A small, steely woman. Her father had insisted, when teased, that there was no hint of romance between them. Shona didn't quite believe him. She wanted to.

'Right. Is Bernie there now?'

'Aye, she is. She's packing me a bag.'

The ferry shuddered, and a garbled cacophony of words over the tannoy announced something. Somewhere deep in the ferry, something boomed.

'You on a boat?' he said, louder. 'I'm worried about leaving MacDiarmid.'

'Yes, Dad, the Gourock ferry! And don't worry about the cat!'

'Grand – that's the taxi now. Speak soon, darling!'

'Taxi?' she bellowed, into silence. The call was ended.

Stricken shambled into view. His jacket and anorak were back on, a bag over his shoulder. 'Is that you calling a taxi, Shona? They've put on a minibus for the wedding party. No need to worry about–'

'Oh, for fuck's sake,' Shona shouted, staring wildly at Stricken.

'Just thought I'd mention it,' he said, backing off. 'Dunoon has arrived. I mean, we've arrived at–'

'Fucking hell, Hector,' she said and shook her head. She closed her eyes and dragged a hand through her hair.

Through the windows, the port had come inexorably into view, as if dragged to them on sub-sea chains.

She texted her father – *Take care Dad. Call me when you can* – and followed Stricken onto the main deck.

As the ferry slowed to the jetty, a text flashed back: *He's fine, I'll let you know how it goes. He doesn't want any fuss, enjoy your wedding – Bernadette.*

'It's not *my* fucking wedding,' Shona said loudly as the ferry quietly slowed to a stop.

Some heads turned, and Stricken whispered urgently, 'You all right?'

'Fine,' she said, shoving the phone into her pocket. She smiled broadly at Viv, who was peering at her from across the room. A crowd of jostling, half-drunk passengers gathered by the door for foot traffic. As Shona pressed to the door, Stricken close by, she could see the pale-faced man; he remained seated, alone at the bar, looking into his drink, turning the little object over and over in his hand.

Stricken turned to her as they stepped through the metal door. 'Who's this MacDiarmid you keep talking about?'

'A cat,' she said.

'Oh,' he said, looking flushed. 'Not a guy, then.'

'No – she's much better than that,' she said and pushed him in the shoulder, to encourage him to leave the ferry.

Shona had phone calls to make, and quickly.

I

Ashley had not intended to go as far as Deepdale, the day she found the shirt.

The last guests had left her mother's bed and breakfast. She tidied and cleaned the rooms, pulled sheets from beds and replaced them, hoovered and dusted. In the en-suite bathrooms she used detergent and bleach, emptied the bins and washed down the mirrors. Someone had left a used condom in the bin. She wrapped it in loo paper and chucked it in the rubbish bag.

The Gildersleve Bed & Breakfast sat on the outskirts of Ullathorne, with meadows on three sides and the vicarage nearby. High trees leaned and whispered over its eaves.

As she cleaned, she could hear the nesting rooks and the buzz of a farmer on his quad bike. Ashley worked slowly and steadily. She had to: her mother had dropped any concessions for her condition years ago.

It was a bright day in Ullathorne, County Durham. Across the market town, which clutched the valley of the River Tyr, the old stones glistened, wet, in the uncommon winter sun. On a cliff overlooking the river, sharp shadows sliced through the ruined castle. The sunlight cast broad shadows on the market cross with its tiled roof and knotted pillars, on the curving cobbled main street and across the roof tops that dropped to the broad, surging river. The town seemed to gleam, as if newly washed, sluiced free of the long winter months of mud and grit and dead vegetation.

There had been snow and ice, only days before. The dale had been transfigured in white, with narrow roads impassable, the schools closed and the river numbed by the suddenly descended beauty.

Under the snow, the town was revealed, became fully itself – a stone town in stony hills, an old settlement for humans to stay warm and fed in the old mountains. By the river, waterfall, tree and standing stones. It had been alive before England. In some form it would endure beyond it.

Jess needed walking, but Ashley was tired. The dog was bouncing around the stone-flagged hallway, emitting tiny yelps, paws skittering.

'We need a few pints of milk,' Ashley's mother, Peg, called from the hot kitchen.

'All right, Mam,' Ashley called back. She briefly looked in the mirror in the hall. Her long hair was bedraggled. She pushed it into her woollen hat and pulled on her wellies with one hand, sitting on the bottom step of the wooden stairs. Jess put her two front paws on Ashley's knees and licked the tip of her nose.

'Give over,' Ashley said, and soon they were out of the old lodge's door, across its gravel drive and onto the narrow path beside the road that led into Ullathorne town.

The land was still. It was a Saturday morning – the market was empty, the children in bed, the bottle factory running its shifts as if the weekend didn't exist. Ullathorne days were the same as Ashley had always remembered them: quiet, the trees moving as much as the streets, the river saying more than the people. Flags snapping on the church roof, heritage flags snapping on the ruined castle. Trucks rumbling over cobbles, cars grinding along the main road to Darlington. The river glinted over the old ford. The morning breeze rattled twigs in the churchyard but did not reach the unmoving silence of the trees in the deep woods.

Ashley walked quickly up the wide county street. Jess, off her lead, trotted beside her – along the path, which ran past the shuttered Masonic Hall, past the old garage, past the solicitors where Ashley and her mother had been read her father's will, past the circular market cross and down the Bank – the steep street of old buildings that led down to the river and the woods.

Ashley was in a dwam, her thoughts screened behind her waking eyes. As if sleepwalking, she walked, sure-footed, to Deepdale. She had not thought of going there, but moving smoothly as if on rails they crossed the river at the metal pedestrian bridge – painted blue-green and creaking slightly in the wind, its Victorian rivets large like plates, its tubular towers like great funnels – then over a narrow road and finally over a low stile to Deepdale. Tyrdale was joined in its fold in the hills by other valleys, valleys that broke off from the main course of the river, and Deepdale was one, a deep cutting that moved west into the Pennines.

It was a tight valley of ancient trees, unfelled since a time beyond remembrance. A beck ran through its heart, but as Ashley trudged into the trees and Jess ran about her, she realised – even though she had been born and raised here – she did not know the stream's name. It chuckled and spat as she headed into the woods.

The path was thick, tacky mud mixed with Durham County Council gravel, and they quickly reached a fork in the way. Onwards lay the depths of the woods, to the right a shallow basin of lighter trees and undergrowth and a path to the moors. The late winter light glittered through the canopy of leafless trees. Snowdrops nodded in sprays of life.

At the junction, Ashley leaned on a tree stump.

'I didn't mean to come this far,' she said. Jess briefly lifted her shaggy head, her nose a black drip of wet, and then ducked down and snuffled on.

Ashley had been walking too fast. She needed to catch her breath. She was tired and knew more fatigue was to come: what was there for her in the days ahead? The weeks and months? More guests to clean up after, more breakfasts to prepare, more rooms to tidy. More small talk with guests. The dog to walk. An emptiness sat in her stomach. A tingling anxiety in her mind. The woods and the trees and the beck and the rocks: they were here when she was a bairn, when she was a teenager, when she went to university; and they were here, unchanged, unmarked by any passing of time, when she came back home with her degree unfinished and her heart sore. It was as if they lived outside time.

Jess jumped up at her, her pink tongue lolling like ham. Her eyes reflected the clear cold sky in sparkling crescents. She smelled of dog and damp, mulch and mud.

'Howay, then,' Ashley said, and they marched on, deeper into the dale. She whipped the spare undergrowth with a thin stick held in her good hand, her weak right hand clenched to a fist and plunged deep in her pocket, as her boots trod harder and faster into the woods.

Soon, Ashley was squelching through mud alongside the stream, splashing in its shallows, as the woods closed in, black and spare.

Jess was up ahead, a quiver of movement in the tangled distance. The beck was swollen from the snow melt of the moors above and swamped the narrow path.

Ashley moved further into the trees, away from the uncertain depths of water. On a slide of mud and stones she almost lost her balance, but her hand quickly found the rough trunk of a silver birch, its skin peeling, and she did not fall. She looked at her hand – there was a tiny roll of bark, tightly coiled, tremulous, clinging to her skin. She blew on it, and it drifted down in spirals into the undergrowth.

She felt like turning around now. She had to go home via the Co-op and load up on milk. A desire clutched at her heart – to hide in her room and write her book. She was thirty-four thousand words in now. She thought about it as she marched on into the trees, which thickened and crowded about her. She wondered how to describe the next scene she planned to write

– it was a party scene, with alcohol and scrapes and kissing and drama. She had been struggling with a passage about the beauty of the land, and how hostile that beauty was. How hostile any kind of beauty seemed. She would return to it later.

As she pushed on through the trees, she knew this was the only way forward – she just had to keep writing. She had to keep living this temporary, quiet, cheap life in this town and finish the book, and keep typing, revising, correcting and getting it right before she sent it to someone, see what might happen next, if anything might come of it. She wanted to be published. She wanted her story – the story of a young woman just like her – to be out there, in the world. So she could feel real.

An unfamiliar concrete wall appeared in her path. Ashley stopped. It was as if it had just been dropped in front of her. She had not been this far into Deepdale before – or, at least, not within her memory – and did not think there were any buildings here. It was a ruin, a roofless concrete block, with one side missing, stained green and brown, throttled with ivy.

She called for Jess, and her mongrel head poked out of a low window, which had lost its frame and glass many years before. Ashley walked around the wall and saw that the insides of the building had been retaken by the valley. There were tall weeds, and the ivy, everywhere, a flung sheet of tangled green slung over the ruins. The concrete smelled damp and empty. There was loss and abandonment. She could not imagine that the building had ever had plumbing or electricity – it was a shell, its purpose lost to time.

There was a growling noise. Jess was now in the corner, pulling at something, her back legs taut and straining.

'Jess, give over,' Ashley said sharply. She did not want Jess pulling at a dead animal, getting guts and muck in her mouth.

She looked closer. In the corner of the ruin was a hole, as if newly dug, and around it were small stones – clean, as if recently polished or washed. Gleaming black and grey and brown. It was as if they had been lifted out from the earth. Maybe the snowmelt had raised them, she thought.

The dog kept on pulling – she was growling louder now, growling at the thing in her teeth, and the weight or knot of something had stopped her from ripping it free and whole from the ground.

'Jess!' Ashley called. Her voice vanished into the overgrowth, into the stands of silent watching trees.

Ashley moved to the dog and peered at the straining clump of saliva, mess and grot in her mouth. Her white teeth were grappling with something murky and black, something made of material that was half-buried in the ground, in the black sludge of time.

'What you got?' she said to the dog, who suddenly let go and whimpered, running around in a jerky circle, the weeds parting about her.

'What you got?' Ashley repeated. The clump of material and grime was half in and half out of the muddy hole. With a wince, she reached out with her hand and pulled on it, and, after something snagged under the surface, it came free.

But she was unbalanced with the force of the pull and landed on her backside in the mud with a soft squelching thud. Jess, all legs and nose and teeth and tail, wriggled over to her and licked her forehead, and then licked at the thing in her hand.

'For God's sake, Jess,' Ashley said, finding a way of pulling herself up with the aid of ivy and stone. The dog jumped up to snuffle the material, but then stood stock-still, tail up, before bounding away out of the ruin and into the woods.

Ashley realised she was holding a sodden piece of clothing, folded up, coated with years of groundwater and mud, of the work of worms and the nameless slime of the forest soil. She took her right hand from her pocket and grabbed hard at an edge of the clothing, between thumb and finger. With her other hand, she shook the folds and creases of the clothing free.

Inside, its concertinaed folds were almost clear of mud. Black and white stripes were revealed, and an elaborate yellow crest – it was a Newcastle United football jersey, torn and ragged. A sponsor's name, *Greenalls*, was written across its chest. In the area where a belly would be, there was a large rip. She turned it over, and on the back the name *Jet* was spelled out in large white letters.

Some small white things fell to the mud – three or four plastic beads, with holes for hanging on a string. They lay in the mud like seeds.

Ashley went back to the corner where Jess had pulled it from. The hole had filled with mud and water, as if it had never been there at all. The earth had hidden it, given it up and closed again. The stones lay around the hole, as if on guard. She picked one up – heavy, solid – and dropped it in the hole. It sank into the meltwater with a splash.

The shirt hanging in her hands was old and heavy, dripping black water. The dale around her was quiet, save the running stream, the wind picking up, creaking the high boughs, the fingers of the trees snickering together.

Ashley peered around the ruin, but there was no sign of anything save plant growth and a cloud of loss. At that moment, the sky turned from blue to grey, and a spot of rain fell on her forehead.

She yelled for the dog, and Jess appeared in a flash, her legs thick with new mud.

'Come on, Jess, let's gan yam,' Ashley said. They made their way back to the path, and the town, Ashley clutching the folded-up shirt in her filthy hands, her legs wet from her fall.

The skies opened as she emerged from Deepdale. The tattered shirt began to smell of something heavier than just mud.

2

The hotel bar was roaring with noise. In the cacophony, music was blaring over the laughter, bellows and shouts of a hundred drunken journalists and ex-journalists – and their girlfriends, boyfriends, partners, second wives and first husbands.

At the bar, Shona's former news editor, Colm, was telling a story about how he had once pursued a famous footballer at a hundred miles per hour down the M8. And, in the scrum of bodies around Shona's table, Stricken was telling the outlandish tale of how he and another journalist, who may or may not have been a spy, had chased a story about drugs and diamond smuggling between Amsterdam and Glasgow.

Shona had only had a couple of drinks and was sitting in the bay window. She looked through the whorled glass to the sea, a mile away, churning black, lights moving upon it. The mountains across the water were dark and impenetrable, their bulk cutting into the star-spattered night sky.

'And anyway,' Stricken was yelling, several drams down, to a gaggle of old hacks who had heard this tale, or a version of it, many times before, 'when we got the story, my contact, old Ken, didn't want to be paid at all, not in cash anyway. He just asked for a blind eye to be turned to the weapon he had bought from a dope-dealer in Haarlem – an AK-47! He kept it under his bed. Hundreds of rounds he had for it.'

Everyone exclaimed, and Stricken took a swig of his whisky before continuing. Shona stared at her phone, stomach tightening, knees gripping her stick.

'Anyway, after we got the job done and I filed the story, we went out, dodgy Ken and me, in Brussels.'

'I thought you were in Amsterdam?' someone said.

'Och, we'd moved on,' Stricken said. 'Anyway, we were well gone – blootered. So, we were chucked out of this bar we were in, and Ken was staggering all over the place. He yelled for a cab, and he got in, and I fell in after him. Literally. Face to the floor. Ken was shouting at the taxi driver, "Take us to the Hotel Metropole!" And the driver was like, "Are you sure?" and Ken was yelling, "Take us to the feckin' Metropole! *Tout de suite!* I have many euros! *Vamos! Schnell!*" And I was on the floor, saying to Ken, "Are you sure the Metropole is not in fucking Holland, Ken? In Amsterdam? Are we driving all the way back to Amsterdam?" And he was yelling at me, "No, it's not. It's our hotel in Brussels, you idiot." And I'm like, "Whatever, I just want my bed. Drive through the night for all I care." And the driver was shouting back, "Minimum charge in this cab, twenty euros! There's a minimum charge!" And Ken was raging, all up in his face. And the driver, cool as anything, just shrugged. Ken was shouting, "Victory!" and I was lying on the floor. So off we go on our epic journey to the Hotel Metropole . . .'

Stricken paused for breath. People were smiling and giggling. Shona had witnessed the retelling of this story at least four times before. She stopped herself from rolling her eyes.

'Anyway! Off we go! Ken had collapsed by now. Eyes rolled back in his head. Goodbye to his SAS training. I was on the floor, breathing in carpet. A week of hard work and a lot of grass and a day's worth of drinking. I was in a state, let's be honest. And the taxi driver pulls into the road, does a neat little U-turn and stops outside the hotel opposite – the Hotel fucking Metropole! On the other side of the street!'

The table groaned. Shona couldn't help smiling. Stricken, red in the face, stuck up two thumbs and grinned. 'Classic,' he said. 'Those were the days.'

Shona looked at her text messages. No update from her father. The last text remained: *At the Western, all good so far.*

B. She had received it hours ago, after she had left the ferry, and after some cajoling from Stricken and Colm that convinced her to continue her journey to the hotel. But she had wanted to turn around and go home.

The wedding was to be held in the hotel's main ballroom the next morning, and, given the state of the party, she figured, would be a sombre and hungover affair. Viv, who was now wearing a pink cowboy hat and a string of Christmas lights around her neck, was standing by the fire, surrounded by her close friends and family. Firelight glowed in their glasses and faces. Viv was laughing, her head back, eyes closed.

Shona closed her own eyes and could see only her father's bearded face, asleep in a hospital bed. He had been tired for a few weeks now. He had slept in until midday recently – the first time she could remember – and had been annoyed. He'd stomped around, slammed his coffee cup down. The old journalist, the old Glasgow socialist, hated being late, or feeling lazy. He had not been up to his allotment for weeks, and it had weighed on him. She could tell he had been frustrated, angry with himself, but had no energy to break out of it. There had been signs of something going wrong. But she had missed them: or ignored them.

As she looked around this room, though – with its press of happy human bodies, the laughter and the drinking, the music and the firelight – she knew he would love it that she was here, this rambling old country hotel in the heart of Argyll. He would have savoured the scent of the roiling sea, the creaking trees, the emptiness of the surrounding land and the cold majesty of the night sky.

'Anyway,' Stricken roared, 'it's my round!' To loud cries of 'At last!' he collected the orders from their table. Red-faced and red-haired, he turned to Shona with a grin.

'JD and Coke, Ms Sandison?' he said.

'I'm all right, thanks,' she said.

'You sure?'

'Aye, just need a bit of fresh air,' she said, standing up, gripping her stick tightly.

Shona moved unsteadily through surging bodies. A hand appeared on her shoulder. She turned her head, and it was Viv.

'Hey there, my love,' she said. 'You all right, doll? Where you off to? Need some air? I think we all need a bit of that.' Viv burst out laughing.

'Aye.' Shona smiled. 'Nice party.'

'Oh, it's lovely to see everyone in one place, isn't it? It's like the old days,' Viv said. 'I'm not sure Wayne has seen so many old hacks in one spot – he doesn't know what's hit him.'

The fairy lights around her neck clinked. The cowboy hat tipped. She looked over to the groom, who was propped, or being held, against the bar by his friends – large men in bright suits.

'Here,' she said, her mouth coming closer to Shona's ear. She smelled of perfume and wine. Her eyes were wide and almost wild. She spoke in a breathless slew. 'I hope your old man is okay, pet, but I'm sure he is, and as you say, he has someone to look after him, and let's be honest, Shona, you need a break from looking after him all the time, and if he's texting you, well, he's fine, isn't he? Sure it's just a wee scare, and, look, tomorrow, after the do, you can run back, get the ferry and you'll be home for tea, so don't fret, it'll all be fine. I am just so chuffed you're here. You need to be here, with me. I love it that you're here.'

Shona nodded.

Viv's eyes were glinting. 'And you have a good time tonight – is your room all right? You're across the hall from my old pal Dan, from back home. Oh! There's Stuart and Donald!'

Viv spun on her heels and collapsed into a giggling, pink embrace with her two friends, one with a salt-and-pepper beard, the other about seven foot tall. They were the only journalists dancing, slowly and drunkenly frugging to their own unheard music.

Shona slipped from the chaos and clamour into the gloomy hallway. When they had arrived at the Poets' Hotel, she had noticed a garden, illuminated with a circlet of white glass globes. She headed there.

The noise of the party faded. Beats became thumps, voices became meaningless, the laughter untethered. In the reception area, excursion brochures flopped out of plastic pots. A sleepy woman was clicking through something on her computer screen. Golden light fuzzed on wooden panels, brass handles and the portraits of famous poets that lined the wall – old men, framed. No women, she noticed.

She made her way outside, into the darkness, and crunched along the gravel track that led around the side of the hotel, past the bay windows and into a small parkland. Beyond was open country and the vast sky, bedazzled with stars, banks of clouds moving slowly over the three-quarter moon.

She walked between high hedges and reached a silent stone fountain, set in a pond. In the still water, the moon rippled and fractured. She sat on the cold stone lip and tried to call her father. It rang out. 'Hugh Sandison here. Leave a message – if you like,' his voice said. She remembered the day she had finally convinced her father to put a proper voicemail message on the phone: a lot of fuss and huffing and, several takes later, this brusque, whispery message.

She didn't leave a message. She hung up and found the number for the Western General. It rang out, too, and she realised she could not face keying the various options and enduring the waiting music. Bernadette would call her if there was an emergency. And it was late now, anyway. Her father would be asleep, and Bernie had probably been sent home.

She looked up to the black and purple vault, the scattering of stars – so many more than she could ever see at home in Edinburgh. And so many more out there, unseen, in the immensity.

The bulk of the hotel loomed above her – three storeys of red stone, heaped in the Scots Baronial style, with four turrets, battlements and flags: a Saltire, a lion rampant, a forlorn EU circlet of stars. They hung limp in the windless night.

A familiar ache crept through her stomach, her chest. It crawled up her neck, like a cold pool of water, slowly enveloping her frail, injured body. She put a hand to her head. These parties, these get-togethers, they were few and far between now. The old newspaper office – her home, her comfort, her life – was gone now. Newspapers were contracting, folding. Many reporters worked from home now. The old *Post* newsroom on Rose Street was shutting. Stricken worked from his dingy flat in Leith. Colm bossed around the news desk from his new-build in Barnton. Fuck knows where the editor, a shaven-headed idiot from Glasgow called Ingleton, lived or worked: probably a basement full of skulls somewhere, she thought.

The newspaper industry, as she had known and loved it – the loud newsroom, the daily deadlines, the jokes, the swearing, the smokers' gallery, the presses, the pubs – had been destroyed. That life – that lifestyle – was dead. This party would be the last gathering. Viv's wedding was a funeral, of sorts, for their lives in newspaper journalism.

So, no wonder everyone was paralytic. The uncertain future was as overwhelming as the vault above. The sweet lulling pleasures of a full bottle of Jack Daniel's struck her as an appealing prospect. So did the deep, endless sea. Her mind reached a sheer black wall and retreated.

She started as feet in smart shoes crunched on the gravel. By their stuttering, long gait, she wondered if it was Stricken. He came loping into view, holding a suit jacket in his hands and shouting, 'Dame Shona Sandison, as I live and breathe.'

She smiled, even if she had not wanted to.

'Why, if I am not mistaken, is that Impatience on a Monument?' he bellowed. He moved towards her and then stopped. 'Viv's going to do a wee speech, thought you'd want to know.'

Shona nodded.

Stricken held up the jacket and grinned. 'And this is not my jacket. I've managed to mix mine up with someone else's. Bit of a bugger. My cash card is in my own blessed jacket. So – alas and alack – I couldn't pay for my round.'

'How awful for you,' she said. 'You must be devastated.'

He moved closer, holding the jacket as if it was a fish on a line, lifted from water.

She put her hand to the suit jacket, with its pale lines barely visible in the dark. 'Have you looked in the pockets?'

'Why would I do that?'

'To find out who's it is, genius.' She took the garment from him. It was light and silky in her hand. Shona looked to see if it had a name tag. It did not. No markings at all. She put her hand in the inside pocket. There was a book of some kind, and something small and hard.

She fished out a small black Moleskine diary. She then pulled out the object. It was a polished pebble, smooth as an eye, with a paler stripe running through it. Shona put it in her pocket, moved closer to one of the lamps and, leaning her stick on the hedge, knelt, so the light fell on the diary.

'What does it say?' Stricken said. 'Whose is it?'

She flipped the stiff pages, but there was no name written within. None of the diary pages had any marks on them either. She put her nose close to the spine – it smelled new. Something was tucked into the envelope slot at the back.

She pulled it out: a folded piece of paper on which were written, in neat black ink, four lines of text:

abdargninetytwo
sorleysays–taketherightpath–
sayyestono–
–thereisnotime–odeadaheado

27

She peered at it for a while. She could not make sense of it: was it a poem of some kind or notes for a kind of creative writing? Maybe song titles? *Odeadaheado*? A nonsense word.

She put the diary in her pocket, alongside the pebble, and folded the jacket over her arm.

'Shona, the speech, come on,' Stricken urged.

When they reached the bar again, Viv was already addressing the party. People were gathered around the bar, in the blazing yellow electric light. The music had been turned off, and Viv was standing on top of the bar. She was tall, and her head seemed perilously close to the ceiling. A round of applause was just coming to an end, accompanied by some whoops and cheers, as Stricken and Shona slipped through the door to the bar.

'. . . and it is also lovely to have the two special people without whom I would literally not be here, my lovely, beautiful parents, here with me in Scotland . . .'

There was more clapping and whooping, and by the fireplace Wayne put a practised hand to her father's shoulder, and her mother dabbed an eye and chuckled. The pale-faced man was there too, his shirt sleeves rolled up, his tie askew. His eyes were half-open, but he was smiling.

Viv waited for the applause to die down and passed a hand over her face. She fiddled with her bracelet. Her voice lowered.

'Of course, and maybe not many people know this, there is one very special person, one wee boy, who cannot be here tonight, and won't be here tomorrow . . .'

There was silence, then someone shouted, 'Wayne's escaped!' and there was laughter. But the laughter was short. Viv wiped an eye and held her drink in the air. She was towering over them all, her hair so close to the lights it looked as if it was on fire.

'. . . so here's to Andrew, taken from us all so soon, so early. I do so wish my brother was here with me, here with us all. He is not forgotten.'

'Hear, hear,' someone from her family said, and everyone

clapped. There were murmurs of support, a rising tide of sympathetic words and nodding heads. Viv recovered her cheer.

'I would love for him to be here, I really would. He would be amazed! His little sister finally getting hitched! Maybe he would be embarrassed. Anyway, we miss you, Andy. I love you, wherever you are.'

There was more quiet clapping.

'I didn't know she had a brother,' Stricken whispered to Shona, his breath drenched with whisky.

'Me neither,' she whispered back, gripping her stick tight, the suit jacket soft in her hand.

'He must be dead,' Stricken said earnestly.

'You think?' she said.

Stricken looked at her through unfocused eyes. 'Well, that's a turn-up,' he said, shaking his head. He stared at Viv and then turned back to Shona. 'Hey, Shona . . . do you think you'll ever be up on there, on the bar, everyone happy for you, at a wee wedding of your own?'

Shona blinked. 'I'm more likely to hammer nails into my head.'

Stricken tilted his head to one side, as if in sympathy. 'You know, Shona, when did you last even *have* . . .'

She glared at him. 'Get to fuck, Hector.'

Shona heard the rest of the speech but did not listen. Someone pushed past her to the lobby, and she lost sight of Stricken. There were several rounds of applause as Viv tried to get down from the bar. Her skirt caught momentarily on a beer tap, a high-heeled shoe came off, a glass was knocked to the floor, and Wayne had to help her down, to much hilarity.

The party resumed.

Shona checked her phone – there were no messages, and it was late now. Somewhere in Edinburgh there were machines blinking, measuring the pulse of her father's heart behind thin curtains, drawn against the darkness.

It was time for her to sleep.

She draped the mislaid jacket on an empty chair, then headed up the two flights of stairs to her room. Her legs ached. There must be a lift, she thought. She paused on the worn red carpet of the first landing. The little pebble had shifted in her pocket. She took it out. In the glow of the wall lamps, she could see it was green – green as a broad bean, streaked with a kind of silver. It was impermeable, complete and smooth, like a tiny planet plucked from deep space. She decided to keep it.

She reached a long, dimly lit corridor that smelled of lemon carpet cleaner. The noise of the party receded into distance and night.

Some doors had names painted on them: HUGHES, ELIOT, WORDSWORTH, TENNYSON, PATERSON, BERRYMAN, MORGAN. Her bedroom was untitled. It was just room 27. She leaned against the wall, fishing out her key card.

But she did not open the door. She was suddenly distracted by a stream of sharp air against her face. A chill. She looked to the end of the corridor. A fire door was slightly open, and, beyond it, a metal staircase. What was out there? The battlements, the flags and the towers. The view across the darkness of Argyll.

Pale light fell on her door – it came from across the corridor. A door was ajar. She thought she heard something: a clumping noise, footsteps, a kind of moaning. But she could not tell where it was coming from.

'Hello?' she called tentatively. She looked left and right, but there was no one around – just the distant bass thump of a song pulsing from the bar.

Shona moved a step forward into the open room. The door, she noticed, had a name printed on it: SORLEY MACLEAN.

She saw a bed and a faint light from the bathroom.

'Hi,' she said. 'Anyone here?'

She thought she heard another moan, and then a deep, long sigh. Raucous laughter suddenly rang out from downstairs.

She took another step into the room. The bed was made, a backpack on the floor beside it. A book lay open on the dressing table. It had been ripped; half a page hung loose and jagged like torn flesh.

With a kind of mental flinch, Shona realised something was on the bedroom floor. She moved closer and could see, spelled out in pebbles and stones, the words: THE RIGHT PATH.

They glimmered with liquid. She bent down and touched a pebble with a fingertip, which suddenly darkened. It was blood.

There was a clanging noise from the hall – the rasp of metal on metal. She moved out to the hall as quickly as she could. In the doorway that led to the roof, something like a ribbon fell into view. It pooled on the floor in a puddle of shadow. She moved to the stairs, as if in liquid, as if in a dream.

There were smears of blood on the wallpaper, lit by a skelf of light. The air seemed to move, like the shimmering around a bonfire. On a metal step lay a pair of silky suit trousers, empty and collapsed. On the next step up, a single sock. Shona moved up the staircase, and the night air was suddenly upon her face, a breeze pulling at her hair.

She reached the top, the battlements low, no higher than her waist.

'There is no time,' a flat voice said.

She looked to her right, and a naked man stood at the edge of the tower.

His white skin glimmered in the light thrown from the garden, from the hotel, from the moon. He was looking out into the night, to the dark mountains and the invisible sea.

Shona found herself unable to move – one hand was on her stick, the other was outstretched, as if she needed to hold the air. She saw her fingers, her hand open, clutch at nothing.

The man turned around. His hands were dark with blood.

On his chest was a tattoo that dropped down from his shoulder blades to his waist: a circle of the letters of the alphabet in deep black, and the numbers 0 to 9. *Yes* on his left shoulder, *No* on his right.

'Say yes to no,' he said, arms outstretched.

'No,' she said weakly.

He nodded. His eyes closed.

He cannot fall. She felt a deep surge towards him.

'Hey, pal, come on, why don't you come to me? Come down, come inside,' she said, in the warmest, most reassuring voice she could muster.

His lean naked body stood between battlements. His face was blank, his eyes closed. She realised it was the pale man who had been drinking alone at the bar. It was Viv's friend.

'It's Dan, isn't it?' she said.

'Ask Sorley,' he said. He opened his eyes. They looked past her. Then he stepped back, into space. Into the night. He dropped from view.

Shona hurried to the edge and saw the end of his fall, the tumbling over, the hurtling into darkness.

There was a loud, wet noise – of solidity meeting softness, of a sudden human breakage. A brief silence – as deep as a sea – and then shouting and a single yelping scream.

His body lay face down, tangled and broken on the hard stone. He was facing the cold earth, the line of the neck dislodged. Legs and arms askew, like the broken branches of a leafless tree.

The music played on, for a while, as doors opened and people gathered. Then the music stopped. And then there were human voices, and the sounds of the deep night, and the murmuring of a small group gathered around the body of Daniel Merrygill.

3

The banquet hall was full of flowers. The morning light glimmered on bunches of pale roses, speared on unused cutlery and glowed on the white tablecloths that shrouded the long tables.

Shona sat at the empty top table, where Viv would have sat, looking out through elegant French windows to the rugged landscape beyond.

The Argyll hills were emerging in a frieze of deep blues and bruised violets. A straggle of dull-eyed sheep lolled in a scratty brown field beyond the fence, huge in their winter coats. A rag of black plastic shook on the fence like a deflated bird.

The hotel's cook, in jeans and a T-shirt, had made Shona a roll and bacon, which sat uneaten beside a large mug of black coffee. He had spoken kindly to her. She had almost broken down.

The police had been at the Poets' Hotel all through the night – bustling around the hotel, sealing off Merrygill's room, the corridor, speaking to staff, interviewing Shona, interviewing Viv. Blue lights had swum around the car park, but after a time they were turned off, and the night had flooded back.

A man in a long overcoat walked slowly across the room to Shona. His polished brogues tapped on the wooden floor. He brushed past an untethered balloon, which bumped gently under a table.

'Ms Sandison,' he said.

She shivered suddenly, as if walking through a cobweb. It was the same officer with the lean face and kind eyes she had spoken to in the early hours. He had interviewed her and taken a statement.

Lorimer, he was called. He was tall, dark and, she may have even said, on a better day, handsome. He had a supple Glasgow accent.

'Thank you for your help, Ms Sandison – we need not detain you any further,' he said. 'Much appreciated, your clarity and candour. You are free to go, although of course we may be back in touch depending on how the case proceeds. There may be further formalities. Right now, I think we have what we need.'

Shona nodded.

The detective stood for a while, hands in his pockets, gazing out at the fields, the sheep, the distant mountains. 'Ms Banks has informed us that the wedding has been called off,' he said, in a low voice.

'No shit,' Shona said eventually.

'Well,' the man said, 'indeed.'

No one would be dancing today. No cake would be cut. No speeches made. No poetry.

'How is she?' she asked.

The detective turned to her, his face calm and unchanging, and then turned back to the window. 'She was very distressed. But she seems okay now. I believe she's planning to travel back to Edinburgh with her fiancé today.'

Shona nodded. She would see Viv on the ferry.

'What was his name again? Dan, wasn't it?' Lorimer asked.

He should know the answer, Shona thought. Maybe it was a test.

'Yes,' she said and poked the soft white dough of her roll.

'Mr Merrygill. Daniel John Merrygill,' he said. 'He was an old friend of Ms Banks. I understand they grew up in the same town in the North of England.'

Shona nodded. She still had Merrygill's book and pebble in her pocket. 'Poor man,' she said flatly. 'It might have been a slip, but still . . .'

The detective turned to her. 'Ms Sandison, you said he turned and fell.'

34

'I did. You're right. That's what he did. He knew what he was doing.'

Lorimer looked at her, levelly, for a moment. He then inspected his nails. 'Nothing's been confirmed,' he said, 'but I think you can probably guess we're not looking for any further evidence. Your account seems to match what we know, and he was full of drink, by the looks of it. Post-mortem to follow but–'

'But what?'

'We found a lot of drugs in his room. Uppers, downers. He seems to have taken a few and . . . intentionally injured his hands with something.' He opened his hands, as if that concluded the sentence.

'Do you think he felt any pain?'

'The medics say he was dead on impact. Broken neck.'

'Naked,' she said.

'As a baby,' he said.

'He had a strange tattoo. On his chest.'

Lorimer nodded. He moved a step closer and looked at her with clear blue-grey eyes. 'Shona, you have the number we gave you if you need any help dealing with this. If you want someone to talk to.'

She nodded. The steam rose from the black coffee, and she reached for the cup.

'Take your time,' he said softly.

She sipped the coffee, and he stared at his watch, as if it was going to tell him something.

'What was the book?' she said. 'In the room?'

'It's bagged up now,' Lorimer said. 'I don't have that information. If I remember rightly, it was a book about geology.'

'Geology? Weird,' she said quietly.

Lorimer sighed and rubbed his face. 'Yes. And all this, on the night before a wedding,' he said. 'But I've seen weirder. You're a pal of Detective Reculver, are you not?'

He peered at her.

'I know him, aye,' she said.

Reculver was her best contact in the force. A large, gruff veteran detective. He usually wore make-up – mascara, foundation. Sometimes beauty spots would appear on his face. He had a large head, rugged as a stump. He dressed immaculately and was often angry as a badger. Like his many pairs of handmade leather shoes, he was both tough and elegant.

'Well, you'll have seen weirder too, then. Okay. I have to be going,' Lorimer said. 'We have your details. Keep your phone on.' He smiled briefly and padded out of the room.

The day became bleary and formless – a mess of organisation, of brief exhausted hungover chats in the lobby and the bar, of looking up timetables, of phone calls, of hurried texts and emails pressed into mobile phones. Stricken had emerged, green with drink, sucking black coffee and talking in a traumatised murmur. People sat around whispering, their faces pale and sick. Viv bundled down the stairs with her silent parents, waved and mouthed a goodbye to the remnants of the wedding party, and ducked into a private hire cab, which whisked her to Dunoon. Wayne had gone already, Stricken muttered, holding his coffee in two hands.

The blue lights had gone. One police van was outside, and a uniformed officer was still at the reception, speaking in a low voice to the receptionist. The hotel manager was there, too, in his shirtsleeves, wringing his hands, his eyes wide as the moon.

Eventually a small fleet of minivans and taxis took guests to the port, and they shambled onto the ferry back to Gourock. White gulls circled over the quay. The sea was an undulating mass of porridge-grey.

Shona had called her father, and texted, but there had been no reply. In the silent café Stricken sat, head in hands.

'Anything from your dad?' he said, his voice muffled by his palms.

'Nah,' she said, shaking her head.

'Have you called that Bernie woman? His friend,' he said, raising his face. His eyes were bloodshot.

'No, I haven't,' she said. 'I don't have her bloody number, do I?'

'Chill, Shona – Jesus. I just thought you might–'

'Why the fuck would I, Hector? Some random woman from the allotment? No. Go back to your sleep.'

The ferry ground its way through the strait. Shona stood up and walked slowly to the metal steps that led to the deck. There was no cheering and laughing now in the wedding party. Just huddled groups staring out at the waves. Shona's head felt heavy, her body exhausted.

The cold air slapped her skin. On the bleak deck she saw Viv, alone, a heavy jacket on, hood up, staring at her phone. A sudden wind whipped about the boat, and the waves began to move and slash white. Seabirds hung above them, as if dangling from unseen strings.

Shona walked slowly to Viv, her stick clipping the deck, and Viv looked up and smiled.

'Hey, sweetheart,' she said softly. She stood as Shona came closer and put her arms around her. Shona could smell day-old perfume and shower gel, stale alcohol and tears. They sat, embracing, for a while, Viv wiping tears from her eyes and cheeks with the back of her hand, a soggy tissue in her fingers.

She started talking. 'He was a good friend at school, Dan,' Viv said. 'Back in Ully, back in them days. Even though he was a couple of years older than me. Poor Dan. Poor, poor Dan. What's he done that for? What's he gone and done that for?'

Viv shook her head and wiped her eyes again. The ferry ploughed on, the sky white, the sea grey, the mountains looming like a congregation. 'But I guess this has saved you having to read that daft poem?' she said, with a smile.

37

'It can wait,' Shona said.

'Ach, doubt it will ever be needed,' Viv said.

'Poor guy,' Shona said.

Viv nodded, sniffed, pulled herself up. 'He used to knock around with our Andrew,' she went on. 'He got back in touch about ten years ago. Lovely man . . . kind, quiet, funny. He led a bit of a lonely life. Looked after his mam till it got too much.'

Something was being intoned over the tannoy, but Shona could not quite hear – it was a garble of words, metallic and meaningless.

Viv blew her nose on the mangled ball of tissue. She sighed deeply.

'Fuck the wedding, it doesn't matter,' she said suddenly. 'Fuck all that shit. That can happen anytime. But what a thing to happen. For fuck's sake. Maybe we should just skip the wedding altogether now – who cares? I don't care.'

Shona held her friend's hand. 'I didn't know you had a brother, Viv. You never said before.'

'He would have been fifty this year, you know. A middle-aged man. But no. He's always eighteen.'

'You never said,' Shona repeated. 'I was surprised.'

She had been more than surprised. She could not imagine Vivienne with a brother. She wondered if he looked like her.

'Maybe I didn't,' Viv said. 'Dan and Andy were good friends. Were tight. Now both are gone. Both gone. No, I probably never said. Andrew would be a big bald man probably, like his dad. Like my dad.'

She pulled her head to one side, as if tearing it away from something. 'How are you, Shona – are you all right?'

Shona looked at her for a while and nodded her head gently. 'I'm fine.'

'I guess you've seen worse,' Viv said, turning back with a crooked smile.

'Don't you worry about me,' Shona said.

38

Viv rubbed her face and spoke quietly and quickly as Shona studied her intensely. 'I don't even know who to tell. Dan was an only child. Where his folks are now, I don't know. I seem to remember his dad was long gone. His mam might be in an Ully care home, but she could be gone, too. Just like Andrew. Like all of us one day. We'll drop into the sea, won't we? We all go down, one day.'

Viv added, rapidly: 'We don't know where our Andy is. I used to walk with Jet, our dog, in the woods, trying to find him. After the police had gone. But nothing. They looked everywhere. It was on the telly. Nothing. It was like he'd melted into the trees. Vanished into the stones.'

Shona opened her mouth to ask more. She felt a pang, both of shame and irritation at herself. Instead, she moved her head and looked out to the sullen grey sea.

'I bet you're dying to know more about my brother now,' Viv said, with a brief smile.

'Maybe another time,' Shona said.

'I guess you think it's odd. That I've kept it a secret.'

'No. And I don't mind secrets. I have some myself. And at least secrets are true.'

Viv smiled and then put her head on Shona's shoulder. 'It was Mam and Dad who suffered the most, not me. He was their baby. It's the not knowing. The waiting. And then the waiting turns into silence. And people forget. Or don't want to remember. They're waiting for an answer, and it never comes, so they switch off, switch out. And then, for us, those who remember, it's just weeks and months and years of nothing. No news. You start to think it never happened.'

The sonorous rumble of the ferry engines was rhythmic and lulling. It quietened them. Viv's head was heavy on Shona's shoulder, as if she was asleep.

'Where's your Wayne?' Shona asked eventually. 'Why are you on your own?'

'I'm not on my own – you're here. Fuck knows about Wayne. He was being annoying. Talking about money. I told him to go and boil his head. But, shush. Let me rest on you a while. You're nice and warm.'

'Aye, that's me,' Shona said, 'I'm exothermic. That's what Dad says. High metabolism.'

Viv murmured something that Shona could not hear. 'You what?'

'Remember that lovely time we went down to Yorkshire,' Viv said, barely audible above the grind of the ferry engine.

'I remember,' Shona said brightly, happy to move onto a good memory. 'Fish and chips in Robin Hood's Bay. Then we went to see where the Brontës lived.'

'We drank far too much, didn't we? You felt sorry for the donkeys in Scarborough and tried to buy one. We got lost for a bit on the Yorkshire moors.'

'I'd rather be lost on the moors with you than most other things,' Shona said, remembering those days – the flat hit of the hammering sun on the bare brown moorland, Viv laughing at their disintegrated map, which had come apart in a mad drenching summer rain the day before. Drinking cider from a plastic bottle at the jagged ruins of Fountains Abbey. Falling asleep together at a cheap B&B in Helmsley, both drunk, both stoned, both sunburnt and delirious. Clapping along to old soul tunes. Yelling, hysterical, to Beyoncé.

'Me too, love, me too,' Viv said softly. 'I'd rather be lost on the moors than sitting here on this fucking ferry boat right now, that's for sure.' She moaned and held her head. 'My folks, Shona, they're distraught. The money they spent . . .'

'I know, love, I know,' Shona said.

'You never even saw my dress,' Viv said.

'I'm sure you would have been a sight to behold.'

Viv gave a husky laugh and shook her head. Her fingers were soft on Shona's soft hands.

As the Gourock port came into view, and houses and roads glided past on the headland, a text buzzed on Shona's phone. *Hugh still in hospital. Give me a call when you can thanks Bernie x.*

Viv stood up and composed herself, flattening her coat, wiping her eyes. She gave Shona a farewell hug. Her parents had appeared on the deck, and she went to join them.

Shona watched her friend stagger away, across the tilting deck, as the ferry rolled into the dock, roiling white foam behind its massive weight. Shona's phone buzzed again – a call. She looked at the screen. It was Ranald, her boss.

She answered. She felt a presence nearby on the deck – it was Stricken, leaning on the handrail.

'Ranald,' she said into the phone.

'Shona,' he said warmly in his Shetland accent, sweet as caramel.

'At your service.'

'So, you said you were at a wedding this weekend?'

'Aye.'

'In Argyll?'

'What you getting at?'

'Was it the DEATH SHOCK HORROR AT HOTEL WEDDING wedding?'

'Jesus fuck. Where did you see that?'

'In the *Record*. Says someone was found dead at the Poets' Hotel, near Holy Loch. A suicide? Reading between the lines.'

'Aye. I saw it happen.'

'Jeez, Shona. You all right?'

'Aye. Fine. Seen worse.'

'You sure?'

'I refer you to my previous answer, Ranald.'

'So . . .'

'So what?'

The ferry clunked into the terminal. Stricken was waving at her as he turned to leave. Viv had gone down into the decks

41

below with her family, with what was left of the wedding party.

'I was wondering if you'd like to write a piece on it. There must be more to it,' Ranald said.

Shona rolled her eyes. But she had the notebook in her pocket, with the strange writing on it, the lines of eldritch text.

'Let me think on it, Ranald. Let me have a think.'

'This report, Shona – it says the man left a message on his body? Is that right?'

'No, no. That's not right. Not sure where that's come from. I saw him.'

'You saw him?'

'I said, Ranald, I would think about it. Hold your horses.'

'Okay, Shona, do that. Give me a call.'

'I will, I will,' she said. She blew out a blast of breath. 'I'm amazed the story's in the paper today. Already.'

'You shouldn't be amazed. Someone at the hotel has blabbed. There's all kinds of detail.'

'Some fucker wanted a bit of cash and got the tip-off fee. Look, I need to go. I'll be in touch.'

The ferry came to its final halt, and the train to Glasgow was waiting. A journey had begun.

4

Hugh Sandison was sleeping now. Shona held her father's frail hand in hers. His steady breath gently shook the long white hairs around his dry lips. His grey chest hair curled from his bed shirt. Her thumb moved over the soft skin of his hand. Blue veins still pulsed, for now. He was pink and tender and vulnerable. Suddenly small.

Bernie had been there. When Shona arrived, she had moved away to another part of the hospital.

'Can you check on the allotment, love?' he had said. At some point past, she thought, he had been weeping. His remaining hair was a little wild, and his eyes were swollen and tender.

'Of course, of course,' she said. 'But you can't go digging around there again for a while. You'll need to take it easy. You can't . . .'

'It's winter now. But it's spring soon,' he said. 'And I've been neglecting it. It's a bit of a mess. I didn't want to say . . .'

'It's okay, Dad. The allotment isn't going anywhere.'

'There's snowbells on the verges, by the cycle path. Lovely, they are.'

'They are.'

'You don't need to worry about me, love.'

'Of course I'm worrying about you.'

'I'm fine. I'm better off in here. How was the wedding? I do like Viv – she's one of your nicer friends . . . and she's a bonny lass.'

'It was fine,' Shona lied. 'Look, you were lucky, Dad, and I'm glad Bernie was with you.'

'Och, she's a star. Did they tell you they're talking about

having something put in my artery, some kind of clip or something? Amazing stuff. Shame my old man never had one. He'd still be alive now. Tough as old boots was Da. A fisherman, like his dad. A Fifer, a fisherman: tough men. Not much give in them. Out on the cruel sea. He didn't want me out on the boats, like him. Didn't want me out there. Oh, no. He was clear about that. He'd lost his brother out there. Terrible business. Tough men. Not like me. He had a dram for his brother every twenty-third February, for Tam. Every year. Said nothing. Tam: his brother. Tough men, they were, out on the boats.'

He had looked out of the window then, quivering, a little bit tipsy with drugs.

Shona had tried to return to the point. 'A stent, yes, the doctor told me. But this was a warning, Dad, a warning to . . .'

'*A warning from history*, isn't that what someone once wrote?' he had said, smiling. 'Ain't that the case?'

'Is that bloomin' Marx again, Dad?'

He had shaken his head, frowning. 'No, no. Maybe. Shona, my love, I'm tired now. I'll try to get some sleep. Can you bring my book in for me? There's nothing to read in here.'

'Is it by your bed? What is it?'

'Oh, it's old Terence. The Eagleton. It's by the bed, love. Yes, that's right. If you could. Thank you. How's wee MacDiarmid?'

'She's been fed, Dad, she's fine.'

'Shona – see your pal Vivienne? Keep her close. Friends are worth their weight in gold. It's not like family, like me. You can't choose your family. Unfortunately for you. That's what makes friends special. You have found them and loved them. If you do love them. Love your friends, hen. It's important.'

She nodded. She could not think of what to say.

'Good, good. I need to sleep now. Takes it out of you, the heart stopping. For a wee moment there.' He had smiled at her, closed his eyes and fallen into a deep fissure of exhausted sleep.

He was still sleeping, his chest moving slowly up and down.

A thread of cotton was caught in the hair of his ear. Shona reached for it carefully, to pull it away.

The nurses were closing the curtains. Shona watched, unmoving, as the fabric swished along the rails. The machines still beeping. The beds, metal and heavy. A tiny ring of rust around a dial. A scar by her father's ear she had not noticed before.

He slept on, deeply. His eyes were moving behind his lids, like an old dog by the fire remembering chases in the high grass.

A nurse smiled and pointed to her watch. It was time to go.

Shona stood up and kissed her father on his forehead. It was warm and solid. She kissed him again, with a hand to his balding head, fugitive hairs between her fingers.

He had nearly left her. Taken the final step into the place where she could not reach him. But he was here. Still here, for her, for himself.

She left the ward and walked through the hospital, passing doctors and nurses murmuring in corridors. She took a lift down to the café, to find Bernie, but she had left.

In a toilet, she put her hands to her face, her stick dropping with a clunk to the floor. She felt the tingle of tears in the corners of her eyes, but they did not come. She rubbed her face. She needed, she felt with an urge overwhelming, to work. She needed this story – any story – to follow, to find, to write. A story to put her name beside. A story to tell to the dark.

The bus journey home across dark and wet Edinburgh was long and slow, grinding between wheezy stops. In her satchel she had the notebook from Dan Merrygill's jacket. She took it out again.

s a y y e s t o n o

What could that mean? Be positive to a negative? Agree to something that is not happening? Maybe it was, as she first thought, a song title. Maybe Daniel had been in a band.

She began an internet search on her phone, as the bus moved down the long straight of Ferry Road, past the handsome houses of Trinity and Goldenacre, and into the closer tenements of Leith.

abdargninetytwo
sorleysays–taketherightpath–
sayyestono-
–thereisnotime–odeadaheado

If they were song titles, they were not by any band or composer that had been recorded. If they had existed, they were gone. The emptiness of a fruitless internet search sat awkwardly in her mind – a fidgety, annoyed sense of something being mislaid, being missed, being lost.

The word *abdarg*. She wondered if it was Gaelic, or the name of a place or person. Again, she searched for it. She could not find anything. It was an ugly word. The *b* and the *d* like eyes with horns.

She realised, as if for the first time, and with a leap in her heart, that she had effectively stolen from a man who had then killed himself. But what did it matter now? No one knew it existed, apart from Stricken – and he had been so drunk it was doubtful he remembered.

The handwriting was neat. The ink was thick and flowing. It may even have been written with a fountain pen. She closed it again and slipped it into an inside pocket of her bag.

The bus slowed to her stop, and she quickly bundled her stick and her bag together and alighted, shouting a quick thank-you to the driver.

From one window of the flat, the bulk of the city's extinct volcano, Arthur's Seat, loomed, and from another, above the brown roofs of housing, the green metal of the Hibernian Football Club's stadium glinted. Her father's room was dark, the curtains drawn. Someone had made the bed; it was neat and had clean sheets. His old blanket had been folded and put at the foot of the bed. His writing table and bookshelves were cleaned, too. His slippers neatly paired.

As she dumped her bag and coat on the sofa, she realised someone had cleaned and tidied the entire flat. The narrow kitchen was spick and span. The living room had been hoovered. Only her bedroom, which doubled as her study, had been left as it was. Bernie must have been given a key, she thought.

There was a note on the dining table. Folded, propped up like a tent: *Wee dinner in the oven. B x*, it said. Shona found herself shaking her head. She screwed up the note and threw it in the general direction of a bin, newly emptied, by the television.

MacDiarmid, a length of warm coiled fluff, raised a tawny head. The cat was female, but for some reason her father insisted on her being named after the poet, so she was MacDiarmid. The cat was on the soft blue chair – Hugh's chair. She raised her head and yawned, her pink tongue curling, her teeth white. She stood up and arched her back, her tail straight in the air like an antenna. Shona scratched her behind the ear and trailed a finger down to her soft cheek.

'How's the wee refugee?' Shona whispered to the rescue cat.

MacDiarmid purred and rubbed her head against Shona's hand. A tiny white skull beneath the warm hair.

'Glad someone's happy,' Shona said and moved to the table and flipped open her laptop. She sat down and searched for Daniel Merrygill.

A few stories came up: the lurid tabloid account of his death, and other, more sober, descriptions of a death at a hotel in Argyll. There were errors and a lack of detail. One description from a news agency was carried in multiple media outlets. It read:

Mr Daniel Merrygill, 49, of Darlington, County Durham, a civil servant, was found dead in his room at the Poets' Hotel, near

Dunoon, the night before he was due to attend a wedding. Police have said there are no suspicious circumstances. The wedding to which he had been planning to attend has been cancelled, it is understood. A spokesman for the hotel declined to comment.

She searched for him, in Darlington. She knew the Northern English town for its railway station and its position on the main east coast line to London, but that was about it. She remembered rows of red-brick houses, a wrought-iron Victorian station, maybe a distant tower.

There was one old link to Merrygill on an employment search company. She clicked on it.

Daniel John Merrygill
Senior Policy Outcomes Officer, UK Government (Darlington: Dept of Administrative Affairs) (21 years)

There was a CV and a small photo. The CV said he had attended Ullathorne Comprehensive, then Manchester University in 1992. Entry-level civil service, a few years in various departments in London, then on to one of the satellite civil service departments based in the North. No other details, and no personal information at all. She searched on social media, but there was not a mark of him. Nothing on any of the major channels. She looked back at the photo. There was a vacancy there. Vulnerability, perhaps, in the open stare, the boyish short-cropped hair.

She sighed and sat back, rubbed her eyes. She could see the scene again: his body adrift in the air, then dislocated on the flagstones. Black blood, pooling about his head like a hideous halo. The letters on his chest, the numbers, the sun and the moon.

She looked out the window. A light was flashing on the tip of Arthur's Seat – the sun had caught someone's glasses, or a camera, or binoculars.

Her computer screen had gone to sleep. She slapped her hand on the table to wake herself up.

Shona knew she needed to speak to Viv. But she could not face it. There was a call she could make first. But before that, she needed a cup of tea. She flicked on the BBC News channel before she walked through to the kitchen. It was a politics show. White men in suits were sitting in a semicircle in a studio. As if prompted by her movement, MacDiarmid slid down from the soft chair to lie in a bar of light.

One of the politicians was dominating the conversation. He had colourless hair, clipped short. He wore a tight grey suit and a blue tie. His face was almost featureless, as if drawn by a child, his voice flat and persistent.

'Fact is, Suzanne,' he said, nodding to the presenter, 'and let's be perfectly blunt about it, this kind of growth-restricting practice belongs to the past. To the failed policies of another era. Unions are by their nature divisive – we are all one nation, one people – are we not? Unions are just clubs to fix wages. Personally, I'd like to look at the idea of a National Labour Force organisation. But that's for another time. Now, free of ridiculous interference, free of unwanted migration cutting off the legs of the proud English worker, we can free our workforces of the globalist obligation to organise in these restrictive ways, work with employers to grow profits and increase growth, target growth, maximise growth. We have to take the right path. There is no time–'

'Mr Watson,' someone interjected.

'Fact is,' he said, waving away the interruption, 'let's take a broader look, a common-sense look at this situation. Common sense, like the way it used to be. Look: we have to reject certain ideas. In a sense, we have to say yes to saying no, to the alien ideas that have somehow taken root in this nation. Because the answers, let's be frank here, lie around us – we should look at the lessons of history. A thousand years ago, this land was part of the Roman Empire. Greatest empire the world has ever seen. There's a bloody great wall built right across the North of England to remind us of their greatness, their industry, their civilisation.' His eyes were flashing, and he had turned to the audience.

'But what brought down the Roman Empire? Now let me tell you, because I'm a bit of a history buff, it wasn't a land battle: they never had their Waterloo. It wasn't a naval disaster: there was no Trafalgar for them. No, the Roman Empire was brought down because of migration. Swarming into the empire from outside. Uncontrolled immigration did for the greatest empire the world has ever seen – until the British Empire, of course – and now, if we are not vigilant and staunch in our vigilance, it will do the same to us. It cannot continue as it has. Common sense just says otherwise . . .'

'We have slightly gone off topic, Mr Watson,' the presenter said weakly.

People in the TV audience were clapping loudly, some shouting their approval. Shona left the room. She flicked on the kettle, and her phone buzzed in her pocket.

'I wondered how long it would take for you to call,' she said.

'Good day to you too, Ms Sandison,' Detective Benedict Reculver rumbled.

'What's the fucking problem this time?'

'Shona, step down from your sweary pulpit for a moment,' he said.

It sounded as if he was walking down a street. She could hear his footsteps on cobbles. She imagined his polished brown brogues on some street in Edinburgh's Old Town, his large frame gliding past stones, spires and archways like an ocean liner.

'I have something to exchange with you,' he growled.

'Not sure I want anything you've got,' she said, pouring the hot water into her old mug with GLASGOW MERCURY printed on its side.

'Hear me out. You might be surprised. Meet me in the Café Royal in forty minutes,' he said.

'Fine,' she said. 'I guess.'

'And before you run for the bus . . .'

'What?'

'How's your old man?'

'See you,' she snapped and hung up.

She nearly tripped over a stretching MacDiarmid as she grabbed her jacket, bag and stick and made for the door.

The cat watched her go, blinked and proceeded to lick a paw languorously, as if there was no yesterday, today or tomorrow.

5

Shona was on the bus when Viv called her.

'Eighty thousand pounds!'

'Hi, Viv – what?'

'Someone's tried to put a load of cash in my bank account.' Viv sounded out of breath. 'Eighty grand!' she shouted.

'Viv, are you okay?'

'No, I'm not okay, Shona! What's going on? Fuck's sake!'

'Where are you?'

'I'm having to go into the bank, amn't I? I'm on George Street. The bank called me. Suspicious activity! I know nowt about it. It's the last thing I need right now.'

'Surely they know who tried to deposit it? Is it an error?'

'It's not an error, Shona. Someone's tried to put eighty grand in my bank account! Now I have to go in and prove it's not money laundering or something.'

'Is it a wedding gift?'

'Shona! Who would do that? No one I know has that kind of cash lying about.'

Shona waited a few moments.

The bus wheezed its way to the top of Leith Walk, where it haphazardly made its way around a messy roundabout.

'Fuck's sake! This is the last thing I need. Where are you anyway?'

'I'm on the way to meet someone. This bus is slow. Milk turns faster. Look – I'll be done in a bit. Do you think you'll still be in town in an hour?'

'Probably! Text me later, and we can meet.'

'Okay – take care – I'm sure it's not . . .'

'Eighty thousand pounds!'

The line went dead.

Shona got off the bus outside the Scottish National Portrait Gallery, a beautiful red stone building that sat poised on the edge of the New Town. She looked up at the statues that adorned its imposing exterior. Their eyes blind and empty in languid faces. Their swords sleeping in carved hands. What couldn't they see? A small woman with a black puffer jacket, leaning on a stick, a laptop bag over one shoulder, a copper streak in her hassled hair.

A cold wind was whipping through the trees in St Andrew's Square, the open space between her bus stop and the Café Royal, and it was getting dark. The sky was cloudless, its light fading to a violet blue. She thought of her father, receiving his supper on a plastic tray in hospital, safe in those white sheets.

The Café Royal stood resplendent in a narrow lane between elegant public buildings. She pushed her way through the heavy door, and her eyes adjusted to pub light – the diffuse air, glinting with brass and glass, purring with the contented murmur of early evening drinkers. The elaborate ceiling was green and gold. Old soul music was cooing through speakers.

Detective Reculver sat in a padded booth under an ornate Victorian tiled mural. He was dressed in a three-piece suit, a red shirt, a big tie, a large overcoat and his usual polished brogues. Today his adornments were limited, it appeared, to mascara and a temporary beauty spot on one cheek.

He sat with an amber pint, his clenched hands, as big as babies, on the table. Shona slumped in front of him. She tipped sideways a little as she slapped down her stick on the seat.

'Shona Sandison, I presume,' he said.

'You getting me a drink or what?' she said, unzipping her coat.

'As ever, it is fairly easy to distinguish you from a ray of sunshine. Some of that awful American bourbon you drink?'

'Yep. With Coke and ice. Ta.'

Reculver stood up, his frame moving solidly to the bar, where he leaned forward to order, as if exchanging a secret.

'I don't know how you drink that stuff,' he said when he returned, sliding the glass across to Shona.

'I open my mouth and tip it in,' she said. 'So, what's cracking?'

'I pity your clearly inexpensive education,' he said and sipped his beer. Behind him, the light was falling in pale beams through the stencilled windowpanes. 'Anyway, I was sorry to hear of your involvement in this nastiness in Argyll. Are you bearing up?'

She shrugged. 'I've seen blood before,' she said. 'I've seen bodies before. The real shame was for Viv, whose wedding it was meant to be. That's all fucked now.'

He nodded. His eyes were dark, unreadable. His lips seemed to be briefly iridescent. The pub murmured and glowed. Men and women in suits gathered around wineglasses and pints.

'She is a friend of yours?'

Shona sighed and flicked her glass. 'No, I was invited to a wedding in the middle of nowhere by a total stranger. Yes, she's an old friend. What does it matter?'

'I assume it was not you, then, who tipped off the papers?'

Shona glared. 'I don't need thirty quid for a lame tip-off to the red tops. I'm not that skint . . . yet.'

Reculver smiled. 'Thought as much. So, I'm guessing you might now be writing about the whole terrible business?'

His voice rumbled like coal being poured from a sack.

'I don't think so,' she lied. 'Why would I do that?'

'You're freelance now, and it's a good story. No doubt some media platform would take a feature on the poor man and the wedding he ruined.'

Shona said nothing. She noticed a small plaster on Reculver's wrist.

'Even if I was going to do that,' she said eventually, 'what could you tell me? The poor guy did himself in for some reason. He chose a bad time to do it. Not that there's ever a good time.'

'No,' Reculver said, shaking his head. 'Although of course there may have been a method in his–'

'So, what is it, this information you are talking about?' she asked again.

Reculver blinked heavily and traced a circle around the lip of his pint glass. 'First, I was wondering if you might tell me something.'

'Fire away.'

'The wedding guests – were they mainly journalists and so on?'

Shona peered at him. 'Why don't you ask Lorimer? He'll have a rundown of everyone in the building, won't he?'

He smiled. 'The brave and handsome Lorimer is many things, but he is not as sharp or as reliable as you.'

Shona shrugged. 'There were a lot of journalists,' she said 'Of course. A lot of old hacks from the *Post* and the *Glasgow Mercury*. Viv's worked in papers for twenty-five years. Some of her fiancé's friends were there, I think. They would not have been journalists. Then there was her mum and dad. Then this Merrygill, who she knew from school.'

'Were there any politicians?'

'Who like? MSPs and whatever?'

He took a swig of beer and nodded. A rime of foam settled briefly on his upper lip. He smeared it away, and a gentle pink shade was moved in a line across his cheek.

'No,' she said, 'I don't think so. I think we would have spotted them. Hector certainly would have, the tedious sod that he is. Nope. I don't think Viv knows any politicians, to be honest. Not her type, not our circle – so, no.'

The drink had warmed her. The buzz of alcohol was flickering in her brain like a guttering candle.

'Who, in particular, are you thinking of?' she asked.

'An MP called Watson,' he said with emphasis.

'Who's he?'

'Member of Parliament for Tyrdale. In the North of England – Durham. Part of the new breed. Got in at the last election, talks loudly about immigration, historic traditions, sinking migrant boats. Wealthy. Widower. His young wife died in a car accident, way back.'

'Car accident?' she said.

'Single-driver crash in Kent. She drove on the wrong side of the road, for some reason. He almost immediately, and most efficiently, threw himself into politics. Likes to stir it up with a bit of the culture war – he's loud about all kinds of things. In his maiden speech he talked a lot about civilisation. He's talked in fringe events about "Anglo-Saxon values" – whatever they are. Not a big fan of the exceptions to his rules. I suspect he and I would have the odd disagreement, should we meet.'

'Sounds like someone to absolutely not invite to a fucking wedding then,' she said. 'No, he wasn't there. What does he look like? Wait a second. He's sounding familiar.'

She looked for the MP on her phone. Many pictures popped up – it was the politician she had seen on television. Hueless hair clipped short. Tight grey suits, a taut gym body and a red tie. A constituency photo showed Watson standing in front of a Union Jack.

'Nope, he wasn't there. Not sure why some English MP would be at my pal's wedding, though? At all.'

'He went to the same school as her – in Ullathorne, Tyrdale.'

'She's never mentioned him. So what?'

Reculver nodded and turned his head slightly, as if registering the sound of a voice from somewhere else.

Shona drained her glass and grinned. 'I know you. You and your friends are watching this guy – what's he into?'

He raised a finger.

'You were with the security services before you joined the force, I believe?' she said, smiling, raising a finger of her own.

They realised they were pointing at each other, and both dropped their hands.

'As I always say, Shona, you are indeed the impossible pencil – both sharp and blunt. I cannot say. But I – we – they – are beginning to be interested in him. A wee bit.'

'Surely a wee bit out of your jurisdiction? He's a Westminster MP. Nothing to do with Scotland.'

'Well, I can't say any more. We do, in general, like to keep an eye on any cream that's about to curdle. However, if you do come across him, in your scurrilous business, I would be most obliged if you could let me know. Here – read this, an interview with the fellow.'

He reached into his jacket and pulled out a piece of folded paper. 'He has his own posse, and they're smart,' he added. 'He has a very good, experienced election agent, and a personal bodyguard, they say.'

She took the piece of paper and slipped it into a pocket. 'Why?'

'As I say – if you bump into anything to do with him on your travels, do let me know. He still runs a company or two in Ullathorne, I believe.'

'Come on, you're not going to tell me anything else?'

'No, darling Shona,' he said and took an extravagant glug of beer.

Shona huffed and crossed her arms.

Her phone lit up and buzzed. It was a text from Viv: *Coffee in 15? Wellington?*

'I've got to go soon,' she said.

Reculver pulled out another piece of A4 paper, folded lengthways, from his voluminous coat.

On the other side of the bar, someone dropped a glass with a brief shattering noise.

'Whoops,' Reculver said, glancing over. 'A slip betwixt cup and lip.' He put the paper on the table. 'Our poor suicide. We ran some checks. Lovely Lorimer over there was a wee bit out of his depth. So: this Merrygill. No partner, no history of ever having a partner, no kids. One parent, still in Tyrdale. Seems he left his job in the civil service recently. Gave no reason and worked out his notice. He also sold his house in Darlington. A terraced red-brick house, two beds – got two hundred thousand for it. Moved a month ago to a caravan on a farm.'

Shona took the paper.

'Looks like he was downsizing,' Reculver said. 'Maybe preparing.'

'Simplifying,' she said.

Reculver leaned forward. His dark-lined eyes glittered. 'Three nights ago, his caravan went up in smoke. Farmer found it burning in the field. Totally wiped out. Merrygill was nowhere to be seen. The farmer's finally reported it to the Durham force. Marton's Farm, isolated place on the moor, halfway between Ullathorne and Appleby.'

Shona opened the paper. There was an image of a small house in a terrace of red-brick houses. A photo of a burned-out caravan in a lonely field, a twisted tree the only feature on a bleak horizon.

Reculver abruptly stood up. 'So, there you go – something for you to ponder. No doubt there's a wee tale for you, Shona.'

'I'm suspicious,' she said.

'You should be,' he said.

'No – of you. Why give me all this stuff? What do you want?'

He shook his head. 'I'm sure you'll be able to think of something. This is our relationship, is it not? I give you things, you give me things. We are but dealers in the underworld of facts, Miss Sandison.'

Shona frowned. She stood up, grabbed her stick and bag. There was a glinting crescent of bourbon and Coke left in the bottom of her glass, which she reached for and drank quickly.

Reculver rose slowly. He plopped a large fedora on his head.

It was beautifully made, sleek, with a purple ribbon around its crown. He looked like a psychedelic gangster from an alternative 1950s. He nodded to Shona and smiled, and then departed, like a tanker exiting a tight strait.

Shona paused, checking her phone for anything from her father – nothing.

She knew she would have to travel to Ullathorne. As she confirmed to Viv she was on her way to see her, she wondered whether her friend knew about Merrygill's fiery caravan in the middle of a shattered moor. She walked quickly through the gathering dusk, across the now dark square, along the elegant, wide George Street, to a basement café on the corner of Hanover Street. 'Hangover Street' they used to call it when the *Post* was in an office around the corner – no more.

Viv was sitting on a high stool, by the window. She already had the drinks ready – a large latte for herself, an Americano for Shona. She slipped off her stool and came towards her, and they hugged. They held each other and asked each other if they were okay. They both said they were and, grinning, shrugged.

'You been drinking?' Viv said, sniffing exaggeratingly.

'Just a wee one. With a contact.'

'You and your contacts. Total mystery, half your sources.'

'Well, they wouldn't be sources if I told everyone who they were.'

'You're a big secret an' all.'

Shona thanked her for the coffee and gulped it down. Her blood was buzzing.

'So?' Viv said, stirring her drink vigorously.

'So?' Shona said.

Viv dropped her spoon. It landed in a puddle of bubbles and cream. 'The money! Don't you want to know?'

'Yes, yes, of course. Tell me more.'

'What's up with you?'

'Dinnae fash. Carry on.'

'The bank, well, they say it was an attempted deposit from a bank in the Isle of Man. Proper bank account.'

Viv produced a slip of paper from her purse. It bore the logo of her bank; below it were details of the attempted money transfer.

'Wow,' Shona said. 'It's a lot of money, Viv.'

'Tell me about it,' Viv said. She threw up her hands. 'The bank was asking questions. Whoever was trying to give me the money didn't have the right account number. Just my name, the sort code. So, I have to wait, or something.'

'Do you have any idea who it could be?' Shona said.

'No, not at all,' Viv said. She was gulping down her coffee like it was water. 'I have no idea what it means or what is going on. I rang Mam and Dad, and they have no idea either. Can't think who it might be.'

Shona put her hand on Viv's hand. 'You've had a time of it,' she said softly.

It was dark outside now. Shona wanted to get home and pack. She needed to call Bernie and Ranald, make plans. But she needed to ask a question. 'Viv?'

'Yes, pet.'

'At the hotel the other night. You made that lovely speech.'

'Thanks, love. Probably the highlight of the whole shambles. Did I tell you they're holding Dan's body? They can't contact a next of kin. For fuck's sake. I think his mam is in Ullathorne. She might not have a phone, mind you.'

'That speech – your brother.'

'Aye,' she said and turned away.

'What–'

'No, Shona,' Viv said, an edge to her voice. Her eyes widened. 'I don't want to talk about that now. Thirty years and it's still too much. I just can't.'

'All I mean is – as I said on the ferry back – I didn't even know you had a brother,' Shona said, retracing her steps.

'He's been gone a long time,' Viv said. 'I thought I'd mention him because . . . me mam was there. She doesn't travel, and poor Dad . . . he . . .'

Viv's face crumpled. She began crying and reached for a paper napkin. Shona, after a moment of hesitation, put an arm around her.

Viv sobbed for a few moments. Then she recovered. She wiped her eyes with the back of her hand. She went to the bathroom and adjusted herself, and they talked of smaller things. Of irrelevancies, of ordinary things. Viv said she was going to spend the money on a long holiday if it ever cleared. Shona said she should buy a house. Viv shook her head – it all seemed too much, too odd, too sudden. She said Wayne was being a bit distant, and Shona bit her tongue.

On the bus home, Shona listened to a stream of electronic music and gripped her stick as if it might float away. Immersed in the mesh of rippling arpeggios, she tried to temporarily forget what she was now determined to do.

6

London, its unending roar, the immensity of it, filled Alison's ears, parched her mouth and drowned her heart.

The children needed to be picked up from school, and in her car the radio was full of noise about the government calling a snap general election. The prime minister was hoping to increase his majority, building on gains in the areas of England previously unknown to his party.

Alison was alone again. And stuck, again, in traffic. White buildings with fluted pillars outside their doors stood silently in the blocked street. All else was movement: the glint of a far plane indented a furrow of vapour overhead. A train thundered past, a blur of velocity, on the tatty railway bridge. There was a woman on a bicycle, and a delivery man on a motorbike. The scene reminded her of an educational transport poster from her youth: all laid out in bright colours on the wall of Ullathorne Primary School – a blue sky, a clean town, all manners of transport illustrated and brightly painted. Happy people, in happy places. Two-dimensional and free of pain.

Up ahead the lights turned to green. She moved forward two metres. The lights turned red again. She thumped the steering wheel with an open hand.

She had to get to the school by 3.35 p.m. and she was running late. Her throat was thick, her eyes were itching, and her armpits were wet with sweat.

Sitting in the hum of her car, Alison Harmire closed her eyes and thought of home. Not the house she lived in now, with two loud children and her soon-to-be ex-husband. Not that. But her real home, where the deep wide river ran from the fells to the dales, through the meadows and the woods, and on to the steel dark sea.

More and more, as she faced the end of her forties, with one career in business over and another career yet to be made, she dreamt of Ullathorne. Not just as a landscape for the inscrutable and absurd night adventures of the mind, but in daydreams – daydreams amid the crash and rush and battle of the city. Memories of her childhood in the old stone town, by the old river. But then her mind would race to her teens and that night in the old mill, and she would be snapped back into the real. Of her loved but insatiable children, and her looming divorce and London, a centrifuge with a gravity inescapable.

London had made her tired of life.

In that moment of awareness, the lights had changed to green and then back to red. It was 3.25. She wasn't going to make it on time. She swore and pulled the car into a space gripped by a double yellow line. She needed water.

She locked the car with a backwards flick and walked quickly down the street. At the junction there was a newsagent. The door caught her reflection as she approached – her body misshapen as if in water. She wondered if she was invisible, if anyone could really see her. Her dark glasses, with wide white frames, distorted her face, as if she was some kind of sea creature. She swam into the dark store. She picked up a green glass bottle of water. There was a man at the till, buying wine, chatting to the shopkeeper.

Her phone beeped. A text from Nigel: *When I'm back we need to talk.*

Nigel, in between allegedly consulting at various financial institutions she had not heard of, had been taking a lot of time off. And as well as shouting at the children, buying new trousers and taking flying lessons, he had been attempting to write a business book with a ghostwriter called Phaedra.

She shook her head involuntarily and inched forward, closer

to the gossiping men. She looked at her phone. She was so late now, but she was desperate for water. She felt her temperature rising. She considered opening the bottle.

Alison glanced at the newspapers, their headlines blaring like red-faced hooligans shouting in the sun. There were European papers too. There was a tabloid paper she had not read before, with a large photo, half covered by another paper. One eye, half a nose, a closed mouth. The mouth was familiar: thin, turned down at the corners. But the eyes had it – so pale and serious.

She reached for the paper, her hands suddenly shaking.

DEATH SHOCK AT HOTEL WEDDING

On the front page was a picture of her old school friend Dan. His face was fuzzed by the cheap paper and unkind magnification. Grey at the temples and thinner than she remembered. But it was him. She had not seen him for years. Not since her wedding. Not long after university, before children, before the stalling of her career. Before she had said yes to Nigel Osbourne.

The words swam and then stilled.

EXCLUSIVE BY JON INNES

A STUNNING BRIDE was shocked last night to have her perfect day DESTROYED by the bloody suicide of a deranged guest.

Blood

The glitzy bash at the Poets' Hotel near Dunoon in Scotland was rocked by the discovery of the body of WEIRDO Daniel Merrygill, 49, who killed himself by HURLING himself from the window of his £300-a-night luxury bedroom.

TRAGIC Dan is said to have SMEARED the room with his own blood and left a shocking message before his bloody death.

Naked

STUNNED guests were horrified to find his NAKED body in the early hours, covered in tattoos of SATANIC symbols.

GORGEOUS media secretary Vivien Banks, 44, was forced to CANCEL the wedding to handsome COPPER boyfriend Wayne Provan after the discovery of TWISTED Daniel in the early hours of the morning by shocked guests at the deluxe hotel in Scotland's romantic Highlands.

Alison put her hand to her mouth.

Glass moved in her hand. She dropped the bottle, and it hit the floor but did not smash. It rolled under the newsstand and lay glinting in the shadows, the water inside glaring like an eye staring from the past.

7

It was the morning after the orgy.

Gary Watson MP was woken by his phone buzzing on the floor. It vibrated across a bed of silvery ripped condom wrappers glinting in the morning light.

He was naked. Alyce, beside him, was also stirring, the light gleaming on her bare legs and feet, the rest of her body covered in a pale silk sheet. On the side table, there were plastic baggies caked with white powder. Other powders and small sprays of crystals lay, scratched and in mounds, on surfaces across the room. Empty bottles had been left by the door. A large tube of lubricant lay on the floor, squeezed into two like a fat link sausage.

Watson pushed himself up. He had a message from his private secretary, Knott: *PM to call GE Be ready*.

He raised his plucked eyebrows, scratched his tingling shaved balls and wiped his scorched nose.

'Well, well,' he mumbled.

He was only mildly surprised. A general election had been on the cards for a while. The Whips had warned him of it, and his constituency team's plans were well advanced. It had been the talk of the back benches, of course. Some of his fellow Northern MPs, sitting precariously on thin majorities, were nervous. But those with safe seats, like him, were looking forward to the six-week holiday until the day of the poll. He scrolled through his phone. There were similar messages from some fellow MPs. Three more from Knott, with links to emails on some mundane practical matters, now that Parliament would shortly be dissolved.

He felt the cocaine burn twinge in his nose and sneezed.

His phone buzzed again. *Get up. PM on way to the palace to dissolve parly.*

Alyce, beautiful and severe, turned over under the sheets. He contemplated the days and weeks ahead. The dissolution of Parliament. A month in the open air, tramping around Tyrdale, being fed lines by the special advisers, shaking hands with farmers and police, meeting small businesses, making speeches at the Party Club, a long arm around the local party chairman, repeating his well-beaten lines, being chummily interviewed by regional television and the local paper.

Watson, a mind full of jackhammers, stood up and stretched and looked about, pulling at his itchy dick. He peered down at it. There were dried clumps of blood around his crotch. With a slight flutter in his heart, he looked to the door of the adjoining suite. He padded slowly across to it and looked in.

He remembered, in hazy slides of memory, the messy exertions of the night before. The single bed had been stripped, and everything removed. A large blue bag of rubbish was full, tied up, ready to be disposed of. An arc of black blood was sprayed across the mirrored cupboard. Watson saw flickering constellations of blue and yellow at the corners of his eyes – the drugs were wearing off. He walked unsteadily to the bathroom.

It was all marble and silver, with a painful, icy clear light. There was a woman sloshing in a full warm bath. The tidal plane of water tipped as she moved. Her eyes widened as he shuffled in. She was middle-aged, her hair cut short. He didn't remember her. She had a collar around her neck.

He stood before a large mirror shrouded by steam. He wiped his hand over it. Behind the condensation was his face, pale and haggard. His eyes were black. He had encrusted dark powder or something else around his upper lip, which he wiped off.

Under his left breast there was a tattoo, with depictions of the sun and the moon, letters and numbers. The sun, with a circlet of flames. The moon, radiating dotted lines of glow.

'How do,' he said to the woman, who was now washing with a large sponge. He ambled to the toilet and unfurled from a distance a lengthy arc of orange piss.

'*Bonjour*,' she said woozily.

He smiled as he drained himself.

People were waking up – the remnants, those who had been overwhelmed by drink, pills or otherwise. Men from business and politics, the media and security services were pulling on clothes, holding their heads, drinking water, checking their phones. An editor of a national newspaper was being unclipped from his restraining gear. Among the paid participants, and those drafted in, there had been some enthusiastic swingers from the Newcastle suburbs, happily filming themselves stolidly rutting in various lubricated combinations.

Watson wandered back into the bedroom. He put a hand on Alyce's side – still warm, still breathing. He pulled back her shroud, and she opened her eyes suddenly. They were violet.

It was not Alyce at all. He did not remember seeing this woman before.

'Hi,' she said.

Watson looked surprised for a fleeting moment. Then his face aligned. 'Here, you from Bulgaria?'

'What?'

'You the lass from Bulgaria?'

'No, Spennymoor.'

'Spennymoor? What – down the road?'

'Is there another one? What time is it?'

'What time is it? Time for you to toddle off, pet.'

'Oh, fuck off, will ya,' she said. She rolled over with a sigh, made a clicking noise with her tongue. 'You fucking people,' she muttered and pulled the sheet over her head.

Watson pulled on a bathrobe and moved to the window. The cold morning light was clear on the fields outside, and on the stone balustrade above the gardens, the carved lips of the fountain. Mist was rising from the stands of trees. The Palladian villa, secluded in the west Durham hills, belonged to one of his wealthiest funders. It was hidden by a half-mile of woods from the moving eyes of the A66 and squatted like a stone toad at the end of a long, winding drive.

He knew he had to leave, to go back to his constituency house near Ullathorne, to begin his campaign. 'To take the right path,' he said.

The woman in the bed was now getting up, pulling her hair away from her eyes. She looked at him impassively and then walked slowly into the bathroom.

He reached for his phone and called a restricted number. Raymond's number. Waiting for the phone to be picked up, Watson looked around the room. Damp towels lay in a pile by the fireplace.

'Gary,' an elderly man's voice said.

Watson's heart picked up its beat. Raymond's voice was a blade of black ice. They had never met. Watson did not want to meet him – he was outmatched.

Raymond ran the project to see certain MPs chosen, elected and protected. Watson took him seriously.

'Morning,' he said. 'That's the starting pistol sounded. Kick-off.'

'I know,' Raymond said, cold as a wall.

'So, the fat man has sung and wants to increase his majority. So off we go. It'll be a doddle.'

'He wants Sally to run, too,' Raymond said with no emotion. Watson winced. 'Sally?'

'His wife, Gary. The prime minister's wife. He wants her to run. In a safe seat.'

'Nice,' he said. 'What a pretty picture that will be.'

'He wants her to succeed him.'

'To suck his seed? I think she's done that already,' Watson said.

There was silence.

'Excuse my coarse humour,' Watson murmured.

'Are you all set in Tyrdale?'

He blew out a sigh. 'Yes, all ready to go. Been on it for months. Knott has his plans. A consultant . . . you know Alyce . . . has been working on the social media campaign with her team. But you know the drill. I'll be present and available in Ullathorne for six weeks. Meet the Women's Institute, the business group, the Young Farmers. Pose pretty. Certain things will have to be done. I'm there now, actually. Funny you called – just getting the house out of mothballs.'

'Knott there?'

'Yep, present and correct.'

'I might visit.'

Watson closed his eyes, as if in pain.

'Is Alyce with you?' Raymond asked.

'No, she's not.'

'Gary?'

'Yes?'

'Remember our chat out in Bayreuth?'

'How could I forget.'

'If there's any more mess . . . or potential mess . . .'

'There won't be.'

'We don't want another Margate, do we? Another shambles. We can't do another Kent. These events strain our capacity.'

The phone line became very quiet. Watson heard Raymond's breath.

'Raymond – come on now,' Watson said, chuckling as much as he could. 'That was a different kettle of . . . and that's my wife you're talking about now.'

Raymond snorted. 'We monitor your interests. Fuck it up again, and we'll have to think on it,' he said, and the line went dead.

There was a sudden thump and crashing noise somewhere

else in the house. A tinkling noise of broken glass. Watson dressed quickly – shirt, suit, jacket – and left the room. The doors on the landing were open, and a trickle of people were leaving. A naked man exited a room with a leather jacket over his shoulder. Watson passed a room with the door slightly open, a slapping noise within.

Three naked people were entwined, steadily fucking on a dishevelled bed. One of them was filming it all on his mobile phone. Glaring above its tiny fierce spotlight, the tall, bald man, another MP from his party, looked demented.

Watson nodded to him with a smile. On the stairwell, he stepped over a sleeping big man, his shoulders as hairy as a badger.

He called Knott on his phone, but there was no answer.

The main room of the house was being cleaned. Two women were tipping rubbish into large bin liners. Empty bottles were being stacked in large plastic cartons. A heap of clothes was gathered by the ripped sofa. A rotating platform was being dismantled. A pair of ripped boxer shorts were hanging like a skinned face from the chandelier.

A stocky figure rolled into view, emerging from the kitchen.

'Knott – fuck's sake. Answer me when I call,' Watson said.

'I've just arrived,' Knott said, unmoved. He held up his phone. 'Did you get my message?'

'Yes,' Watson said. 'Have you seen Alyce?'

'Alyce? She left last night,' Knott said, wiping his hands.

'Did she?'

'Yes. Around one, when I did. You said goodbye to her.'

Watson didn't remember. 'Oh, yes, of course,' he lied.

'I'll follow. I need to make some calls,' Knott said.

'No, I need a driver,' Watson said and clicked his fingers.

Knott stared for a moment and then nodded.

Watson walked away, his footsteps silent on the thick white carpet, like a cat. In the long, mirrored hallway, a cleaner was swabbing the tiled floor. A young woman in a large puffer jacket, red tights and high heels was weeping on the shoulder of another.

Outside, in the cold, he paced quickly through the austere beauty of the surrounding parkland. Knott crunched behind, murmuring into his phone.

The world was asleep. The fields were flat and empty. A diffuse scramble of birds rose suddenly from the high, leafless trees.

Watson checked the news on his phone: stories about hospitals and Brexit, football, some celebrity or other. He looked at the news in Wales: nothing. He flipped to the Scottish section and stopped.

DEATH AT WEDDING IN ARGYLL
PA Reporter

Police have said there are no suspicious circumstances around the death of a guest at a wedding at a hotel near Dunoon.

The naked body of Daniel Merrygill, 49, was found in the hotel grounds in the early hours.

It is believed he had taken his own life.

A guest at the wedding said that Merrygill, a civil servant, had written a message in his own blood on the hotel wall.

'It was a horrible thing to have at what would have been a beautiful wedding,' the source said. 'We were all partying and then the body landed in the garden. I recognised him. He was part of the wedding party. He was naked and covered in tattoos, all letters and numbers, like a Ouija board. It's clear he was dead from the fall. I pity the bride, that's her big day ruined. How can you get over something like that?'

A spokesman for the Poets' Hotel, Argyll and Bute, declined to comment.

*The wedding, of a Ms Vivienne Banks and Mr Wayne
Provan, has been cancelled and police have ruled out any
further investigations in the case.*

People walked past him as he stared at his phone. A woman
giggled as she carried her shoes. A man spoke in Russian.

Watson was frozen. He shook his head.

'Sir?' Knott said, stopping beside Watson. His breath was
silver in the air.

'Where's Bax?' Watson said eventually.

'At Scar Top, I assume.'

Scar Top was Watson's home in the Tyrdale valley.

'You know, we should start thinking about Bax's
responsibilities. His capacity,' Knott said. 'He takes on a lot for
you. For us. How much do you pay him?'

'I don't. But he's a soldier, he can take it. He's loyal. But
where the fuck is he? I need to speak to him.'

'I'll give him a call,' Knott said. 'Now the big game is afoot.'

'Can you let him know I need a word, urgently?'

Knott sighed and checked his watch. 'I will. What's the
urgency?'

Watson shook his head. 'Let's get out of here.'

In the car park, hidden behind frosted topiary, they found
Knott's large dark car.

Watson slumped in the back. The car hummed to life. He
looked out the windows as they drove through the woods.

'Did Raymond call?' Knott said impassively.

Watson nodded and closed his eyes. The glass moved in his
mind. Gliding over words, over combinations and paths, tracing
its own occult parabola.

Words could not be unsaid, and sights could not be unseen.
But he had to take the right path, as Sorley said. As Sorley
always said. Right, and right, and right again. And the right
path led to Ullathorne.

As Knott hit the main road, Watson opened his eyes and phoned Alyce.

The phone made a strange beeping noise. He took it from his ear and looked at it. The beeping continued.

'I'm sorry. This number is no longer available,' a metallic voice said, as cold as the dead.

8

It was three in the morning, and again Shona could not sleep. The streetlamp's corona glimmered at the edges of her window. A faint glow on the wall, cast by a tiny light on her charging laptop, pulsed weakly. Dim lights, small lights, all faint in the dark.

She could check on her father, who was being released from hospital in the morning. But she decided not to.

She sat up, her black T-shirt draped over her knees. She felt alone. She felt alone because she was alone. The world outside was vast and hostile, and here, this place of safety, was changing. It was drifting, untethered. The walls about her suddenly seemed to be cardboard, paper – temporary. Her father, probably safe now, and warm and dreaming of gardens and skies – temporary. One day, he would be gone. And then what?

'Fuck's sake,' she said.

She stood up and rubbed her side. At the window, she pulled aside a blind. Nothing out there amid the parked cars. An ice-cream van. The short strip of shops was closed and shuttered. The sick yellow light of the sleeping city tainted the sad, heavy clouds, like cotton wool soaked in piss.

There was a sudden loping movement. A fox, russet and sleek, snuffled in the street. It ducked between two hedges and was gone.

Shona thought of her mother. Long gone. Dead in her youth. Her father weeping, and a dark church, filled with more weeping. What could she remember of her? Just an uncertain smile and reddened eyes looking down from a metal hospital bed. No grave. Her ashes, cast by her father, somewhere in the hills. Shona pushed it all away, as she had always done. She turned around. There was another movement in her room.

MacDiarmid leapt onto her bed and yawned, and then in a sleek instant formed a neat furry circle in the residual heat of the sheet. Shona sat beside her, stroked the short hair around her cheek. MacDiarmid leaned into her, rubbing Shona's fingers with a heavy head, eyes half closed, the tip of her tail twitching.

'Dopey cat,' Shona whispered.

She lay beside the purring feline and looked to her side table – there were two folded papers from Reculver. One was an interview with Gary Watson MP. She reached for it and flicked on the lamp, which flung sudden shadows across her room. The furniture gained edges, surfaces, weight and mass.

'What's this fucking nonsense, then,' she said to herself, opening the document.

It was a printout of a short online interview with the *Northern Recorder*, a mass-market tabloid. There was a prominent picture of Watson. He had shaved the sides of his hair, and the longer hair on top had been swept into a kind of quiff.

He beamed from the page, teeth white and straight, tie knotted tight, neck and shoulders gym-toned, skin unmarked by age or illness. His clothes were immaculate.

WESTMINSTER FOCUS:
QUESTION TIME WITH TYRDALE MP GARY
WATSON
The outspoken MP talks to Northern Recorder's
political editor Paul Tankard.

How you doing, Gary?
Never been better, Paul. You call me in my office in Westminster; been a busy day doing the people's work. A few key votes, but as I said to the PM from the stage of the Tyrdale vote – you'll never need the Whips to speak to me. I'm fully on board with the project. Blood, sweat and

tears: that's what I am prepared to give. But today's been a good day. We won the votes handily – it always feels that way when you know you have taken the right path. But as I always say, any day spent outside Tyrdale is not a perfect day – looking forward to racing back up for constituency work in the recess. Can't get home soon enough.

What are the key priorities for the year ahead?
There's many – fulfilling our manifesto must be the main commitment: we put in that document many promises, many pledges, which we have to see through. We must honour those. So, there's immigration reform – hopefully, we'll see the back of that. There's the Safe Seas Charter for protecting the south coast from refugees – very close to my head and my heart, as you know. There's the Constitution Act to protect the Union, unravel the error of devolution and bring back some measure of sensible control back to the centre. The major free trade deal with the nuclear powers. And, of course, I'll be fighting for the Tyrdale people, especially traditional families, protecting them from others who may do them harm, restoring their faith in nation and honour, and ensuring their healthy, decent numbers grow. But there is no time. We have to work for it – to strive, to fight and to win.

You're a Tyrdale lad – is your voice heard in Westminster?
I am indeed, and proud of it. I've always said my vision for the nation started on the banks of the Tyr and the generations my own family have spent in and around the dale. It's in your blood, that soil. My childhood in those vales was idyllic.

From the Pennines you can see for miles – and I've always said you can see the future of Great Britain from there. As you know, there's a cadre of Northern MPs now, and we have the Say Yes to North group at Westminster. Some say I am their leader, which is very kind. I am the chair of the group in Parliament. I wouldn't say we are acknowledged as a major force as yet, but the PM knows we are there and, to be fair to him, he spends time with us and knows what we're all about. He is sound, that way. I think he's smashing it, despite the doubters and the weaklings.

You're a backbencher right now – what are your ambitions for higher office?
We all have ambitions, Paul: didn't you always strive to be at the top of your game? I'm no different – I am ready to serve King and Country in any way that the PM sees fit. If a role of duty was to be offered to me, I would put my all into it. But, first and foremost, my ambitions are for this country – to be a lean, mean machine of a modern country with an empire of opportunity behind it and ahead of it. A great, strong, unashamed nation – tough as teak with both feet set in the glories of our past and our blue eyes set fearlessly on the time when tomorrow comes.

How do you relax, Gary?
To be brutally honest, Paul, I try not to. Since my wife, Sarah, passed, I mash the sixteen-hour work days, wherever I am. That's how I was brought up and that's what I expect of myself. I expect and demand rigour and discipline within myself, and thus, Paul, those around me. I do like to read when I can – mainly the Romans, the Greeks. Big fan of the Stoics. Look them up. Top advice. And I like to listen to audiobooks on my train journey north – innovative business theory and a spot of modern hard rock when I need a lift. I slap on some of the heavy stuff when I'm cracking on with the irons. I like gyms. But you would know that if you've seen me!

Thanks, Gary.
Over and out. Got to crack on. See you round the 'dale.

'Fuck's sake,' Shona said, shaking her head.

The cat opened her eyes and mewed. Tiny teeth gleamed in a pink mouth. She trilled. It seemed as loud as a roar in the night.

'Shut up, fatty,' Shona whispered. She dropped the paper onto the floor, turned off the light and closed her eyes again in the restored darkness.

She needed to sleep, even if, at its end, she would have to endure waking up again.

9

There was a lot to do and a train to catch. Shona needed to pack.

Her father was now home, watching TV, slumped in his corduroys. Bernie was there, too, bashing pots in the kitchen and loudly singing 'Hares On The Mountain'. Shona, holding her half-empty travel bag, raised a theatrical eyebrow to her father as Bernie ululated.

Hugh Sandison had shaved off his beard. It made him look older, his jowls pink and tender, and he had a small white scar on his chin she had not noticed before. He acknowledged his daughter's mild display of sass with open hands.

'She has a fine voice, Shona,' he said. 'What can I say?'

Shona was kneeling on the carpet in their living room, trying to extract her laptop charger from a complicated mass of cables that coiled in and around a table leg.

'Well, she has *a* voice,' she said. 'You're right there.'

'Aye, well, young lady,' he huffed. 'As I see it, you're buggering off to that England chasing some story. Ms Comfort, on the other hand, is volunteering to look after this old man while he ails in his dotage, so I think I can bear an old folk song now and again.'

Shona pulled angrily at a white cable, which only made a loose tangle into a fast knot. She noticed a large pair of headphones attached to a plug socket, charging.

'Are these Bernie's?' she said, pointing to them.

'No, she bought them for me, to listen to my music,' he said. 'Grand, aren't they?'

Shona nodded briefly and yanked at the cable. 'For fuck's

sake,' she muttered. 'This is a fucking snake's wedding.'

'Your language, my love, is still abominable,' her father said, smiling. 'You wouldn't catch me using coarse words in that manner.'

'Dad, you called that Henry at the allotment an arrogant cunt a wee while ago, so don't have a go at me,' she said.

'That was a factual observation. I've heard enough about his onions. He was saying my patch is getting too messy, out of control. The cheek of it.'

'Is it?'

He shook his head. Then, reluctantly, he nodded. 'But maybe there's some benefit to having the bugs and insects in the long weeds. I hope.'

'Didn't you say there's a load of old junk to get rid of?'

'There is, but it's none of Henry's beeswax. You should see the state of his shed: solar panels! Cunt.'

Bernie was trilling away in the kitchen. She sounded happy.

Shona looked to her father. His eyes were watery. His ears seemed larger. 'Well, maybe you were slowing down with the gardening because you weren't feeling too good, and–'

'Mind yourself,' he interrupted. 'I haven't been slowing down. My allotment just needs a wee tidy-up. A bit of moving things about. Bernie will help me.'

Shona took a deep breath and finally freed the offending cable.

'Anyway, when's your train, and when do you get back again?' her father said, sounding tired, looking at the TV.

'There's one every hour,' she said, pushing away a stray lock of hair. 'And I'll be back in a few days. Got a place to stay in the town. Ranald wants a news feature – if there's a story there.'

'Ah, so you've been commissioned?' he said, with a sudden burst of informed interest. Hugh had been a journalist in his day. Decades at the *Herald*, including ten long years as night editor, and a few before that in local press in Fife. He often said he had printer's ink under his fingernails. He knew the trade inside and out.

'Yep. Ranald wants it sooner rather than later,' Shona said, noticing the change in his mood.

'Can you rustle it up in a week?'

'I'll bloody have to, won't I?' she said, jamming a pair of damp socks into her bag. 'And let's face it, Dad,' she added, rolling a top and sliding it down the side of her belongings, 'we're bloody skint.'

'Need the cash,' he said, nodding. 'That's no lie.'

Shona was running late. She bent over and stroked MacDiarmid, who was lying regally on a bill from the council, which had been discarded on the carpet. MacDiarmid evidently thought it was her new bed.

'So, it'll be one of those human-interest tales? Because in my experience, love,' her father went on, 'the story behind a suicide is not often dramatic or of interest to other people. Sad, tragic, devastating to the family, but not of interest to readers of the papers. We used to avoid them, back in the day. Not in the public interest.'

Shona knew this – which irritated her – but knew there was more to this story. The messages, the stones, the burning caravan, the money appearing in Viv's bank account. There was something else. Beyond her ken. But not for long.

'So, what's your plan?' her dad asked. His eyes were back on the snooker. Perfect coloured globes clinked on a small jade lawn.

'I'm meeting one of Ranald's freelance snappers at Darlington station,' she said, 'and going to the caravan place, then he's dropping me at Ullathorne. So, I'll be on my phone the whole time. If I need to turn around and come back, I will – okay?'

She zipped her bag, rested it on the table and knelt beside her father.

His attention moved from the screen to her. His eyes were

pink-rimmed, watery. His newly revealed skin looked tender. He raised a trembling hand to her face. 'Best of luck, my love,' he said softly. 'I'm fine. Don't you worry about me. Get the story. But come back soon now.'

'I will, Da,' she said. She kissed him on his forehead. He smelled of soap and coffee.

With tenderness, he moved to tuck her hair behind her ear.

'I'm badly in need of a haircut,' she said, smiling.

'Looks like someone has already done it badly,' he said.

'Dad.'

'Off you go. Get the story,' he said, winking, 'and haste ye back.'

She stood and kissed him again but could not say goodbye.

'Bernie!' she called to the kitchen, as she rushed to her room to grab her mobile phone.

Bernie stopped singing for a moment. 'Yes, dear?' she yelled.

'Don't let Dad cook,' Shona shouted. 'And don't let him on that allotment.'

'Shona?' Bernie called back, and Shona heard footsteps and her father loudly complaining.

Bernie appeared in the frame of her bedroom door, pink rubber gloves aloft. 'Are you in charge of the shopping around here?' she said quietly.

'Yeah, why?' Shona said, grabbing her phone from the bedside table.

'It's just I've been going through the cupboard and there's a lot of out-of-date food there. There's some tins well past their sell-by date,' Bernie said.

She had an oval face and deep brown eyes. Her long grey hair was held back in a tortoiseshell clasp. She looked as if she held something profound in her small busy body.

'Well, you'd know about things being past their sell-by dates,' Shona said, opening her bag again and tossing in her phone charger.

Bernie blinked and carried on. 'I mean there's a tin of tuna there that will soon be getting a telegram from the king . . . And Shona, my dear' – she produced a wooden bowl of fruit from behind her back – 'you don't rotate your fruit. The fruit at the bottom was rotten. You should make sure the older fruit is at the top, new fruit underneath. Then everything's eaten in its right time. You need to rotate your limes.'

'Rotate my limes,' Shona said, struggling with a zip.

'Yes. I don't think Hugh has the energy to rotate the limes. I hope you don't mind, but I'll do a wee stock take, a little bit of an update on your larder essentials,' Bernie said.

Shona zipped the bag, looked up and smiled as broadly as she could manage. 'Sure. Knock yourself out. See you later – oh, and Bernie?'

'Yes?'

'Don't eat that tuna.'

Within the hour Shona was travelling south from Edinburgh. She was on the King's Cross train that passed through Newcastle and Durham before stopping at Darlington. It was a weekday afternoon, and the carriages were not busy. No one else sat at her table, and she watched with a surprising sense of rising alarm as Waverley station and then the outskirts of Edinburgh slipped away. She texted Bernie and asked for her to call if anything changed.

A message – *Don't worry he is fine fast asleep after big brunch* – came back immediately.

She plugged in her laptop and watched the landscape pass by for a while. There were grey fields and low hills, and then suddenly on the left, the sea, a plain of steel to the horizon. The waves were engraved, barely moving, with light in fine lines, like tiny wires.

Shona texted the photographer who was to pick her up at Darlington. Shona did not drive any more. She just could not face the stress and physical discomfort of being behind the wheel of a car again. Her left side ached at the thought of it. The photographer was called Terry Green. She texted him a message to check everything was okay, but there was no response. She opened her laptop and logged on to the internet.

She had put it off, but she began to search for what she could find on Andrew Banks, Viv's brother. There were some businessmen of that name. But she could not find an Andrew Banks related to Ullathorne. Screeds of useless web pages scrolled before her. A sinking desert of digital sand.

Tyrdale's local newspaper, the *Tyrdale Times*, came out every Wednesday. It had an old gothic masthead and still carried news from cattle marts and livestock auctions. It had a clear, frequently updated website. For an independent local, she thought, it wasn't all that bad. A former colleague of hers, John Fallon, had worked on it, many years ago. He had been features editor at the *Glasgow Mercury* when she had been a junior reporter. That had been the first broadsheet she had worked on – now it was nothing but a website. A ghost. Fallon was long gone, his whisky-poisoned body found on a bleak scrag of island in Loch Lomond. Another body, another face, another needle of pain pricking from the past.

As the train neared Newcastle, she looked at the *Tyrdale Times* archive online. There was nothing for Andrew Banks. There were many pictures of Ullathorne. It was unchanging: two wide main streets, a market cross marked by a conical roof, large stone houses with square windows. Cobbles and lanes. A ruined castle on a cliff and, below, the River Tyr. In the background of every photo in the paper – be it a story from the market or a football match, a factory opening or petty rural vandalism – there were the dark stands of trees and the distant moors.

The archive only went back to 1999, for some reason. She slapped the laptop shut. Newcastle went by, its broad river and bridge-spanned quayside reminding her of Glasgow, and next, Durham, with its castle and cathedral on their hill. The old strongholds stood still, the modern world swimming about them. Shona remembered reading how Scottish prisoners had been held in Durham Cathedral, back in some pointless bloody war, many years ago.

She was in England now. Scotland and its concerns were another country. She was a stranger now – people would notice her Glasgow accent. She wondered what it might conjure for them.

The accents of the other passengers changed with each stop. Looking for their seats, they spoke in flat vowels, the arrested roll and clipped restraint of the North of England. Outside, there were streets of red brick, lifeless business parks, large fields brown and dull green, and glimpses of motorways. To the west, vast clouds moved in drifting inky shadows across the dark hills – the spine of England, the Pennines.

Somewhere in those blue folds, the River Tyr ran from its source as a stream over moorland rocks, down through a green rich dale and then disappeared, ancient and deep and slow, into the swallowing sea.

Somewhere in that crease of country, old rules and old secrets prevailed. And maybe old reasons why people now were doing strange and violent things – why a man might throw himself to his death from a hotel roof. Why he might suddenly destroy his life and carry messages, rhymes and legends on his body.

Out of a plastic wallet she took a front page, ripped from the *Record*. Merrygill's white face above the story of his death. His eyes like dried-up puddles on a sunless day. Lips thin and pursed. His face was a mask concealing something awful – or perhaps nothing, nothing at all. Just emptiness, a life wasted, and at the end, a short burst of needless pain and hot, pooling blood.

Darlington arrived. A steeple rose above a grey town huddled on dreary flat land, and as Shona wearily descended from the train, her stick smacking on the door, cold air slapped her face. The train departed like a slow injection and left her alone on a dirty platform wet with rain.

Preparations were being made for the coming election. But Watson had slipped out, into the wild.

He had taken his sleek silver motor and driven quickly to the rendezvous. He had to be back in time for an online meeting with the Say Yes to North group of MPs. They would be talking about strategy, joint hustings during the run-up to the election and the latest press lines from the special advisers in central office. Watson wanted to re-emphasise the grip of his leadership. The PM knew he led the cadre. And after election day, he would impress on the Whips how influential he now was: twice elected, he would be. In the media, and in the Commons, he would be the voice of the wall of Northern MPs who held seats from Wallsend to Carlisle. He would be a Carl himself. A king, or at least, a kingmaker. He already was vice-chair of the Intelligence and Security Committee; more power would follow.

He had sped through the gathering gloom of the wintry afternoon. Silver flashed in the puddles beside the quiet country road. Shadows grew in the tangled hedges. His stomach was tight, his shoulders hunched.

Up ahead, on the low glacial hills of the lower dale, stood the standing stones. Out of sight, high above the river, clear above the tree line. He had never received messages from Sorley here, but he thought he should, one day. The signal would be strong, a granite receiver – stone circles being, he had read, the primeval Ouija boards of the rock-inhabiting dead.

The darkening, rising fields blurred past: first the low winter grass, streaked with brown and lush ochre mushrooms, then the dead stubble, then the trampled mud, then thistles, peat and rocks. He reached the empty car park, switched off the engine and slid out from his seat. He pulled up his collar, pulled on a black beanie and walked quickly past the information sign.

Shoes crunching, he made his way up the steep gravel path, the smell of pine and mud around him. Tall conifers ringed the bare hill like a monk's tonsure. No one knew how old these stones were. They stood jagged like the torn nails of an embedded giant's hand.

He stopped halfway up. A figure was moving within the stone circle. Above, cold stars were just beginning to glitter as the dusk gathered. He looked back to the west – the sky was a sick yellow.

Bax could wait. He reached inside his jacket. There was a gram of cocaine in a plastic bag. He tipped a line onto his shaking hand and snorted it violently. Stars and a shiver, like the thinning tines of a splintering orgasm, surged around his face and eyes.

He shook his head and leapt up the remaining steps to the head of the hill.

Bax appeared from behind a standing stone, as if stepping out of it. A former soldier, bearded and all in black, he was all hard ligaments, quick twitch and clenched potential. He had been with Watson for the last few years, appointed by Raymond as an aide, a bodyguard, a fetcher, a carrier, a booker, an office clerk, a cleaner.

'Sir,' Bax said, nodding.

Nine stones stood in the wide circle, wider at their crests than their roots. Three more were broken, uneven, spattered with lichen. In the centre, like the pupil of an eye, a low stone was slumped.

The valley lay below them. The course of the Tyr was wide here, and slow. Trees hugged its edges. The bruise-blue distant hills had already become one with the falling night.

'Election,' Bax said.

'Yes, all ready to kick off. PM's going to the country. You ready?' Watson said, sniffing. The inside of his nose was aflame with chemical embers.

'Of course,' Bax said, nodding.

'Where've you been?' Watson asked. He moved to the central stone and sat on it. He ushered Bax close to him.

'Brussels,' Bax said, shrugging.

'For Raymond?'

Bax walked slowly towards him and nodded. 'I'm back now,' he said, smiling his lopsided grin.

Watson plunged his hands into the pockets of his thick black jacket. 'Well, we have some urgent business.'

'Always do, boss,' Bax said.

'I read somewhere – a good operator like you is like a good poisoner: anonymous. A bad one becomes famous. Look, I have something a little different to your normal kind of job, Bax. It's a bit of a tricky one. Delicate.'

Watson took out his phone and brought up a note on its screen. He tapped the screen, and the note was sent to Bax. Watson deleted it.

Bax's phone buzzed, and he peered at it. Its blue light was gentle on his hard face. 'What's this?'

'Last weekend, that fellow at the top of the list – he fucking died,' Watson said evenly.

A hawk spiralled above in the last thermals of the short day. A breeze rose and fell. The grass ruffled and settled.

Bax nodded.

'Topped himself, like a twat. Those other people, they knew him – and knew me,' Watson said.

'Knew?'

'Know,' Watson said, tilting his head.

Bax waited.

'This is the thing. This is the urgent thing, Bax. They cannot be troublesome to me now. Not in the coming weeks.'

Watson sniffed and rubbed his hands together. From the stone circle, he could see the whole valley. He had read, somewhere, that you could trace a straight line between the waterfall at the top of the dale, through the old Coine Tree, to this hill. An eldritch geometry. He shook his head. No. A swell of black anxiety and anger rose through his chest, like acid, like ichor.

'Look, this loser has gone and done it around people who might know me. And he's gone and done it with my fucking tattoo on his chest. Mine. He's gone and stolen it from me. And Sorley. From me and Sorley.'

Bax frowned. 'Does Knott know?'

'No. Forget fucking Knott. Fucking outrageous, right? To do that, to me, the selfish prick,' Watson said. 'So, that sad little waste of space is one thing. The other is the location: the wedding. A gathering of halfwits. Someone, somewhere – they might not, but we cannot risk it – might make the connection between him and me. I don't want that. We can't fucking have that.'

'Right.'

'Not now, not before I'm elected.'

'Raymond?'

'Raymond doesn't know about this. It's way below his pay grade. And I don't want his pals at MI6 tapping on his sarcophagus about it. All right?'

'Raymond isn't MI6 no more,' Bax smiled, with slow blinks of his grey eyes, like a resting cat.

'You don't need to tell me that,' Watson said. 'That list – learn it and lose it. You've got their details, right there.'

'Who are they? Politicians?'

'No, worse than that. They're amateurs. They probably think they have a clue. Worthless people, Bax. Empty people. Pitiful. Losers. They're all still lying around the dale like unflushed turds, apart from Ali – apart from Alison – she's in London. I just want them to be out of my mind. For me, for us. For the future of this nation – do you understand? I need rid of this.'

Watson had been slapping the stone with his hands, he realised. They were now smarting. The clean conifer air was painful in his swollen nostrils.

Bax looked at him impassively. He was now all shadow in the gloom.

'Am I important to you, Bax?' Watson said in a low voice.

'Of course.'

'How important am I?'

'Very.'

'Where we're going, you know, few Britons have been before, Bax. A new land – burnt free from the old. A cleansed slate, a revived and deloused population. We're going slowly because no one will want to see the destination right now. They won't be able to stomach it, will they? No. We inch there. The cities could burn. Redundant towns might wither away. But places like my Ullathorne – ancient, hard, safe – will prosper and survive. Thing is, we have the guts for it, and they don't. So, we win. We win.'

'Yes, sir.' Bax nodded.

'But, Bax, before all that, I need these people to be quiet. To stop what they're doing. To not meddle, you know?'

'Okay, got it. But do you know what they're planning? *Are* they planning?'

Watson shook his head. His mind was full of fierce light. It was if the acid of his stomach had risen past his throat and into his brain. His mind was now ablaze. 'I just can't have them all gathering together. I can't have them laughing at me. Giggling little girls in their little lives, their tiny pathetic landfill lives – do you understand, Bax, do you know what I mean here? I can't have it.'

The moon was up and clear now, its scars threaded and interlinked. It seemed the only light in the sky. It was a circular doorway. It could have been an entrance into a galaxy of bone.

Watson went on. He was jabbing at the air. 'Obviously that

prick was trying to get at me, do you see? He was trying to put me off. To make me nervous. To put me off my game, Bax. That's my tattoo he has. It's pathetic. Fucking outrageous, really. If I'd known, I would have got you to stave his head in. But, no, he goes and makes his fucking *death statement* in Scotland. But the others – we can't have the others jabbering on, blabbing to the press, now he's done this. About what they know or don't know. Understand?'

'Yes, boss. You want rid.'

'Yes! I want rid,' Watson gasped. 'I need that.' His chest hurt – a solid, throbbing pain, like something was trying to get out of his rib cage.

'I can sort it,' Bax said. He folded his arms.

'You sure?'

'They won't get near you. They won't say owt. Is there a danger, though?'

'What danger?' Watson hissed.

'Well . . . by making them quiet, we make them loud. If you know what I mean.'

'People go silent all the time, Bax,' Watson said. 'People fall by the wayside. That's just the way it is.'

He clapped his hands together. Beyond the bend in the valley, the streetlights of Ullathorne were glowing. They tipped light up to the fell, to the gathering clouds.

'And you know, Bax, that Sorley's been with me from the outset. From the very start. And he's always got it right. And he's telling me that this is what we need to do. This is the right path. And Raymond's backed me, even after . . . other things. Bumps in the road. So . . .'

Watson reached into his jacket. There were pills in a foil twist. He took one out and swallowed it.

Bax looked away.

A light rain began to fall. The stones slowly blushed black. The grass gently bent, and a freshness rose from the earth.

Across the dale, sightlines shortened, distant peaks receded into grey.

Watson rubbed his throat. The acid dipped away. OxyContin breathed warm kisses.

'You can do wrong things for the right reason, Bax,' Watson said. 'Wrong things for the right reasons. That's us. That's me.'

'Yeah.'

'We're just plain Englishmen, putting the country first.'

'Yes, sir.'

The stones about them seemed to move in the descended night. They were swaying, their edges smearing. Watson's eyesight began to frazzle. The moon repeated: it was doubled, like two owl eyes.

'I need a lift,' Watson said. 'I can't take the Tesla.'

Bax nodded.

As he left the hill of stones, Watson looked towards the deep forest in the valley.

For one suspended moment, caught in a flare of moonlight, he could see the upper branches of the great Hollow Tree, and caught in their mass and tangle, the plunging tumult of the Great Fosse. White water, hammering down in fury, held by black unyielding branches, encircled by living stones.

But no: that could not be. It was not possible. The geography, the geometry, the distance was all wrong. You could not see the Coine Tree from here. You could not see the great waterfall.

He blinked hard, and perspective and depth returned. The real world. All there was in the dale was darkness, and the drive of the valley delving into the earth. Its sides, like huge, cupped hands, a trough of hard flesh, gulping blood.

Terry was driving, her eyes fixed on the road. They had left Darlington and were heading west, into a land of small villages and whitewashed farms and, as the hills rose, the deepening valley of Tyrdale.

Terry had turned out to be a woman. She was slim and tall and had closely cropped white-blonde hair. She had greeted Shona with a wide smile and a heavy handshake.

Her car was a mess – the back seat was home to a large battered camera bag with multiple torn pockets and worn compartments, several cameras and lenses, a tripod, a light, several umbrellas, discarded takeaway coffee cups, fast-food wrappers, a distraught map, a pair of dirty green trainers, a couple of anoraks and a plastic supermarket bag which contained old clothes and boots thick with clumps of wet sand.

For a while they drove in silence, as Shona tried to find Marton's Farm on the map on her phone.

'So, star reporter, you worked for Ranald for long?' Terry said cheerily, as the road bit deeper into the hills. A broad river ran to the left of the road. The Tyr, Shona's map said. They were sixteen miles from Ullathorne. Terry's voice was lightly accented. Shona could not place it.

'About six months,' Shona said. 'Can't find this farm on this bloody map.'

'It's up on the moor, past Stainton. I found it earlier,' Terry said. 'I did a recce. No one was about. Saw the big burnt-out thing.'

Shona glared at her. 'Did the farmer see you?'

'No one was about.'

'Right.'

'You from Glasgow?' Terry said, speeding up as the road straightened. The hills were higher and more wooded now, the fields held by drystone walls. Barns and feeding pens slumped in mud. In a distant field, sheep moved as one towards a gate, harried by a black dog, its mouth agape. The moors loomed like the return of a bad memory.

Shona felt the landscape briefly overwhelm her – the emptiness, the scale, the far horizons. There were no streets here to shorten perspective, no junctions and paths to cut the earth into journeys and neighbourhoods. Just a silence, and space, and hidden life behind and within the folds of the earth itself. She was far from the wrecked and gorgeous Glasgow of her youth. Far from the neat parks and languid crescents of Edinburgh.

Terry's question had been left unanswered, and Shona remembered. 'Aye, Glasgow,' she said at last. She gave up looking for the farm and shoved her phone in her pocket.

'My old man is from Glasgow. Bearsden, you know it?' Terry said.

'Yeah. Dump,' Shona said.

Terry laughed. 'That's not what he says.'

'Yeah, I've been six months with the Buried Lede. Ranald pays my invoices on time,' Shona said, attempting to change the subject.

'He does, aye,' Terry said.

'He never said you were a lass, though,' Shona said.

'Why would he?' Terry switched on the radio, which unfurled a liquid silver rope of electronic music. She flicked a look at Shona. 'How long you had the stick?'

'Since I was a kid,' Shona lied.

Terry raised her eyebrows. She'd heard a different story. But she let it go.

They came to a roundabout near a large country pub with a large black sign of a Victorian prize bull.

'Aye, it's a right here, I think,' Terry said, taking the turn.

The road narrowed to a B-road and headed steeply through high hedges through the foothills of the Pennines.

Shona looked into the back of the car. 'Your car's a midden.'

'Hah, that's what my ex used to say.' Terry grinned. 'Well, I'm a snapper. That's how it is. I need all this shit.'

Shona smiled. 'Right enough. Wait a second . . .'

'What?'

'So, you're Terry.'

'Yeah,' Terry said.

'Short for Theresa?'

'Right. Theresa.'

'So, your name is Theresa Green?'

Terry looked to Shona, unsmiling, and then quickly nodded. 'Trees are green. Funny, right? My parents are idiots.'

Shona laughed. She felt something hard and tight leave her chest as she did. She blushed. 'I'm sorry for your troubles.'

'I bet.'

'There was a girl at my school called Iona Carr.'

'Really?'

'Nah,' Shona said, smiling, looking the other way.

'Listen, Ranald said you were stabbed back in the day. In the line of duty. Is that the reason for the stick?'

'Jesus fuck, what's with all the medical queries? Wee Ranald should keep his neb out,' Shona said, irritated, tapping the top of her stick.

'Right. Of course. Look, sorry,' Terry said. She held up a hand.

'Aye, I was stabbed by . . . I was on a job,' Shona murmured.

'Well, that's shite.'

'Wasn't the best night of my life, but–'

'But what?'

'Got the story, didn't I?'

They looked at each other briefly and then turned their eyes to the road.

'So, you live in Darlington?' Shona said.

'Nah, not in Darlo,' Terry said. 'I'm in a village, Newsham. Not far from here. Do stuff for Ranald now and then, but mainly it's *Yorkshire Post, Northern Echo* – *Guardian* sometimes. Do some commercial stuff as well – pays the bills. No weddings, funerals or bar mitzvahs.'

'Ever been to Scotland?'

'Aye. Went to Edinburgh Art College. Did I not say that?'

'Ah, right. Nice.'

'It was. A degree in fine art,' Terry said, shaking her head. 'A lot of good that did me.'

The fields weren't fields now, but wide rolling acres of unfarmable land – dull marsh, gorse and rocky hills. The sky was vast. Cold becks ran in rocky runs, and dilapidated houses and outbuildings, long abandoned, holding volumes of darkness and stench, dotted the desolate heath, which ran to the arc of a white horizon.

They came to a halt beside a hard, rocky, high-cambered track, which bent raggedly off the main road.

'It's here,' said Terry. They turned into it, and the car bumped along the track. They saw a large farm half a mile away – a central stone house, outbuildings, a concrete yard, parked tractors. But before the farm, there was a field, with a black mess near its edge amid twisted trees tortured by the moor gales.

As they slowed, the black mess became clearer – it was the burnt-out caravan. It was listing on burst, melted wheels, its sides folded in, and charred metal parts lay sunk in the mud and ashes and mess. It was black and ruined and open to the sky, like a metallic animal, gralloched and charred.

Terry pulled the car around so that it faced the main road. 'You speaking to the farmer?'

Shona nodded. She left her bag on the seat and, holding her notebook out and with her Dictaphone app on her phone turned on, started to walk down the road to the farm. Her feet, in trainers, were ungainly on the road. Her stick banged on myriad tiny hard surfaces.

The farm seemed to be empty of life. There was no one in the yard. Nothing was moving. She looked back, and Terry was doing her work – photographing the remains of the caravan. She was crouching, elbows out, the lens an extension of her hands, her eyes.

'What's all this?' a deep voice said.

A man in blue overalls appeared. He was in his late teens, fresh-faced, with a large bucket in one of his pink hands.

'Hi, maybe you can help me – is Mr Marton about?' Shona asked.

The youth rubbed his hair and looked behind him at the stone house. 'Nah, he's away in town,' he said. He pointed to Terry. 'What's all this?'

'We're from the papers, just doing a piece on the fire,' Shona said.

'*Tyrdale Times*?' the boy said, pulling at an ear. He looked down at her stick and furrowed his brow.

'No, we're freelance,' she said. 'Do you know when Mr Marton will get back?'

'He'll be a bit,' he said. 'I don't think he wants any of this business. I'd come back another time.' He stood looking at Terry, shaking his head. 'Aye, I'll tell him you've been, like. Come back another time.' He sucked his lower lip. He looked concerned, his cheeks blotching.

'Were you here when the fire happened?' Shona asked.

He studied his fingernails.

'Did you help put it out?'

'Nah, it was all out by the time I shipped up,' he said. 'All out. You could see it, like. Marton had called in the engine, but he'd got the foam on it from the house. Near put it out. The fella had removed the gas tank. Or it would have gone up.'

'It did go up,' Shona said, with a smile.

The boy kept staring at Terry.

'I hear he's died. Something like that,' he said quietly.

'That's right – what was he like?'

'Quiet.'

'Would you say he kept himself to himself?' Shona said, wincing at the cliché. Stricken would have laughed at her.

'Aye.' He gestured to Terry. 'Is she done?'

'Think so,' she said. 'How long was the man living here for?'

'Oh, couple of weeks. Maybe three. Maybe a month. He went away for a bit – down south, I think – then he was back. Then we heard he was in Scotland. He was no bother. Never saw him. And then the news. Marton was happy he wasn't in there when it went up, mind. Are you off now?'

'I'll be giving Mr Marton a call,' she said.

'Right, well,' he said, peering again at Terry.

'Did the man have a car?' Shona asked.

'Aye, police took it. But it was scrap, even when it were working. He had a bike, too. That was probably in the fire, like.'

She nodded. 'What kind of bike?'

He shrugged. 'Red one.'

'And what's your name – so I can tell Mr Marton you told us to piss off?'

A flicker of a smile played across his mouth and eyes. Then it was gone. 'Tell him you spoke to Mark and I told you both to get lost,' he said.

'Fine,' she said.

'Maybe,' he said. He scratched his nose.

'Maybe what?'

'Maybe you should speak to Old John. He was friendly with the fella.'

'Who's Old John?'

'Old guy lives down there, on the fellside. They were always talking, like. That's him,' he said, pointing past Shona.

She turned round. Past the burnt-out caravan and across the moor road there was a track leading further into the valley. Amidst a small stand of firs huddled a cottage. Smoke rose from the chimney.

'Well, that's me,' he said and, without a change of expression, stomped off across the yard. He did not look back and disappeared through a large door into one of the barns.

Shona walked up the track again. High clouds were smeared across the sky, and it felt colder. She noticed remnants of snow on the high moors, white lines across long banks of rock.

Terry was taking general views of the area with a different lens. She was standing on a large flat rock, blotched with lichen.

'That's me done,' she said. 'Farmer about?'

'No. I think he'd probably tell us to piss off anyway. I'm just going to look at that house over there. There's some old guy who used to speak to Merrygill.'

'Oh yeah? I'm going to take a couple more GVs. Call me if you need me over there. Caravan was well and truly torched, wasn't it?' Terry said, tilting her camera in the direction of the pyre.

'I like it when snappers state the bloody obvious once in a while,' Shona said.

'You what?'

'It's kind of comforting,' Shona said.

'Give over,' Terry said. She resumed her work.

Shona walked down the track and crossed the main road, her stick skittering on the gravel. As she neared the cottage, in a copse of twisted firs, she could see a raked slate roof, tiny windows and a tatty fence around an overgrown garden. Abandoned outside lay an old green bicycle, mud-spattered, with rusted wheels. Its basket held an open canvas bag of sooty potatoes. Out the back, she glimpsed a pile of clapped-out machinery and white goods, a shattered caravan and a gross oil tank amidst knots of high grass.

Beyond it, the watching moors rose. This could be the first house of the moor, or the last.

The front door was peeling. Sunlight hit the brass door knocker beneath a foggy, diamond-shaped window: a bearded man. She looked closer: the beard was vines and leaves, the eyes acorns, and the knocker between his teeth was a curved tongue. On a board attached to the door were painted the words: THE GROVE.

She knocked on the door and, to her surprise, it boomed, hollow and deep. She looked up to the main road, but the lie of the land meant Terry, the burnt-out caravan and the farm were all out of view. They may as well have not been there.

Shona banged the knocker. Again it boomed as if behind the shabby door there was a tunnel dug deep into the guts of the earth. Then she rotated it clockwise. The door opened. A shadowy hallway, with dim shapes of bulk and weight, lay ahead. The marble eyes of a dead rabbit stared at her, chilly teeth in its open dead mouth. Its body was laid, with other mounds of fur, on the top of a sideboard.

Shona moved into the hall, her feet and stick tapping on bare floorboards. There was a thick smell, a sweet soup of mould and spores. Her eyes adjusted to the gloom and began to itch. There was dark wooden furniture everywhere – a large wardrobe, several chests of drawers, a stand filled with walking sticks, some of which were topped with the brass heads of dogs and deer. Heavy coats hung from hooks, and, beneath them, a sloppy pile of waterproofs, flung on top of filthy wellies.

'Hello?' she called. No answer. Just the ticking of a clock, somewhere, and a wheezing noise. There were paintings on the wall: hunting scenes of men in red on horses chasing invisible foxes. There were blotchy scenes of rural disarray. There was one large portrait of a woman, pale and severe, in a high-backed chair. She was in black, with a large ruff about her throat. Her head looked decapitated, as if presented on a plate. The eyes had been scored out with a knife. Circles of bare wall showed where the pupils should have been.

She looked up: the rough ceiling was stained with smoke and grime, and a field of mould in dark patches, tiny black spots, scattered like acne.

Halfway down the hall, an open door revealed an empty room flooded with light. She peeked in. In a neat circle on the wooden floorboards were various stones. Shona looked at the strange arrangement. The stones – brown, orange and grey – had been cleaned or polished. At the centre sat a candle, a wooden cup and a small pile of gravel and pebbles.

Leaning against a plain white wall was a full-size mirror. Something was written on it in white paint, or correction fluid. Shona looked closer. There were two oval shapes, like empty eyes, inches apart, five feet up the glass. Two white dots where a nose might be. Where the mouth might be, someone had written: *sorley*.

She heard a loud snort and jumped.

'Hello?' she called again. She moved back into the hall. The wheezing was still there. She listened closely. It was breathing. There was a steady propulsion to it, a pneumatic certainty.

She reached forward and pushed at the door at the end of the hall. It moved inwards with a creak. She put her head around the edges, smile fixed, ready for human contact. The small, dark room throbbed with warmth. Low flames moved behind the sooty window of a squat iron stove.

Covered in a woollen blanket, a large old man slept soundly on an ancient couch. It was burst, the stuffing hanging in shags from its green seams. Across deep brown wooden surfaces there was a sea of rumpled papers and open books. On either side of the stove, recessed shelves were jammed with antiquarian volumes and yet more papers, rolled and tied, folded and open.

The chaotically bearded man had a shock of white hair with tawny streaks. His lined brown face was at rest, his lower lip hanging, his mouth slightly ajar. His eyes were screwed tight, like two walnuts pushed into a warm dough. He was wearing heavy overalls and several pairs of stringy woollen socks. His hairy hands were clasped on his chest over a rifle with a wooden stock. Its metal gleamed dully.

On the floor beside him was a glass of brown liquid and a dropped book. There was a heap of chopped wood by the fire, and the contents of a box of firelighters trailed across the floor. On a circular table, bottles of alcohol stood, many without corks or lids: wine and vodka, whisky and rum. Some had no labels and were fastened with stoppers.

The smell of damp was sweet and thick. Shona looked to the unshelved walls; there were stains rising up from the floor and down from the corners. The paint was blistered and popped, and behind the flaking paint, the exposed plaster was black as a wine-stained tongue.

'John?' Shona whispered, looking intently at the gun. The man slept on, and a log gently broke and slid in the fire.

She stepped fully into the room, and her leg glanced against a pile of newspapers, which slithered to the floor and spread in a fan. The old man did not stir. She bent down to look closer at the papers: they were all from the 1980s. She could now read the title of the book that had been dropped: *The Occult Roots of Nazism*.

Shona moved to the middle of the stifling room and wondered what to do.

She moved as quietly as she could to the bookshelves. There were many volumes in German and French. The covers were a dull green and grey, heavily creased, spines askew; some were ripped and torn, with tiny binding strings sticking out like fish bones.

One slim volume had been set, open, on a shelf, as if it was a lectern. Shona reached for it. It was titled *The Thanosophy of Stone: On the Allotment of Souls in Clay, Granite, Marble and Sedimentary Rocks*, by a Dr J. Kinninvie. She flicked through it.

It had been published in 1989 by Kinninvie Publishing, in one edition.

The frontispiece said: *This Thesis and Thanosophy is my contribution to the Study of Afterlives and the Spiritual Realms and represents a Life Work. It contends, supported by objective evidence and Representations from the Incarcerated Dead, that there are no human souls in any Heaven or Heavens or any Hell. It proves that, after Death, mankind's Eternal Lights migrate to the Stones, Shelfs, Rocks and Mantle of the Earth As It Is. In the following chapters I shall prove . . .*

The man wheezed on in his deep sleep. She flicked through the book. There were depictions of rock formations, of the layers of the Earth, and diagrams showing the souls of humans – depicted as small, almond flames – flattening, reducing and moving as if in flight to illustrations of various stones, rock types and formations.

At the back of the book was a list of further titles on the subject by Kinninvie: *The Distribution of Immortal Light in Igneous Rock*; *A Study Upon the Settlements of Animal and Human Child Souls in Pebbles, Gravel and Sand*; and *Dinosaur Souls, Primal Souls and the Movement of Continental Plates*.

By the stove, she noticed, was a chart of some kind, tacked to board: photographs of stones, with strange markings beside each, and writing in another language. On the mantelpiece were more stones, arranged neatly in a regular line. Cold grey and deep black. Red stone and marble. Sandstone and igneous rock.

Old John wheezed on. She moved closer to him. His toes wriggled. He smelled of sweat, of unwashed flesh, of mud and alcohol. A thick, earthy, acrid scent.

She did not want to touch him, to wake him. She certainly did not want to shake him. Not with that gun in his arms. Not with his size and drunken slumber. So, she moved to the windows instead and pulled back a shutter, to let the cold light fall on his face.

It settled in a pale line along the gun barrel. Old John did not stir. His chest rose and fell steadily. His hands remained over the gun, as if holding a pet dog. Shona thought of her father, lying somewhere. Hopefully warm and dry. In their flat in Edinburgh, clean and sane and cared for. Not alone like this, lying alone in a filthy shack on the top of a bleak moor. She wondered if Old John had anyone to care for him. She wondered how old he was. He could have been in his fifties, he could be over a hundred. He could be a body stolen from time by faeries and left here to wheeze for ever.

She suddenly decided to leave. She took her notebook from her bag and wrote down on a page her name and contact details in capital letters, and that she wanted to talk to him about Daniel Merrygill. She gently tore it off and slipped the paper under his drink, then stepped gingerly over the books and papers on the floor and went out to the hallway.

She pushed the back door, and she was outside again. The fresh air cut away the fug of mould. A mess of dereliction spread before her. A window frame and several mirrors, stacked against a wall, reflected the garden back upon itself, shimmering with shreds of displaced sky. A heap of full black bin bags slumped by the door, soft and yielding like wrapped bodies. There was a stench of mulch and bin juice and rot. The chaos unnerved her. A plastic bag, caught high on a twisted tree, flapped and snapped like a flag.

She looked once more around the backyard, before turning to go. Something was glinting in a clutch of twisted thistles – a red bicycle, dropped in the mud and surrounded by boot marks. She turned back.

The bicycle was broken – its greasy black chain was ragged and loose, and one of its pedals was missing. There was a rime of rust around its joints. But it was red. There was a heavy black pannier attached to the back.

Shona reached down and pulled at it. It refused to open.

'Anything in it?'

Shona jumped in alarm.

Terry was right behind her, peering at the bag.

'What the absolute fuck?' Shona gasped.

'Hello to you, too. I just followed you.' Terry stuck a thumb back over her shoulder. 'Anything inside that shambles?'

'There's a man asleep by a fire. It must be the old guy the farmer mentioned. He's surrounded by a load of weirdness.'

'Shall I wake the old codger, then?'

'No, he has a gun.'

'A fucking gun?' Terry said loudly.

'Shh! Jesus wept,' Shona hissed. 'I'm not risking it. I left a message for him. And then I found this.'

'Okay, Sherlock. Well, let's not hang around. Not sure I want to surprise some old fucker with his own artillery. Let me have a look inside this thing,' Terry said, looking around, 'I want to get out of this place.'

'I think I can manage,' Shona said, trying to detach the bag from the bike. It was fastened tightly by a flap and a plastic lock.

Terry was already on her knees beside her, and her hair and warm head brushed against Shona. There was a sweet scent from her, a nip of limey shower gel. They were both kneeling on the soggy grass now beside the bicycle, as if praying at a shrine.

'Ach, I can't move it. It's stuck tight,' Shona said.

'Not for long,' Terry whispered. She reached inside her camera bag and pulled out a penknife. With a fingernail she flicked out a blade.

'What are you doing?' Shona said, looking about.

'I'm about to murder you,' Terry said lightly and started cutting.

'Hurry up, then,' Shona said. She looked behind her. The back door remained open. There was darkness within.

Terry sliced through the material around the lock and pulled the bag away. 'Go on, have a look.'

Shona reached for the bag. 'There's something's inside.'

'Now who's stating the fucking obvious?' Terry said, closing her knife.

It began to spot with rain. Cloud lay like a grey sheet over the landscape. A wind blew over the empty moor. They needed to move.

They both stood up and looked back at the house. Smoke still rose from the chimney. The windows were dark. Nothing was moving.

'Let's get out of here,' Terry said quickly, standing up.

Shona held the bag tightly.

The back fence was bent low, pushed almost horizontal by years of gales and snow. They struggled over it and tramped over springy moor grass and heather, trousers sodden, heads wet in the slew of light rain, back to the car.

As they set off along the tarmac road again, the small car filled with the smell of earth and mud and grass.

'What's in it?' Terry said. The swish of the windscreen wipers moved shadows across her face.

Shona opened the bag. It was a brand-new pannier and, apart from its torn fastener, was intact. Inside, there was what looked like a lens from a pair of spectacles: a circular, convex sliver of glass. The glass was held within a plastic ring, as if it were a monocle. There was also a large, unsealed brown envelope, bloated by bubble wrap, with several new stamps on it. There was something hard inside.

'Interesting,' Shona said.

'Open it,' Terry said. She had lit a menthol cigarette and was blowing smoke out of the opened window.

'Mind the road, not my business,' Shona said.

Inside the package was a small, boxy disposable camera.

'An instant . . . haven't seen one of those for ages,' Terry said.

Shona held it, turned it over in her hand. 'It hasn't been developed.'

'Nope,' Terry said. 'Or it wouldn't be around. You hand in the whole thing to the chemist's. Or that's how it used to be.'

'Can you develop these things?'

'No, it's a machine that does it. Take it to the Boots in Ullathorne. What condition is it in?'

'It's old,' Shona said, peering at the fading packaging, the dated font and design. 'But it's dry, it's not deformed.'

'Old, dry, but not deformed. Sounds like Ranald,' Terry said.

Shona smiled and put the instant camera in her satchel.

Soon the car was climbing a steep slope on the edge of an old country town. There were weathered stone buildings, with small windows and slate roofs. There were church spires, a blocky business park and the drab bricks of a large modern school. The ruin of a medieval castle, with a shattered cylinder of a main tower and the remains of a craggy sheet wall, sat on a cliff above the slow brown river.

The sign on the edge of the town, as Terry slowed at a bridge, was painted clear in black on metal: ULLATHORNE.

Ashley was ready to go out.

Her mother was downstairs, welcoming a new guest. She had arrived in someone else's car and had a stick. She spoke with a strong Scottish accent and seemed to be fed up about something. The woman had asked if they had Wi-Fi, as if Ullathorne was still in the Dark Ages. Yes, we have broadband, her mother had said, far too kindly. We also have electricity and indoor toilets, Ashley thought.

She had spent a quiet afternoon reading and writing. Now it was after six o'clock, and she was meeting Amy for a drink in twenty minutes. Amy was an old school friend, now a hairdresser, who lived in the town. Suddenly, Ashley remembered the old football shirt she had found that morning. On the way out, she stuffed it in the black rubbish bag by the kitchen door – tomorrow was bin day.

It was Folk Night at the Lion pub. Ashley liked folk music now – she had barely known it growing up. There was no folk music on her mother's radio, and none was taught or even mentioned at school. It was only at university that she had heard proper folk-rock from the 1960s and realised that 'Matty Groves' had probably first been sung in Tyrdale. She had begun listening to a lot of the old records and had fallen in love with Sandy Denny's voice.

There was a knowledge and an endurance in the old songs, she thought. They were from the past, alive in the present, and they would endure into the future, too. The old songs did not age, or rise and fail, even if societies did. They rang true, singing from a world of wounding, and loss, of those who thought themselves superior, and those who were deemed inferior, and the cruelty that flowed from such a reckoning. Much the same as now, she thought – much the same as ever. So it was no discomfort to sit in the cosy Lion and drink with Amy and listen to someone sing the old songs.

The sign tacked to the pub door: TONIGHT – BUNDLE OF TWINE.

Amy was already seated in a booth by the window, with drinks ready for both of them. They hugged, and Ashley sat down. Her mam was babysitting for the night, Amy said excitedly.

On a low stage, at the far end of the pub, a PA hummed to life. Bundle of Twine were a three-piece – a singer, a guitarist, a drummer. The singer was a woman with a long dress, many bangles and dangling earrings. Her hair was streaked with grey. Ashley knew she had been at school with her mother – Beverley, she was called. Beverley Moore. Which was apt, as she lived on the moor.

The band began to play. The barman – shaven-headed, with a black beard, a jerkin covered in patches – pretended to put his fingers in his ears. The pub was half full; some sullen teenagers slouched around a long table and a clutch of old men leaned on the bar, nodding.

Ashley, too, was nodding to the beat and the sway of the melody and she turned to Amy who was doing the same. They had a quick catch-up between songs. Ashley was 'fine but bored'; Amy was the same. The snow had been madly deep and fierce, but spring would soon come. The music stopped, and the large, heavily bearded guitarist held up his hand in apology as he retuned. People went to the bar for more drinks.

'"Little Musgrave",' the singer whispered into the microphone eventually, and the audience clapped. The singer wiped her wet eyes. She fanned her hands down the front of her dress.

'I'm sorry, we've had some bad news today,' she said. 'But it's good to sing. This one's for Dan. A little bit of "Little Musgrave" for him. He liked this old tale.'

Ashley and Amy turned to each other and shrugged. They opened a packet of crisps and listened to the sad song. After a time, the guitar ended its rhapsodic echoing chime and the singer stood away from the microphone, leaving the song, its tragedy, to stand like a dagger in the soil. There was a silence. Then people clapped and roared, and the band nodded in appreciation, and the singer called to the bar for a pint of cider.

'That's Bundle of Twine, ladies and gentlemen,' the barman whispered over a microphone, and people clapped again. 'Appearing at the Dentdale Folk Festival in June! And regular here at the Lion. Now, lads and lasses, a break.'

The pub filled with the hum of chat and drink. Quiet music played over speakers. A TV came on over the bar – the prime minister, talking about a new general election. It was quickly muted; no one was interested.

Ashley and Amy began talking in earnest.

Ashley liked Amy. She was warm and easygoing and didn't ask her about what happened at uni, or what her plans were, or what she was thinking about her future. Amy was laughing, telling a story about her little boy's first word being 'Dada'.

'Dada! What about bloody Mama! Don't you know your dada is a fucking dick? Who's feeding you, eh?'

'Classic,' said Ashley.

'He never sees his bloody dada. And that's his first word?' Amy said, eyes wide, shaking her head.

The singer from Bundle of Twine stalked over from the bar and sat down at the girls' table with a grunt and a loud sigh. She smiled at them both. Her eye make-up was smudged, but she was smiling, a light sweat on her forehead, her hair now tied up and swept back from her face. Even sitting down, she loomed over them. She was a tall woman, big in frame and bone.

'Hi, Ashley,' she said, her deep voice rolling.

'It's Beverley, isn't it? Loved the music,' Ashley said.

'Aye, it were right good,' Amy said.

'Thanks, my loves. We're getting there. Karl is a great guitarist, isn't he? The great lummox. Anyways, look at you, what a pair of darlings,' she said and sipped from a fizzing pint of coppery cider.

'Give over,' Amy said.

'Oh, to be beautiful and young again,' the singer said.

Ashley laughed.

'You cracking on to us or what?' Amy said.

'Amy!' Ashley gasped.

'You'd be so lucky, madam!' Beverley said, poking Amy's hand with long painted fingernails. She turned to Ashley. 'Sorry to disturb, but I was wondering if you might pass a message to your mam,' she said, looking to her with wide eyes.

'Sure,' Ashley said.

'Just tell Peg that Beverley asks if she's heard the news about Dan. Daniel Merrygill – he's passed away. Your mam knew him, back in the day. Could you do that for me?'

'Dan Merrygill. I will do, Beverley,' Ashley said. Beverley's eyes filled with tears. 'I'm sorry to hear that,' Ashley added.

'Just let her know. It's been a long time, and there's not many of our year left in Tyrdale now. Class of ninety-two – that's what they would say in America! God's sake,' she said, looking into her pint. Bubbles flew vertically to the surface, popped and disappeared.

'I promise,' Ashley said. 'What happened?'

'He was an old soul, was Dan,' Beverley said. 'He was sensitive. To all kinds of things. So, it's no surprise, in some ways. I didn't know he was still friends with Viv and her family. He died when he was with her. But it figures. I guess they leaned on each other. Supported each other. So that makes sense. I know he was living in Darlington, but he may as well have been on the moon – I hadn't seen him for years. Doubt your mam had either.'

Amy had left the table. She was walking to the bar, talking on her phone.

'Who's Viv?' Ashley asked.

'Oh, sister of a friend of ours. Viv Banks. She's up in Scotland now. Her brother Andrew – you might have been told about him.'

Beverley was running her finger around the pint glass now, her eyes focused on something else, far away. The flames from the log fire glittered on her jewellery, in her eyes.

'No, I don't think so,' Ashley said. 'That was a lovely song, earlier.'

'Ach, that's a bad old song. Just like all the folk songs,' Beverley said. 'They never teach folk songs in school, do they? You know why? Because they're all about the same things that are happening now. The poor people hooded and blinded. Look at that arsehole. He pretends to be on the side of the people, an' all.' She pointed to the prime minister on the silent TV. 'Nowt's changed.'

'You're right enough,' Ashley said. She felt nervous now, her back prickling.

'You know that song we sing? *Buck and doe, believe it so, a pheasant and a hare, Were set on earth for everyone, quite equal for to share.* There's truth in that. That's why we have to keep singing them.'

Amy had returned with two more drinks.

Beverley suddenly looked surprised that she was sitting where she was. She looked about her, as if awakening from sleep. 'I'd better get back, pet,' she said, reaching across to pat Ashley's hand. 'Tell your mam about Dan, won't you, love.'

She stood up and wandered to the bar, her jewellery gently clinking. The huge guitarist at the bar bent and kissed her on the forehead.

Amy raised her eyebrows and said, 'Looks like you've got yourself a new friend.'

'Give over,' Ashley said. 'She seemed a bit upset.'

'Pissed more like,' Amy said. 'What was she on about?'

'Have you heard of Viv Banks, Andrew Banks?'

Amy nodded. 'Oh, aye,' she said and drank from her tall glass.

'What's that all about, then?' Ashley said.

'Oh, it was ages ago,' Amy said. 'Some local lad – he went missing. Disappeared. Big search for him up and down the dale, but no sign. It was in the papers for a bit. It was on *Crimewatch* or something like that. Anyway, he probably ran awa. Joined the navy.'

'Disappeared?'

'Aye,' Amy said. 'Without a trace. Sad. But that was the old days. People go missing all the time. All the time. After a while, everyone stops looking. Everyone except for the family. It's too much bother, isn't it?'

Ashley looked across to the bar. Beverley was staring at her.

Shona had slept fitfully.

Now she was hissing at her laptop in the breakfast room of the Gildersleve B&B as it tried to connect to the Wi-Fi. A hot coffee was steaming by her elbow, and she had picked at some bacon and eggs. She'd texted her father. Bernie had replied on his phone: he was still sleeping, she said.

The woman who had met her and given her breakfast said her name was Peg. She wore a T-shirt and jeans. Her hair was scraped back in a bun. There was a younger girl, too, who had slipped out last night as Shona was arriving. She had a blue streak in her unruly hair and, like Shona, walked with a slight limp. Shona wondered why.

The late spring light flooded the breakfast room of the old lodge, glowing on the stone walls, on the wooden tables, the crockery on the shelves. Framed scenes of old Ullathorne depicted the mill, the castle and men in flat caps gathered beside a white bull, its vast sides like a canvas. Outside, a murder of crows cawed in high branches. Someone, somewhere, slammed a car door. But all else was quiet. The stones settled in their mortar.

There was a sudden shout from the kitchen next door. Shona, startled, caught her coffee cup with her elbow.

'Fuck!' The coffee spread like blood across the white tablecloth. She righted the cup and swabbed the spillage with a napkin.

Her phone buzzed. It was a text from Terry.

How's the digs? You going to the newspaper archives? Let me know if you need pix ta T.

That was Shona's plan for the day. She was going to visit

the *Tyrdale Times*, to look for cuttings on the death of Andrew Banks. Where she would go from there, she did not quite know. She texted Terry back: *Fine. That's the plan. Might need your help later if you're free?*

Never free, Terry texted back immediately. *Can do snaps for cash.*

Shona smiled. She could hear more raised voices in the kitchen. Peg was arguing with the young girl.

'I was going to show it to you later,' the girl said.

'Were you heck-as-like,' Peg said sharply.

'I just forgot. Anyway, it's for the bin. Just an old football shirt. So what? Jess found it.'

'In Deepdale?' Peg said. 'Where in Deepdale?'

'I don't know,' the girl said, whining a little. 'Deep in the dale. There's an old building there.'

'There's no old building there,' Peg said. 'In Deepdale? What you on about?'

'Aye, in Deepdale. You follow the beck instead of the path, and then there's this old building. It's all ruined.'

Peg's voice softened. 'What, like a water maintenance building or something?'

'Yeah, maybe. Anyway, Jess was digging away in the corner and she pulled it out. What's the big deal? It's ancient.'

Shona heard a rustling sound.

'It's not ancient. I remember the Newcastle shirts with that design. Here, what's this on the back?'

'Just a name,' the girl said.

'Was it buried?'

'Nature claims things, doesn't it? It's all overgrown there.'

'Jet,' Peg said. '*Jet.*'

'What about it, Mam?'

Shona heard a sigh and the sound of a woman sitting heavily.

There was a long silence. Shona listened intently. There was a shuffling of feet.

'Where was it again, Ashley, love?'

'I told you. It was half buried, in the corner of the old building. Jess was pulling at it. Maybe she ripped it.'

There was silence again.

'There's been floods in Deepdale, has there not?' Peg said.

'It's always wet there.'

'Floods disturbing the ground.'

'Floods from the snow melting.'

Shona picked up her plate of half-eaten food and went to the kitchen door. She stepped through.

Peg was standing by an Aga, looking at a dirty old football shirt which she had lain out on the range. The shirt had once been striped black and white but was now almost entirely green and brown, with a series of dark blotches around a deep rip. The young girl, holding one hand in another, was by the sink, and looked surprised when Shona entered.

'Oh, hi there,' Peg said. 'You can just leave that. I'll get it. Did you have enough?'

She spoke with a flat Northern English accent. Brief and plain, as if the language's corners had been rounded off. An old, tempered sound, like something hardy and weathered, that had survived.

'Lovely, thanks,' Shona said. She put the plate down on the table.

The kitchen was spacious and stone-walled. As well as the Aga, there was an electric oven and two large fridges. The walls were lined with cooking implements and shelves of plates and pots. A magnetic strip was laden with large knives.

'That needs a bit of a clean,' Shona said, nodding to the shirt.

Peg looked at her, as if waiting for something, and then answered. 'Aye, it does that.'

'Dog found it,' the girl said.

The three stood, unmoving. Peg ran a hand through her hair. Somewhere in the fields, a dog barked.

'I was wondering if you might help me?' Shona said.

Peg answered with a smile, as if relieved to change the subject. Shona asked where the office for the *Tyrdale Times* was, and Peg said she couldn't miss it, it was on the high street, next to the Lion pub.

'Meanwhile,' Peg said, sighing, turning back to the shirt, 'I think I have some calls to make.'

'About that?' Shona said, glancing at the football shirt.

Peg flicked her a look. 'You've got to be going, I guess?'

In a short while, after a quick shower and tidy up, Shona headed into town. As she left the B&B, she heard crunching on the gravel behind her. She turned her head, and it was the girl.

'Hiya,' she said to Shona. 'I need to get some supplies for Mam. I'll walk you in. Not that you'd get lost, mind – there's only three roads here anyway.'

'Thanks,' Shona said. She looked at her phone – a missed call from Stricken. That night in Argyll already felt a long time ago.

'I'm Ashley,' the girl said.

'And I'm Shona.'

They walked on the broad silent streets. The road was broad and cobbled in stretches. Ashley walked alongside her, down the elm-lined streets, staring at her phone, making little movements on its screen with a cramped right hand. She was dressed all in baggy black.

Shona's stick clipped on the pavement as the centre of the town neared – there were church spires and snapping flags. Between the buildings, the distance could be seen – ranks of trees, the dip of the river channel, the blue moors, watching.

Ashley kept looking sideways at Shona and her stick. 'You down from Scotland, then?' she said.

'Aye. Here for a job – I'm a journalist.'

'To work at the *Times*?'

'No, but I do need their help with something.'

'Man, I don't think there's much to report in this town,' Ashley said, smiling. 'Nowt happens here.'

'Why you here, then?'

'Wonder that myself. I left uni. Taking some time to think on what happens next. Did you go to uni?'

'Yeah. Back in the day. Glasgow Uni, then Strathclyde for the journalism course. Fun times – what I remember of them.'

'I want to write,' Ashley said. 'Not sure journalism is for me, though.'

'You should check it out,' Shona said. 'It beats working for a living.'

The road they had walked along had gradually become lined with shops and offices, and now they were in the centre of Ullathorne: a wide cobbled market square. People walked the streets, but no one was talking. A car waited at a pedestrian crossing as two riders on gleaming chestnut horses slowly clopped past.

'Horses,' Shona said, surprised. She found herself pointing at them.

'That's right,' Ashley said. 'That's what they are.'

Shona laughed. 'I don't see them often. Look, before I go to work – want a coffee or something? I could do with some background stuff on the town. Can you help?'

'Aye, all right – let's go to the Market Caff.'

As they crossed the road, Shona looked downhill to the river. At the bottom of the Bank, amongst modern housing, was a large ruin, a shambles of roofless stone and brick.

'What's that building down there?' Shona said.

'Old Ullathorne Mill. Been a wreck as long as I remember it. Used to have a big water wheel. There's been plans over the years. Someone wanted to turn it into flats, then there was talk of a bookshop or something. There was a fire there a while back. Mainly, the sixth formers go there and get pissed.'

The café was small, with five tables and nothing on its plain walls. A pale teenager covered in freckles shouted at them from the till, asking what they wanted while dangling a phone from one hand. They ordered two coffees.

'Fine,' the teenager bellowed back, slamming down her phone.

'Latte, eh? Fancy,' Shona said.

'I know, right? That's what Hull Uni does for you. Forgetting my place,' Ashley said in a singsong tone.

'Hull? Jesus wept.'

Ashley laughed. 'Give over! Larkin was there. It's all right. I quite liked it. City of Culture.'

'Don't give me that. So was Glasgow, so I know what a load of fuck-all that means,' Shona said.

The drinks were thumped down by the teenager, who retreated into her rage behind the counter.

'Can I ask you something?' Ashley said, dropping sugar into her coffee. Fugitive brown granules clung desperately to the white foam before falling through bubbled tunnels to their melting end.

'Fire away,' Shona said.

'Your stick – do you have hemiplegia? CP?'

'No. What's that?'

Ashley held up her right hand. One of her fingers sloped across the others. It was half-closed. 'One side of your body is weaker than the other. I have it on the right side. It's cerebral palsy, really. I have it mildly. That's what they say.'

'So, you had a stroke?'

'In the womb. They called it an "insult to the brain". Which it is, really.'

Shona nodded. 'You type one-handed? Fair play to you. I can barely type with two.'

'I use my right thumb and forefinger for the mouse – slowly.'

Shona smiled. 'Well, you're doing all right. You've been through school, to uni, and you want to be a writer. If you need any advice on journalism, ignore my cynicism and ask away.'

'Thanks. I saw your stick and wondered if you had the same.

If you were the same. Sorry.' Ashley shook her head and looked out the window, suddenly shy. She winced, as if remembering something painful.

'No, I just had an accident,' Shona said. 'And don't say sorry.'

'An accident? That's shit.'

'It is.' Shona nodded. 'As you get on in the world, you'll realise most things are, to be honest. But you'll be fine.'

Ashley nodded and sipped her drink.

'That football shirt,' Shona said. 'Where did you find it?'

'I was walking Jess down Deepdale. It was in this old building. Dunno why me mam's so mad about it. She gets crazy now and then.'

'What's Deepdale? Is it near here?'

'Aye,' Ashley said. 'It's over the river, a beck, goes right up to the moors. Jess loves walking there, all the smells, I guess.'

'Near here?'

'Aye, just over the county bridge. You'd be there in ten minutes from here. But Deepdale goes on and on. You could walk for twenty miles, then suddenly you're on the moor top. Old trees there. Gets a bit spooky at night. I like it.'

'Are there signs for it?'

'I don't know, maybe – but you don't need one. You just go down to the river, cross the bridge and road. There's a stile, and you can see the path and the trees – walk into them.'

Shona cleared her throat and said, 'I was wondering if you might help me. Have you heard of someone called Dan Merrygill?'

Ashley's mouth opened and then she put her left hand to her face. 'Fuck!' she said, loudly enough to make the teenager at the till look up from her phone.

'What's up?' Shona asked.

'I was meant to tell my mam something and I never. Argh,' she said. 'I have heard that name – just last night. Bev told me to tell my mam that – wait, why do you ask?'

'I'm doing a story which involves him.'

'What kind of story?'

Shona lifted her cup and peered over its steaming lip. 'I'm not sure yet.'

'Bev said he was dead,' Ashley said. 'I'd never heard of him. He was at school with me mam.'

'Right.'

'Was he dodgy?'

'He's certainly dead.'

'I haven't told Mam yet, so could you wait before you mention it to her? How long you in Ully for?'

'I'm not sure. Yes, of course I'll wait. I might want to ask her what she remembers of him.'

'Right, well,' Ashley said. She suddenly stood up. 'Good luck. I better get going. We can gan down to Deepdale later?'

They said goodbye, but as Ashley stood up, Shona asked, 'Who's Bev?'

'Beverley Moore – she was at the pub last night. Sings in a band. I'd better go.'

Ashley pulled up her hood. Shona watched her walk away. She ordered another coffee from the angry teen, listened to her clattering about for a moment, and then called Stricken.

Outside, a large green tractor rolled past. Shona was surprised by its bulk and the hugeness of its tyres. It rolled past like a tank.

'Shona!' Stricken yelled.

Shona held the phone away from her ear briefly. 'Fuck's sake, Hector. You know I hold the phone right next to my ear like a normal person. You trying to deafen me? I missed your call.'

'Sorry. I need a bit of help. Thought you might oblige.'

'I'm fucking doubtful,' Shona said.

'Right.'

'But carry on.'

'Your pal Detective Reculver – do you know how I can get hold of him? He's changed his number.'

Shona tapped the side of her mug, annoyed. 'You've asked me this before. As I said last time, and the time before that – no. You can go through the police press office, like any other hack. He's changed his number for a reason.'

'Ah, but, Shona! I just really need a word with him for this story.'

'What story?'

'Och, just this story I'm trying to work on.'

'On what?'

Stricken's voice dropped. 'Human trafficking.'

'Ah, right, nasty.'

'Yeah,' he said.

Another coffee appeared before Shona, crashed down before her with a jolt and a slop.

'So?' Stricken said.

'No,' Shona said. 'Look, sorry, Hector. But I can't give you his number. In any case, if I did, and you called him, he wouldn't help you, and, worse, he probably wouldn't help me any more. I'm not burning my contacts book for you.'

There was a loud exhalation of breath. 'Right, okay, I tried. I'll get him some other way. Man, I'm knackered.'

'From thinking too hard?'

'Ha ha. It's this new digital-first regime that this prick of an editor has brought in. Did I not tell you at the wedding? We're all on digital shifts, seven in the morning till seven at night. Regurgitating wire copy, nicking stuff from the BBC, putting up our own headlines and pictures – there's no picture desk any more, no subs checking anything. We're just constantly shovelling copy up onto the website, slapping a clickbait headline on it and moving on. I've been working on these proper stories in between all that shite. In my own time, at night, at weekends. I'm fucking exhausted.'

'That really is shite.'

'It's not journalism, Shona.'

'It's churnalism. And, no, I hate to disappoint you, but you won't get Reculver another way. He's a secretive type.'

Stricken sighed and swore at the same time. 'That poor guy at the wedding – I saw he was from Ullathorne in County Durham. Isn't that where old John Fallon was from, back in the day? You know, the features editor?'

'Aye, Fallon's old stomping ground. But he's long gone now, isn't he? He might have been some help.'

'Help? For who?'

Shona's heart quickened a little. 'For Viv, maybe.'

'I suppose so. Well, better go. Shall we go for a drink soon?'

'Nope.'

'Right, okay then . . .'

'Wait.'

'What?'

'Do you know what *Odeadaheado* means? Ever heard of it?'

Stricken made a whistling noise and asked her to spell it. She did.

'No, means nothing to me. Is it some kind of fantasy thing? Science fiction? Like a character from a film or something?'

'I've looked – it means nothing.'

'Well, you've answered your own question, then. It means nothing. Why do you ask?'

'None of your beeswax, Hector – bye.'

Shona paid for the coffees, left the café and walked to the *Tyrdale Times*, only metres away, down the quiet main street.

As she walked, she felt a creeping, tensing chill in her shoulders. She was alone again. By herself again. The stone buildings leaned in on her. The white sky was smaller.

She opened the door to the newspaper office.

A tiny bell sounded as she entered, tolling tinnily in the forest of quiet, like the chimes of Mass at the Eucharist in an empty church.

14

'Do you want me to get Colin?' the woman said, putting down the celebrity magazine she'd been flipping through. She was wearing thick glasses and smelled of lavender. A small white badge on her orange blouse said WATSON WINS.

'Er . . . no,' Shona said. She did not know who Colin was.

'Oh, I thought you might want to speak to the editor. Colin Mickle?'

'No, no, thanks. Just some family history to look up.'

'Oh, lovely. Are your family from round these parts?'

'That's what I'm trying to find out.'

The woman smiled and introduced herself as Angela, then ushered Shona through the shop – which sold that week's edition of the paper, as well as Tyrdale calendars, postcards, maps and sweets – to a bare whitewashed room. A rank of filing cabinets stood under a sloping ceiling. A single microfiche reader – with a boxy screen and a large plastic hood like an ancient computer – sat on a table in the corner. Alongside it, there was a magnifying glass on a metal stand.

Angela, delighted to have a visitor, told Shona that the *Times'* archive was only digitised from 1999 because of the strict and random stipulations of a millennium project grant. Before that, the microfiche and paper records of the newspaper went back to 1914. And before then, single printed editions were stored at Durham University.

Shona explained that she wanted to look at newspapers from the 1990s.

Angela opened one of the cabinets. Fifty-five editions a year, she said, were stored here. 'They're all filed by week and month and year. I'll leave you to it,' she said. 'Now, would you like a cup of tea? Where did you say you were from?'

'Stirling in Scotland,' Shona said. 'A cup of tea, milk and two, would be lovely, thank you.'

'Stirling, how lovely, and what do you do there?'

'I design luxury yachts,' Shona said.

'How lovely,' Angela said and padded away.

Shona put her gear down and laid her stick against the microfiche table. A shiver of something moved through her: this was journalism, real work, with paper and pen and the potential for discovery.

The papers for 1992 took up most of one filing cabinet drawer. She looked to the middle of the year, when classes were breaking up for the summer, grabbed the first six months in two tranches and put them on the table. The papers were held together with neat, metal-tipped strings, like laces, and the typography looked old-fashioned – a gothic title and many stories crammed on each broadsheet page.

As Shona flipped over the pages, the paper rolling and whispering, and saw the stories pass by – the commonplace and the trivial, the serious and the comedic, births, deaths and marriages – her mind drifted. She wondered if she should jettison her anxious freelance life, work for a local paper in Fife or the Western Isles or maybe even Northumberland, move to the sticks, edit a weekly. Make friends with a flinty but twinkling local policeman, report on fishing and farming, mild crime and milder entertainments, put the paper to bed on an early Thursday night, then sip coffee with someone on a wind-blasted beach and watch the birds wheeling over the mercury sea. Interview the local MP over a dram in the distillery and sleep at night lulled by wind and sea, the cities far distant, a fire burning beyond the horizon. Her father, happy somewhere, smiling as he pulls potatoes from the ground. And maybe there would be a river, too, in this new life . . . implacable, relentless, like the Tyr, here in this old dale, an intractable old God, ever present and ever moving, a constant murmuring living deity . . .

Angela broke the reverie, planting Shona's tea, brown as a kidney, in a large mug beside her.

Shona thanked her and continued to flick through the papers. She was looking for a photo of the sixth form at Ullathorne Comprehensive. There were none in May, June or July 1992. Just prize winners with awkward smiles and little trophies. Then Shona realised – the class photos would be from the beginning of the school year, in 1991.

She hauled the papers back to the cabinet and looked for papers from the late summer and autumn of the year before. She looked through August – nothing. But she remembered: summer holidays were different in England. She flicked on. September: there they were, a page of class photos: first year, second year, third year, fourth, fifth. The images were all in black and white. Rows of faces, pale as petals, young and open. All the children lined up on the parquet floor of the gymnasium. Some were smiling, others were blank, some were serious. Some stood out. A boy with a manic grin, a girl with a hand over one eye, a boy looking hard to the left, a girl in the front row looking down at her feet, the top of her head showing her fiercely parted hair. All in school uniform: V-neck sweater, stripy tie, dark skirt or trousers. All stilled in time. Beside each group of children was a teacher: there were smart suits and floppy suits, long skirts, perms and flashy jewellery. Smiles and scowls. Big hair.

There were plenty of photos, but none of the sixth form. She opened the paper for the first week in October. The headline on the front page was something about a local company escaping charges for dumping sewage in the river.

And there, at the back, before the classified ads for cars and furniture, puppies and flower arranging, was a small photo of that year's upper sixth class.

The teacher was a man with long grey hair, maybe in his

sixties, tall and lanky, half-sitting on the table before which the pupils stood. It seemed there were only seven students in the year – all going into their A-levels, all soon to leave school. They were arranged in two rows.

Shona pulled over the magnifying glass and placed it over the picture. A caption in splodgy old type, ink sunk into the cheap newsprint, read:

> *This Year's Upper Sixth at Ullathorne Comprehensive, led by U6 Head Mr Norloch. From L to R (back row) Daniel Merrygill, Beverley Moore, Alison Harmire, Andrew Banks, (front row) Gary Watson, Margaret Gildersleve, Robert Stang. Miss Harmire is the Sixth Form Captain for 1991/2 and Head Girl.*

Shona realised she was holding her breath. She leaned in. At the back and on the left stood Dan. His clothes were neat, and he was not wearing a tie. His face was softer, plumper, and he had more hair, but there he was – pale, poised, taut. Beverley, next to him, was a tall girl with long hair and a long face. Alison was shorter, pretty with her hair pulled neatly back, smiling in a smart uniform. She had a Nike swoosh on her sweater. There was a sense of ease and optimism about her. Then, the lost boy – Andrew – with wavy hair and large dark eyes. He was handsome. He looked like Viv. She looked closer. His eyes sparkled, or maybe he had just been crying. There, in the front row, was the MP: unmistakably a young Gary Watson. His eyes like chisel dunts in stone. He wore an ironed shirt and a straight tie and an air of impatience. Next to him, looking nervous, was a youthful Peg, from the B&B, with a frizz of red hair. Then there was a large boy, Robert, with thick thighs and arms, staring out, defiant. He seemed to have the smudge of a moustache at the corners of his mouth. He looked ready to run out of the picture and thump someone.

Andrew, Dan, Gary, Peg, the others . . . all together for one captured moment. And something still held them all together. Something from thirty years ago, or maybe longer. Something from the past living inside the present.

She pulled the newspaper out of its loose string binding, folded it over and put it to one side.

She was closing the folder of papers when her eye caught something in the rippling pages. There was the same picture, the same photograph – but enlarged. The front-page splash of the paper, from July 1992:

SEARCH FOR MISSING ULLATHORNE TEEN
Family call for information on search for
Andy Banks, 18

THE FAMILY of missing Tyrdale boy Andy Banks, 18, have appealed for more witnesses as the search continues.

Andrew did not return home after spending a night out with friends on Friday.

The popular Tyrdale student had recently completed his A-levels and was looking forward to his summer holiday before his planned attendance at the University of Kent, Canterbury, to study History.

Friends and family have been left distraught by his disappearance.

Last week, police confirmed they had searched the river and the mill – popular with local teenagers.

Andrew's father Ken said: 'Caroline and I, and Vivienne, his sister, are beside ourselves. We would like to appeal to anyone who saw Andrew that Friday to come forward with any information. Even a small detail could help us find Andrew again.

'He is a friendly lad but no fool, and we don't believe he would have got into someone's car. We hope he has just been having an adventure, but we want him home now.'

Shona pulled out the edition, and the other, and walked quickly back to the shop, where Angela was hovering by a photocopier.

'Found something?' she said.

Shona looked down at the papers. 'Aye, some interesting bits and pieces. I need to make copies.'

'Sorry, love, the machine's broken at the moment,' Angela said.

'Oh, is it? Its lights are on,' Shona said, pointing.

'It's broken. I'm getting a man in. Why don't I take those and photocopy what you want, and you can pop back in later and pick them up?'

Shona eyed Angela, who stood as innocuous as a glass of milk. Shona said that would be fine and noted down the images she wanted copying, spelling out the pages and the dates.

Angela slowly folded Shona's note and put it on the countertop. 'Ta-ra, then,' she said.

Shona said her thanks, gathered her belongings and made her way to the Lion to find out more information about Beverley Moore.

As she walked, her thoughts moved over the faces in the picture, from side to side, and up and down, and again over the words in the caption, as if her mind was an eyeglass empowered by something beyond its time.

Moving over the faces. Moving over their names and words. Spelling out messages that she did not understand.

It was a bright, cold day in Tyrdale. The snow had long melted away, and the world was wide and empty, the valley brown and enfolded upon itself, clutching its trees and river.

Robert Stang woke from another nightmare. The sweat of it was wet in his armpits, in the small of his back. His mouth was dry and thick.

He had seen bodies, limp, heavy as rocks, being tipped into pits. Heavy boots kicking them in. The dull thump of body on body. The clunk of skulls. A dark forest of silent pines and a row of graves. And then, a single quavering candle in a circle of frightened eyes. A wheel of fingers resting on a glass as it moved over letters and words.

Moving, and no one could deny it. Moving, but no one knew how or why. Just movement, with no explanation. Moving, like the Earth around the sun, or vast rotations of the galaxies in flight – with silent movement and unseen, implacable force. Mass and speed and gravity.

Bobby rubbed his eyes. In the living room, his daughter Becky was watching a cartoon. He had a day off work, between shifts at the bottle factory, but she still needed to go to school.

He made a coffee in the pin-clean kitchen. Becky, still in her PJs, ate a bowl of cereal on her knee and laughed at the TV, as, after a jolt of caffeine, he laid out her ironed school clothes and made her snacks. Her mother, Karen, would pick Becky up today. He just needed to see her to school, down in the dale.

The house was in a small cul-de-sac of former council houses, pebble-dashed and squat, halfway up the valley. Behind them, a barren hill led up a thistly bristle of land to the moors. Below, the tree line was a sheer drop to the Tyr.

'Teeth,' he reminded his daughter, who moaned and reluctantly padded out the living room to the bathroom.

He looked at the news again, on his phone. He had read it late the night before and was certain it had led to the nightmare. Little Dan Merrygill, dead. Dead in some place in Scotland. He recognised Viv's name as well. They must have kept in touch. It made sense as they were friends. He had not seen Dan since that night, all those years ago. After, it all went dark. He had not seen Viv either, not since her brother went missing. He wondered what she was up to and how she'd ended up in Scotland.

Dan: dead, by his own hand. In the army, he had seen it. A body in a shed, deep in a Balkan ravine, a man with his head missing, a gun between his knees. An open neck, and the roof blown open.

He was curious about one detail – Dan's body was reported to have been heavily tattooed. He did not think Dan had it in him to get a tattoo. Not his kind of thing. Not something he could imagine Dan enduring.

Bobby rubbed his arm over his own regimental tattoo, as he was wont to. Deep blue, it was now. Deeper in his skin than all those years.

Bobby's phone blinked – out of battery. He swore and plugged it in. But he wouldn't need it for the school run.

Becky danced through to the kitchen, immaculate and tiny, and he picked her up in a swoop. She giggled, and he looked at her face – clean apart from toothpaste at the corners of her mouth. He pressed it off with a finger.

'Okay, Little Miss Freckle,' he said, 'school for you.' He kissed her forehead.

In the car, Becky chatted and played with her hair as the cold dale rolled by. Stone walls black with moss. The sky huge above, the clouds a soft, slow paving of vapour and weight.

A black 4x4 joined the empty road at a junction and stayed close behind them – too close.

'Get out of my backside, tosser,' Bobby said.

'Language, Dad,' Becky said.

'There's a right halfwit behind me,' he said.

'Who is it?'

'Someone looking for a clip around the ear.'

They came to a crossroads. Ahead, the roofs and spires of Ullathorne nestled in the valley. Bobby looked across the fields to the business park where the bottle factory lay and slowed the car to a halt.

'At holiday are we going to Scarborough again, Daddy?' Becky piped up.

'We can do, love. I've been saving up.'

'I like it there *a lot*,' she said.

'Me, too, pet,' he muttered, peering into his rear-view mirror.

'Do *you* like it there?' she said, searching for something.

'I like it there when I'm with you.'

'We can get a caravan,' she said.

'We can get a caravan,' he said quietly.

The black car stopped behind them, inches from his rear bumper. Its windows were tinted.

A line of bright blue had emerged in the southern sky. It would be brighter later, Bobby thought. He waited for a horse box to turn at the crossing, and then he followed, putting on speed.

The black car kept close.

'God's sake,' Bobby said.

He slowed and rolled down his window, waved the car on.

'Go on then, soft lad, overtake,' he said.

The black car just slowed down and stayed behind them.

'Are we going to be late for school?' Becky said.

'No, pet, we're fine,' he said.

He drove quickly down the long straight road to the town,

then dropped his daughter off outside the primary school, indicators clicking. She skipped out, grinned and waved to him before joining her friends.

'Remember, yer mam is picking you up,' he yelled after her, and his deep voice made a few small heads turn.

She looked back with a furrowed brow and mouthed, 'I know,' then disappeared into the school.

Bobby knew the black car would be waiting on the main road. The drive to the school was a dead end, and there was no way out without driving past it again.

The school car park was for teachers only. 'Fuck it,' he said. He parked and left the car. There was a narrow footpath between stone houses, leading away from the school grounds. Bobby walked down it, hood up, hands deep in his pockets.

As he left the footpath and entered the main street of the town, he could not hear any footsteps behind him. He looked over his shoulder as he turned. No one there. He had nowhere to go in particular, but he pounded down the main street, arriving at the market cross and then carrying on, down the Bank, shaking his head. 'Being daft,' he told himself. 'Paranoid.'

But he carried on. Down past the toy shop where, as a child, he had begged his grandpa for soldiers. Past the crooked old shop where, legend had it, before the tarmac was laid and electricity threaded through the town's stones, Oliver Cromwell had slept overnight. Past a boarded-up shop and down to the road that ran alongside the river. The mill was ahead, its empty windows gaping, its smashed portal a door into the dark. There, where something in him changed, where his path to uniform and service and death was laid. He had not been in there since.

He turned right, past another pub, its whorled windows swollen like an old drunk's eyes, and walked along the river. He stopped for a while, leaning his large body against the wall. The south bank of the river was all trees and bungalows, windows glinting like teeth between bare branches.

The black car turned onto the road alongside the river. It slowed steadily as it reached him. Grinding on the tarmac. A shadow behind the wheel.

Bobby set off again, walking faster along the side of the churning river. Over the county bridge and onto the other bank. He crossed the road which led to the moors.

The car was crawling over the bridge. Bobby was being hunted. He jumped over the stile that led into the depths of the Deepdale woods and moved quickly along the beck, into the tree line, and was gone.

The black car mounted the grassy verge, and a tall, bearded man stepped out. He locked the 4x4 and followed Bobby into the trees.

As he entered the wood, crunching on the undergrowth, splintering a rotten branch underfoot, he drew a long blade from a sheath.

16

Bobby could see the tall, lithe, bearded man walking slowly into the woods, something glinting in his hand.

He knew he had to run. He knew this terrain, and his hunter did not. Bobby was heavy, but he was fit, and he could move. He heard the snap and whip of the man crashing through the undergrowth. Bobby knew he had an advantage. He was a soldier, and he knew this ground. His heart was beating fast, but he was thinking clearly.

Bobby veered hard off the main path and scrambled and dived into the trees. He crouched in thick bushes. He could see the man, now only twenty yards away, standing still on the track, knees bent, holding a sharp blade, looking from side to side.

Bobby could not move now. The man would see him. His nose was close to the earth of Deepdale – it was wet from the rain, deep and ancient.

The bearded man moved slowly forward, keeping his shoulders low. Bobby's legs were exposed, but his body and head were hidden in the tall weeds and thorns. If he stayed still, the man might not see him. But if he did, he was vulnerable.

A tiny green insect settled on his wrist. He noticed, in his dive from the path, he had ripped the back of his hand. There was a ribbon of ripped skin, and new blood flooding the wound.

Who was this killer on his trail? Bobby was angry. Angry because he had panicked and run. He should have stood his ground. Angry, too, for his daughter. Angry at the violence which, like an animal, was entering his life again. He had moved back home to be free of it. Now it was here, dressed in black, armed, ready – for some reason – to harm him.

Bobby looked closer at the man's weapon. It was more like a stiletto blade than a hunting knife or a machete. If it pierced him, it could breach the walls of his heart or slice open his guts. Bobby sized him up. The man was tall, but not that big. Bobby could overpower him.

Images flitted in his skittering mind – the rapid click-clack of machine-gun fire in the fir trees of Bosnia. Splinters about his helmeted head. The thump of mortars. And later, much later, the thunder of strikes in the desert. The vicious sucking of air. Mangled bodies, humans wrenched inside out. A basement full of choked bodies in T-shirts and sportswear. A man, at a distance, decapitated by rifle fire.

But here he was. In the woods of his hometown. His injured hand closed on something hard: a strange, sickle-shaped rock jutting from the bracken. He grabbed it.

The bearded man at last moved. He walked forward tentatively, and then quicker, crouching, along the path. Then he stopped, and turned, and faced the thicket where Bobby lay. Then he turned again, all black clothes and lethal poise, to face the way he had come.

Bobby gripped the rock and rose to his feet.

The bearded man swung around, but the rock had already left Bobby's hand, flung with force. It flew lower than he wanted and thumped into the man's chest. The man grunted and staggered back.

Bobby charged him, his head down, shoulders square, pushing his weight forward to crush the bearded man. But his foot snagged on a root in the undergrowth and he tripped. The bearded man stepped aside deftly and, as Bobby tumbled past him, plunged his blade down.

Bobby felt force, not pain. The bearded man raised the blade again in a clear arc, and Bobby, prone, kicked out at him, hit something solid and pulled himself up.

For a moment, they stood, both crouched, one armed, one

wounded, and stared at each other. The bearded man, his eyes fetid as pond water. Bobby, huge and wild – and bleeding.

'What are you doing?' he found himself saying.

The knife swung again, on a deadly arc – and it missed Bobby.

He turned and ran. Deep into the deep of Deepdale, as hard as he could, knees high, headlong through bushes and undergrowth. Thin branches whipped and snapped. The ground rolled and jutted beneath his feet. Up ahead was another path, coming down from the edge of the dale to this wooded valley. He looked back. He could see a figure flitting through the trees. There was no time. He needed to do a U-turn and make his way back to town.

For speed, he followed the beaten path. It pressed uphill, a steep slope. The man would reach it soon. Bobby reached for his phone as he pelted along the track – jumping over rocks and boulders – but he had left it behind, charging in his house.

On his right was a barbed-wire fence; over it, there were thinning trees and flat fields. To his left lay the darkness of Deepdale. He did not want to try the fence. And the open fields were a killing ground. He came to a muddy stream, a trickle of water leaking brown from the field, and took off, helter-skelter, down into the trees again.

But the hill was steep and treacherous underfoot. And Bobby was weakening. He shot forward, fell and came to a battering halt at the base of a thick tree.

He was still and blank with pain. Before he could move, the man was at him. There was a moment of violence and confusion. The bearded man's breath was in his face, his elbow chopping back and forward. Pain ripped through Bobby's side, in his guts, and a fiery heat spread fast across his belly and down his thighs.

The bearded man stood up, unsmiling, and nodded. His glove was red with blood, dripping death. And then, he was gone, like a blown shadow, disappearing into the trees.

Bobby pulled himself up. He felt his side. He raised his hand, and it was shockingly wet with hot dark blood. He looked down at his jacket, and in it there were savage rips, its stuffing hanging out in wisps of white. He pulled up his ripped sweatshirt. There were ragged apertures in his flesh. He was suddenly exhausted. He was punctured, leaking. He bellowed.

In slow motion, as if caught in mud or wading through water, or a living dream, he crawled down the thickly wooded slope, his eyesight blurring. He was deep in the woods, the sky only flashes of ice-blue in the canopy.

He knew that if he lay down and slept, he would bleed out. He had to refuse the sudden warm offer of the long night. That would come, anyway. Right now, he refused.

Staggering to his feet, he lurched forward to a concrete wall that emerged out of the thick green branches and trunks. He had been to Deepdale many times before and not seen this building, this abandoned place. In his slipping mind, he wondered why it was here, so far from the town, from roads and people and civilisation. Maybe the woods themselves had built this ruin. Or it had grown out of the mud, out of the stone.

Bobby knew he could not stop moving. He had to get back to the town. He lurched left again and headed the way he thought Ullathorne lay. It would be easier if he found the beck – the beck would lead him home.

Trees ghosted past him. Thorns tore at him. Weeds gripped his legs. He held his side, held his sides inside, held his blood in his wounds, and suddenly found himself lying in the water. His blood was flowing into it – swirling and misting, a nebula of blood, blooming.

Momentarily, his mind stilled and narrowed. Past his eyes he saw something ghostly move – marching feet, muddy feet and legs, matted and filthy. He smelled the stench of old skins, human bodies, sweat and leather.

Prone, unmoving, he looked wildly into the trees. Dark eyes

moved between bare branches. The trees had thickened, and the beck was now wide, a river. On the far shore, there was a silent procession. People were moving, carrying a long stretcher. On it was a dead king, with coins for eyes, clean-shaven, with a glittering circlet beside his cold and wounded head. Many hands held him. The dead king seemed to lie in suit trousers, a white shirt, his arms folded, his hands holding branches of ash, elm and yew.

All this passed through Bobby's eyes and mind: women mourning in green with heads bowed, and children walking silently, their faces painted. Men strode, low and loping, with bronze glimmering and iron held fast. As silent as a dream they moved through the bars of trees.

His eyes filled with light. He did not blink and did not sigh. He felt warm and calm. He lay, his face half under the cold water of the Deepdale beck, the branches low about him. His fingers were white and gently wrinkling, his boots cleaned of the mud and dust of life.

After what seemed a long while, but passing only in seconds, he sensed movement nearby, and the sound of soft feet on moss and pebble, a rustling through nettles and weeds. Beside him, there was now a man in soft garments. He had a face like creased leather, his eyes were dark as wet stone, his hair long and black and braided. He seemed to say something quiet, something kind, in muffled words that he could not quite hear, and he touched Bobby between the eyes with consoling fingers wet from the stream.

And then he was gone, and Bobby knew he was alone, lying in the beck, dying in the mud.

He thought now only in torn shreds and disconnected fractals. But in those fluttering shreds was Becky. She was at school, working her way through lessons, laughing with her friends. Her day advanced beyond the moment of her father's death. Like love, he was now outside time.

Robert Stang, in the cold stream, opened his mouth to call his daughter's name, and then his mind stilled, his eyes closed, and he dropped into the sea of everlasting dark.

the hollow tree

Earlier that day, before the sun had crested the hilltops, in the clearing of the hollow tree, there had been darkness and silence. Without the sun, the giant tree cast no shadow. It was sunk deep into the enclosing dark, like a bone inside a body.

The hollow tree stood in Tyrdale, as it had age after age. Its roots held the earth and rock. It drew water, and drank it, and breathed it, feeding it to the sky. Dumb, but not numb, it was as alive as the world, but still and silent. It was dead and alive, motionless, yet always moving. It was a bridge between the soil and the sky. A home – a tower – a vast flower.

Then, the world had moved, and the sun's light had come again. The hollow tree had stood for countless unremembered dawns like this, where the sun slowly blushes the eastern sides of the Pennines. A fresh sheet of light laid over the plunging fells and the tumbling white-teethed ghylls. Dew lay in tiny pools on bark and limb. A rime of moisture shivered on cold branches and many-knotted twigs.

A single brown bird emerged from a feathery hold. It opened its mouth and croaked. A gentle wind had risen, bringing the smell of the nearby river, its mulch and jetsam.

The bird was not alone. Across the waking forest, the hunters, the mothers, rose and peeked from their nests.

A drifting owl skimmed through the upper canopy of naked branches. It drifted on a rising heat and looked down upon the giant tree, black and alone in its own clearing, the surrounding woods standing back, giving the old ogre space.

The rising sun and the fading moon glimmered in the owl's round eyes – it saw all as it soared on the opening air, and it sensed, higher, a swifter killer.

There, the hawk, lolling on the heat of the exhaling earth, gently tipped its weight below the cloud line. The river below was a running ribbon being pulled into the sea, and the fields about it glistened. A sudden gleam caught its deadly eye.

It dipped, its body as light as a knife, and below, in the old woods it scanned the clearing of the hollow tree. Human sweat was there, and footprints. And inside the tree there was dark, and an iron hardness, and things the hawk did not want to, and could not, disturb. It rose again, observing the lightening fields, the mist now gathering like frost in the hollows of the valley.

The hawk had a home, and it turned in a tight arc towards it, barrelling down in wide circles, the world tilted as if turning on a hip socket.

It spiralled on, a ranging dot above the morning glade of the hollow tree, where tiny insects stirred and hovered over the fern and thorns, flitting in fizzing flight between beech and red oak, between old firs and sweet chestnut.

A tawny squirrel, skittering about in its quick-twitch business, clung to an old fir. It had run on the hollow tree's bark, once, several moontides ago. A memory clung to the silver innards of its bubble skull. It had reached a rent in the tree skin, and in it had crept, trembling, to the lip of the crevasse.

No food was there, in the dark inside. Down into the sunless, moonless dark, the swift rodent had stared into the wreckage of bark, of wood death and fungus rot. Its gleaming eyes had seen the circlet of yellow bone, a hanging human jaw, a tumble of teeth. Finger bones dislocated and adrift in the enclosed soil.

Because deep below, deep enough never to be found, were the remains of a human body in a rotted bag, a sacred gift long faded and frayed. A stomach of barley, flax, glass beads and pig. A curled corpse, clean-shaven, one arm missing, long since given to the hollow tree.

The sun was high now, and the rabbit, the owl, the hawk and

the squirrel were long gone. The river ran loud, and the cars of humans began to grind on the nearby road. The giant tree cast a shadow aslant the glade.

A man walked into the shadow. He walked slowly, dressed all in black. Insects moved on, unmoved by the bulk and the weight. The birds flustered and flew.

The man looked around. He looked up. His cheek was red with blood, a line scored out by a sharp twig dragged across the soft flesh. He shook his head. He said something loud, and paced, cursing to himself.

Perched on the arm of a nearby oak, a blackbird watched with its yellow-ringed eye, as the human walked back and forth, back and forth. It smelled him: sweat, sweat from his armpits, from his thighs, deep sweat from his trousers. The metallic ions of deodorant. And mixed with that was the scent of crushed bracken, of mud from another dale. And blood: the iron tang of it, from this man, and another.

The murderer ripped off his bloody gloves. He folded them together. He looked around and above. He saw the apertures in the sides of the hollow tree and pushed them in, and pushed them down.

The gloves, balled, tacky with drying blood, fell into the gloom of the inner tree. In its fall it gathered dusty murk and fungal spores, clogged moss hairs and thicker cobwebs. The gloves tumbled down to a damp cave within, brown with wet flopped mushrooms. The gloves lay now in the darkness and would, in weeks, be covered and shielded by fallings, by droppings, by sheets of webs and spots of mould. They would not be found.

The man paced. He suddenly clapped his hands. The sound shook through the undergrowth and up into the trees, but nothing stirred. The world was silent and waiting. He turned on a heel, digging a sudden semicircle into the mud, and left the glade.

The day began to pass again, in and around the hollow tree. The fingers of the farthest branches arced towards the sun, still growing, still breathing, still reaching for the light.

17

Terry pulled up outside the entrance to the ruined castle.

Shona stuck her head into the open passenger window. 'You're late.'

'Thanks for coming all the way from Richmond to pick me up, Theresa, thanks very much,' Terry said, putting on a ridiculous Scottish accent. 'Thanks for coming thirty miles out of your way for me.'

Shona clambered into the car, dropped her stick and shook her head. 'Och, wheesht,' she said.

Terry burst out laughing.

'Right,' Shona said. 'This woman, she lives further away, into the hills.'

'Up the dale?'

'I guess so.'

'Fine. Up the dale.'

'Where?'

Shona squinted at her notes. She had told the barman at the Lion that she wanted to speak to the singer of Bundle of Twine for a newspaper article. She had flashed her National Union of Journalists card, and he had given her Beverley Moore's number. She had spoken to Beverley, told her she wanted to talk about her band for a feature for the paper, and, after a long pause, in her deep voice, Beverley had given her an address.

'So, it's in a place called Thorsgill,' Shona said.

'Oh, aye, halfway up. Be there in forty-five minutes, longer if we're caught behind a tractor,' Terry said. She turned the car around and guided it through the streets of Ullathorne.

Shona rang her father.

'Morning, Shona,' Bernie replied.

Shona snorted. 'Can you please stop answering Dad's bloody phone for him?'

'But he's asleep, darling,' Bernie said.

'It's just annoying,' Shona said. 'Is he all right?'

'There's no need to be so rude,' Bernie said. 'I'm not at all rude to you, am I? But anyway, yes, he's fine. He was very tired. MacDiarmid is asleep on top of him. It's so sweet – you should see the pair of them. She's purring away, the wee thing.'

'Fine. Can you say I called, please?'

'Shall I tell that to the cat or your father?'

Shona drew her breath sharply. 'Both. And can you not call the cat Mac, please? That's not her fucking name.'

'Shona!' Bernie exhaled. 'I mean, honestly?'

'Bye.' Shona hung up.

Terry smiled and put a luminescent yellow cough drop in her mouth. 'Someone taking your cat's name in vain, eh? Something to rage about. Good use of your body's finite resources of energy.'

Shona looked out at the deepening valley. 'My dad is poorly, and she's supposed to be his nurse. Instead, she's wibbling on about the cat.'

'I'm sorry to hear that – how old?'

'About a year. Just settling in.'

'Your dad.'

'Nearly seventy-five, going on sixteen. Him and his *girlfriend*.'

'I've got a cat.'

'Amazing. How nice for you.'

'He's old now – getting thin, losing his teeth.'

'Fascinating.'

Terry shook her head and flicked on the radio.

They drove on, following the course of the river.

'Has this woman agreed to have her photo taken?' Terry said.

'About that – I've said we're shipping up there for an article on her folk band,' Shona said.

'It's not, is it?'

'No, course not. Who gives a fuck about her sodding folk band? But she went to school with Dan Merrygill. She can tell us more.'

'You going to be angry all day?'

'Probably.'

Terry suddenly pulled over into a passing place. She turned off the engine, and the radio fell from a burble to nothing. 'Can you hear that?'

Shona listened and couldn't hear anything unusual. Birds were singing in the roadside bushes, hawthorn and blackthorn, and a brave pioneer bee was bumbling between thistles in the pasture beyond the wall. Then she realised what to her was the usual roar of life in the city was now somehow present here. Coming from somewhere beyond the high trees in the crease of the valley above.

'That's the big waterfall, the Great Fosse, up there in the trees,' Terry said. 'It's where the Tyr falls about eighty feet. It's pretty bloody loud when you get near it. I've had some nice jobs there over the years. There's a big hotel beside it, the Fosse and Rainbow.'

Shona could hear the distant rumble, but without seeing it, she could not imagine the waterfall, its relentless power, its constant cloud of spray and foam. 'Can we get going?'

'Aye,' Terry said, 'Green Northern Tours continues, after the break.'

'It's grim up north,' Shona said. The car moved on. 'You have to remember, this is south for me,' she said, tapping the top of her stick.

'How you finding it?'

'Nice landscape, shame about the people.'

Terry grinned. 'Fair enough. I blame William the Conqueror.'

'Oh, aye, what did he do, then?'

'Tried to kill everyone north of the Trent, I do believe. The Scourging of the North.'

'I'm sure he had his reasons.'

'It's all right for you rebellious Scots,' Terry said. 'We're stuck with the fuckers, still lording it over all of us today.'

Thick stands of bare budding trees pulled in around them.

'Down that way is the Coine Tree.' Terry pointed to a gravel track that led into the woods. There was a green sign which Shona could not read. They sped past.

'The what?'

'The oldest, biggest tree in England, they say,' Terry said.

Shona sighed heavily.

'What now?' Terry said.

'Well, it's probably good colour for the article,' Shona said. 'For my feature. Can we go back and see it?'

Terry smiled. 'No bother.' She reversed and turned on the tight road.

They returned to the gravel track, and Shona could read the sign now: THE COINE TREE: THE OLDEST TREE IN ALL ANGLE-LAND.

They pulled into a parking area beside the road. Shona stepped out, and her stick felt slick and heavy in her hand, as if the valley had its own gravity, or by some unsaid kinship the wood in her hand was drawn to the trees around her. She waited impatiently while Terry pulled her equipment from the car: a black bag of cameras and lenses and a tripod, folded like a gun.

They set off down the path. The world closed in on either side. Roots straggled over banks of rock. Ferns and green moss as bright as jewels glimmered wetly.

'It's a yew tree,' Terry said, lumbering a little with her gear. Shona was crunching along the track, her stick skipping and tapping.

'Would yew believe it!' Shona said and looked to Terry for a smile, which was not forthcoming.

156

'It's massive – must be about eight metres around,' Terry said.

They tramped in silence and arrived at a large clearing. In the centre was a monster – a huge, wide tree, which looked like a tightly knotted clutch of wooden towers. The growth of its trunk over hundreds of years had split it into multiple bodies: it was several trunks all intertwined. It was like a petrified family of giants, back-to-back, facing out to the world.

There was a large slit in its side, dark and wet, and Shona could see that its largest trunk had a cavity within. The trees in the woods looked like children around it. Feeble and scared.

Shona moved closer. The Coine Tree towered above her. It looked like it had grown in the wrong world. It was too big. She looked up to its canopy, shorn of leaves in the long winter. It was a maze of twisting black branches, crisp and clear against the sky.

'Jesus,' Shona said. 'That is a big tree. My dad would love it.'

'The druids worshipped it, they say,' Terry murmured, staring at the back of her camera.

'I'm not surprised. I feel quite close to uttering a prayer myself,' Shona said.

They stood for a while before the hollow tree. Shona wondered if there was something missing in her – she felt as if this vast entity should be telling her something. Offering an insight. All she could sense was its sheer scale.

There was something else there, though, that she could not immediately fathom. She did not have the means to measure and understand it. It seemed to be timeless. She, on the other hand, was stuck with time. It was passing even as she considered it. She was rootless and soft. This thing was gripping the earth, and it was as hard as stone or iron – as hard as death.

Terry started taking photographs, complaining about the poor light.

Shona put her hand to the bark. It was cold and smooth,

rippling like a frozen waterwall. She noticed there were other doors into the hollow trunk, apertures into the darkness within.

'Why is it called the Coine Tree?' Shona said, peering through a hole into its depths.

'Go around the other side, Sherlock,' Terry said, without looking up from her camera.

Shona slowly walked around the tree. The tree trunk glittered, studded with curved edges of metal. Coins had been forced into its skin.

She moved closer and could see a galaxy of thin pennies that had been pressed into the bark over centuries. Some were now green like algae, some were bent, some were almost submerged in the growing bark.

'People push the coins in and make wishes,' Terry said. She was standing with camera in hand, cocked like a gun.

'People,' Shona said quietly, running her hand over the coins. They were like scales, like rusted armour on a sleeping giant in the woods.

'People, yeah.' Terry looked at her watch. 'The coins are killing it. They had a sign up a few years back, asking people not to stick the coins in any more, but people ignored it, and so it just carries on. The coins are poisoning it.'

'People are idiots,' Shona said and turned back to the path. She found herself glancing at the tree, as if it may move or disappear.

At the car, they settled into their seats.

'Nice tree, eh?' Terry said.

'It's not bad,' Shona said. 'How old is it?'

'Thousands of years.'

'Poisoned or not, it'll probably be here when we're long gone.'

'It already is,' Terry said, as the car pulled away.

They drove on, and the weather brightened, and the valley widened as they moved higher. The fells on either side were wide and gentle. They passed farms, isolated houses, until, at last, they came to Thorsgill.

They pulled over beside the village green, which had a roofed well at its centre and neat stone buildings clustered around. A small road led up the side of the fell to a group of newer houses. Beverley Moore lived in one of them.

They walked to the last house in the row. The pebble-dashed semi had a large garden with a low fence about it. Dream catchers swung on low branches, chimes dangled from two gnarled cherry trees, and a wicker lantern hung from an apple tree, swinging in the light breeze. Around the sides of the two-storey house, vegetables were grown – all harvested months ago. A stone badger stood by the front door, and several figures made from concrete and wire – bearded, in robes – huddled in the long grass. They stared with blank eyes to the north of the dale.

Shona and Terry opened a creaking gate and walked up the path to the door, which had been painted purple and had a yin-yang painting above the knocker.

'So, what gives here?' Terry said.

'I'll knock and see what happens,' Shona said. 'Don't get your camera out.'

'Aye. I've done this before.'

Shona rapped on the door.

A deep voice sounded from within. 'Wait a minute!'

There was the sound of padding feet and the door opened. A tall woman with long grey hair and a yellow smock stood in a colourful hallway decorated with many small mirrors. She wore a lot of jewellery and had a hand-rolled cigarette in her hand.

'Oh, hello,' she said, her voice low and sonorous.

'Beverley?' Shona said. 'We spoke on the phone. I was hoping you'd like to talk to me. I'm a friend of Viv Banks. We worked together. I was at her wedding. I was there when Dan died.'

'Oh,' Beverley said, raising her thick eyebrows. 'So, you're the lass that called.'

'That's me.'

'So, you're not really here to talk about my band, then?' Beverley said, her voice hardening.

'We can talk about that too.' Shona smiled.

Beverley took a short drag of her cigarette. Sweet marijuana smoke drifted in a whiskery trail.

'And who's this young lady?' she said, nodding to Terry.

'Terry's a photographer. I'd just like a word. I'm trying to find out about Daniel. About what happened.'

'Well, if you were there, what more is there to know? It's already been in the papers,' Beverley said, folding her arms across her body.

There was a silence, and the three stood, waiting.

Shona decided to grin at her. Beverley seemed to take in the grin, like a gift. Her body moved back, as if receiving something unwanted but painless.

'*About what happened,*' Beverley repeated. She took another drag.

'To Daniel,' Shona said.

'Who do you work for?'

'Myself. I'm freelance.'

'So, for nobody or anybody,' Beverley said.

'Well, exactly,' Shona said.

Beverley smiled. 'And this pretty one an' all?'

'I'm just happy to be here.' Terry beamed.

Shona found herself grinning again, amused by Terry's sudden perkiness. 'Beverley,' she said, 'I'm just looking for background – for information. I'm not here to interview you on the record or quote you. I'm just trying to find out what might have led to Daniel's death.'

'It was at his own hand, love,' Beverley said. 'I'm not sure I can really help you.'

'I know. But I'm thinking there must have been reasons. Maybe going back a long way. Going back to his school days, maybe.'

'Maybe,' Beverley said.

There was silence again. A bird was singing overhead. Terry peered at her camera lens, as if it had something to say.

Shona pressed on. 'I'm just looking for background,' she said. 'You were there, back when he was a lad. You might provide some context for me, some facts, some accuracy.'

'No quotes, no interview – just the gen,' Beverley said, seemingly to herself.

A large man suddenly appeared behind her in the hallway. His face was ruddy and almost entirely covered in a curling grey beard. He had tattoos on his neck and his arms. Fine hairs stuck out of his ears and from his eyebrows. He resembled a bear, or an outsized owl.

'Everything all right, love?' he said. His deep voice burred like timpani.

'Aye, Karl, love,' she said. 'Put the kettle on.'

He disappeared again after a stiff nod.

'That's my Karl,' Beverley said. Then she seemed to peer into the distance and make a decision. 'Come in, then.'

Shona felt a rush of relief. She crossed the threshold, with Terry not far behind.

They passed a large metal Buddha in one corner of the hall and then walked into a sun-filled living room. There were windows on three sides. Leaning in a corner was a large decorative axe, with a leather handle and blade etched with runes. Orchids stood stiff in decorated pots, and a crocheted blanket had been draped over a small television in another corner. Heavy wooden shelves were filled with vinyl records and CDs. A large rug covered bare floorboards. A scented candle, black and huge, stood on a metal holder, emitting a heavy perfume. Music was burbling from a small radio, next to a statue of the Virgin Mary near the stone fireplace. The Virgin, in blue, looked sorrowfully down, her face cracked, robes flaked and stained with age and smoke. Two acoustic guitars sat beside the fireplace. The light glimmered on their tigerish red and orange varnish.

'They say never let the Devil cross your threshold,' Beverley said brightly. 'But here we are.'

She asked Shona to sit, and she did, on a wooden chair beside the coffee table. Both looked homemade, and the table was slightly higher at one end than the other. Terry looked around the room. She mumbled something about the light and waiting outside, and quietly left. Shona watched her leave with a frown.

Beverley asked Shona to call her Bev. There was small talk about the weather, the delayed spring, and Bev asked Karl to make something more substantial for an early lunch when he brought through their tea and laid cups on the table. He rumbled that he would and returned to the kitchen. They spoke of Shona's journey south and how she knew Viv, and Bev asked how she was, kindly.

Shona looked around. There was a large painting of astrological signs. There was a framed poster from the 1980s which said: *Before Margaret Thatcher came to power the UK stood on the edge of a precipice – since then we've taken a step forward.*

'We're old socialists. Old Labour,' Bev said, catching Shona's eye. 'Sorry about that. You feel the need to apologise these days.'

'Not many of you left, is there? You and my dad,' Shona said.

'Problem with fascists,' Bev said, 'is you'd have to beat them all. It's too tiring. So, we give up.'

Shona moved her cup to make room for her pad and pen. It slid sideways.

'Unusual table,' she said. It was higher at one end than the other.

'No need to buy expensive furniture when you can make it yourself,' Bev said. 'All that traipsing to the shops. What a rip-off. My soul dies a little in those IKEA places – you have to put the bloody stuff together yourself. What a scam it all is.'

'Thieves,' Karl called through from the kitchen. He had put some folk music on. A beautiful woman's voice was lilting over electric guitars, and Karl was humming along.

'Karl makes our furniture. Makes sense to us.' Bev put out her joint with a solid fizzle in a clay ashtray and sipped her tea. She peered at Shona. 'So, you saw poor Dan?'

Shona nodded.

Bev pushed her hair behind her ears and pulled out a neatly prepared joint. 'Poor Dan,' she said. 'Poor sod.'

'Had you seen him recently?'

'No, love,' she said, inhaling and exhaling. The dope smelled sweet and strong.

'That smells good.' Shona smiled.

'We grow it ourselves,' Bev said.

'Don't tell the cops,' Karl shouted through.

'Karl, can you get on with lunch and leave us be?' Bev shouted.

Shona asked again: had she seen Daniel Merrygill recently?

Bev shook her head. 'No sight nor sign of him, not recently. Maybe a year ago, saw him in Ully. Maybe visiting his mum in the care home. He was never for talking much and he didn't then, either. I never knew he was still friends with Viv. I had no idea.'

'He was in sixth form with you, though – had you not seen him since then?'

'Not really. Not since Andrew's funeral. The one with no body in the coffin. It was more of a memorial, really – not a funeral. In ninety-eight, I think, or was it ninety-nine? Years after he went missing. Years.'

'What about Dan after school? You were in a small sixth form with him – Viv told me.'

Bev blew out more smoke, tilting her head up. 'Pet, this is ancient history, really. But, yeah, sixth form was daft. Looking back on it. It was so small. After the GCSEs, everyone left. There were all these people, loads of friends, and then they left. Off to trades or apprenticeships, off to sixth form in Darlington maybe. Who knows where? So, suddenly, there was just a handful of us. That final year, there were even fewer of us. Bobby and Andy, Dan, myself, Alison and Peg, Watson – that was it.'

'All doing the same subjects?'

'No. Let me remember now. There was me, Andy and Alison all doing English. Can't remember what Gary Watson did – maybe some business or sciences. Maths. Bobby was just doing General Studies and something else by upper sixth. Andy did History, I remember that, and so did Dan, I think. We'd spend most of our time in the library or the common room, just hanging about. It was all baggy clothes in those days. Paisley shirts.'

She sipped her tea, and so did Shona – it was hot and brown and sweet.

'No mobiles or laptops then, remember, love. This was ninety-one or ninety-two. So, we'd be listening to the Stone Roses and Happy Mondays on a small cassette radio we had. Gary would put 808 State on and some crappy rave tunes. Andy would play older stuff – The Beatles and the Stones. We'd nip off to the Old Well sometimes at lunchtimes or after school and have a pint and a game of pool. I snogged Dan in the fields once. I think I gave him a fright.'

'How did the exams go for you all in the end?'

'Oh, I did all right. Seemed so important then, though I don't know how important it was, really. It was going to be the last summer before real life began, but then it happened. Andy disappeared. We never really spoke again. Went our separate ways. You have to remember there was no emails, no texting, no internet, no social media, in them days. It was easy to lose touch back then. Seems nuts now.'

'But you came back to Tyrdale.'

'Yeah, I came back eventually. I got sick in Liverpool. Then

I got homesick. Got a job in the council, been here ever since. Planning, of course. Got married to a prick, got divorced, all in eighteen months. Then I met Karl at Glastonbury. He moved here to be with me, didn't you, Karl? Daft apeth.'

Karl rumbled something inaudible from the kitchen.

'I was in two bands by then,' Bev chuckled. 'Not that we had any success, of course. But we had fun.'

Shona smiled, tapped her notepad with a finger. 'Your ex-husband, what was his name?'

Bev shook her head. 'He's irrelevant. I intend to keep him that way.'

'Right. So, what about the others? Do you know what they got up to?'

'Bobby went off to war, didn't he? Can't remember seeing much of him. Was he in Bosnia? Might have been in Iraq or Afghanistan. I know he was in Germany mainly. Saw him in the Lion once with a crew cut, looking massive.'

'Always was a big lad,' Karl boomed from the kitchen.

'Yep, always a big lad. He lives over the way now. Works at the bottle factory, got a wee lass. Quiet. Then Alison – I don't think we saw her again, after that night. She went down to London and stayed there. She was always a smart cookie. Bright. I saw on Facebook she's married, but I don't think the wedding was up here. Her dad, he had some bad times. Think it knocked the family.'

'What about Daniel?'

Bev peered at her for a moment, but then carried on. 'Not sure what was going on with him. He just vanished. Maybe something to do with his mum. His dad had buggered off years before. Peg – Peg had a kid. She went off to catering college, I remember. She runs a B&B now in the town. Nice, is Peg. I like her. Had some problems with her girl, but what's new. She's got palsy. Nice girl, and bright too, like her mum. Poor Peg's husband died – cancer.'

'And Gary went into politics after business – an MP now,' Shona said.

'Yeah, suits him,' Bev said, flicking away some ash.

'Tosspot!' Karl shouted from the kitchen. 'All that nonsense he talks and what-have-yer.'

'Karl!

'That cunt needs fucked up,' he said, in a low but audible tone.

'Anyway,' Bev went on, shaking her head sadly. 'We could see that all coming. Gary had a briefcase in third year! Always talking about his mam and dad buying shares in BT and British Gas. Had a Filofax, the daft bugger. He was one of the more well-off kids. Didn't have much time for anyone else – not for me anyway. Ambitious.'

'What did his parents do?'

'They owned the abattoirs first,' Bev said. 'And some other businesses, by the end of the eighties. They bought the bottle factory. Video stores, too. Watson's Videos – chain across the North East.'

'So, he was as ambitious as his folks?'

Bev tapped her finger on the sloping table, and her voice quietened. 'Yes, but . . . I do remember one night that was a bit different with him . . . There was what we kind of called a rave. We all piled into someone's car. Gary came. Tunes all the way over in the car. We ended up in some old quarry over by Appleby. It were mad. Gary was out of it. We all were. It was pretty great – we were only seventeen, eighteen. Seemed like the world was changing. Of course it wasn't – but the music and, I guess, the drugs . . .'

'Ecstasy,' Karl hollered.

'Yeah, all that. It felt . . . optimistic, you know? Probably for the last time. Anyway, that night Gary was weird. Quite emotional, I remember. Maybe it was the music. Anyway, he was crying there, in the corner of the tent. Weeping. I think his

166

dad was a right arsehole, to be honest. He liked dressing up in army uniforms in his spare time. He's dead now – the old twat. His mum was a scared little thing. Anyway, Gary was upset that one time. He maybe had a rough time. Especially around A-levels. Maybe felt the pressure. So, I do remember that one night. Never saw that side of him again.'

'Loaded,' Karl shouted.

'Yeah, they were,' Bev said. 'Didn't seem to make them very happy, mind. Think they sold the whole chain of video stores for a sackload. Helped Gary set himself up as what he is now. He still owns a load of businesses – the bottle factory. Not the abattoir, though; they closed that down for whatever reason.'

'Wanker,' Karl shouted.

'An MP,' Bev said. 'He's quite a big deal, I guess. Not my kind of deal, though. I think he got married, but she died in a car crash.'

'Rum do, that,' Karl shouted.

'So,' Shona said, 'you said "that night" there – what night?'

'Did I?'

'Yes. You said you didn't see Alison again after "that night".'

'Oh, *that night* – the night Andy went missing.'

'What happened that night?'

Bev looked out the window. Her eyes reflected the sun outside. She pulled at an earring and sucked her joint. Karl came into the room and put a plate of thick sandwiches on the table. The plate slid a little on the slanting surface and then came to a halt.

Karl pulled a large conical joint from behind an ear. 'I'll be outside, love,' he said. He opened the back door and disappeared into the garden. Shona could hear him greeting Terry, and then their voices rising in laughter.

'Have a sarnie,' Bev said. 'We make our own hummus. Cheaper than the supermarket. Tomatoes from the greenhouse. Karl makes the bread; it's delicious. I don't tell him that, though. It's the only dough he makes around here.'

'Thanks,' Shona said but ignored the food. 'So, Karl is out of work?'

'He's always worked in the garment industry.' Bev shrugged. 'Good with his hands. But that's all gone to buggery now, hasn't it? Out of Europe, and now the business is cost-cutting. Corner-cutting. He lost his job a year ago. Like everything else: he was lied to.'

There was a silence.

'Have you spoken to Viv about her brother?' Bev asked.

'You know, I didn't even know she had one,' Shona said.

'She had a brother. Maybe everyone has forgotten about how he disappeared. Certainly no one in Ully speaks of it now. Viv's away in Scotland. The police have forgotten. Those that worked on the case, they've all retired or died. Alison's dad – he was a copper here – he led the search. It was all in the papers back then, but the police downgraded it after a while, stopped looking. It all seemed half-hearted at the time an' all. No internet, of course. No social media. It was on *Crimewatch* on the telly, I do remember that. Then it was gone and forgotten. As if everyone wanted to forget.'

Shona was taking notes in her pad. Little ticks, swoops and flicks of shorthand.

Bev added: 'He was a nice lad, Andy. Lovely big lad. We all liked him. He was going to be an engineer, he said. Had something lined up, some kind of summer job. Handsome, like Viv is pretty. He had the most beautiful eyes, you know. Long eyelashes.'

'When was the last time you saw him? What were you up to?'

Bev blew out a gust of sweet blue smoke. 'We were all bored with town. Bored with Ullathorne and school. Bored with living in the sticks. Bored with modern life. It's a terrible feeling, boredom, when you're young. But, you know, we were maybe scared as well – scared of leaving the town, of leaving Tyrdale.

Even though we knew we had to. Look at Bobby joining the army – he was desperate to get out. Mind you, his parents were hard work. Alison and me, too. But also . . . it's a hard place to leave. We'd get drunk to try and avoid all the choices, all the inevitable things we were going to have to do. The exams. Uni. Jobs. Money worries. All that. Some hormones, too! I was fancying everyone at the time. I even fancied Peg for a bit . . . Don't tell her.'

'So, you were all getting drunk a lot?'

'Aye, of course. Like you Scots. English people can't bloody live without alcohol. Stops us all jumping off a cliff, I think.'

Shona pressed on. 'What else was there – you had parties? Those raves you mentioned?'

'Well, of course there was the drink, as I said.' Bev shook her head. 'We were minced at the weekends. Cider and black. We used to drink this mix – Castaway and Diamond White. We called it Blastaway. In pints! Jesus! And Aftershock – we would get trays of them at the Lion. Gary was always on the lager. I remember Dan liked rum and Coke. Andy couldn't hold his drink – it was funny at the time.'

'So, there was a final party? Like some kind of going-away do?' Shona asked.

Bev looked outside. 'Has anyone told you about *the sessions*?' she said.

'Drinking sessions?'

'No, not that kind of session.' Bev paused and crushed the joint into the clay ashtray. The light dimmed. The sun was occluded. A shadow fell across the room.

'Ouija boards,' Shona said quietly.

Bev blinked hard. 'Was that a guess?'

'Not entirely,' Shona said. She remembered Daniel's tattoo.

Bev stood up and nodded to Karl through the window. Then she slumped back down again. 'It was all daft. We shouldn't have. But we did. We should have said no, should have said yes to no. But we carried on because it was scary, and a secret, and that's exciting. When the glass moves! When you think you're speaking to the dead. Or something. Or someone.'

'Who was doing this?'

'All of us, even Gary. I used to think he was messing with us, but he was well into it.'

'What, in the evenings?'

'No. You won't believe it, but we started doing it in the sixth-form common room, during the day. We had these empty study periods – hours long. There was this round table we had – the top came off the metal legs. So, we took it off and flipped it over, got some chalk from the classroom and drew out the board. The letters and the numbers.'

'Hello, goodbye, yes, no,' Shona said.

'Yes. The sun and the moon. And we'd do little sessions in these break times. And then flip it back over when the teachers or other kids came around. Sometimes we sneaked into the backstage area in the main hall. Behind the curtains. It was pretty dark back there. Sometimes the glass would move, sometimes it didn't. But it was stopped.'

'Stopped?'

'Yeah, someone found out. Not sure what happened. But the head teacher found out – got us into his office, gave us all a fucking telling-off. Gary shit himself. Alison was embarrassed, didn't want her parents to know. Her dad. Anyway, we were all told we had to stop doing it at school. Peg got scared. She kind of drifted away from the rest of us a wee bit. She got into The Cure! I remember her big hair and T-shirts.'

'What would happen in these sessions?'

'You ever done it?'

'No,' Shona said truthfully. 'Were you not moving the glass? Surely someone was moving the glass. Is it not just suggestible . . . a kind of game?'

Bev took a long swig of tea. She was thinking on something.

She shook her head as if that was the end of it, then murmured: 'The glass moved. Of course, there was a lot of mucking about – Bobby mainly.' She shivered. 'Actually, it's freaking me out thinking about it now.'

'What did the Ouija board say?'

'Nothing,' Bev said firmly.

'Nothing?'

'No. Just jumbles of letters. All gibberish.'

'Really?' Shona said. 'So, why keep doing it?'

'We were desperate to get something, some message or other. But we never did. It was crazy, really. We were just this little hysterical mad club, for a bit.'

Bev stood up. She was momentarily unsteady and rested her hand on the back of a chair, which rocked slightly on uneven feet. She tottered out of the living room and into the kitchen.

Shona reached for her stick and stood up. She moved to a window and looked outside. She could see the rest of the garden, separated from the hillside by a wooden fence. There were more vegetable patches, a polytunnel with plants of some kind inside and a greenhouse. Terry was sitting on a bench with Karl, getting stoned. Her cameras lay untouched in a bag beside her.

Something moved into Shona's head – a notion. It formed fully and clearly. The names of the six students: Alison – A, Bev – B, Dan – D, Andrew – A, Robert or Bobby – R, Gary – G. *Abdarg.*

Shona looked into the kitchen. There were wooden cupboards and shelves. A large poster of a hare pounding a tabor. Pans and skillets hanging from hooks – an electric oven, two microwaves. Knives were glinting on a magnetic strip near the toaster. She heard footsteps.

Bev was behind her, in a coat that seemed to be half leather, half wool. 'Let's have a little walk. I could do with some fresh air.' She opened the kitchen door and shouted to Karl that they'd be back in twenty minutes.

'Let's gan up the hill,' she said.

Shona looked to Terry, who gave her a thumbs-up. Karl was now bent over in the garden, his hands rummaging among the wintering plants, his beard tickling the soil.

Shona and Bev climbed over the garden stile and tramped over a barren, steep field. Thistles sprouted in patches. In the far corner, a knot of shy grey sheep slumped.

Shona silently cursed her shoes – trainers – which were sinking into the soft, wet turf. Her stick was useless here. Tiny brown balls of sheep shit lay scattered like seeds.

They walked quietly for a while up the steepening field. The width and depth of the valley opened as they rose. Cars flashed on the road. All above, the sky. A vastness, and a silence.

In the next field there was an abandoned barn, its doorless entry black, the grey stone streaked with yellow lichen. Propped against the outer wall was a bench.

'Let's have a sit here, save your legs,' Bev said.

Shona slumped down. She could feel her toes were damp. Her shoulder was sore. They sat beside each other, a metre apart, looking out over the dale. Below, Bev's house was tiny, like a toy house dropped from above.

'It's strange talking about all this now,' Bev said.

'I'm sure it is,' Shona said. 'I'd like to say thanks for all this – for your help.'

'That last night . . .'

'The night Andrew went missing?'

'I wish I could remember more. But I was so drunk. I was rat-arsed. I told the police the same at the time. Alison's dad. He didn't take many notes, I remember. And the years . . . they've not been good on my memory. It's funny – I remember it like pictures.'

'Like pictures?'

'Some are faded, some are framed, and some are treasured. Some are torn up and thrown away . . .'

A vast shadow moved across the fell. Shona looked up: a cloud like a dirigible was scudding on an invisible current.

Bev began to speak again, picking her words carefully. 'We'd all been in the Lion. Drinking at the end of the week. Me and Alison and Peg. Andy with Dan. Bobby. Gary with his numbskull pals. But somehow we all came together. It were warm. We walked down to the mill in pairs, or in separate groups. I remember telling the cops: it was me with Ali, Peg went home, Bobby on his tod, Dan and Andy, and Gary came down later. I was wasted; we all were. Nervous about the summer, about exam results, about going to uni. Bobby was all signed up, ready to ship himself off to Catterick garrison. To the army.'

She reached inside her jacket and fished out a packet of cigarettes. She offered one to Shona, who shook her head. Bev lit up, sucked and blew smoke up into the windless air.

She smoked for a while more, and Shona waited. She had learned, long ago, that silence was often worth waiting through. It was best to not interrupt or second-guess what might be said next.

'It's hazy now, it really is,' Bev said. 'We were in the basement of the mill, sitting on our seats – deckchairs, folding chairs from school. Gary had a little stool. It were late by that point. Did a little session with the board – nothing doing. Then we all left. Andy was on his own. I remember him climbing those stone stairs, and his silhouette against the blue night sky – it were nearly July – and then he was gone. No one saw him again. I remember him waving goodbye, a thumbs-up and a smile. He was wearing his Newcastle top, as per usual. Loved his football.'

'Did the police ask what you were up to? Down there in the mill?'

'Yeah, course. We said we were drinking. Which we were – cider, beer. Ali was petrified, I think. I don't know what Gary said. It's not like we were ever interviewed as a group. We were never asked to go to the station to make statements. It didn't seem to matter to them.'

'So, what do you think happened to Andrew?'

Bev ground her cigarette stub into the wet grass with her boot. 'I think he went in the river. I don't know why, but I think he went in the water. Out at sea, now.'

'Why's that?'

'Well, he was mangled with drink. He might have gone down by the river there, for some reason, and fallen in. I don't know. He wasn't picked up by someone – he only had a ten-minute walk home. He just needed to go up the Bank, into the town centre and up to his estate. I mean, maybe a twenty-minute walk. So, he wouldn't have accepted a lift from some nutcase. Why would he do that?'

'What was Dan doing?'

'I never really saw him,' Bev said, slurring her words a little. 'He left the mill after Andy, but he went straight home, back to his mam's. He was seen in the chip shop, buying chips and gravy. Then it was Gary – he drove home, I think, pissed. Shame he didn't crash. Then Ali left, and I walked into town for a bit. I think Ali said she was sick before she got back to her folks.'

Shona was taking notes. Bev did not seem to care.

'They never found Andy's body,' Bev said, almost whispering now. 'And there were no sightings. He just vanished. There was a search, there was the telly stuff – and then nothing. There was nowhere for the thing to go, so it died. And then the family held the memorial a few years later. That seemed to be the end of it all. Andy's parents sold up, moved on. Viv went to uni – in Glasgow, I think? Yeah, Glasgow. She's not been back here for ages. Why would she? Nowt here for her.'

'No?'

'No. What is there? There's nothing holding anything together. It's just families trying to get by, isn't it? The dream's over . . . You got kids?'

'No.'

'Well, probably for the best – that's what I tell myself an' all.' Bev sighed, long and hard. She rubbed her face. 'And that's me, Shona. That's all there is. I'm really sorry – I don't know any more.'

Shona nodded. 'Thank you. I know you weren't expecting to talk about this today.'

'You never know what a day might bring,' Bev said quietly.

They walked without words down the hill, through the scraggy field. The sheep were now gathered around a large metal feeder, crying.

Shona remembered something. 'Bev, I was wondering, why did Dan have a tattoo of a Ouija board on him?'

Bev glanced at her. 'Did he?'

'Yeah, on his chest. I saw it.'

They paused before the stile into the back garden. Bev's eyes flickered for a moment, and she looked away. 'I don't know about any tattoos, love.'

'Do you know why Dan might have spelled out a phrase in his . . . in the suicide note?'

'What phrase?'

'"Take the Right Path"?' Shona said. 'He also wrote "Say Yes to No" and "There Is No Time" and a name, "Sorley". Was he a friend? Sorley?'

Bev moved away and climbed over the stile. Karl was poking at something in the garden with a shovel – he looked up as she climbed over.

'No, love, sorry,' she said. 'I've no idea. And your friend there seems nice, but I'm not posing for any pictures for you or your papers.'

Shona followed her silently to the house.

Shona and Terry gathered their belongings as Bev waited by the front door.

'Nowt in the papers, now,' Bev said. Her face had hardened. Her eyes were glassy. She wanted them to leave.

'There won't be,' Shona said. 'Not of you. Not about you.'
She nodded at the ornamental axe. It looked heavy, deadly,
ridiculous. 'What's with the exotic weaponry?'

'That's Karl – his fantasy stuff,' Bev said, rolling her eyes.
She added: 'The band's playing at the Lion this week – you're
welcome to come.'

'If I'm still here, I will,' Shona said.

'Time for them to go, love,' Karl called.

Bev opened the front door. 'Aye, off you trot. Take care.'

She stood for a while, watching them, and then suddenly
turned and closed the front door.

Shona and Terry walked silently back to the car. Terry slung
her gear into the boot. Shona leaned against the bodywork and
tapped her muddy stick on the tarmac.

'Did you get what you needed?' Terry said.

'I don't know.'

'I got the feeling she wouldn't play for pics.'

'You felt right.' Shona chewed a fingernail. Something was
wrong – and something was missing.

'Where to now, boss?' Terry said.

'I need to get back to the town. I need to visit someone.'

Gary Watson MP was watching himself fucking.

It was one of many recordings. He watched his toned hairless back rising and falling, under hard bright hotel light, a pair of bobbing ankles high around his ears. He watched, his eyes unblinking, his mouth hanging open, a hand down his black silken pants.

He was startled by a bleep from his other phone. His mouth snapped shut, his hand stopped moving, and he shut down the video. He peered out over the valley from his stone-and-steel kitchen at Scar Top.

Scar Top was the Watson family's mansion on the outskirts of Ullathorne. Set back behind a gated drive, within woodland, it stood on its own hill overlooking the town. In recent years, it had been refurbished, redeveloped, extended. Now, its interior was all white concrete, polished stone and glass. Pristine surfaces, wipe-down marble and vast planes of blue sheet glass, yet it retained the old cellars and hiding places.

He moved closer to the window. A notification bleeped again on the phone lying on the long glass tabletop. Shadows moved in the glass as if it was water.

He hoped it was a message from Alyce. But no. It was an encrypted text: *call*.

Raymond.

Watson read it, and it was instantly deleted.

He made a strong drink and moved through to the living-room area, divided from the kitchen by a change in flooring from black stone to lush cream carpet. The television was silent. There was a large dark stain on the rug. Knott would sort it.

He took down a slim silver tablet from the stone mantelpiece and opened it. He looked over the election plans. Posters and flyers. Social media messages. Five proactive news releases. Reactive lines already cleared with his agent and the Whips. A question-and-answer document, already written, running to ten pages. Top lines in bold and underlined, key facts in boxes, statistics in italics. All ready.

Watson had access to the Party communications grid, and it was full, had been for months. There was a map of his constituency, broken down into smaller areas, each with a campaigning target. The section on social media was long and colourful: dozens of messages for microblogs, short videos, blip-ads. Targeted scare-messaging for older voters. Wheedling, anxious lines for middle-income households. Smart short ads with big lies for the undecideds and the ignorant. He smiled and shut his laptop with a hard tap.

He was ready. He looked at the list of forthcoming events. A speech outside one of his family's factories in Ullathorne for the cameras. A launch speech to small businesses and supporters at the Great Fosse. A chat to the Territorial Army at the old drill hall named after his dead father. He considered his win a formality. A ministry awaited – and then the new dominions.

The front door opened and closed. He moved back through to the kitchen. He expected to see Knott, but, manifesting like a shadow, it was Bax.

'Fuck's sake, man,' Watson said, his heart skipping in his chest.

'Reporting in,' Bax said.

'You shouldn't be here.'

Bax barely moved.

'Yet here you are. Get yourself a drink,' Watson said to his man.

Bax nodded and reached for the bottle of vodka by the sink. He poured some into a long glass and scrunched into it some ice from a nozzle in the freezer. It squealed and popped.

Bax's shoes were covered in mud, and there were thick smears on his trousers. He leaned against a marble counter, opened his mouth to say something, but changed his mind. He carried on drinking. He wiped blood away from a vivid unhealed scratch on his cheek.

'Shall I get your robe? You'll catch your death,' Bax said, nodding at Watson's naked torso.

'Not me,' Watson said. He stretched. His shoulders popped. He stretched his fingers. Under his fingernails was a grotty line of scum. He stared at them for a while.

'Is Knott here?' Bax said.

'Briefing the leaflet team,' Watson said.

'So . . .'

Watson waved a hand. 'Don't need to know.'

Bax shrugged and sucked his drink. He looked at his hand, as if there was an answer.

'Remember, Bax: Sorley agreed with all this.'

'Aye?'

'He said, "Mute." I know what he means. He's led me this far. I'm not going to start ignoring him now. Not now. He's not been wrong about owt.'

'He has been . . . vague about stuff.'

'Not to me, that's the important thing,' Watson said.

Bax put his glass down, empty, and blinked heavily.

'You look worried,' Watson said.

'I'm not worried.'

'Sure?'

'Sure.'

'Any word from Alyce?'

Bax shook his head.

Watson looked closely at Bax, to see if he could divine more. His eyes were two small dark marbles. 'What has Raymond been saying?'

'Nothing much.'

'Much?'

'He was saying you're on the cabinet list. But you know that.'

'Ah, Bax, my friend. You know as well as I do: they need a Northern MP in there. They're thinking long-term on localities, on regions. Waiting for Scotland to go its own way. Matter of time. And then you have a northern border, all of a sudden. We'll need a watch on the Rhine. A tower on the Tweed.'

Bax nodded. He looked outside, into the forest. His hands were entwined, fretting.

'I had Chief Whip on at me yesterday,' Watson said, a sheen of sweat still on his bare chest. 'Prodding around my "interests".'

'And you said . . .'

'You know the drill. Kept it vague. Anyway, fuck that old twat – my voting record for this lot is immaculate. On the NHS I'm more hawkish than they'd like right now. You know how I stuck my head above the parapet on abortion. But I kept the pot simmering. Ready to boil. And Raymond has my back. We know that.'

Bax, fidgeting, moved closer. Watson could see mud and dirt in the pores of his face. The slash of blood was still tacky, red. Watson wiped his lips with the back of his manicured hand.

'I'm making progress,' Bax said.

'Good, good,' Watson said, raising a palm. 'I just don't want to hear . . . I just want to reiterate the importance of it, to me.'

'I understand,' Bax said, looking down at his hands.

Watson regarded Bax with admiration. 'Look at that beautiful skull of yours.'

'What?'

'Your lovely skull. It's ideal, isn't it? Your nose, your blue eyes. You must know you can admire it. Your ideal form. How it should be. How it will be. You're a handsome lad. You remind me of someone . . . it's the eyes, the cheekbones. You know, you should have a bit of fun with my friends sometime.' He burst out laughing. He traced his fingers over his own hairless chest. 'You'd be very popular.'

'No, no. Not for me,' Bax said, almost whispering.

'Let's be honest: you're a picture, my lad,' Watson said. 'One day, one day – we'll be masters again. We'll be masters, and that lot – they'll be servants. Just as it was, it will be. Where did you say your old man was from? Bristol?'

'Cirencester.'

'Lovely town, lovely town,' Watson said. 'Full of the right kind of people. Stout villeins and maidens. My late wife was from near there.'

'Was she?'

'You'll know about the incident in Kent,' Watson said. 'Adds to my CV. Everyone these days loves a bit of personal tragedy. An obstacle to overcome. Some kind of emotional redemption storyline. It's all a load of fucking shite. But I'm happy to milk it. They lap it up.' Watson sipped his drink. 'The thing we always have to remember, is that we are winning. The other side lost the will to fight years ago. We're winning, and they don't even fucking realise it.'

'Yes, sir.'

'We're going to fuck them all to death,' Watson said, swilling his drink, staring at the marble counter as if faces could be seen in its swirls and clouds. 'You know how we're going to win this thing? Not with policies. Not with fucking details. Who cares about the fucking details? With a war of anger. That's how we win. All emotion. All reaction.'

Bax nodded, his eyes blank as stone.

'Right. Get one of the glasses,' Watson said. 'Let's do this. See what he's saying.'

'Sir.' Bax reached for a small pink shot glass on a high empty shelf.

Watson lay down on a long black leather sofa. Outside, the

sun was beginning to slowly drop behind the Pennines. Liquid copper light gleamed on bark and rock and twig.

Bax walked over and took off his heavy jacket. He stepped around a pool of thick vomit which sat, stinking, near the sofa.

'Man,' Bax said, shaking his head.

He sat down beside Watson and pulled up his shirt cuffs. The room was now in dusk. Night had fallen.

Bax put the glass on Watson's chest on the tattoo of the Ouija board. He placed it carefully on HELLO. Watson did not flinch. His head lay back on the leather, eyes closed. His arms lay limp and flat, his fingers soft and relaxed on his chest.

'Okay, let's talk,' Watson said.

'Do you ever think someone will find out?' Bax said.

'About what?' Watson was lying back, as if entering sleep.

'About all this,' Bax said.

'How would they? And I trust you, Bax. To make sure no one does.'

Bax and Watson each placed a finger on the upturned glass, which rose and fell with his shallow breathing.

After a time, the glass appeared to move across his hairless flesh. The message came: *hello gary*.

Shona and Terry were driving back to Ullathorne on the tight and winding dale roads. Terry was changing radio channels with one hand, looking for some music she liked. Shona was on her phone, exasperated, listening to Bernie.

'The committee says in this letter that we have two weeks to sort it, Shona, or they're going to consider taking your father's rights away. Hugh opened the letter before I could get to it. He was awfully upset, and he's gone to bed.'

'Is he all right?'

'No, he's not, Shona. As I said, he's very upset.' Bernie's voice quavered a little.

Shona bit her lip. She looked out the window at the uncut verges. She felt a great emptiness.

'What does the letter say *exactly*?'

'I'll go and fetch it,' Bernie said, and there was a clunk as the phone was put down.

'Fuck this! No radio reception,' Terry said.

'What music you got?' Shona said.

Terry scrabbled in the glove compartments: there was a scramble of CDs, in and out of their covers. Light suddenly strobed rainbows on the plastic discs.

A large truck, full of catatonic sheep, was stationary at the crossroad in front of them. Terry pulled up. Mournful heads stuck their snouts through the slats of the filthy truck.

Shona held her phone close to her ear; she could hear Bernie thumping around her flat.

'The Stones?' Terry said, putting a disc into the CD player.

'No chance,' Shona said, scowling.

'Why not?'

'Hate those old fuckers.'

'Jeez,' Terry said. She ejected the CD and looked at other options.

'I can't see what the hold-up is,' Terry said, trying to peer around the truck.

'Your music is shite – that's the fucking hold-up,' Shona said.

'Here: what about The Smiths?'

'I think not.'

Terry smiled and cast Shona a bemused look with glittering eyes. When she smiled, dimples popped in her cheeks.

A sheep turned its trapped brown head and stared at Shona. Its eyes were jet black, and it had black patches around its mouth. It looked satanic.

'Have you any electronic music?' Shona asked.

Terry threw some cases onto the back seat. 'Not really – how about Kate Bush?'

'*Hounds Of Love*?'

'Yeah.'

'Fine.'

Terry put the CD in and picked a track. The truck engine ground, the baffled sheep bleated and birds chattered in the high hedges. Then a beautiful song began, and Shona closed her eyes. It reminded her, instantly, of her mother.

Bernie huffed back to the phone. 'Found it.'

'I thought you'd gone off and died somewhere,' Shona said.

'Shona Sandison!' Bernie said, aghast.

'Go on, then. I'm stuck behind some sheep. What does the letter say?'

Bernie started reading in her singsong voice: '*The council considered that your allotment garden, plot seventeen, is in a poor state and condition, being untidy with an accumulation of items behind and to the side of your shed, and two large buddleias on two sides of the allotment garden which require cutting back substantially and are a nuisance to neighbouring tenants.'*

'Is that true?' Shona said. She did not know what a buddleia was, but assumed it was a weed.

'It's very overgrown,' Bernie said, 'but "a nuisance to neighbouring tenants"? My foot! They're going to take it off Hugh if it's not tidied.'

'Does it actually say that?'

'They say they're going to inspect his patch next week. It's signed by a Mr Colin McCall, Allotment Officer. He says they're going to *engage a contractor to undertake the remaining tasks and claim the full cost of this in damages from you.* I don't think Hugh has the money or wherewithal for that. Damages!'

'And he definitely read this?'

'Yes.'

'What a bunch of fascists,' Shona said. 'Do they know Dad's been sick?'

'I don't think they care. I don't know how to respond. I bet it was that man with his solar panels who reported him. I'm furious. Hugh's furious, too, but he hasn't replied yet. He can't lose his allotment, Shona. It would be a disaster for him. He'll be absolutely scunnered – he loves that place–'

'I know, I know,' Shona said.

'And in his condition–'

'Yes, I know.'

'I mean, it's cruelty, that's what it is–'

'Bernie! I know!' Shona said loudly. 'Look, can you use email?'

'Yes, of course I can, I'm not demented,' Bernie said. 'I email my son all the time.'

Shona suddenly laughed. 'Newsflash! I didn't know you had a son!'

'There's a lot about me you don't know,' Bernie said primly. 'I bet you didn't know I used to be a nun, either.'

'You what?' Shona said, after a moment. 'How did you have a son, then?'

'It's a long story. Oh, I think I hear Hugh rising. I'll take a picture of the letter and send it to you. Can you ring the council? I'd love it if–'

'I'll sort it, Sister Bernadette,' Shona said.

There was a silence.

'You and I need to talk,' Bernie said, and the call ended.

'What was that all about?' Terry said. Rising ahead were the grey, black and brown buildings of Ullathorne, and the ruined castle staring on its bare cliff.

'A nun,' Shona said. 'A nun who had a son.'

'Sounds like the beginning of a song.'

'Or the end of one,' Shona said.

'So, Beverley – wasn't that interesting?' Terry said, as the town moved around them. Cars were parked on cobbles, and shoppers drifted on wide pavements. There was a queue outside the butcher's – men checking notes on paper, a young woman shouting into a mobile phone.

'I wouldn't say that,' Shona said. 'There was something about her . . .'

'That you didn't trust?'

'Yeah. On the one hand, she volunteered a lot. But how much was true, I don't know. There was something she wasn't saying. But then, I was asking about things she probably didn't want to talk about that much. Did you get any pics at all?'

'Aye, on the down-low, when you were talking and I was smoking weed with the big guy. Some clear ones of her. I could crop you out.'

'Great. I need to meet someone now,' Shona said. 'But I'll need some general views of the town – and the mill at the bottom of the Bank. Can you find the time?'

'Could do, could do,' Terry said. 'I'll let you know how I get on.'

186

'Fine. Well, drop me off here,' Shona said. They parked at an angle on the cobbles, and Shona grabbed her things and almost rolled out of the car.

'Thanks, see you later,' she mumbled, and Terry drove off. Shona watched her drive away for a while, her blonde head disappearing, and then walked into the tangle of stone buildings, following the map on her phone.

St Mary's Care Home was in the centre of the old town. A low building with a pitched roof, set back in a neat garden, it looked like it had been built in the 1970s. The glass on the large windows shimmered in orange and brown.

Shona pushed a nagging irritation out of her mind. She had missed a phone call while talking to Bernie – it had been Viv. Her heart had leapt a little. She'd call her later.

Shona refocused on the task in hand. She straightened her clothes and hair and walked up to the main door of St Mary's. She pressed on the button for the intercom, but before she could speak, she was buzzed inside.

From the reception area, Shona could see an adjoining corridor. Pictures of flowers and landscapes hung in matching frames, and a trolley with rows of white cups on it sat outside a nearby door. The floors of the corridors were uncarpeted.

Shona checked her clothes again. Buttoned jacket, black jeans, black shoes, her stick: it would do. She walked over to the desk, where a woman asked if she could help her.

'I hope I have the right place,' Shona said, changing her voice slightly. She sometimes put on what she called her 'posh Scots' accent when she felt it might be useful. In her mind's ear she now sounded like a confident second-year law student at St Andrew's University.

'I think you have my email. My name's Eliza . . . I'm a friend of Dan Merrygill, and I was hoping to speak to his mother. I saw him last week before he . . . before the incident. I'd love to speak to her, even if for a short while.'

'Martha Merrygill's boy?' the woman said quietly.

'That's right, Daniel. I've come down from Scotland. I was at the wedding where he–'

'Yes, of course,' the woman said. She put a hand on the phone and said she needed to speak to someone. 'Eliza what, love?'

'Field. I won't bother her for long, I just need to tell her something that Daniel said.'

'Okay.'

'Something he wanted his mother to know.'

'Okay, pet,' the woman said, as she waited for someone to pick up an internal line.

Shona's stomach was churning. There was a small table in this foyer, with a truculent stack of old magazines lolling on it, waiting to be thrown away. There was flock wallpaper and sturdy chairs.

'No,' the woman said. 'Well, she's here right now. She's come all the way from Scotland.'

Shona took a seat. She placed her bag neatly on her lap. The woman had been speaking for a few minutes now. Shona eyed the door. She could leave and no one would know her, or what she was doing. A clean, swift exit.

'A young woman,' the woman said, louder, looking at Shona. 'Yes, she was at the wedding when . . . yes.'

Shona smiled back, as sweetly as she could manage.

'Okay,' the woman said and stood. She flattened down her blue tunic and walked around the desk. 'If you could come with me?' she said.

'Thank you,' Shona said. Her stick pecked the carpet silently and then tapped as they made their way down a brightly lit corridor. A door was open as they passed – she looked into a large room, with windows looking onto an internal courtyard. Several pensioners sat slumped in massive chairs pointed towards a muted television.

The woman stopped at an office door, rapped it lightly, and they walked in.

A large woman in a trouser suit was sitting behind a desk. Shona was ushered in, and the door closed behind her.

'I'm Fiona Cox, the assistant manager,' the woman said. 'And you want to see Mrs Merrygill?'

'Yes,' Shona said. 'I am – I was – a friend of her son Dan. I came to speak to his mother. To talk about him.'

Ms Cox nodded. 'It was terrible news. It's not often the children of residents die before them. So, you were at the wedding where he died?'

'That's right.'

Ms Cox looked at her steadily.

Shona smelled flowers and cleaning fluid. The room was square and airless. The carpet was clean, the surfaces were clean. 'A terrible thing,' she said quietly.

'Of course,' the woman said. 'What is it you want to tell Mrs Merrygill? You could leave a note, send a card, send flowers.'

'I'd rather not . . . share. It's something Dan wanted her to know. He told me to tell her.'

'And you've come down from Scotland especially?'

'Yes, from Leven.'

'You could have emailed or called.'

'I very much felt the need to be here in person,' Shona said, as sadly as she could. 'Some things are too important. I had to come.'

'Well, as I'm sure Daniel will have told you,' Ms Cox said, lowering her voice, 'his mother is very frail and can get confused. Daniel valued the care and support we give her here. He used to visit every week. I never would have guessed.'

'No.' Shona put a hand to her eye, as if to wipe a nascent tear.

'But who knows these things?' Ms Cox said. 'People can be in trouble, in deep pain and–'

'Not show a thing,' Shona said.

'Not give a glimpse of it to the outside world – to their friends or partners. I think it was that way with Daniel. You'd never know what was going in that head of his. And he was so pale. So pale and quiet. Like his mother.'

'He mentioned how much comfort he got, knowing she was here, being looked after,' Shona lied. 'Still in his hometown.'

Ms Cox smiled. 'Well, I'm not sure he thought much of Ullathorne, but he did visit. Is it true he sold his house in Darlo and moved into a caravan? I think I read that somewhere.'

'I didn't know about a caravan,' Shona said, suddenly nervous. 'He never told me that.'

'I'm sure it was mentioned in the piece about him in the *Echo*. Anyway, Mrs Merrygill will be having an afternoon snack soon and then we'll be playing bridge. So, you're lucky to have arrived when you did.'

'Thank you,' Shona said. 'I won't take long. How is she?'

Ms Cox looked at her hands for a moment. 'I think it's fair to say the news will take a while to sink in. You've come a long way, and perhaps at the right time – before it does sink in.' She stood. 'Do you mind my asking – how did you come by that walking aid? Is it temporary?'

'I had a mountain climbing accident,' Shona said. 'When I was a kid.'

'I'm sorry to hear that.'

'We all have our crosses to bear,' Shona said.

'Just like Daniel,' Ms Cox said. 'You know, he was never the same after his dad disappeared. He was just a bairn then. Martha won't talk about that, of course.'

'Where did his father go?'

'Away travelling. Not sure if they ever got divorced. But it wasn't a happy home. Dan took his mother's name.'

'Oh, really? What was the married name?'

'I can't remember,' Ms Cox said briskly and, not looking

at Shona, bustled out of the room. 'Come this way, ' she said huskily.

They came to a door in a row of doors. Ms Cox stopped and knocked gently before opening the door slowly and looking around its edge.

She turned back to Shona and nodded, and then pointed to a large digital watch on her wrist. 'Ten minutes. No longer.'

Shona nodded.

'Ten minutes,' Ms Cox said to a passing nurse.

With Ms Cox behind her, Shona entered the small room. There was an immediate sense of clutter. There were dark bookcases, a writing desk with flowers in a pot, framed pictures and a large metal-framed bed covered with a patchwork quilt.

Near the bed, in a large armchair with wooden arms, sat a silent, unmoving elderly woman. She was wearing a dark blue tracksuit, with a blanket over her lap. She was looking out of the netted windows to Ullathorne, blurred and indistinct outside.

'Hello, Martha,' Ms Cox bellowed. The woman looked up, revealing a deeply lined face and pale blue eyes. 'This is Eliza, a friend of your Daniel. She's popped by to have a word.'

'Hello,' the woman said, her voice as fragile as crêpe paper. 'Come and sit by me.'

'Ten minutes,' Ms Cox repeated. The door shut with an airless clunk.

Shona saw a low wooden stool by the bookcase. She put her stick to one side, took out her phone and turned on the Dictaphone app. Then she darkened the screen again.

She crouched down on the stool. 'I am so sorry to hear about your son, Martha,' she said.

Martha's hands were crossed on her lap. She had two rings on her ring finger, one with a small diamond. The skin around her eyes was as grey as a dove.

'He's gone now,' she said, speaking more clearly. 'But he said, you know, that he'd always been there.' She moved a hand upward; in it was a crumpled tissue. She wiped away water from her eyes.

'John was too hard on him – far too hard, I always said. "Spare the rod and spoil the boy," he said. But he was too hard on the lad. And me an old mother. I'm sorry, I'm forgetting my manners – can I get you tea and a biscuit?'

'No, thank you,' Shona said.

Martha turned her head and looked at Shona. 'I don't know you.'

'I'm a friend from Dan's work.'

'I don't know you,' Martha said again, and looked to the window and the inaccessible world beyond. 'I knew what he was doing. And now he's gone.'

'What was he doing?'

'When he were a lad, he used to cry a lot. He was a shy boy. Afraid of his own shadow,' she said. 'He used to wet his bed. Piles of sheets in the mornings.'

She turned her head a little but did not move. Dust drifted through the light. Books sat stacked on their shelves like blank gravestones.

'He was quiet,' Martha said. 'Such a bonny baby. Then his father left, and he was never the same. Never the same. He missed his daddy.'

'When did you last see him?'

'He was a sickly child. He had whooping cough, the mumps, suffered terribly with the measles.' Martha blinked slowly.

'When did you see him last?' Shona persisted.

'He used to go into that room of his,' Martha said.

Shona's phone buzzed: a text from Ranald. She ignored it.

'There was always something going on in that room of his,' Martha said. She turned to Shona again and looked past her. 'His room was full of letters.'

'Did he write a lot? Of letters?'

'He would lock himself away,' Martha said, shaking her head.

Shona rubbed her face. Her time was running out, and she needed more. 'Did you know he was sad?'

'He came and saw me on the eve of Epiphany,' Martha said. 'He held my hand and said I would be taken care of. He'd sold his house, he said, was moving into a caravan. He would be happier there, he said. He said he was nearer to the stones, to the rocks.'

'A caravan.'

Martha smiled. 'It is lovely. Have you seen it? He showed me a lovely picture.'

'No.'

'He's growing vegetables. He's saving up, he said. You wouldn't know Ullathorne. Not with that accent. Ullathorne gets very dark. Winter is like a cold hearth. I think people from outwith Ully do not understand it. How cold it is, how hard it gets.'

'He was telling me about something terrible that happened when he was young, about his friend Andrew,' Shona said.

Martha turned her face the other way. 'Poor bairn,' she said softly. 'Poor wee bairn.'

'Terrible business,' Shona said.

'Police came around. I remember the blue lights in the kitchen. John upstairs, writing. Police came – Harmire – to speak to Danny, but of course he knew nowt. How could he? He left with his friends. He was scared. I was scared. But then . . .'

'But then . . . ?'

'It all went away. It all went away, didn't it?' Martha smiled. 'The inspector never came around again.'

Shona sensed a body by the door outside. Someone was going to open it. A shadow fell.

Martha's eyes began to glisten.

'Did Daniel leave Andrew with his friends, that night?' Shona prompted.

'He came home. Left his chips by the front door. I remember: the police saw them. Chips and gravy.'

The door opened, and a nurse appeared. She said, 'Time now, Martha,' and nodded to Shona.

Shona stood up. 'I am so sorry about your son.'

Martha put her hand out, and Shona held it. It was weightless.

'Will you come again?' she said, with a half-smile.

'I live in Scotland, but I'll try,' Shona said, and her stomach turned over. Everything was too awful. She wanted, suddenly, to be at home with her father.

'I'd love a visit,' Martha said.

'Now, now,' the nurse said.

'I'd like another visit.'

'I will,' Shona lied, smiling.

Martha was crying without moving. A tear slowly rolled down her smooth cheek. She gently pulled at Shona's hand and moved closer.

'"I'm talking to myself, Mam," he would say,' she said quickly. 'He said he was talking to himself – in his room. That he could speak to himself. That he was already dead. That's what he said. He told me one night after Jack left me. Off to write his books, and never came back.'

Shona felt a deep shiver run through her. Martha's eyes had become hard. She felt the woman's breath on her face.

'Come on, Martha,' the nurse said, bustling into the room. 'Let's not start all that daft business again.'

Shona withdrew her hand, like taking her fingers from a soft pocket.

'That's no way to talk to me, is it, nurse?' Martha said, annoyed, looking up, turning her head to watch Shona leave. 'That's no way to talk, is it?'

Martha's words could be heard all the way down the corridor, fading softly as Shona walked away.

The hard light rolled over Shona in waves of destruction.

Alison was leaning on her kitchen island, her face in her hands. Margaret Gildersleve had emailed her. Alison could not shake Peg's words from her mind.

Her children were in the dining room, hunched on the sofa, watching images roll and flash on their phones. Planes moved heavily across the blue London sky, slowly knitting a cat's cradle of jet trails.

Nigel was back from his alleged business trip. He said he had something to tell her.

She looked about her unlovely house. It was tall and narrow, and in central London: it would sell for a lot of money. They would sell this place, and she and the children would live somewhere else. Away from the city and its incessant demands. From the noise.

They would move into a place of quiet, where a deep river ran and old trees overhung. Where rock and stone stood, and the hills embraced a valley, and time slowed, and there was time to think, and do, and be. The children would not miss their overpriced, demanding, average school. They would not much miss their empty, hectoring father.

Nigel walked into the kitchen, his flip-flops slapping. He was tanned and tall and was still damp and pink from the shower, his heavy head of hair gleaming.

'So,' he said curtly, as if addressing a meeting.

She stared into the stone spirals on her kitchen countertop.

We've found something in the woods, Peg had written.

'Well,' he said, clapping his hands together. He lowered his head, and his eyes grew wide. His voice became his version of low, and soothing. 'I think it's time we had a little chat.'

'You know at some point you need to move out,' she said.

He blinked heavily. 'Can we talk first? We need to. I think now is the time for the conversation.'

She knew what it was. She felt it in her body. There was dread in her, but there was no sorrow. She had searched for it, but there was none. Alison had felt deep and angry sorrow before, and this was not the same. This was another feeling – closer to an extended irritation. The heat and itch of a slowly emerging spot.

She turned to look at the children in the dining room. Their tawny heads. All she needed was them. Their frail hands held back the darkness.

'Let's go somewhere else,' she said.

'To the pub?' he said.

She looked at her husband's face. It struck her, as it had before, as less the face of a grown man, with all the lines of loss and painful joy that might feasibly mean, than a movable screen built for melodrama. She felt a passing twinge of sorrow. She had learned, over the years, that instead of deep convictions, or real emotions, he had only a thinly felt series of poses.

'No, not the pub. Somewhere out of sight – away from the children,' she said.

She slipped off her high chair and walked past him, checking her phone. Nothing new. No more news. She had texted and received no reply.

In Deepdale, Peg had said. *We've found something.*

She padded past the newly carpeted stairs, the large, framed portraits of the family taken in a white studio, a stand of tennis rackets, lacrosse sticks and golf bags. All the future landfill of their comfortable, unsustainable lives.

She went into the front room. He did not seem to have followed her. There was no television, and the room was rarely used. She had once thought that adult guests could gather there and talk seriously about the world. It never happened. Instead, three large cream settees sulked around an elaborate fireplace, under a chandelier, and encircled a table with heavy books glossily advertising things she did not really care about: architecture, international travel, business, the Himalayas.

A paperback book about self-improvement was on the sofa, something Nigel had been reading since he told her their marriage was over. Alison took the book and threw it across the room. It landed behind a chair.

She looked at the rest of the books – she would burn them all. She sat down and crossed her legs, and Nigel loomed in the doorway.

He mouthed almost silently, 'Are the kids okay?'

'They're fine. Fed and watered.'

'What was that noise?'

'Nothing. A car.'

Nigel was now barefoot. 'How's your mother?'

Alison's mother was fine, a widow living in a bungalow in Cornwall, as far away from Tyrdale as she could manage. She went to church twice weekly and was involved in committees. She refused the policeman's pension and lived frugally.

'Mum's fine. Still a big fan of Jesus. Why?'

He sat down and began to wring his hairy fingers.

Alison knew, or nearly knew, that Nigel had met someone else. Finally, someone else to inflict himself upon.

There had been a period when they met, when he had been long-haired and handsome, and his scattergun red-trousered enthusiasms had seemed the interests of a man in love with life and all it could offer. And after the religious silence of her mother, the lies and corruptions of her father, his world seemed something to marvel at: something vast and multicoloured. But the endless swirling confetti clouds of his interests, she realised, were just that, a two-dimensional whirl of nothingness.

'Alison,' he said.

'Nigel Osbourne,' she said.

To think, she remembered, she had been unsure about marrying him, this erratic, foolish man. Until the board had told her: *Say Yes to No*. And so she had said yes to N.O. – the letters still speaking to her long after the glass had stopped moving.

Gary had always taken its messages so seriously, all those years ago. She wished she had not.

'You look so tired,' Nigel purred.

'Nigel, let's get this over with,' she said. 'For both our sakes.'

He turned his head slightly, as if reluctantly accepting a bad offer, and carried on. 'Ultimately, Alison, I see this as good news. This is, in fact, wonderful news.' He patted his hands on his knees. 'For both of us. But there is no easy way to say this . . .'

Alison suddenly felt violently impatient. She stood up.

'I have met the most wonderful person . . . the most wonderful woman,' Nigel said with a tremulous voice.

She felt herself begin to shake. She looked to the fireplace. There were hard black fire irons there that could easily shatter his skull. Despite his height, he was as weak as a gosling. She was stronger than him. She could break open his face, drag the body to the ornamental pond, sink him in the water and drive away. It would be a long time before he was found.

He was still talking. He had clearly practised this speech, as he was now gaining confidence and his voice was clear.

'. . . we understand each other, ultimately, in a way which really speaks to me at this time in my life. And, to be frank, we have fallen in love! Which is a wonderful thing, isn't it?'

He shook his head, as if in wonder. 'Do you not want to know who she is?' he asked, as if surprised.

'No,' she said, staring into the fireplace. 'I do not give a flying fuck.'

He looked momentarily stunned, then carried on. 'We should now move on to the next phase: make our arrangements, disinvest, decouple, disentangle, recombine. We can talk to

Derek. We can talk about our assets, about the house, the children . . .'

She nodded. Then she began to speak – about the children, about their house – and was pleased with how calm and focused she was. She was making sense. She was not expressing anger or disappointment. Her tone was even and unemotional. She agreed they should speak to their financial adviser, talk about the house, the assets, the money.

As she spoke, she was aware that another, cool, eyeless part of Alison was looking at the table, and the shape and solidity of its surface. Then she realised she had said her piece, and there was nothing more to say.

Nigel's words rolled on. 'Maybe we can consider boarding them, so that . . .'

She thought of Daniel, dead on the pages of the newspapers. That pale face – from memory, from a time now lost and gone. Maybe there was no time, and he was still alive, and she was dead. Her children were both alive and dead. And Nigel, this stranger, was both alive and dead, both from the past and the future, as well as the instant and the present, which was now already gone.

She was sitting on an expensive sofa in her temporarily intact house, which was also a house of ashes, a house sunk in mud by the swollen river, a house of stone, a house rendered by fire, a house of weeds and ivy. She briefly saw a white body in water, a detached arm spiralling in foamy eddies.

'. . . slightly more than half of the house, given my investment in it over the years . . .'

We've found something.

The heavy face of her dead father, the police inspector, the man who had led the search for, and not found, Andrew all those years ago, rose to her eyes.

Her father, who had not interviewed her, and not interviewed Gary Watson, and not interviewed the friends all together, who had closed the case while Andrew's flesh was still on his bones.

Her father. Dead now. Dead in his disgrace.

Don't you worry, our Alison, this will all blow over, he had said.

Now Nigel would blow out of her life, too, and she had to return to the source of her discomfort. The place she had left and rejected but still called to her in dreams and daydreams. Tyrdale, the North, was still with her now, in the South, in London. She had to make it real again, she had to return. She had to leave the life into which she had escaped.

'. . . and seeing their daddy in love – really in love, for the first time – can only be good for them, to be around my own personal joy.'

She needed to go back there, now. Andy had been gone for years. Now Daniel was gone. Who remained? Who else was there? All the faces of the past were rising from the mud of time.

We need to talk, the message had said.

'Okay, thanks. I think I need to go,' she suddenly said. 'I'll be away for a couple of days. Can you cope with the kids?'

He held a hand to her. 'Darling,' he said, his eyes brimming. *It says Jet.*

'Fuck off, Nigel,' she said. She left the room and walked slowly upstairs, to pack.

The past was suddenly here again. It was as if it had been pulled, crashing through the coulisse of intervening years by a sudden yank on its ropes. And now it was fully present, there, in front of her, as real as a stone, or a moor, or a tree.

She ran down the stairs, flung her belongings in her car and drove north through the day and the evening, moving relentlessly forward down a lightless tunnel, as if she was speeding down the course of a vein.

Bax had moved too far and too fast. He was unsure of the path he was following. But the only way was forward.

He parked his car a mile from the house, in a mossy dark lane behind a stone barn and beneath overhanging trees, and then walked quickly in the deepening twilight towards the distant village. His lithe body was wrapped in black. He climbed over walls and crossed fields, agile as a cat, avoiding the roads, to reach the house at the end of the row. As he drew closer, he could see someone moving inside.

He had left Watson at Scar Top. The glass had been moving. Their friend had been speaking. And the MP, as was his way, had drawn comfort. Thinking of it, Bax shook his head.

Bax halted by the back wall of the garden. He waited. A dim light glowed within the house. The garden was darkening, the trees and outbuildings becoming silhouettes, the light moving from the outside to the inside. Natural light withdrew and electric light advanced.

His flexed his fingers within his black gloves. He drew the knife and moved it from palm to palm. It weighed little. Lighter than a gun and, unlike a firearm, untraceable.

He moved again, a shadow within shadows, through the garden. He reached for the back-door handle, and, as he knew it would be, it was open. He turned it slowly and crept into the kitchen, blade in hand.

He stopped and listened. There was noise above – water was filling a bathtub with a slow and constant rumble. Music was playing somewhere. A man's voice was humming along to guitar and pattering drums.

Bax leaned against the fridge for a moment. There were photos attached to the door of a couple in various years and states: on holiday, at a beach, drinks aloft at a birthday party, hugging old relatives. There was one of a young girl, the same woman as in the other photos, but in a school uniform, her face anxious.

He moved slowly to the door. He smelled cannabis, and the folk music was louder now. Upstairs, the running water had stopped.

The music was now a woman, singing sadly over minor chords. He could not pick out the words. There was a golden light flickering around the edges of the door.

Bax gently pushed and then moved around the door, his knife drawn and held high, ready to strike. The music was coming from a large set of speakers. Candles had been lit. Shadows hung tremulous around the room.

He turned quickly, sensing something large and moving. But it was too late.

A large, bearded man with an axe brought the blade down with force, and it caught Bax full in the face. His face collapsed. His skull cracked and splintered into itself, imploding from the weight of iron and muscle. There was a gasp and a crack, a popping noise, and his blood fell in a sheet.

His body crashed to the wooden floor. Bax's face was now a sudden open envelope of bone and blood, cartilage, tongue, gum and teeth. The knife in his hand gently dropped onto the wooden floor.

He had fallen into a small occasional table. Candles had fallen. Some had been snuffed out by his warm blood. Wicks hissed. Others still flashed and flamed on the wooden floor. Their light shook on Bax's remaining eye. Candle wax dripped on his unfeeling skin and hardened to a new coating.

Karl, astonished, dropped the axe with a loud clunk. Blood dripped from his beard. A tooth rolled to a stop in the doorway. Sloppy liquid fell from the ceiling.

'Fuck me,' he exhaled. Something wet and thick was gathering on his forearm.

He stepped heavily over what remained of Bax and yelled up the stairs, 'Bev!'

'What? I'm in the bath. Have you broken something?'

Karl ran a blood-spattered hand through his thick hair. 'I think you need to come down, Bev.'

'So, where are we then?' Ranald said, down a clear line from Shetland.

Shona was sitting on her bed at the B&B, laptop beside her, her stick on the floor. 'Well, where the fuck are we, indeed?' she said. She ran through, in brief, her travels, her discussions and discoveries.

'So let's recap: we have this guy who killed himself, from this school in the North of England, and this tragic class of which he was part,' Ranald said. Somewhere in the background, dogs were barking.

Shona flung herself back on the bed. 'Yeah. Dan, our suicide, was part of this tiny group of sixth-form students. Early nineties.'

'Who else was there?'

'Andrew, Viv's older brother. He went missing ages ago and is still missing. He's dead, of course. But no body found. The police basically gave up. Viv spoke about him at the wedding that never was.'

'Does she know you're there?'

'No chance.'

'Is she likely to find out?'

Shona rubbed a hand over her face.

'I haven't really thought about it properly yet,' she lied.

'Okay, who else – anyone interesting?'

'There's Beverley, part of that same class. I interviewed her. She told me about the Ouija sessions. She lives in a village near Ullathorne. Council worker, folk singer, partner, no kids. Not sure I believe everything she says.'

'Good copy?'

'Yeah, nice material, but all background.'

'Fine, all right,' Ranald murmured.

'Then there was this other lad, Robert Stang – Bobby. Big guy. He joined the army, is also back in town, works at a factory.'

'Have you spoken to him?'

'No, not yet. I've only just got here.'

'Okay . . . maybe you should.'

'I will. Then there's this other lass, Alison, who was the star of the class. She moved to London, made herself a successful career in finance.'

'Goody two-shoes.'

'Exactly. Head girl. Her dad was a police inspector in the town. He was involved in the search for Viv's brother.'

'Oh, aye? What was his name?'

'Harmire.'

'Name rings a bell, but not sure why.'

'And then there's something quite interesting. The local MP was in the class, Gary Watson.'

'What – "sink the boats" Watson?' Ranald said. He seemed to whistle, away from the phone.

'The very same,' Shona said. 'I don't know how close he was with Daniel, but he was there. In that class.'

Ranald seemed to think for a while. 'This makes it all much stronger already: it shouldn't be too hard to get a comment from him. That's a story in itself. We can do a full backgrounder for you. I'll get someone here to do a cuttings file and ping it across while you're there.'

'Thanks – anything about his childhood in particular,' Shona said.

'He's one of the coming stars, isn't he? He's been on the Top Ten MPs to Watch lists for a while. His voting record speaks for itself. It's as you would expect. He's on the telly a lot. Good speaker. Can you meet him? Has he commented on our suicide?'

'No. No one's made the connection, I don't think. Why

would they?' Down the line, Shona could hear him tapping a pen against something.

'Oh, and I have words from the mother,' she said quietly.

'The suicide's mum? Fabulous! Any help?'

'I don't know. She's in a care home, and I'm not sure we can use them.'

'Right, okay,' he said uncertainly.

There was a silence.

'How's Shetland?' she said, after a time.

'It's braw today,' he said. 'What's it like there?'

'I'm a city girl. All this space and silence makes me itchy. It's pretty, but rural, repressed and hard.'

'I had a girlfriend like that once,' Ranald said.

'Funny.'

'How you getting on with Terry?'

'She swears too fucking much,' Shona said.

Ranald laughed. 'Look, I think you need to speak to Watson. And this Daniel, you said his caravan was burned out?'

'Immolated. Oh, we . . . came across some of his stuff.'

'How?'

'I won't incriminate you by association. It was in the shack I mentioned. There's a camera – a disposable one, it needs developed.'

'Well, that could be something?' Ranald said, unconcerned about where or how it had been found. 'You definitely need to get that developed. Look, Shona, I think there's something going on here. I mean, you've almost enough for a colourful feature as it is, what with the death, the tattoos, the house sale, the caravan, the shack with the tramp, the Ouija board sessions, the school link and so on, but . . .'

'I need more on Watson,' she said. Outside, the town's lights were slowly coming on. A string of white lamps lit the main road beyond the trees. The sky was dark but sprayed with an arc of stars, more than she had ever seen in the city.

'Can you stay a couple more days? Get Watson if you can. Surely he's doing some kind of election stuff. Oh, wait . . .'

'What?'

'Here on the old interweb – your man Watson is doing his campaign launch at a hotel in Tyrdale. Near a waterfall? It's on his website. Some place called the Fosse and Rainbow? Near the Great Fosse . . . Is that–'

'Yeah, that's a massive fuck-off waterfall. When is that?'

'Friday – two days.'

'Fine, I'll try to pin Watson down there.'

'It's a plan. Make sure Terry is with you. And until then, dig as much as you can. We need more colour: school friends, relatives – all that palaver.'

'Thanks, Ranald.'

'How's your old man?'

'Och, Dad's on the mend,' Shona said. 'He has a fucking nun looking after him.'

'How do you mean? What – a real nun?'

'Yeah, she used to be a nun. Now she harasses my old man. I'll tell you more another time.'

'Okay, I need to walk the dogs. What you doing next?'

Shona could hear keys being jingled. She had not visited Shetland for many years. She imagined Ranald in a self-built house on a cliff edge, staring out at the immense steely sea beneath a massive sky.

'I think I need to go on a long walk or get a long drink,' she said. 'Or maybe both.'

'Sounds like a plan. Look, thanks for all this, Shona. We're getting somewhere. You're good,' Ranald said.

'Well, I knew that already,' she said, smiling, and hung up.

She looked out onto the darkening world. She needed some air. She felt the dead breath of the care home still in her mouth, settling in her lungs. She realised three things: she missed her father, she needed a walk and she was hungry.

The street outside was dark and wide. Shona walked hesitantly at first, wondering whether to follow the main road into the marketplace or take another route into town and find another path. She remembered seeing a chip shop on the main street, so she headed that way. A car passed slowly.

She walked on, the only noise her feet and the tap of her stick, to the marketplace. A man was smoking outside the Lion. A couple of youths were leaning on the wall outside another pub, the Green Man, chatting and drinking from bottles.

A wave of loneliness suddenly filled her. She thought of Viv and felt a nauseating wave of terrible dread. She stopped walking and leaned against the door of the butcher's. She felt a sob building within her. She held her face with her hand for a while and gripped the stick as hard as she could.

'Fuck off,' she said. 'Fuck off, fuck off, fuck off. Idiot.'

She opened her eyes, wiped her face and looked out, beyond the town. In the city, Shona was often lonely. In the countryside, she felt alone. She felt tiny in this place. Walking in a world on a greater scale than she could fill, or within which she could have a sense of meaning. Beyond these old stone houses was the ancient silent dark. The silence sank into everything – the air, the light, the stone, the surrounding trees. Even the river was silent now, running darkly somewhere out of sight. Edinburgh, her home, was quiet, introverted, interior – but not like this. Glasgow, where she had grown up, was never quiet. Everything was noise there. She missed it. But she was also hungry. And she had only half a story.

And so she wiped her eyes and walked on. The chip shop's glow was exaggerated in the darkening evening – a puddle of rich golden light. She clattered up the steps. There was another customer waiting, short and bulky. He was wearing a long grey winter coat with its collar up, a suit and shiny black shoes. He looked out of place. Behind the glass of the serving area, a small, pink-faced man was shovelling chips like a stoker feeding an engine. He had a small white cap on his head. He was sweating, his arms a blur.

'Two fish,' he suddenly barked.

The suited man nodded and said, 'Aye.'

Shona waited by the door. He turned and looked at her. He had a boxer's face. A nose broken years ago. Small white burn scars around an ear.

'How's Mr Watson?' the chip man said, swaddling the food in brown paper. He flipped the package around in his fingers.

'Raring to go,' the man said. He flicked another glance at Shona. She opened her phone and pretended to look at it.

'He'll walk it,' the chip shop man said. 'He's a good solid Ully lad and speaks plain sense. I knew his old man. Fine man.'

He handed over the food, and the man paid with a fifty-pound note. Shona moved out of his way as he barrelled past her, trailing the smell of expensive cologne.

The chip shop man looked up from behind the blasting heat of his work. 'What you havin'?' he said.

Within a few minutes, Shona was jamming slimy hot fish into her mouth and her pocket was lumbered with a can of cold Coke. Her mouth blanched at the tang of vinegar and salt, the crackle of hot batter. She walked slowly to the park beside the ruined castle. It was on a height, crowned by trees – the edge of the woods.

Her phone suddenly buzzed. She swore, sat on a park bench and put the fish and chips and her stick to one side. She licked her fingers and picked out her phone. Distant lights glittered on a far road in the darkness.

It was Viv. The phone buzzed on. Shona did not want to answer. But she answered.

'So, Shona,' Viv said. Her voice was hard and high.

'Hi, Viv. I–'

'You're selling my fucking story to the papers?'

Shona took the phone from her face for a moment and gulped a dry gulp. Then she returned.

'Out with it,' Viv snapped.

'No, I'm not.'

'Aye, you are. Shona. Jesus fucking Christ.'

'I'm trying to–'

'Write me up. Write my family up. Sell it to the papers, Shona! Jesus.' Viv choked back a cry.

'Viv, I'm not. Will you just listen to me. Listen,' Shona found herself pleading.

'Can't believe it, to be honest. Cannot fucking believe it.'

Shona stood up. Alone in the dark.

'And to think you were going to read my poem!' Viv spat.

Shona closed her eyes tightly. She balled up her strength and purpose.

'Viv, listen – I'm not writing a single word about you. Nothing. I'm trying to find out about Dan. I was commissioned. Someone asked me to. So, I'm looking into–'

'I'm not a fucking idiot, Shona. I'm not as clever as you, but I'm no fool. A pal of mine has seen you in the town. She said you were looking into what happened to Andrew. What happened to our Andrew! And you're going to write it all up again and hook it on Dan's death. Drag it all up again. What's the peg, Shona – what's the fucking peg? My fucking wedding that never was! My wedding. That's the peg. Or, as we both fucking know, without Dan topping himself like a twat, there's no story. Because we both know my poor brother's vanishing act is not news now. Not interesting. But Dan fucking offs himself and suddenly Andrew's there again for you to rake up. I know he's gone. I know it. But there you are – in Ullathorne, my hometown – scraping around for a story. Fuck's sake, Shona. I can't believe it.'

There was a silence for a while. Shona opened her mouth.

'Writing about my family. The worst thing that's happened to me. To my mam and dad. And you're there, asking questions, dragging it up.'

'Viv–'

'And if you dare speak to Mam, I will find you and–'

'Viv, I'm not going to do that. Look–'

'No!' Viv shouted. 'I don't want to hear it. I can't fucking stop you, I know that, but God help me, I've seen what you do and how you do it. There's no stopping you. Even if the bodies start fucking piling up.'

'Viv . . . look . . . Maybe you can help–'

'Shona! Get to fuck, seriously. No. I don't want to speak to you again. Never a-fucking-gain.'

'Viv–'

'You going to write about the money as well?' Viv suddenly shouted.

'What money? No–'

'*What money*? You know fine well what fucking money. You make me sick. Just fuck off.'

The call ended with a sudden, sharp click.

Shona sat down and was quiet and motionless for a while. She took her stick and kicked it. It skittered along the tarmac and then landed softly on wet grass.

Shona dumped the rest of the fish and chips into a bin. The castle ruins glimmered. The moon, yellow as a scab, appeared behind ragged clouds.

Shona stood up and walked slowly, alone, back to the warm emptiness of her B&B, through the silent streets of the town, in a senseless fog as if drunk, as if she was concussed.

B ut she did not get there. A car drew up alongside her as she was crossing the main road.

Terry wound down her window and stuck her head out. 'Howdy, stranger,' she grinned. 'Fancy a drink?'

Shona stood still. Her hands were greasy, and she smelled of vinegar. She realised she was shaking. Or she felt she was shaking.

'You all right?' Terry said. Her car was humming and warm. Lights were gold on the dashboard.

'I'm fine,' Shona said. 'Drink where?'

'I know a place.'

'A pub?'

'A place. I have some booze in the car. It's been a long day – let's have a drink.'

Shona's stick rapped on the car door as she got in. The car was warm and the seat soft beneath her. She felt tiredness soak her body.

She sat quietly as Terry drove into the darkness. They moved down the Bank, past the mill, sombre in the darkness, and out along the river. Listening to the radio burbling, but not really listening, they crossed the Tyr and moved through black fields and trees in parallel to its wide slow course. The town drifted like an illuminated ship in the dark behind them. They eventually pulled up alongside a gate to a field that sloped down to a silhouetted copse and the river.

'Here we are,' Terry said. 'Hop out.'

They left the car, its lights clicking off, plunging the gate and the wall, the field, back into the waiting natural dark. The darting insects that had swarmed temporarily in the car's light blinked back into their hidden minute lives.

Terry climbed over the gate, with a clanking tote bag of tins and other, undefinable, items. Shona stood, stick in hand, satchel over her shoulder in front of the gate. She felt afraid for a moment, here in the rural vastness, and with an obstacle before her. A long way from home.

'Ah, sorry,' Terry said. She fiddled with the gate's fastening for a second, and it swung open.

'I can climb, you know,' Shona said.

'Well . . .' Terry began to say something, then shrugged. She pointed down to the river. 'There's a beach down there.'

'What's wrong with an old boozer?' Shona said, peering down the field, plum-purple in the dim light.

'I am an old boozer,' Terry said, laughing, and, swinging the tote, she started tramping down the field to the river. Halfway down the meadow she reached into her bag and pulled out a camping light. She clicked it on and, like an archaic cleric, led the way, by light, to the water.

Shona looked up. There were no clouds, and the moon was encircled by a dim silver aura. The stars were arrayed in chaos and constellation, and a faint arc of the Milky Way could be seen.

She followed Terry, followed the swinging light. When it suddenly dropped out of sight, Shona picked up her pace, her legs damp from the grass, until she could see it again, stationary on the riverbank. There was a short drop to the beach, but a smooth route had been gouged from earth and sand and grass, and she took it down to the shingle beach.

Terry was already sitting cross-legged, leaning over a circle of blackened stones. 'I think we might borrow this old fire,' she said. From her bag she pulled some kindling and firelighters.

'I hate barbecues,' Shona said.

'Why's that?' Terry smiled, her face suddenly lit by a cigarette lighter. Her cheeks orange, her eyes flashing yellow.

'If I wanted explosive food poisoning, I could just go lick a door handle,' Shona said.

'Fine. But I'm just lighting a fire for us to sit beside. To keep us warm. I'm not going to rustle up your tea. Go and get some dry wood, make yourself useful.'

As she scooped up driftwood, Shona could smell the river, its swirling soil and deep brown water and carried life. Her eyes began to adjust to the light. She saw curved pale twigs, dropped from the trees above. They were jointed and smooth, like parts of a dismantled tiny skeleton. She gathered them one by one, moving hesitantly, as Terry lit the fire with gusts of breath and handfuls of kindling.

The fire began to bloom, and the flames licked light onto the beach, flickering gold and scarlet on their faces. The blackened spindles of twig and stick crackled, the firelighters burned hard, and gusts of sour smoke rose on the windless air.

They opened green cans of pre-mixed gin and tonic and watched the river pass by.

'So, a big day?' Terry said.

'Average,' Shona said, after a long pause. 'Did you get general views of the town, of the mill?'

'Yes, boss.' Terry nodded. 'How's your dad?'

'Fine.'

'Can he save his allotment?'

'I have to. I'm not sure what he'll do if I can't. It's his world. I'll need to get back to Edinburgh and sort it. But instead I'm stuck here, sitting in the middle of the sticks where no fucker lives.'

Terry chuckled and threw a handful of twigs onto the flames.

'What?' Shona said.

'You have a way with words.'

'If I didn't, I'd be fucked. It's all I have.'

'Come on now.'

'No, seriously. You must know journalists.'

'I do indeed.'

Shona drank a gulp of gin. 'You'll know, then. We're refugees from society. Some are desperately trying to be important: trying to get *in*. Showbiz for ugly people, as someone said. Some are trying to escape, to get *out* of normal life. To view it all from a safe distance. Others, they just cannot do anything else. Clever misfits, the disenchanted, smart-arse oddballs and misshapes – like me.'

'Like you,' Terry said, nodding. She tipped back her gin and tonic and opened another one with a hissing clink.

'Wait a minute, you're driving, aren't you?'

'Ach, yes. But we'll be fine.'

'How far is it to walk from here? Ullathorne.'

'Half an hour?'

'I think I'll walk back, then, if it's all the same.'

The flames popped and spat. Terry leaned over and blew into it. They were on an island of fire and light in the watchful dark. The broad river ran silently over rock and stone. She turned to Shona. 'What's your story, then, Shona Sandison?'

'What's *your* story, Theresa Green?' Shona said.

Terry's eyes were very clear. Her hair was cropped back from her ears, swept away from her temple. She looked sleek, like a water creature.

'Nowt to tell,' Terry said, shrugging. 'Grew up in Richmond – the original Richmond, down the road, not the one in London – then Edinburgh art school: it was fun. Did some travelling, did some newspaper work . . .'

'Where?'

'The *Mirror*, *Daily Record* for a bit, and then some right daft bugger convinced me to live with him in Newcastle – so the *Chronicle*, *Northern Echo*, *Teesdale Mercury*, the Tyrdale paper. *Yorkshire Post*. *Guardian* northern edition.'

'Nice. Good work.'

'Has its moments.'

Shona looked out over the river. It was glossy and black now, like plastic. A smooth rock at its centre stood out, and the water turned white as it flowed around it and gently slopped over it, grinning suddenly like a smile and then disappearing into the black again.

'The daft bugger saw through me in the end, though,' Terry said, now poking the warm fire with a stick. 'So, I'm freelance in more ways than one.' She stared hard into the fire. Her eyes became tigerish with flame.

'The North. It's beautiful, it's bleak, it's a bit broken down. But it can be lonely. It can be lovely. I moved around. Lived in Durham. Spent quite a lot of time in and around Hawes.'

Shona burst out with laughter. 'I beg your pardon?'

'It's a wee town in Yorkshire!' Terry said. '*Hawes*, not whores.'

'Maybe I should visit Hawes,' Shona said.

'You should. You'd love it. There's a cheese factory. Anyway, what about you?'

'Nothing much to tell,' Shona replied, pulling her legs up to her body. She drained her can and opened another. She looked up. The trees, whispering, listened. Nothing moved apart from the high branches, the water and the two huddled humans by the flames.

Shona breathed out. 'Glasgow born, bred, schooled. Southsider. History at Glasgow. Mum died. Journalism at Strathclyde and Caledonian. Got a job at the *Mercury* – it went bust. Got injured. Had a time-out. Moved with my dad to Edinburgh – got a job at the *Post*. Made redundant by their bastard of an editor. Won the bloody Reporter of the Year nonsense. Freelance. Signed up with Ranald and his mob. Live with Dad, still. Getting old.'

'Tell me about the injury, then,' Terry said. 'I think I heard about it. You were doing a story about some weird shit, weren't you?'

Shona sighed and winced. The fire was red at its centre, the twigs entwined in their slow destruction, and an arch had been formed within, a gateway to the heart of the fire, a holloway to the furnace. The heat bloomed on both their faces.

'Yeah. I was on a job,' Shona said wearily.

'And?'

'It was complicated. There was this . . . I'd been tipped off that there was this man in Glasgow with all the signs of the stigmata. The wounds in the hands, the feet, his side.'

'The wounds of Christ?'

'No, of Tintin. Yes, of Christ.' Shona drank more gin and tonic, crushed the can and dropped it on the shingle.

Terry handed her another, its green and silver glinting in the firelight. 'Go on.'

'He was an old priest, before he had become this mystic, this prophet. And anyway, to cut a long story short, I found him. He was hard to find.'

'Where? Was he being hidden?'

'Only by himself. Up a high-rise. A condemned high-rise that was about to be blown up.'

'Oh, wow.'

'Wow, indeed. Most of the high-rises are coming down. So, it was a weird situation.'

'I bet.'

'It's hard to imagine a high-rise just now. Just looking around here . . . in this darkness. The countryside. The trees, the open land, the river. The idea of a high-rise, the idea of boxes of concrete stacked on top of each other for people to be contained in, to live in . . . it seems absurd, doesn't it? When you're here. It seems fucking horrific. All the space here. All that crushed humanity there.

'Anyway. I found him, just hours before the demolition guys were ready to press the button. Pull the trigger. Whatever. And when I found him . . .'

'What was he like?'

'He was wrapped in a blanket. Skinny as a rail. Covered in dried blood. Starving, stinking. He had written this big mad book. A third Testament. There was no glass in the windows of his flat. So, birds had flown in. There were birds everywhere. He was sleeping on this old clapped-out sofa, in his own blood. I interviewed him, got it on tape for the paper, then I called an ambulance to get him out of this bloody ticking time bomb. There were literally charges all set up in the tower. This tower in the north of the city, looking down over Glasgow. But then he attacked me. He just flipped.'

'Bloody hell!'

'Yeah, he had gone mad, attacked me. I was there on my own. No snapper. So, he went for me. And got me.'

Shona threw her empty can as far as she could. It clinked into the darkness.

'I'm sorry,' Terry said.

'Aye. So, he stabbed me with something – with a long nail. It went into my side. Second stab missed my spine by yay much. Third one into my hip, did some sore damage. I passed out. I was a goner.'

'Fuck me, what a bastard,' Terry said.

'I woke up bleeding outside a burning house in the Southside. Don't know how I got there, don't know if I ever will. The man was inside the burning house. His body was found there. I was taken to the hospital. But I got the story. I filed it all by phone to the news desk from A&E. That was that.'

'Jesus,' Terry said. 'I think I remember some of that now.'

'Well, it was some story.' Shona nodded.

Terry became quiet, contained, and slowly fed the fire with twigs and grass.

'I came out of the hospital with a limp and a stick,' Shona said, almost to herself. 'And a massive fucking desire to leave Glasgow. My dad fell ill, too. Maybe the shock of it all. We needed a change. I was offered a job at a paper in Edinburgh, so we both moved there. That was that.'

'The attack, though . . .'

'I tried to carry on as if it hadn't happened. I tried to forget it. But I've been led to believe that's not healthy.'

'I couldn't move home like that. I like to know my home, know the place where I live. I'm a bit of a homebody. I like my wee place in Newsham. I like falling asleep to the silence. Don't mind the trips to Newcastle and Carlisle and whatever for the papers, but then I need to be back in my cave, my home. Newsham is tiny. It probably hasn't changed for a thousand years. It has a blacksmith, for God's sake.'

'Is that why you like getting hammered?' Shona said.

'Nice.' Terry rolled her eyes.

'Look, Edinburgh's fine. It's quiet, it's orderly, and that's fine. I like the beach at Portobello. My dad has his bloody allotment. Shame my paper made me redundant, fucking twats, though I probably deserved it.'

She threw a pebble into the fire.

Terry looked at Shona sideways, her eyes pale fire in the light of the flames. 'You have anyone else, apart from your dad?'

'In what way? I have a cat.'

Terry sighed. She took some dry bark scraps and threw them into the fire. They flared and crinkled at the edges, and tiny flares of steam rose from their scabby backs.

Shona spoke quietly. 'My friends are mainly hacks. I know how their minds work. This place, though, Ullathorne? I can't get under the skin of it. I've got half a story, and . . . I suspect that's it.'

'You didn't answer my question,' Terry said. She had her phone out and was staring through its camera into the fire. 'Caverns of light, cathedrals of flame,' she said, taking images with quick dabs of her thumb.

'Surely the contrast with the night . . . You'll not get a decent picture.'

'Leave it to the professional.'

Shona felt drunk. The black trees shook, the river tipped and settled. She rolled up her coat and lay back on the shingle. Tiny touches of cold stone on her neck. She opened her mouth to speak, and then didn't. Then she felt an urge to speak, to answer. She spoke quietly and quickly.

'To answer your question, no: no relationships. No relay-shun-shups. God,' she began to suddenly shout, as if released, 'I hate that fucking word anyway.'

Terry reached into her bag, pulled out another can and opened it with a crack. 'Look at that moon,' she said, looking up. 'Looks like genuine cheese. So yellow tonight. You can see every crater.'

'You're genuine cheese,' Shona said. 'You're also a nosey parker.'

Terry grinned. Shona felt an urge to leave. But she remained lying back on the stones.

'No, no. I just like all the gen. I like to know who I'm working with,' Terry said. 'But I think I knew the answer anyway.'

'I think I need to be getting back,' Shona said. She sat up straight.

Terry held up her hands. 'Sorry. I'm sorry. I'm a little drunk and I've enjoyed working on this story today. We can talk about what else we need in the morning. I've been through some of the pictures, but we can review more tomorrow.'

'Ach, it's all right,' Shona said. She was feeling off-kilter, and she would probably not see Terry again after the weekend. She wondered if she minded. She began to speak again, with that feeling of release, of a lightening.

'There was someone, once. But it didn't work out. Five years of it. Bad timing. On their part, on my part. It was a bit sad and agonised by the end. I still haven't made amends, really. Anyway, they're married now, got a kid. What-the-fuck-ever. There's an email I still have, apologising. Saying sorry. I should have sent it. But I never did. The days slide by. Suddenly you're older and tired. Everyone's older. Everyone's tired.'

She was looking into the fire. The golden edges, the heart of throbbing red. Her eyes blurred. The heat warmed her face.

She stood up, the world swaying a little. 'Enough of this chat,' she announced. 'Now I must go. Thanks for the booze.'

She bent down and picked up her stick.

'You can't bloody walk back,' Terry said, her face half in darkness, half golden.

'Well, I'm not being driven by a pissed snapper, that's for certain.'

'You don't know the way. You're in the middle of nowhere.'

'I'll follow the road, genius,' Shona said. 'Or maybe just follow the river. Just like in the old days.'

'In the old days, a single girl wandering alone in the dark wouldn't have got far,' Terry said, standing up.

But Shona had already stepped away from the circle of light and warmth. She turned, waving, and made her way to the riverbank. She needed to move, away from here, away from this conversation, from the darkness. She had a sudden yearning for a warm bed, a ceiling and walls.

She was already across the field as the night closed in around her and Terry called after her.

She walked past the cold parked car and turned left on the country road, heading back to Ullathorne.

Shona walked as quickly as she could as the hedges grew high on either side and the road rose and fell. She expected Terry to follow in her car, but she did not. There was silence, apart from the fall of her feet and her stick. The moon glowed in the vast sky. The trees were still and black, cracks in the starfield.

She stopped. Tiny reflections of the moon shimmered in minuscule puddles on the tarmac. They looked like stars. Up ahead, there was a dim glow above a rise in the road.

At its height, she saw a figure standing. A large man, alone.

She could not sense him looking towards her, or anywhere. He stood, for a moment, black against the faint glow, and then descended the hill, out of sight.

She walked up the rise, and, glowing in orange and white, the lights of Ullathorne glittered ahead. A clutch of electric eyes gathered in the darkness.

There was no man on the road.

She passed a sign, which said DEEPDALE, pointing to a lane into the trees. Then she heard an engine, as loud as a shout, and stepped woozily onto a narrow kerb as a motorcycle buzzed past, its beam sharply illuminating the path.

Shona found herself at the river and then on a heavy stone bridge. Skeins of light flickered on the river's flow. In the shadows of the banks, it was deepest night. Under the bridge it flowed slowly and intently, where the river was deepest, following its surest path to the sea.

Shona was cold now, and the alcohol in her seemed to have settled somewhere. She did not feel drunk. She looked down into the river.

What had happened in this town? All those years ago.

She thought it through. Bored of the silence and the emptiness, the limits of the town and the limits of its life, a small group of teenage friends had toyed with Ouija boards. And one of them went missing. Who had been there, and what had happened to them? Alison ran off to London. Bobby trudged off to war. Beverley left and came back, but in the company of Karl, the giant. Gary Watson: now a politician, the MP for this town and this dale. And Dan seemed to have lived a bloodless life until he emptied what was left of himself onto the flagstones of a hotel in Scotland.

What had the Ouija board said to them? Was it the phrases on that note in the suit?

Shona shook her head. Words on a paper, words conjured by hands on a board. She just did not feel the connection.

What had been moving the glass? They had been, of course. The teenagers in the common room, the bored sixth formers behind the curtain of the assembly hall. Their fingers on the glass, pushing and pulling. Nothing more.

She thought of her own youth, of studying physics, biology, chemistry – had she ever really felt that this world, or this existence, contained more? She did not, could not. She looked into the river again and passed a hand across her face. Why did she think in this way? Maybe it was her father. Hugh Sandison, the warm old socialist, had instilled in her a respect for the material of life, for hard surfaces, for science – for classifications and distinctions, for facts and theories, for observable truth and measurable volumes – and an awareness of class and the distributions of power and privilege. And their absence. Maybe there were enough demons and angels in those calculations without the need for spirits from another world.

Staring into the dark rushing river, she thought: did she even believe in the soul? A conscious flame set in some way in the midst of all this soft and breakable flesh? Did she believe in her own? Her mind moved away from it. She was not ready to answer, even to herself.

Instead, her mind moved to her mother. Dead now for more than twenty years. Had she ever contacted her daughter from the beyond? Come to her in dreams? No. Nothing. Not even as Shona lay, her side rent, incapable, dropped past her senses, in the Southern General. There had been no visitations. There had been no comforting meetings in the passing softness of a shifting dreamworld. No long tunnel of light, with loved ones waiting at its end. And if her own mother could not or would not contact her from beyond the wall of death . . . who else would feel the need to? No. After death, there was nothing, the same as the nothing before birth: just the obliteration of time.

The river ran beneath her, roiled under the bridge, and then passed on its way. She walked on, along the main road, and up the Bank. No cars passing, no one on the street. She stopped outside the church. It was lit by floodlights set in the grassy graveyard spread about it. Its clock tower, detailed in gold, told her it was nearly three in the morning.

Shona tapped her pocket to check she still had the room key. She didn't. She looked in her other coat pocket – no. She swung her bag from her shoulder and, under a streetlamp, checked it. No key. She must have left it at Bev's, at the care home or, more likely, on the beach. Terry might have it, but Shona did not want to speak to her right now. She'd probably driven into a ditch by now.

As she approached the Gildersleve B&B, she could see a light in the breakfast room and figures moving within. A large black car was parked on the gravel drive. She stood at the shoulder of the car and peered into the room.

A tall woman with neat, cropped hair was talking to Peg. She was in gym clothes: a grey hoodie, matching leggings, expensive trainers. She had a car key in her hand and was gesticulating. Peg, wrapped in a dressing gown, was standing, her face drawn, arms tightly folded.

Shona could not hear what they were saying. A door opened, and Ashley wandered into the room, her eyes fuggy – just up from sleep in a large purple T-shirt. She raised an arm and said something snappy.

On the breakfast table, half in and half out of a bin bag, was the stained Newcastle United shirt, turned on its face. The word JET was visible on its back.

The tall woman was pointing to it. Her face changed, her eyes crumpled, and her shoulders began to shake. She bent over, her face in her hands. Peg moved to her swiftly and put an arm around her. Ashley retreated to the doorway.

Shona moved to the front door, pressed the bell and waited to be let in.

24

They had discussed it most of the night, but by three in the morning they had decided to bury the body in the garden.

Bev was determined. She seemed to know what she was doing. Karl was surprised by her businesslike manner. Her lack of fear. It was like she had done it before.

So, they would not be calling the police. They would never do that. Karl would be charged with manslaughter, at least. She could not bear to part with him, she said. She had explained, at length, that she did not think he would get through the process of interrogation, of arrest, of confinement, of the legalities, even if eventually he was freed. She could not bear to see that big, bearded head shake with weeping and fear.

They could not transport the body somewhere remote and unfindable – it would inevitably leave a sea of inexpungable DNA in their house, in their car, on their bodies and on their clothes.

The man had little on him to identify who he was or where he came from. Holding a tea towel to her mouth, and after having covered his smashed head with a bin bag, Bev had searched his pockets. There was nothing apart from a slim black mobile phone, which she decided to destroy with the meat tenderiser. She knew the phone was trackable. But here, in the dale, perhaps not precisely. She slipped it into the pocket of her flowery nightgown. Bev knew there had to be a car nearby, and with Karl still crying and beside himself, she would have to go and find it.

The man was all in black: black jeans flecked with mud, black socks, black boots – still glinting wet from walking across fields. A black zip-up, a black waterproof jacket. A kind of neck roll, tight and light, that could be pulled up over the face like a mask. Now, there was no face to cover.

The body had to be hidden. A body that would rot, she knew, could not be hidden in the house. But they had a large garden. Nothing overlooked it, apart from the empty moor. There were two sheds, a greenhouse, a compost heap, rows of vegetable patches – some fallow, some prepared for the spring.

The sun would be rising in a few hours. There was no time. They would have to dig a hole and tip him in.

Karl was now in the kitchen, staring out of the window. Bev held him again. He had showered, but he still smelled of sweat and tears. She asked him to dig a hole in the garden, in the scrap of ground next to the path that snaked between the sheds. They could put the body in and then cover it up again with earth and the detritus of the garden: the old mower, the bags of mulch, the roller. Karl could dig a hole in a couple of hours. And it would focus his mind.

'All right, love,' he said eventually, wiping his eyes with the back of his hand. 'All right.'

'I'll get us a smoke,' she said. She found one, pre-rolled, in the drawer under the microwave. She lit it with a match, and the tip crinkled and curled, and sweet smoke coiled to the ceiling. They smoked it in silence, passing it back and forth, looking out to the dark garden and the eyeless hills beyond.

'*In the deep dale, there are many wild creatures*,' she said.

Karl nodded. He knew the old Saxon poem.

'Who the fuck was he?' Karl said eventually.

'We'll never know. A burglar?' she said.

'He was an assassin,' he said. 'What the absolute fuck.'

'Assassin no more.'

'Come to kill us.'

'Maybe he came to the wrong place. You got him first. We'll never know. The most important thing is to hide it all away. Cover it over. And forget.'

Karl put the kettle on, and as the water began to bubble, he pulled on his waterproof trousers, his wellies, his waterproof jacket, gloves and a woolly hat.

'Just leave the kitchen light on,' he said. 'That's all I need. To dig a massive fuck-off hole.'

'A massive fuck-off hole is what we need, love. Thank the Lord we got rid of the carpet in the front room,' Bev said.

'We'll get bin bags under his head – let's worry about that after.' He kissed Bev gently on the head and headed to the garden. He looked to their only neighbour: Mrs Flintergill was in her eighties and slept late most days. That's why, according to Bev's reckoning, which he did not disagree with, he was safe digging a massive hole in his garden in the early hours of the morning.

He stepped out into the night, the light from the kitchen watery on the earth and plants, the small apple tree, the sheds.

Karl set to work, his body relieved to be moving again. As he moved the detritus from between the two sheds, his shoulder twinged. He had hit the man with all his force. The sharp judder of the blade meeting the skull had been harsh and sudden. He felt his shoulder for a while, breathing hard, and then began to dig with his best shovel. The earth gave way easily, as if it was eager to eat the body.

Inside, Bev looked down at the man again. The blood had pooled hours ago and was now congealing. She noticed the knife, as if for the first time. It had flown across the room and now lay on top of a small pile of LPs, its blade across the faces of King Crimson.

She went to the kitchen and pulled on a pink rubber glove, returned and picked up the weapon. It was surprisingly light.

She realised she did not know what to do with it. She looked down at the calm, intent faces of King Crimson. She looked outside, into the starless night. Karl was out there, digging the grave.

She moved to the corner of the room, where a large concrete Buddha sat, his face fat and happy. It was a hollow statue. She put the knife down on a shelf and tilted the Buddha a little, moving it from its place. Little crumbs of concrete fell onto the hardwood floor. After a moment or two of wriggling and lifting and adjusting, she slipped the knife inside the statue. A weapon of murder hidden inside the avatar of peace and enlightenment, she thought, and smiled.

She sat on the sofa and pulled the man's phone from the pocket of her nightgown. There was only one bar of service in this part of the dale. Plenty of shadows and blind spots.

She did not know the access code to the phone. It did not matter. As soon as she tipped it, the screen flared up. The background pattern was rows and rows of helmeted heads at a military rally in the 1930s. She decided to turn it off and keep it, just in case. Then Bev stood up, and with Karl digging furiously in the garden, she went to find some black bin bags.

25

S hona was woken by her phone buzzing. It took a moment for her mind to surface. Light was low in her bedroom. She had fallen asleep in her clothes, her muddy trainers by the door. The phone was on the side table, beside her laptop, which was open. She could not remember writing late at night, but maybe she had been.

The phone buzzed again, and she reached for it. 'Yep?'

'Wakey, wakey!' Ranald said cheerily. 'A warm welcome from Fladdabister. I have some news for you. How's my ace reporter?'

She made an incoherent noise.

'Did I wake you up?'

'No, no, I'm just back from my morning run.'

'Do you run?'

'Of course I don't fucking run, you dick,' she said, happy to be swearing so early in the morning.

'Ah, right. Sorry, yes. Anyway, I looked a bit more into the disappearance of Andrew Banks. There was some national press – not much, mind. National Library had some paper cuts.'

'How did you get them when you're in Ultima Thule?'

'Shetland mafia, Shona. Its tentacles range far and wide. Even as far as Edinburgh. Anyway, PDFs were emailed to me last night. The main article is from the *Mirror*. It has quotes from a lead officer of the Ullathorne Police, Harmire. It says here his daughter attended the same school. Is that your Alison?'

'Harmire?'

'Yes,' he said, then spelled it out.

'The very same,' she said, yawning.

'Anyway, what else is cracking? Have you spoken to the local?'

'The local what? There's a lot of local around here.'

'The local paper – what's the name again?'

'*Tyrdale Times*. I went to their archive. I didn't speak to the reporters – wasn't sure I wanted them to know I was in town, to be honest.'

'Might be worth it, though. Maybe speak to the editor, mention Merrygill's death? They're bound to know about it. If nothing else, we can quote them in the piece, give an extra lick of local colour.'

'You want me to lick people now?' she said.

Ranald laughed. He seemed to be in an uncommonly good mood.

'Fine, I'll speak to the paper,' she said, propping herself up in the bed. 'An old pal of mine worked on it, long ago, strangely enough.'

'Yeah? Well, drop her into the conversation.'

'He. John Fallon. He was my boss at the *Glasgow Mercury* before it went bust. He taught me a lot.'

'Oh, aye, the name rings a bell – where's he now?'

'In the ground. Died a while back.'

'Ach, joined the majority. Well, see if dropping his name will help grease the wheels a bit.'

Ranald ended the call.

Shona undressed and showered. She remembered she quite liked staying in hotels, bed and breakfasts: they came with bathrooms that she didn't have to clean herself. Fresh towels. New shampoo. Sometimes even bathrobes. She pulled the white robe on and looked into the mirror in the shower room. She wiped her hand across it.

When she had been young, not long after her mother died, she had taken to staring into mirrors. Until her eyes blurred and her face disappeared, the background and foreground becoming one. Her face would merge with shadow and blur and smeared vision. The reflection became a hole, an aperture into nothingness. Then her eyes would hurt, and she'd have to squeeze them shut and shake her head. And then she would check in the mirror that she was still there, and she would understand that nothing in reality had changed. Her eyes looked back at themselves, reversed. Nothing else. Her mother never walked into the frame of the mirror.

Shona's phone buzzed. 'Oh, fuck off,' she said, leaving the shower room to pick up the call.

'Is Dad okay?' she said immediately.

'Hello, love, yes, he is,' Bernie said. 'But he isn't.'

'Which?'

'Well, my love, we had another letter from the allotment people today.'

'Right?'

'It says they're going to terminate his tenancy and charge him for a contractor to clear up the mess. It's a horrible letter.'

Shona swore under her breath. 'Okay. Well, there's not much I can do from here. I'm busy. I'll be back at the weekend.'

'But we don't have much time to sort it out, Shona. I went down there last night, and it really is a state. I mean, those wooden pallets holding the compost, they've all collapsed, and the bushes are out of control, and I'm convinced there are rats in the shed. It's such a mess. And you know he has his enemies on that allotment. There's been nothing done for months, and with you away–'

'He's been in hospital after a heart attack! Of course it's a mess. Maybe I can call them. Is there a number?'

'It wasn't a heart attack, it was angina. There's a difference.'

'What-the-fuck-ever,' Shona muttered.

'No number,' Bernie carried on. 'It's an official letter. I don't think you realise, Shona. If Hugh loses his allotment' – and her voice suddenly became a hard whisper – 'it will be awful for him. He lives for the place. And you, of course. He won't have a reason to leave the house.'

'I know. Well, he can leave the house to see you.'

'That's nice of you to say. But he really needs that patch of earth.'

There was a silence. Bernie wanted Shona to do something.

'Look, I'll see if I can find a gardener or someone who can get to work on tidying it up before the allotment Gestapo arrive next week.'

'Could you come back now?'

'No, I'm working. I have a job to do.'

'But your father—'

'I understand. I'll see what I can do. I'll be back in a day or two. Okay?'

'There's no time, Shona,' Bernie said.

'I know that.'

'Well, all right.' Bernie sighed. 'I might see if any of the other allotment people can help, but I doubt it. I mean, we're all pretty old and decrepit, and your father with his heart and me with my hips, and no one really has the energy any more even for our own patches, although there's a young family over by the alders who have—'

'Okay, Bernie,' Shona cut in. 'I get it. How is Dad?'

'He's just up, watching the cricket.'

'Cricket? Jesus, he must still be sick,' Shona said.

There was some mumbling in the background, the sound of Shona's father saying something. Shona asked what he'd said.

'He said it's still an English preoccupation and he wants to understand it more,' Bernie said.

'Look, I will sort something, but I have to go. Bye!' Shona was beyond an acceptable limit of irritation.

She dressed swiftly and went down to the breakfast room.

Through the doors that opened onto a small garden overlooking an open field, Shona could see the tall woman from last night. She was deep into a heated phone conversation – her head nodding, her eyes screwed up.

Ashley appeared and asked Shona what she wanted for breakfast. She noticed Shona looking at the tall woman and lowered her voice. 'One of Mam's old friends. Turned up last night out of the blue. Lucky we had a room free.'

'Oh, aye?' She moved closer to Ashley to appear appropriately conspiratorial. She could smell the girl's shampoo and perfume.

'Yeah,' Ashley said, her eyebrows rising, 'there was a right carry-on.'

'About what?'

'That old shirt I found in the woods – well, that Jess found. I brought it back. I wish I hadn't. Mam's been fretting over it, and Alison there went plain mental when she saw it. They were hard at it last night, so I went to bed. Bloody hell.'

Shona asked for a couple of bacon rolls and a coffee, sat down and looked out the open doors to Alison, still mid-conversation. She heard the name 'Nigel' and something about children, about money. Alison was a handsome woman, with sleek hair. Her clothes were simple and expensive.

While waiting for her breakfast, Shona looked at her phone. Ranald's email had arrived. It was a massive file, with ten attachments. She opened one, and slowly the PDF unfurled.

It was a picture of a cutting from the *Mirror* from 1992. There was splodgy typeface and a black-and-white photograph. It was page thirty-four. An even page, at the back of the book. The headline read: MYSTERY AS BOY, 18, VANISHES.

The article outlined the story, in simple, effective and direct tabloid writing, of Andrew Banks. How he had been out with friends, drinking in the 'small northern market town', and then gone missing. Police had searched parked cars and gardens and dragged the river where they could. Posters had been put up. Tracker dogs in the woods. A helicopter from Cumbria had swept the moorland. Nothing found. A short quote from the family solicitor. No mention of Viv, or her parents.

A policeman, Harmire, was quoted. He said: 'We appeal to Andy to come home. His family are beside themselves. He may have gone to visit friends and stayed over – if so, please get in touch. No one will think less of you if you turn up now.'

As she read on, Ashley arrived with her breakfast. There was a picture of Harmire in uniform, fuzzy and indistinct. A long face, intense eyes. He was smiling. The caption said: *Cops: No sign of teen.*

Shona expanded the photo with her fingers and looked over at Alison, who was now facing the doors of the breakfast room. The same face, the same penetrating eyes.

As Shona ate, distracted, she was suddenly struck with what she once described to Stricken, who recognised it well, as 'news panic'. It was the desperation to get the crucial interview for a story – the overwhelming, consuming need for it. Her skin began to tingle around her eyes. There was tension in her shoulders. She needed to speak to Alison. Alison was outside, and as far as Shona could see, the only way into the building from the garden was through the French windows of the breakfast room. So, she waited.

A small brown dog with a tight curly coat and a face of joy trotted into the room. Its paws clipped on the stone floor. Ashley followed behind, wearing an anorak. She had a dog lead wrapped around her weaker hand.

'This your last day here, then?' Ashley said.

'Think so. One more night,' Shona said, 'maybe two.'

'You been busy?' Ashley asked, pushing the dog – who had suddenly stood up on two legs – down.

'Busy enough,' Shona said.

'You'll be glad to be out of here and back to the city.'

'Maybe.'

Ashley looked at Shona and blinked slowly, as a cat might

do. 'Well, I'm off to walk Jess here. Hopefully she doesn't find any more relics this time.'

Jess was beside herself now, running around in a circle, hopping up and down.

'Will your mum take the shirt to the police?' Shona asked.

'I don't think so,' Ashley said, suddenly distracted. 'Ta-ra, then.' And, along with the prancing, bouncing dog, she left. The front door slammed.

Shona looked to the garden again, but Alison was gone.

'Fuck's sake,' Shona said, rising from her seat, grabbing her things and moving to the open doors. She saw that in the far corner of the backyard a small gate led to the fields. A track wound its way across a field and down to the tree line and the river.

Shona followed Alison. The air was sharp. The wet grass tickled the skin between her socks and her jeans. Her stick sank softly into the earth.

The path, although not paved, gravelled or mown, beat a clear way across the field down to the river. As the field dipped steeper, Shona saw a drystone wall with a gate set in it. Beyond, there was another field – overgrown and abandoned. It was full of tall thistles, and somnambulant sheep, shaggy and dyed, were rooting in the grass.

Alison was staring into the river. A dog-walking couple moved past her in matching red waterproofs. The man may have nodded to her, but she was unmoved.

Shona approached her, squelching on the lumpy ground, her shoes wet. The only sound was the river's roar.

Alison did not turn as Shona approached. Shona had long learned to, if not ignore, then just roughly ride over nerves when speaking to strangers. She found volume helped.

'Hi!' she said, on reaching Alison.

Alison looked round. She had been crying. Her eyes were watery and red, and the edges of her nostrils were inflamed.

'Hi,' she said, then turned back to the river.

White bubbles floated steadily on its brown surface. A large branch was rotating steadily on its way downstream. In the eaves of the far side, several ducks bobbed.

'So, you're the news reporter,' Alison said.

'I'm the news reporter,' Shona said. 'Guilty as charged.'

'Peg told me you were in town.'

'I was at the wedding.'

'Where Dan died.'

'Yes. I found his body,' she half-lied.

Alison's face was unreadable. 'What do you want from me?' she said. Her voice still had the flatness of the North in it, but it had been stretched and remoulded by decades of life in London.

'A chat.'

'I'm not one for chatting,' Alison said. She turned away and glanced at her watch.

'What are you waiting for?' Shona said.

Alison shook her head. 'Can you leave me alone, please?'

'I'd like to speak to you about Dan,' Shona said.

'I don't want to talk about poor Daniel.'

'I'm trying to find out why he did what he did.'

Alison looked at Shona. 'Good luck with that.' Her phone bleeped, and she took it from her pocket and began to speak into it. 'Yes, Derek?' she said and moved away, following the path downstream.

Shona thrust her hands in her pockets and watched Alison. She pulled out her phone to check where she was. For a moment, the marker pulsed and flared, the GPS not knowing her location or how the signal could be tracked in the large empty land. But it soon found its coordinates, and beside a stretch of water – River Tyr – she found herself represented by a small blue dot on a yellow path. Closer than they felt, the town's buildings spread out behind her, a featureless grey diagram.

Alison was walking down a path marked on the map. Shona zoomed in on it with her fingers. The path went past the town's sewage works and over more fields, until it came to a bridge which carried two-lane traffic over the river. Over the bridge, about a mile from where she stood, was a ruin. Angleton Abbey, the map said.

Alison had now disappeared into the tree line. Shona wondered if she was heading for the abbey. She began to follow her, and the river, downstream. The thistles here seemed abnormally high, their thorns as long as steel needles. The riverbank was high above the water and ragged: here and there, it had collapsed into the brown river.

She picked up her pace. The river had become shallower – shoals of stones were showing above its waters. She glimpsed Alison ahead of her, walking steadily, talking into her phone, following the path, which darkened as the trees thickened.

As Shona walked on, peering ahead, the river made a deep growling noise as it battered, suddenly furious, over the steps of stone. Hearing the rush of the rapids, she felt a sudden pang of cold fear.

And through the thickening trees, as if to match the violent waters, a black stone bridge rose threateningly through the trees. She could see Alison climbing the path towards the stone bridge, her head down. If she crossed it, Shona would follow her to the other side and on to the ruined abbey. If she did not, Shona would turn back and see her later at the B&B.

Her phone rang. She swore and fished it from her pocket.

'How do,' Terry said jauntily, albeit with a voice slightly thickened by a hangover.

'So, you made it home alive,' Shona said.

'Where are you? You sound like you're in a tunnel.'

'By the fucking river again. I'm . . . working.'

'Don't believe it. Yeah, made it home. No alarms and no surprises.'

'Fuck's sake, Terry, that's not right. Drunk driving. You'll kill someone.'

'Och, I'm fine. No one was about. Anyway, it seems this town will be in the news again soon.'

'Why's that?'

'I think it's you, bringing death and destruction wherever you go. They've found a body in the woods.'

'What woods?'

'Woods over the other side from the town – Deepdale. Somebody was out walking their dog this morning and found a dead body in the stream. Just heard it on the local radio.'

'Fuck,' Shona said. 'I was going to go and have a look at that place. Any more details? Who is it?'

'Nope, just that the cops have declared it a suspicious incident. The main path to Deepdale is taped off. I could get in from the western end, park up the high fell . . .'

'Maybe it's just some poor old sod who had a heart attack. Dropped dead in the woods. I don't think it's worth spending the effort trying to get near. It isn't really why we're here.'

'Maybe so. Deepdale is ancient woodland. You can get lost there. Anyway, this MP thing tomorrow, the campaign launch, you want me to come and get pictures?'

'Yeah. We'll need snaps of Watson on the stump, doing a speech, whatever. And a full formal portrait. It's near the waterfall, isn't it?'

'Yep, dramatic. I think I have a number for his election agent – someone called Knott, if I remember from last time. I could ring ahead, get some time squared off for us? And you need a lift, I take it?'

They arranged a time to meet and ended the call. Shona watched Alison's head bobbing along the parapet of the bridge as she crossed over to the other side.

Shona followed. The path was steep now, and her stick kept slipping in the wet undergrowth. She crossed the river.

Emerging through trees, on the south bank of the Tyr, the shattered Angleton Abbey stood, resplendent in its ruin. Its nave still stood, huge but broken and roofless. Its chapterhouse was long collapsed, its stones taken in days long past for farms and outbuildings. Henry VIII had destroyed this abbey in his fury, and its monks were dust and bone. At its centre were the remnants of its quad, and beside it, the only intact space – a small chapel.

Alison Harmire was there.

Shona struggled uphill to the abbey. Her side was sore, and her gin hangover was now hanging heavy on her tired limbs. Her stick was clarty with mud. She walked slowly around the towering walls. They were stark and sad, with no sign that humans had ever lived there, slept there, ate and worshipped there.

But it was not all rack and ruin. The central chapel stood as if new. She pushed through the door and stood at the back of the nave. Instead of a stone altar, there was a bare wooden table. On it was a brass crucifix and two simple candles. A bible was resting on a folded pale cassock, which glittered with gold stitching.

There was a large modern stained-glass window above it – a vertical slide of captured light. It had a splaying pattern of diamonds, of leaves, of spear heads, arrow heads and light flares. Purple and blue, diamond and emerald.

Alison, still, tall, was sitting in a pew.

As Shona walked slowly down the aisle, her stick tapped on the flagstones.

'So, you followed me,' Alison said, unmoving, facing away from Shona.

'Yes, of course,' Shona said. 'I'd like to speak to you. And it was a pretty walk.'

'Bonny, as you Scots might say. Do you think you'll go it alone, then? An independent Scotland? That's what I hear.'

Shona shrugged. 'I didn't think we'd be talking politics.'

'I didn't think we'd be talking, full stop,' Alison said.

'To answer your question: I think so. Eventually. We'll be a normal country, like everyone else.'

'What's normal?' Alison said, as she turned around. She had been crying again. Her eyes were red and liquid. Her nose had been blown and was pink. A tiny smear of mascara was black on her cheek.

'You all right?' Shona said. She sat on the opposite side of the aisle, a row back. Her feet were wet and ached. She looked up – the roof was high and clean, waterproof, windproof. The chapel walls were old, but the roof was new, its heavy gleaming doors likewise, with steel locks. An old place had been renewed.

'Hardly. No, not in any way,' Alison said. She wiped her eyes with the heels of her hands.

'I'm sorry,' Shona said.

'No, you're not,' Alison said. She turned around, her arm resting on the back of the pew. 'I know your type. You want a story. I'm not sure what story you want, but that's what you're here for. So, no, don't tell me you're sorry. Don't bother with that.'

'Fair enough,' Shona said. 'But I am sorry you're upset about something.'

Alison looked at her for a moment. Shona could feel her assessing her appearance, her demeanour. What it meant to her. Whether she had to give anything, or if anything was due to come to her.

'Glasgow or Edinburgh?' Alison said, at last. She pulled a scrunch of tissue paper from her sleeve and blew her nose. It echoed around the chapel.

'Both,' Shona said, smiling.

Alison nodded, unsmiling. 'My mum has a stick now,' she said. 'She had a fall. She mainly uses it to swipe at the dog.'

Alison looked up at the window. Light moved across her face in a dim pattern. Her eyes glistened. 'It's beautiful, isn't it?'

Shona agreed.

'They put it in for the millennium. And the new roof. Everyone thought things were going to change, didn't they? Get

244

better. But they didn't. They got worse. Worse and worse. Do you remember the millennium bug?'

'No.'

'You were probably too young,' Alison said. 'Everyone was in a panic about it. A complete collapse of worldwide computer systems. The bank where I was working at the time spent a pretty penny preparing for the apocalypse. It never happened. Life just carried on. It was just a number on the calendar, here and then gone. No apocalypse. Just the usual steady stream of disasters. Most of them forgotten now. No one remembers. No one needs to.'

'Did you come to this abbey when you were a kid?' Shona asked.

Alison frowned at her, as if Shona had said something idiotic. 'Yes, of course. We used to come here with the dogs. My dad would make us walk here. A round trip from Ully and back again. Miserable in the winter, of course. But the river is beautiful. And the abbey, too, in its way.'

'There's a lot of beauty around here.'

Shona moved to the front row of seats, so she was directly opposite Alison. 'I'm here because of Daniel, because of what he did,' she said quietly.

'You said,' Alison said. 'What did he do, then?'

'You know – he killed himself at Viv Banks's wedding. He threw himself off the roof of the hotel. I was there.'

'I know,' Alison said. 'I read the papers. Was that you writing that? Was that your doing?'

'No, Viv's my friend. I wouldn't write about it.'

Alison folded her arms. 'A friend? Not for much longer if you're snooping around here.'

Shona stared up at the stained-glass window. Her eyes burned with its incandescence. She wanted to leap into it.

'Did he ever talk about suicide?' she said.

'God's sake, I'm not talking about Dan. None of your

business. No.' Alison shook her head. 'Fancy doing that to yourself at a party full of journalists. It's not like no one's going to write about it. He should have got drunk and walked into the hills. Settled for the night with a bottle of whisky and waited for the weather to do its worst. In the Cairngorms. Or here on the Pennines, up at the top there. It can freeze your blood. It's like hell.'

'Like an empty hearth,' Shona said.

Alison peered at her. 'Who else have you spoken to?'

'I haven't spoken to Robert Stang yet, but I am going to speak to Gary Watson. I think I've got enough for a story.'

'Bobby won't speak to you. He's army: not liable to go shooting his mouth off.'

'And Gary Watson?'

'He won't want to talk about the past, that's for sure,' Alison said, looking into the light.

'You went to school with him. Was he political then? He's the darling of his party now, isn't he? Tipped for the cabinet.'

'I guess so. They weigh his votes around here, rather than count them. He'll win easily. No, he wasn't political back then. I think his dad was. I don't know where this country is going. Mind, if someone like Gary is close to the levers of power, then God help us all.'

'I don't think God gives a flying fuck.'

Alison let out a short laugh and shook her head. 'I saw some graffiti in New York once. It said: "No God, Only Satan." What a thing to write on a wall. Mind you, it would make sense.'

'Was it a description or a warning, do you think?'

'Both. So, you're definitely going to interview Gary?'

Shona leaned over. 'Why are you in Ullathorne, Alison?'

'None of your business,' Alison snapped.

'The thing is: I want to talk to you about Andrew Banks, too, as well as Dan. And about your little group. Back then, in sixth form.'

Alison's was still for a moment. Her hands clenched. 'What do you mean?'

'Back then,' Shona said. 'I need to know about it.'

Alison stood up. 'No,' she said, shaking her head. She strode down the nave, her feet heavy on the floor, opened the door and slammed it behind her. The sound exploded in the air and disappeared.

Shona was alone in the chapel. Something moved across the sun, and the room darkened. The light dimmed in the stained glass, and the crucifix cast its shape across the stone floor.

She thought of following Alison, but the moment had passed. So, she sat in the silent chapel, and after a while, it began to rain.

'Is that Colin Mickle?'

Shona was on a green wooden bench overlooking the river. She had tramped slowly back to the town, along the south bank of the Tyr and past a quiet caravan site, and now sat opposite the old mill. The high walls bore signs, warning of danger.

At the ground level, there were barred windows. There was darkness beyond them as deep as space. In there, the glass had moved across the board. In there, the friends had had their last meeting.

Her legs ached, her trainers were drenched and her jeans were splattered with mud, whipped by weeds and the tall meadow grass.

'Aye, that's me, love,' a jaunty Northern voice said.

'Great.'

'Many a mickle makes a muckle!' he yelled.

'Sorry?'

'Nothing, pet, never mind. Carry on.'

'I was wondering if I might ask for your help, professionally,' Shona said.

'Oh, now then – that sounds terribly serious,' Mickle said. 'Go on.'

Shona gathered her thoughts as she spoke. She was hesitant, at first, and Mickle asked questions. But eventually she laid it out – she was in town as a freelance reporter following the death of Dan Merrygill, trying to find out more about his background. She outlined – vaguely – that she had learned of the tight-knit group of teenagers back in the early 1990s. That one of his friends, Andrew Banks, had disappeared. All those years ago.

'So, I was wondering if you could help in any way. If we run anything, you could have an extract as an exclusive for your paper,' she said. 'I could talk to my boss about that.'

'It's all a bit before my time, to be honest,' Mickle said quietly. 'And I'm not from Ully, so don't remember it. I'm from the other side, Westmorland. Have you looked in our archive?'

'Not yet – thought I'd call you first,' she lied.

'Ah, right, well, there might be stuff in there. It goes back to the nineties. Why don't you come in? We can have a natter. Paper's gone to bed for the week, so I've got a moment or two.'

'Thanks, Colin – I'll come around later.'

Shona then checked a text that Terry had sent her: the details of whom to call to arrange an interview with Gary Watson. Someone called Knott.

She tapped in the number, and it rang and rang, and then a prerecorded message said to leave a message or call another number.

Shona dialled the new number. Again, the number rang out.

She left a voicemail explaining that she was a freelance journalist who was interested in interviewing the talented and interesting Gary Watson for a piece to run in a UK national broadsheet newspaper. She left her name and number and a suggestion that she have twenty minutes, a face-to-face interview, with Watson after his campaign launch, the next day.

She hung up and breathed deeply. The sun cleared some clouds and a warmth fell on her shoulders. There was a chopping noise, a hollow *whop-thok* in the air. A helicopter thrummed overhead and flew up the dale. An ambulance siren briefly sounded, and then was gone, lost in the stone and the trees.

Shona called her father, but there was no response, and she didn't leave a voicemail. She wondered how he was, all those miles away. She thought of his tender head, his messy allotment, his wounded heart. She hoped Bernie was looking after him – she knew she would be. The blessed nun, she thought, was probably blessed in some way. At the very least, her father would be safe until she got back.

She rose with an involuntarily moan from the bench and walked down to the metal bridge that spanned the river. The morning, and the chasing of Alison, had been frustrating. Shona wondered if she really did have enough material now for a story. She thought back over the previous days. Yes, she did. For a news feature of a few thousand words or so? More than enough. If some outlet wanted a clean, short, follow-up news story, she could probably provide one as well. Add in her own experiences at the wedding and it could stretch further, if needed. After all, no one else had been there when Daniel fell. That was an exclusive, she knew.

But she knew, too, with a sense of vacancy, an ache, that the heart of her story was still empty – the disappearance of Andrew Banks, the Ouija sessions, that circle of friends and what they had done. There was a central darkness – an obscurity.

She was not a detective: she could not succeed where the police had failed. She could not find Andrew. He was almost certainly dead. Daniel was dead. Alison was hostile. Bobby – she had not tried to speak to him yet. She had not mentioned anything to Peg yet. Bev was the only friendly contact she had made. And she had the words she had found in Daniel's jacket – whatever they meant. She swallowed hard. Viv would see, eventually, that she did not want to stir up the deep soil of old pain. That she wanted to shed light, not inflict further wounds. Viv was angry now, but she was smart, and reasonable. She knew how newspapers worked. She would come round. Shona told herself that. She had to.

She jumped. Her phone was buzzing in her pocket.

'What is it?' she said.

'Hello to you too. That body in the woods . . .' Terry said. There was music playing, and she was driving. Somewhere on a road, barrelling between high hedges and watchful trees.

'What about it?'

'PR man at the cops told me something.'

'A friend of yours?'

'Kind of. They're going to publicly identify him this afternoon, in time for the news on *Look North*. It's Robert Stang.'

'What the actual fuck?'

'Bobby. From the same group of friends as your suicide.'

Shona's heart leapt. 'Any cause of death?'

'Not that I'm being told. But all the forensics folk are in the woods. It's not a suicide. Where does this leave us?'

Shona looked to her feet and, through gaps in the frame of the bridge, she could see the river running. On the streams of light and shadow tiny shreds of forest flotsam spun over and over on their circumference.

'Well,' Shona said at last, 'even if he has been done in, it's not necessarily part of my story. But I'll need the detail of what's happened to him to add to the article because he and the others are all linked by the same past. Ranald will be on about it, no doubt about it. I'll want to have answers to the questions before they're asked.'

'There'll be a news release from the cops, but it's not like we can get anywhere near the body,' Terry said. 'We could try for a "collect". He has an estranged partner and a lass. But if the wee girl is with her mother—'

'Yeah, no chance of getting a photo from the mantelpiece. Unless the cops release one from the family.'

'Aye. I'll ask the press officer. Man, it's dark, isn't it? This bunch – they have a bloody hex on them.'

Shona nodded. Something like a hex.

'He was a veteran, wasn't he?'

'Yeah. Army. As far as I've heard, he was a solid citizen. Not mixed up in anything dodgy. Worked at the bottle factory. Foreman. Big lad.'

'Poor guy,' Shona said, her mind moving on. 'Look, this

interview tomorrow with Gary Watson: you still okay to pick me up? I need to get to Darlington station after.'

'You definitely heading home, then?'

'Yep. Time for me to return to reality. This place isn't it. Or it has its own reality. But it's not mine.'

'Right. Well, I will once again be happy to be your personal chauffeur service.'

'See you tomorrow. Buzz me on approach.'

'If I get any more on this Stang thing . . .'

'Yeah, send it over. Speak in a bit.'

Shona walked slowly back to the B&B. Her mind was fogged. She did not hear her phone ring or buzz, but as she got to the door of the Gildersleve, there was a text from Bernie from her father's phone.

I have prayed on it, and I have had an idea about how to make things better, which I want to share with you. In the meantime, I will have to act. Not only prayers, but deeds, Shona. We both hope to see you soon. B x

Shona kicked off her muddy shoes in the hallway and slumped upstairs to her room. She lay down on the bed and threw her stick onto the floor.

She looked around the room, as if for the first time. The wallpaper was a tangle of tiny green and pale pink flowers, entwined and repeated. Tiny stems, linking and unlinking across the pale wall, like a forest, like an alien world consisting only of vine and flower, of root and branch, repeating to an obscured horizon.

She had an idea.

She opened her laptop and emailed Ranald.

I need a cuts check. Can you check the public comments, speeches, statements, quotes or otherwise of Gary Watson MP? I want to see how many times he has said these phrases: 'Take the Right Path', 'Say Yes to No' and 'There Is No Time'. See also if he has said anything about Andrew Banks. Need it by the earliest a.m. Ta.

A heaviness fell over her like a weighted quilt. She had to sleep. Shona turned on her good side and, too tired to move, left the curtains open. The sun would dim in time.

She soon fell into a deep sleep, her mind playing monochrome shreds of fractured dreams –

A shot glass moving over a tattooed alphabet.

A boy on an island staring at the setting sun from a lonely beach, the sand glowing with light.

A distorted man on fire, twisting like an acrobat in a flaring flower of agony.

A fire on an empty moor, the smoke rising to a blank paper sky.

The face of a grey king in a white shirt, his eyes replaced by coins, carried on a stream of hands into the spiking gloom of a darkening forest.

A body in a suit underwater, swimming towards her, three black eyes in his face.

Her father, in hospital, his mottled shoulders bare, staring out of a window with watery eyes. His hands as black as charcoal, his mouth full of crushed glass. His eyes, turning to her, as colourless as peeled eggs –

She woke with a start.

It was pitch-black. There was a loud, repetitive noise.

Someone or something was knocking on her door.

28

Her door trembled slightly as the knocking went on.

'Hello?' Shona said groggily.

'It's me,' a voice said.

Shona, tendrils of her mind still drifting in dream-heavy sleep, swung her feet from the bed. She looked to the window – streetlamps were buzzing on the silent road.

'Who is *me*?' Shona whispered.

'Ashley,' the voice said.

Shona opened the door. On the dim landing was Ashley, clad in baggy clothes, ashen-faced.

'What's up?'

'Can I come in?'

'Sure, but why?' Shona said, widening the door.

Ashley moved past her, her socked feet silent as a cat on the thick carpet, and sat on the bed. Her hair was mussed and tangled.

'See that thing I found in the woods?'

Shona closed the door and leant against it. She was vaguely aware she had now blocked Ashley's exit.

'The thing you found in the woods? The shirt, you mean?' Shona said. There was a mild irritation in her mind.

'Yeah, the football shirt. I wanted to tell you something about it. Mam has it now. She's away out with it, with her friend.'

'Why are you telling me this?'

'I saw you walking across the fields, following that Alison. You're a journalist – you must be after something.'

'I am, and you're right. I'm always after something.' Shona smiled and ran a hand through her hair.

'Are you hungover?' Ashley asked with a sudden grin.

'Not any more.' Shona sat down on the chair by the dresser. 'Tell me about the shirt, then?'

Ashley looked down at her hands. She held one with the other. 'It was a weird thing to find in Deepdale, right enough.'

'Yeah, and your mother has it?'

'She's kept it. I think she was going to take it to the police, but she didn't. I saw it in the kitchen cupboard. Now she's gone out with Alison, and she's taken it with her.'

'Right – so why are you telling me this?'

'Because of that name – Jet.'

Shona leaned forward. 'Right.'

'Well, thing is, last night, when she and that Alison were talking – when you came back late – they said how they used to go into Deepdale with their pals. About how they would go there and drink cider or whatever.'

'Yeah?'

'Alison said the shirt belonged to their friend, the one who went missing. She said it was definitely his. Because of the name on the back. Jet was Andrew's dog. Then they had a row over what to do, and now they've gone off with it.'

Shona's heart was pounding now. She felt suddenly hot, almost feverish.

'What has your mum told you about Andrew?'

'Just that they were pals,' Ashley said. 'I don't know. Mam did have other friends, but mostly she spent a lot of time with my dad. By sixth form, Dad was in Darlo, at the college, so she spent a lot of time there. He was studying accountancy. But, yes, she knew Andrew, and she's mentioned before how she was part of that group. And how sad it was when he disappeared.'

'Has she ever mentioned what they got up to, that group?'

Ashley smiled and faintly blushed. 'What do you mean?'

'I mean, what did they do together?'

'What, having it off and that? Gross. No.'

'No. I mean, has she ever mentioned them doing weird stuff?'

'What, like drugs?'

Shona stood up and walked to the dresser. In the mirror she could see them both, reversed. Both dishevelled, in their own ways. Her stick on the floor by the bedside table. Her bag thrown in the corner.

'No, I don't think so,' Ashley said quietly. 'Although–'

'Although?'

'There was this old story she used to wheel out now and then when *Songs of Praise* was on the telly, or some religious thing on the news. I remember we were watching *The Exorcist* and she mentioned it.'

'And?'

'Oh, just about when they were all in sixth form. One of the lasses, one of Mam's friends from church, she came into the sixth-form common room and threw holy water on that Gary Watson.'

'She what?'

'Yeah, she was evangelical. Can't remember her name now, Mam would tell you. Anyway, she steamed into the common room. Watson was asleep, apparently. She marched in and chucked the water over him. Mam says she was half-expecting Watson to melt away on the spot.'

'Holy water?'

Ashley shrugged. 'That's how the story goes.'

'Now why would anyone do that?'

'Maybe because he's a total prick? I don't know. Did you see what he said about, eh, disabled people?' Ashley said quietly.

'I didn't. What did he say?'

'He's denied it since, mind.'

'I'm sure he has. What was it?'

'There was a thing in the *Mirror*. He was at some posh lunch in London, and he said disabled people should think about whether they contribute enough to society. He asked whether we were just *ballast*. Mam went tonto.'

'What did he mean by it, do you think?'

'I think he thinks we're worthless,' Ashley said. 'A drain on society. A burden.'

'Well, if he thinks that, he's a fucking cunt,' Shona said.

Ashley burst out with a sudden, shocked laugh. 'You Scottish people don't mess about.'

Shona dipped her head in acknowledgement. 'We can't afford to. And anyway, where did your mum go? With Alison?'

'They might have gone to the pub. Bev's band are playing again, I think. Maybe they went to see them. Are you going to ask her about the shirt? Can you please not say you heard about it from me?'

'I knew about it already.'

'How?' Ashley's eyes were wide.

'I have my sources.' Shona tapped her nose.

Ashley turned to Shona with pleading eyes. Her lips were wet. She had become pale.

'How, though?'

'I saw it in the kitchen when you were discussing it with your mum.'

'Oh, okay. So, you can say that.'

'Yes, I can say that. But I didn't know Jet was the name of Andrew's dog.'

Ashley looked hard at Shona. 'Well, you do now. But you didn't hear it from me, right?'

'I can say his sister told me. I'm a . . . friend of hers.'

Ashley stood up and moved to the door, but paused, her hand on the plain white doorknob. She was looking down at her feet. As if remembering.

Shona sensed there was something else Ashley wanted to say. 'Was there anything else your mum and her friend said last night?'

'There was,' Ashley said, almost to herself.

Shona waited.

'Mam said they had to do the right thing. No, to take the right path. And Alison said they had no time to waste, or something. Then she said something a bit weird.'

'And what was that?'

'She said they had to do what some other guy said. They had to speak to him. Some guy called Sorley. Mam kind of shivered all over, and then you came back, and it all stopped.'

'Sorley?' Shona said. Her mind seemed to suddenly turn in on itself, like the snap of a blown sheet in a sudden gale.

'I don't know who Sorley is, like. Must be another friend from school.'

'Maybe,' Shona said, to say something.

'Well, okay, see ya then. Ta-ra,' she said and suddenly left. Her feet pattered in the hall.

Shona washed her face and got ready to go back out into the night. Before she left the room, she texted her father: *Dad, hope you're OK. Is Bernie looking after you? Coming home soon. Love you S.*

The night was cold, winter lingering in the darkness.

Where would they be? Peg and Alison were here somewhere. They might be in a pub, but the town had several. She might have to try them all. She decided to start at the Lion, where Bev's band were playing.

She realised, as she crossed the cobbles to the pub, that she should have called the *Tyrdale Times*. Tomorrow, she told herself.

There was music playing in the pub, but it wasn't a band. She could hear from the street a single acoustic guitar chiming its way through minor scales.

She entered the pub. On a low stage, a large man was sitting, bowed over a guitar. With one hand he was tightening a string, his eyes low to the frets. At the bar, a man was drying glasses, looking up at the TV, which was showing the evening news with subtitles. The prime minister, pushing back his lank hair, was making a speech outside Number 10 about the general election, which would be held in six weeks. His wife – immaculate, impermeable – stood beside him, surveying the gathered press corps. The barman was shaking his head.

There were a couple of old men by the bar, damp and antiquated in tweed, muttering to each other over short drinks. One had no hair; the other had too much, squeezed under a green bunnet. Near the slot machine in the corner, which madly flashed in Technicolor, a middle-aged couple were playing dominoes. By the stage, some teenagers in black were sombrely reading their mobile phones.

The guitarist looked up as he prepared to sing his next song. Shona recognised him. It was Karl, Bev's partner. He stared at her for a while and then spoke breathily into the microphone: 'This is an old one and a true one – "Rufford Park Poachers".'

He played a skeletal riff on the guitar, his large fingers moving spryly over the strings. He plucked a lonesome arpeggio. As he sang, the beautiful melody rose and fell, and the guitar chimes held and supported the melody for a time, drifted underneath and then let go. Karl sang with a clear tenor that rang true.

Everyone was watching and listening, even the old men at the bar, and Shona realised she was standing in the middle of the taproom by herself. She moved to the bar and ordered a Jack Daniel's and Coke.

Her phone vibrated in her pocket as the barman served her drink. By the time she had paid him, the phone had stopped. She had missed a call from a private number. But then it buzzed again: a voicemail.

She suspected it to be a work call. But Ranald always called from his landline or his mobile, and Stricken usually texted. It was likely a call back from Gary Watson's PR team. She pressed the button to listen and put the phone to her ear, just as Karl's song came to an end and the crowd clapped.

The message began. There was the sound of rushing, of air moving in a stream over obstacles and around barriers. A keening – a whine of gale moving over the moor. Then a voice – deep, uneven – rolled over the howl.

'Sandison . . . I'm fine now. I can talk. He left me a lot of money. He left the banks a lot of money. It was a settling of debts. He was ready for his final journey. To go beyond, so he could come back.'

There was a pause.

'I am here if you want to know more. He has seen what will happen. He's seen it already. He's in the stones – in the rocks and stones. Goodbye, Sandison.'

The voice ended, and the wind returned. Just the flow of air through rock and heather, over lichen and stone. For a minute the sound of the wind continued and then, with a clunk, it was gone.

Shona stared at her phone.

'What the actual–' she said to herself. She couldn't even call back, as the number had been withheld.

A large figure was suddenly in front of her. It was Karl.

'So,' he said.

'Nice tunes,' Shona said. 'Can I buy you a drink?'

She noticed his right hand was shaking, his eyes pink and tired.

'I guess you're looking for Bev, and what-have-yer.' He leaned on the bar; he looked ready to collapse.

'I am,' Shona said.

He pointed to a bottle on a shelf and the barman nodded.

'You all right, Karl?' she asked.

He stared ahead. 'Aye, right enough,' he said flatly. 'Get a bit nervous when performing, like.'

'Fair enough. Was that an old folk song or one of yours?'

He poured the bottle of amber drink into a straight glass and took a sip. 'No, it's an old one. About the rich fucking the ordinary folk. Nowt's changed there.'

Shona nodded. She thought of her father. He would love this chat. And Karl and Bev clearly thought alike. They were a close couple.

'I thought Bev would be on tonight,' Shona said.

'The band were meant to be on' – he nodded – 'but it's just me tonight. Bev has something to do. She said it couldn't wait.'

'She's meeting Alison and Peg,' Shona said, looking at him directly.

He stared at his drink. He said nothing.

'Is that right? A reunion?'

'I don't know,' he said, his hand shaking.

'Karl, back on in ten?' the barman said, tapping his watch.

'Aye, sure,' Karl said.

'Karl, I just want to catch up with them all together, for my article . . .'

'About that poor Daniel, I know,' he mumbled.

'Do you know where they're meeting?'

He leaned towards her, his massive head creating a shadow, his hairy face haloed with harsh pub light.

'I'm not going to say this twice,' he said, 'so listen on and reckon.'

'Okay, Karl,' she said gently.

'There's something weird going on in the dale. Something dark. Since you've been here. Or since Dan topped himself. There's been . . . incidents. I can't say more. Bev and them are down at the mill. Fuck knows why. I just want everything to go back to the way it was. You know they've found a body?'

'Where?' she asked. There cannot be *another* body, she thought.

'In the woods. Deepdale. Bobby Stang,' he said.

'Ah, right,' she said. 'Yes, I heard.' She suddenly wished she had spoken to Robert Stang first. But now he was gone, too.

'Did you hear he was stabbed? Stabbed to death. There was . . . there *is* someone going around killing people. That's a bigger story than poor Dan, isn't it? Bodies fucking everywhere, and a murderer. Not poor Danny – that's not a story.'

'I know what a story is. What do you mean, bodies everywhere?'

He looked at her. His eyes were wide, his face flushed. There was a tang of sweat.

The barman said Karl's name again, and his shoulders sank.

'I'm off,' he said and sloped back to the stage. Some people clapped, and he wiped his brow and raised a hand.

Shona looked outside. It was dark, with loneliness in every shadow.

Karl picked up his guitar again. He strummed his way through three more songs: all sad, all forlorn, all in the minor keys. One of them, 'John Ball's Blues', was very long, building to a heavily strummed climax.

'When Adam delved and Eve span, who was then the gentleman?' he sang, over and over.

Shona could tell that Karl was upset. There was something clenched in his tone, something nervous in his body. At the house he had seemed full of bonhomie, bulky and capable. Here he looked diminished and scared.

She sat at the bar for twenty minutes, drinking bourbon, and was on the verge of texting Terry about nothing in particular – she could not think of a subject matter – when there was a smattering of applause as Karl's set came to an end.

'Nice one, Karl,' someone hollered from a dark corner.

Karl put his guitar in a battered case and looked over at the bar. He saw Shona and wiped his forehead. He nodded at the barman, who poured a pint instantly.

Karl lumbered over as piped rock hits began filtering through the pub's PA.

'Still here, then,' he said.

'Looks like it,' she said. 'I just want to chat a bit more.'

'What for?'

'Well, I think you have something to tell me.'

'Oh, aye?'

'You're talking to me now, aren't you?' She smiled.

He looked around the bar. His massive neck was red from sweat, hair plastered on it.

'Where's Bev?'

'There's a place out back,' he said, as if not to Shona, but into his pint. He trudged to a fire exit near the jukebox. Shona followed. The door opened into the cool air and silence of the night.

She was in a lane between the pub and the adjacent building, and at the end was a sliver of electric light, where Karl was standing now.

There was a backyard, filled with empty beer barrels, pallets and boxes and recycling bins. Past a low wall was a sheer cliff face, heavy with trees, and the river. On the other side of the Tyr, the streetlamps glowed orange and the streets were empty. A single lamp glimmered on the wall.

'You never heard it from me,' he said, at last. Karl was smoking a joint, and the sweet smoke was blown from the river back to Shona and the lane behind.

Shona leaned against the wall and waited.

'Okay,' she said softly.

'It were called Sorley. Funny, right?'

Shona's heart bumped again, but she did not show any emotion. The smoke dragoned from Karl's joint. It drifted across her vision of the land below the cliff, as if the town's lights were gleaming in a cloud.

'The thing they were talking to,' Karl said, 'Bev said he – or it could have been a she, I guess – was called Sorley. That's who they were talking to, on them Ouija board sessions and what-have-yer. Back in the day.

'She told me about it at Glastonbury. She was a bit freaked out by something we took. Magic mushrooms. Bad acid. She told me all about it. Said it had given her years of bad luck. Until she met me.'

'This Sorley—'

'When you showed up the other day, asking questions about back then, well, it made me think of what they were up to. Maybe it's brought me bad luck an' all.'

He shook his head and took a long draft of his joint. He shot out smoke from his large nostrils.

'In what way?'

'Ach, something that's settled now.'

She didn't know what he was talking about. 'So, this Sorley?'

'Backstage at their school, that Alison, Bev, that poor Dan, the boy who went missing, Big Bobby, that other prick – they met once a week. Regular, like. I'm not sure if they were friends as such. Maybe Bev and Peg and Alison. Andy and that Dan were meant to be close. That's why he was at the wedding.'

He sat down on a beer barrel, breathing hard. 'Bev won't thank me for this, but I think they were addicted to it. They got in right trouble for doing it at the school, so then they started meeting in the basement of the old mill. The ruined one down by the river there.'

'Why are you telling me this?'

'Because I heard your question to Bev. About those messages – the lines you were saying.'

'"There Is No Time", "Take the Right Path" and "Say Yes to No".'

He blew out a jet of smoke. He rubbed his eye with a palm. He nodded.

'Bev said their sessions eventually got a bit boring,' he said quietly. So quietly, Shona moved forward. 'This Sorley, repeating the same messages. Those lines. The glass would move so quickly, sometimes their hands would come off it. Sometimes it seemed to be floating off the table. Bev said that, sometimes, the glass would only spell out fragments, bits, of those sentences.

Bit like a parrot who only remembers some of what it's been taught.'

'Have you and Bev ever done a session?'

He looked at her, his eyes tawny in the electric light. 'Not a fucking chance. That stuff scares me, to be honest. I don't want to talk to the dead, with spirits or what-have-yer. Do you believe in all that? The afterlife?'

'I don't think so. Do you?'

He shivered suddenly. He picked a scrap of tobacco from his lip. 'I believe Bev. She doesn't lie to me. Plenty of people have, but she hasn't. But I think them messages are cursed. They're bad. Like hexes. They shouldn't have seen them and they shouldn't have said them. But they were young and they were fucking idiots for dabbling in that stuff.'

'Why are you telling me this?'

'I shouldn't be, really,' he mumbled. 'But, you know, I love Bev. She's turned my life around. I would be dead in a ditch by now if not for her. Life is hard. I just know she's in the mill right now, with them lasses, and I'm worried it all might kick off again. Dan's topped himself, hasn't he? There's a body in the woods. There's bad shit going on. Andrew was never found. You're here, kicking around the bones and the dust. It doesn't feel right to me.

'And,' he added, 'I just didn't like Bev lying to you about them messages.'

He rubbed his hands and moved to the wall. He stared down through the dark trees to the murmuring river. A moving shadow amidst the shadow.

'You should probably go now,' he said quietly.

'What are you going to do?' she said softly, as she looked at the great bulk of Karl, staring down into the darkness.

'I'm going to get my guitar and drink myself stupid and wait here for Bev to join me.'

'I'm going to go to the mill.'

'Well, you know now.'

'I do, and thank you.'

He reached into his shirt pocket and fished out another joint. 'I don't want to sound over-dramatic and what-have-yer, but this never happened.'

'What happened?' she said, smiling.

He laughed softly.

Shona turned on her heel and made for the lights of the town.

The stars glittered through the ruins of the old mill, which stood, shattered, on the dark banks of the River Tyr.

Shona walked down to the edge of the building where it bordered the river, but she could not hear or see anything moving. There was no way in – just a sheer wall and boarded-up windows like thumbprints in the stone.

But there, by the river's edge, a thin ribbon of light flickered on the passing water. She looked up. The moon stared back, a scarred bowl of silver, but it was not casting that shiver of colour.

Shona looked down. It seemed to be coming from a low barred window. How to get to there? Shona thought. There was no path down from the bridge. Cross to the other side and wade across the river? she thought madly. No chance of that. The water was deep and driven. She would be carried away.

Maybe she could get to the other side of the mill and then clamber along the riverbank to the window. She set off back up the Bank for a short distance and then down a cobbled street, the bulk of the building to her right.

Stomping past a parked car and its hidden driver, Shona continued down to the river's edge. There was a short drop to the rocky shore. The river ran wide here, slow and deep. Lights glittered on the far bank. The night was silent.

She looked over the edge, then she sat, put her stick down, turned around and inched down to the riverbank. Her trainers hit the scree hard.

The world seemed suddenly changed. The smell of the river was about her, and the world of men was obscured.

The path along the riverbank to the mill was dark, pitch-black in the eaves. With a curse, she realised she had no torch. But she had her phone. She switched on its torch, and it cast a sharp light on pebbles and rock. If she aimed it at her feet and her stick, she would be able to see immediate obstacles.

Suddenly nervous and clumsy, she made her way along the stony bank, her stick prodding into the darkness. If she fell, she would fall on unseen rocks or tip into the river and be lost. She stopped for a moment to catch her breath. The river ran beside her, wide and dark and relentless.

Above the flow she heard voices. She walked further on, almost to the bridge, which now loomed nearby.

There was a semicircular, glassless window close, at shoulder height. She crunched along the shore towards it. Inside was an intact basement room, and there was light: a white fuzz from a camping lamp set on a trestle table. Three figures were around it. On the table was a plastic bag with something inside it.

Bev, Alison and Peg were murmuring. Shona took out her phone and switched on the Dictaphone. She set it to record and dropped it in her pocket.

Peg turned to the window and saw Shona. She lifted her hand to the others and walked over.

'I thought it might be you,' she said. She stepped up on something in front of the window and held out a hand. 'Come in, then.'

Shona passed through her stick, which Peg took. Peg then grasped her hand, and Shona climbed through the empty window frame. The brickwork scraped her hands and knees and tore at her thighs.

'Fucking hell,' she said as she landed on the damp basement floor. 'That's the most exercise I've had for years.'

'Hello, again,' Bev said.

'Good evening,' Alison said.

Peg handed Shona her stick. 'I've got some drink,' she said. 'It'll warm you up.'

Peg moved to the table and rummaged inside the plastic bag. She took out a flask, which she unscrewed and passed to Shona, who, nodding at the others, took a swig. It momentarily crossed her mind that the drink could be poison. But it stung her throat and sent a fire up her nose – it was whisky. She handed it back to Peg.

Alison had a small glass in her hand. She put it in her pocket.

'So,' Shona said.

'Hi,' Peg said.

'So?' Shona said.

'So, what the fuck is going on? Is that what you mean?' Bev said.

'She knows what the fuck is going on,' Alison said.

Shona moved forward and laid her stick against the table. 'I'm a bit disappointed. I thought you might be having a wee Ouija board session.'

They all stared at her. Bev looked exhausted. Alison was watchful and severe. Peg looked ready to cry.

'You know, for old times' sake – a wee game of spin the glass,' Shona said, the raw whisky spiking alarmingly in her blood.

Alison drummed her fingers on the table. 'Okay, we haven't got all night.'

'Well, we have, actually,' Bev said, looking out to the darkness.

'Tell us what you know,' Alison said.

The camping light shone harshly on their faces. The floor was uneven concrete, with dank pools of water here and there, the ceiling a rough cast from which hung strands of muck and cobweb. A door in the corner led to a staircase. Outside, a wind was picking up, shaking branches.

Shona took a deep breath and then, omitting some details, ran quickly through the events of the past few days. She concluded by saying she was going to interview Gary Watson at his campaign launch in the morning.

Alison crossed her arms and looked at the floor. Bev stared out of the window. Peg leaned on the table's edge, fiddling with the plastic bag.

Shona pointed to it. 'So that's Andy's shirt, isn't it?'

Alison nodded. 'Yeah. He was wearing it the last time.'

'Some things should stay in the ground,' Bev said. Her voice carried through the half-moon window and across the water.

'Ashley said the dog found it in some building in the woods,' Shona said.

'Yeah,' Alison said. 'I think I know that building.'

Peg looked at her in surprise.

'Gary took me there once. It's a fake ruin – it's not a real building.'

'What you on about?' Bev said.

'Gary's dad – he was in the Territorial Army,' Alison said, still looking at the floor. 'Awful man. They built it as a pretend ruin, to defend or capture or whatever the fuck they do.'

'I've never seen it,' Peg said.

'Didn't know owt was there,' Bev said.

'You can find it if you look for it,' Alison said.

'Gary took you?' Peg said. 'When?'

Alison shook her head.

'What are you going to do with the shirt?' Shona said.

'Bury it again,' Bev said.

'I think we should take it to the police,' Peg said.

'I want to show it to Watson,' Alison said.

'Why?' Shona asked.

Alison's face hardened. Her eyes flashed. 'What does wee Viv think of you being here? Does she even know you're here?'

Shona bit her lower lip. She pressed on. 'Look, the shirt has been found. I know about the Ouija board stuff. I know a little bit more about Daniel. So, I'm going to write about all this anyway.'

Silence fell. Bev leant on the edge of the window and looked out at the river.

272

'I know you will,' Alison said eventually.

'Why,' Shona said, 'do you think Dan did what he did? It makes no sense to me. He led a quiet life in Darlington. Saw his mother in the home. Was at his friend's wedding . . .'

Alison took something out of her inside pocket. It was a packet of cigarettes. She fished out a pink plastic lighter and lit up in a sudden blaze of fire. New shadows flashed around the stonework and were then gone again.

'And he was clearly obsessed with the Ouija board. It consumed him, didn't it? He had one tattooed on his chest,' Shona said.

'No, he never,' Peg said, aghast.

'I saw it,' Shona said. 'I saw his tattoo. I saw the mess in his hotel room. The messages. The stones. I saw all the words he'd written. It was like he wanted them to be found. Like he wanted someone – someone like me – to follow the trail back, back to here. Back to Ullathorne: "Say Yes to No", "Take the Right Path", "There Is No Time".'

'You're deluded,' Alison said. 'He was sad. He was sick. That's it.'

'You're lying to yourself,' Shona said.

Bev was nodding at something. She turned round, her earrings glittering in the dark. '"Say Yes to No", "Take the Right Path", "There Is No Time",' she said quietly, nodding. 'That's what he always said. That's what they always said.'

'Dan killed himself because he was in despair,' Shona said. 'He had reasons all of his own. They died with him. We'll never really know why. But when he did, he wanted to say something, too. He picked a public event – the wedding of his friend's sister. He stripped off to show the world his tattoo. He left those messages in his jacket for someone to find. Accidentally or deliberately. He knew Viv worked in the papers. He knew that journalists would be there. He was pointing to something. He was pointing to Ullathorne.'

'How can you say that?' Peg said.

'I'm here, aren't I?'

Peg shrugged.

'It was the wedding of Andrew's sister,' Shona said. 'He didn't do it on the spur of the moment. He didn't throw himself under a train. He didn't take an overdose. He didn't slash his wrists in his caravan. He went to the wedding, stripped off, jumped from the roof, left messages. And I'm going to write about it. I'm going to write about it all. I'm going to write about this thing – this thing you might call Sorley. I don't quite know why he was pointing here. But I have my ideas.'

'Sorley, eh?' Bev said. She chewed a fingernail.

'I'm going to say it,' Alison said to Bev.

'You'll sound bloody mad,' Bev said.

'It is mad,' Peg said.

'Dan *is* Sorley,' said Alison.

'What?' Shona said.

'Sorley is Dan, in the other world, in the afterlife. Whatever you want to call it,' Bev said.

'Another plane,' Alison said.

'Pardon?' Shona said.

'This is what we think,' Peg said.

'This is what's happening,' Alison said.

'Sorley – your pal from the Ouija board?' Shona said. Bev flicked her a hard look, but it passed quickly. 'How can Dan be this Sorley thing? He was with you when you contacted it. Or it spoke to you.'

'There is no time,' Alison said.

'That means – you see, it means,' Peg said, stumbling over her words, 'that time as we know it, here – in Ully, in Durham, in our lives: it seems to go forward. From the past to the present to the future.'

'Like the river, from a trickle on the moor to the beck to the sea,' Bev said.

'But when you're dead, you're outside time,' Alison said. 'You can be in the past, in this present and in the future. Dan is Sorley. Dan is outside the river now. He is on the banks. Or in the beck. Or on the beach. Or in the clouds. He has pulled himself from the flow. Out of the current.'

Shona immediately thought of old Martha, in the drab netherworld of her care home. Talking about her son talking to himself – to his dead self.

The shadows deepened. The lights seemed to recede. The world seemed to briefly refocus, as if a lens had been added or subtracted from her inner apprehension of the reality about her.

She shivered. 'His mother said he was always talking to himself in his room.'

'His mum has always been a fucking pain,' Alison said. 'No wonder his old man scarpered.'

'His mother is sick, Ali. Yes, Shona, we think he was talking to himself,' Peg said. 'He was talking to his dead self. He was talking to Sorley.'

'So,' Shona said, 'have you been speaking to Sorley? Have you been . . . ?'

They all nodded.

'When?'

'None of your business,' Alison said. The lit end of her cigarette glowed like a single red eye.

'Sorley is just saying the same things, over and over,' Bev said. 'The same things as he did thirty years ago. Those three messages . . . that's it.'

'You told me the messages said nothing,' Shona said to Bev.

'I lied,' Bev said.

'Lots of lies going around,' Peg said quietly.

'Look, we all got obsessed. We thought it meant something,' Alison said. 'We figured they were orders. Advice. Guidance.'

'So, how seriously did you all take the messages?' Shona said.

They avoided her glance.

'Some more than others,' Bev said eventually.

'Not all of us. I hated it,' Peg said vehemently. 'I hate it. And I never thought they were instructions. Never thought they were orders.'

'You weren't one of Abdarg, were you, Peg?' Shona said.

Peg shook her head, as if she did not hear.

'Andrew, Bev, Dan, Alison, Robert, Gary – ABDARG,' Shona said.

'I don't know what you're on about,' Alison said. 'We never called ourselves that.'

'But we did take it all much too seriously,' Bev said. 'We read into it what we wanted to read into it. Gary, too, I reckon.'

'I made some bad decisions,' Alison said, reaching for the flask.

The three women looked to each other, as if trying to divine each other's intentions.

'Do you know what Odeadaheado means?' Shona said.

'What? No,' Alison said.

'Never heard of it,' Bev said.

Shona suddenly felt very cold. She reached for the flask and poured herself more whisky. 'So, let's try and take a wee moment here. What you, the Abdarg crew, are saying is: Dan killed himself, so he could die and become Sorley.'

'Yes,' said Alison and Peg at the same time.

'Is this not a bit insane?' Shona said.

'None of us are mad,' Alison said. 'I'm finally getting divorced. That proves I'm not mad.'

Bev chuckled.

'We saw it then, we see it now,' Peg said. 'All this. I knew there would be consequences. I knew it would come to bad. I never wanted Dan to be the one. Never wanted that. Poor man.'

'He couldn't become Sorley unless he died,' Alison said, blowing out a jet of cigarette smoke.

'He never had much of a life,' Bev said. 'He knew he wanted

to say something in his death. And if you think you're already dead, it doesn't take much to get there.'

The river rushed outside. The wind blew the scent of drift and jetsam from the water.

'We need to talk about Andrew and that shirt,' Shona said sharply, her head beginning to buzz with the alcohol.

'Maybe we do,' Bev said.

'It's evidence, that shirt,' Peg said. 'I didn't think so at first. But I'm glad Ashley found it.'

'Not sure about that,' Alison said. 'Why's it been found now?'

'The earth has given it up, Ali,' Bev said. 'It has offered it up from its grave.'

'We should absolutely take it to the cops,' Peg said.

'You know what will happen,' Alison said, harder of voice. 'They'll say thanks, and it'll be forgotten – it'll get filed away in a box, in a room with no windows, locked away. Forgotten. It's useless, anyway: after so many years, there won't be anything on it – no DNA, nothing useful. How many winters has it been underground? Soaked by rain. Frozen. It's only because it's made from polyester that it's survived this long. Nothing will happen, Andrew won't be found, and nothing will change. And maybe that's fine.'

Shona was becoming more anxious. She knocked her stick against the wall unintentionally. But it got their attention. 'Did your dad think it was all fine? Did your dad do fuck-all about it because you were involved, Alison? You were one of the last to see Andrew,' Shona said.

'Fuck off,' Alison said. 'Fuck right off.'

'Leave her father be, Shona,' Peg said. 'He had his troubles.'

Alison looked at the floor. Her eyes glistened. 'He brought it on himself.'

'I still think we should hand it in,' Peg said.

'We can't ignore it,' Bev said.

Shona held up her hands. 'Ladies, I will write about the shirt – either way.' She tried to sound reasonable. She let a moment of time pass.

The other women looked to their hands, or their shoes, or the window. Bev bit her fingernail.

Then Shona said, 'What really happened that night? The night Andrew went missing. I'm guessing you've not talked about it since then.'

'I'm going to say it,' Alison said. 'It seems to fall to me again.'

'Go on,' Shona said.

'I think Gary did something to Andy,' Alison said.

Bev put her head in her hands. Peg looked away. The river murmured.

'*Did* something?'

Alison nodded.

'How so?' Shona said. She was suddenly aware of her phone in her pocket, the green light of the Dictaphone app still running.

'I was with Gary last. I was with him on the old bridge,' Alison said. 'After we left here.'

'Snogging,' Bev said with disgust.

'Not a crime,' Peg said quietly.

'Snogging, yeah,' Alison said. 'Down by the river. Then Dan and Andy turn up. They'd followed us. Everyone had a laugh, mainly at my expense. No one knew me and Gary . . .'

'I had a fucking good idea,' Bev said.

'. . . were having a carry-on,' Alison said.

'And?' Shona said.

Alison rocked a little, and Peg moved forward, putting a hand on her shoulder. 'It's all right, it's all right,' she said.

'It's fucking *not* all right,' Bev said, fierce.

Shona waited. Alison's shoulders were shaking. She grasped her body with her arms.

'Fucking Gary, and Andy,' Alison said. 'Gary had a bag of pills. Andy was delighted. He wanted to get mashed. So, they

278

went off, across the river, into Deepdale. I saw them cross the road and go into the woods. Me and Dan, we watched them. Then we just walked home. Dan saw me home. I liked Dan. He was so gentle, wasn't he? He waved goodbye and said he was off to get chips and gravy, that he was going to talk to Sorley on his own. Sorley spoke to him, he always said.'

'And the next day, Andy was missing.'

'The next day, he was gone.' Alison nodded.

'And we just all fucked off, didn't we? As if it never happened. We took the right path – for us,' Bev said.

'I was in the search parties,' Peg said, 'beating the woods.'

'I take it you and Alison were not,' Shona said to Bev.

Bev shook her head.

'I never said a thing,' Alison whispered. 'I was scared. I told my dad I never saw anything. And he said not to worry. "Don't you fret, our Ali, this'll all blow over," he said. I somehow knew he would make it blow over.'

'Bloody hell,' Peg said. 'I can't even remember speaking to the police. Not sure I did.'

'We need to tell someone,' Bev said, her voice gravelly.

'I'm seeing Watson tomorrow,' Shona said.

'You show him this,' Peg said, suddenly behind Shona. She handed over the plastic bag. 'You show him this and see what he bloody says.'

Alison made a gasping noise. She downed a whisky and wiped her eyes. 'I should have said, I know that. But I was scared,' she said, suddenly gulping with tears. 'I was so fucking scared. I just wanted to leave this town. I'm sorry.'

Peg put a hand on her shoulder. Then she drew her in. Alison collapsed into her and wept, tears running hard. 'I *hated* him,' she cried, through snot and tears. 'Hated them both. I hate them.'

Bev eventually moved over, too, and put a hand to Alison's head. 'Come on, lass,' she said, her voice deep and kind. 'It's all right now. It's all right. Nothing we can do.'

Alison turned to Shona. Her eyes blazed in the darkness. 'I want to know what he says,' she said. 'I want to know what that bastard says.'

30

Gauzy shadows flowed down the bedroom wall like water. It was early, and Shona had slept badly. She wanted to get going.

'Here, Reculver,' Shona said, the phone clamped to her ear.

A rumbling voice emanated from what sounded like a deep pit. 'Is that how you greet me these days, Shona – hailing me like a dog?' Detective Inspector Reculver said.

'Sorry, I'm in a rush. I need your help with something.'

'It's the crack of dawn! Help in return for what?' he said. He sounded like he was outside.

'Where the hell are you?' she said.

'I'm in London for the birthday of my sister's son.'

'Wait, you have a sister? And a nephew?'

'Shona, why do you sound permanently surprised? It's the Glasgow accent, isn't it? Yes, my beautiful sister, who, rather aptly, has a beautiful son. I'm with them. I am sure you are astounded. What do you need?'

She slumped on her bed. She could hear raised voices in the kitchen below. Ashley's voice was loud. There was the crash of a pan on the Aga. The dog started barking.

'I'm interviewing Gary Watson, the MP, today,' she said.

'Wait,' he said quietly. She could hear movement, a door closing. 'Right, that's better,' he said brusquely. 'Ah, well, good luck with that. I hear there's some noise about him, some trembling on the wires. And I hear he has a temper when pressed. But he is the Coming Man. Nothing but good press about him at the moment, I see. From certain quarters.'

'A temper?'

'I just said that. Yes, we hear he has a reputation for it in Westminster. Volcanic. But the Whips keep it all hush-hush, of course. You're asking him about the suicide?'

'How do you know these things?'

'Old friends, old ways and byways,' he intoned.

'We need to speak about your contacts in more depth one day. Look, have you ever heard of a senior policeman in the North of England called Harmire, John Harmire?'

Reculver laughed. It was a bright contrast to his speaking voice. It tinkled like breaking glass. 'Oh, my!'

'What?'

'Ah, the fragrant names of John Harmire, Bob Hilton and Sir Bernard Vane?'

'What are you on about?' she said, irritated now.

'Have you searched for him on the interweb, my favourite award-winning investigative journalist?'

'Not yet,' she conceded. 'I'd rather ask you–'

'You should. There'll be plenty of information, and I don't have the time right now. He was one of three force colleagues who were all rolled up like dirty carpets in the early noughties. Big corruption case in the North, all kinds of mess and murk. Lots of pay-offs between businesses and cops. They got "got", though. Not sure we got all of them, but they were the big names. I assume you don't know what I'm on about?'

'No. Haven't a clue. Never heard of any of it. Man, I wish I'd known this last night.'

'Why so?'

'Ach, never mind . . . Oh, fuck.' She realised she didn't have Alison's number. 'This Harmire, he was the father of a woman here, Alison, who was connected to a disappearance years ago. He led the investigation, but it went nowhere.'

'If he was involved, I would be instantly suspicious, to be honest,' he said. 'Nothing worse than a dirty copper. And he was filthy, especially where money was concerned.'

'There's plenty of things worse,' she said.

Reculver seemed to huff, then sigh. 'Look, I can hear you're in a fankle. Let us reconvene next week – the Café Royal, Monday? I can walk you through it all.'

'Fine. But not the Café Royal. We're always there. How about the Canny Man's?'

'Fine. And good luck with Watson.'

'Harmire,' she said, 'is he still around?'

'Oh, no – died in prison. Best place for him: the cleansing flames of purgatory,' he said cheerfully. 'Better go! The wee man calls. Toodle-oo!'

Shona stared at her phone. She rang Terry.

'Ay up,' the photographer answered quickly. 'I'm on my way. I'll be early. What's up?'

'Remember those old photos of the sixth-form class and the stories about Andrew Banks in the local paper? Can you go in and take some photos of them from the hard copy? I'll need them for the piece. Let me give you the dates.'

'What, this morning? Sure. Wait a minute . . . let me write this down. I'll need to pull over.'

'Do you know this Mickle guy? The editor.'

'A bit, aye,' Terry said. 'Enough to let me in early. Not sure the place will be open at this time of the day. Right, give me the details: fire away.'

Shona gave her the date of the paper she needed – October 1991 – and hung up.

'For fuck's sake. So, there was nothing there?' Shona rapped her stick against the dashboard. 'How come?'

Trees moved by the window as if on casters. Terry was driving, and Shona was making a call. They were driving to the Great Fosse. The launch of Gary Watson's electoral campaign was at 11 a.m. at the hotel near the falls, and they were finally on their way. The clear sun cut sharp shadows on the road and fields. Light and dark had been divided. Terry was dressed all in green – a multi-pocketed heavy jacket, a T-shirt with a glittering moon on it and khaki trousers. She looked like she was about to leap into combat.

Terry had just told Shona some inconvenient news: when she got to the *Tyrdale Times* office, the copy they wanted was not there. It was 'no longer in the archive'. It had been removed.

'Did you ask–'

'Yes. I asked that dim bulb, Angela, to look for it, but she said there was no record of it. Then she said, "There were a wee woman here the other day asking for the same paper, and it wasn't there, either." And it's not on their digitised record. That only goes to–'

Shona looked fiercely at Terry. 'To 1999, I know. And that "wee woman" was me, and I did see it! Fuck's sake. It had the picture of the class. She said she would photocopy it for me.'

'Did you take a–'

'No, I never took a picture with my phone,' Shona snapped. 'Because I'm a numpty.'

'Well,' Terry said, after blowing out a hard breath, 'that's shady as fuck. Mickle is up to something, I reckon.'

'Was he there?'

'Nah, I asked. He was heading up to the hotel for the launch.'

'I bet he is. Shady as all fuck.' Shona nodded, slowly relenting from her anger. They drove deeper into the valley, leaving Ullathorne behind.

'Look, I do have something for you,' Terry said, glancing at her passenger.

Shona grunted.

'I've found out something quite interesting,' Terry said.

Shona wasn't listening. She was phoning Watson's election agent. The phone rang for a while and went to the answering service – again. She swore.

'I said, I've found something out,' Terry said.

'Congrats – put it in an email,' Shona said, redialling Knott.

They passed the sign to the Coine Tree. Shona's eyes flicked to it as the car barrelled up the dale.

'You're really quite obnoxious,' Terry said, shaking her head.

Shona angrily slapped the phone down on her thigh.

'Why are you like this?' Terry said, half-smiling. 'Have you ever considered therapy?'

'I don't need to be fucking audited like a spreadsheet, no. Tell me, then: what is this thing you've found out?' she said. She glanced at Terry, who was gripping the steering wheel tightly for a change.

'Right! Well. That old guy, Old John–'

'Dan's smelly old friend.'

'Where we found the camera. Which, like your character, is probably still rather undeveloped.'

Shona suddenly smiled. Her irritation began to drain away. 'Nice. Yes, it's still in my bag. What about it?'

'That auld guy is Dan's dad. Old John is Dan's father,' Terry said, looking across to Shona.

'Pull over,' Shona said.

'You what?'

'Pull over. I can't think in a moving car.'

Terry slowed down and parked on a grassy verge. They were near a village, which was half hidden in the trees. The square tower of an old church rose from the tangled high branches.

Shona turned to Terry, who was suppressing a grin. 'How the fuck do you know that? I thought he was dead.'

'Nope, not dead. We maybe assumed that. He's just mad and old. He left Dan's mother many moons ago – they divorced. John is his dad.'

'So, that's why Dan took the caravan up there,' Shona said. 'To be near his father. They weren't friends, they were father and son. How did you find out?'

'Well, I know this guy up the dale,' Terry said, looking out the window.

'I'm shocked,' Shona said.

'It's a long story,' Terry continued. 'But I was looking through the pictures of Marton's Farm, and I kind of remembered I had been up there before. It's the back of beyond, you know that. But if you keep going on that road over the fell, you come to some farmed forest – conifers – and there's a mad place, a lonely old pub. I know a guy there. I rang him up the other night after our campfire–'

'I'm amazed you were capable – and that he answered.'

'I asked him about the caravan fire, and he said he thought it was an insurance job. He didn't understand why he didn't just move in with Old John because that was his dad. He said Old John would cycle to the pub in all weathers, come in with a book and sit by the fire. He'd talk about his son, how proud he was of him. Said he was coming to live with him soon, in a spare room. My pal didn't think anything of it. He thought Old John was a bit cracked.'

'Shit!'

'What's up?'

The voice on the phone. The message she received, in the pub the night before: it had been Daniel's father. Hailing her from the howling moor.

'Old John left a message for me on my phone,' Shona said. 'It must have been him. He said someone had left a lot of money to the banks.'

'Maybe he meant Daniel had given money to the Bankses – the family. Andrew Banks.'

'I'm a fucking idiot,' she said.

'You have your moments.'

'Eighty thousand pounds,' Shona said. 'Eighty grand was put in Viv's bank account. From selling his house.'

'Quite a lot of cash.'

'A settling of debts, that's what the old man said.'

Terry nodded and shrugged.

'Who knows what he was thinking?'

Shona looked into the trees beside the road. It seemed as if they were holding something that she should know, that they had seen things they could not tell.

'So, where had John been? Why did people think he was away – or dead?' she said eventually.

'He'd been a teacher – a master – at the big private school in Ullathorne. But he took early retirement, apparently. Wanted to quit the dale. Did a lot of travelling. Collected books. Then came back six years ago and bought that tumbledown place on top of the moor.'

'Definitely his dad?'

'I checked the electoral roll. John Kinninvie Merrygill, The Grove, Marton's Moor.'

'You looked on the roll? Was it a double-barrelled name?'

'I don't think so. Kinninvie's a village near Barnard Castle, down the road. But it looks like it's his middle name.'

'He wrote some weird books about rocks and stones under the name of John Kinninvie. Occult stuff – which makes sense.'

'Oh, aye?'

Shona's phone suddenly buzzed. An unknown number. 'Shona Sandison,' she answered.

'Knott. You called?' a voice said.

'Oh, Mr Knott, how good of you to call back.' Shona put on her friendliest voice.

Terry smirked and lit a menthol cigarette and rolled down the window.

Shona explained she was the North of England stringer for a news agency, and she wanted to use the opportunity of Gary Watson's campaign launch to ask a few questions and write a profile. She said she was already in the dale and would only need twenty minutes.

'He's got about ten minutes,' Knott said thickly. 'I've not heard of your agency, but our people can check that out. Mr Watson is being interviewed at length by a local journalist. Maybe we can squeeze you in after that. He needs to get away to Bishop Auckland for a party event. You got a snapper?'

'Yes, I'm with a photographer, Terry Green.'

'Never heard of him, either. But come to the launch, make yourself known. I'll have to contact our special advisers in London, though – they might have you on our no-fly list.'

'Are you his election agent, Mr Knott?'

'Something like that.'

'I look forward to seeing you at the hotel,' Shona said and closed the call.

They drove on, further into the hills.

The sun flashed through the trees and spread bars of light and dark from the serried gate posts and fences onto the road. There were countless tiny caves in the mossy drystone walls. Shona looked up. A ragged sickle of high birds straggled across the cold sky. They passed Bev's house in Thorsgill and began to climb through emptier fields, knotty with thistle and nettle, the high ground shaking with ferns.

'Not far now,' Terry said. The road climbed. The trees about them huddled and gathered, and suddenly they were in forest. Old forest, deciduous and dark, with split rocks gaping amidst the towering trunks.

Terry pressed a button, and Shona's window slid down. The air was cold as it flooded the car. The hum that threaded the air became a churning roar.

Shona could see a cataract. Beyond the line of trees, a huge volume of water was tipping in smooth and massive velocity over a sudden ledge of hard rock, into a hidden bowl of crashing white fury below. The old river, severed by the cliff.

'That's the Great Fosse,' Terry said, 'and this is the venue.'

On the side of the road was a large, whitewashed hotel, its forecourt thick with cars. A broadcast van was outside, its satellite dish pointing to the sky. Above an open double door was the sign: THE FOSSE AND RAINBOW HOTEL AND BAR.

They parked and got out. People were gathering. Old dale men in old suits, young men with Gary Watson haircuts in tight-fitting new suits, middle-aged women with blood-red lipstick and neat bobs and farming gentry in tweed were leaving their Range Rovers and 4x4s, chit-chatting, smiling, filing into the hotel. Some had flyers in their hands, with WATSON WINS written in black over an image of Gary Watson against the backdrop of a rippling Union Jack.

Terry shouldered her heavy photographic kit and smiled briefly at Shona, who was adjusting her satchel and holding her stick tightly.

'Howay then, lass,' she said softly.

'Could be the big one,' Shona said.

There was a press of bodies in the lobby. Men with pink necks in blue suits, young party staffers, a large woman in pink with a huge floppy hat. Rows of posters had been neatly pinned to the walls. Two roll-up banners on either side of the entrance to the function suite showed a life-size image of Watson, thumbs up, smiling. There was a murmuring buzz, a fizzing wattage of excitement.

Shona looked around the room. By the doorway, a man with a buzz cut and a black suit was checking off invitees' names. There were paintings of the Great Fosse on walls and on leaflets in piles on the reception desk. Music began to play in the function suite – an orchestral version of 'Jerusalem'.

Terry was behind her. Shona had a notepad in her hand, a well-bitten plastic pen jammed into its rings, more as a sign of her occupation than as a symbol of intention. Her stick was held firmly in her other hand.

They reached the doorway. Shona could see a large wood-panelled conference room with high stone windows, with chairs set out in rows in front of a stage concealed by curtains.

The audience were sitting down, either staring at their phones or leaning over seats talking to each other. Everyone seemed to know each other. There were no strangers. A camera had been set up at the back of the hall.

At the door, the shaven-headed man asked for her name. She gave it, with a smile, and waved her notebook.

'Oh, aye,' he said. 'Mr Knott mentioned. Stand at the back, don't ask any questions during the event, and we'll grab you after. There's a room upstairs: you'll get ten minutes.'

'Thank you ever so much,' she said, smiling.

'And you, flossy,' he said to Terry, 'no pictures in there. You can get a portrait after, upstairs. None in the room.'

'Thanks, mate,' Terry said, following Shona into the hall.

They leaned against the back wall as the room filled. Shona looked at them. There was an air of anticipation. There were short grins and raised eyebrows. From another door two uniformed policemen entered and stood against the wall near the stage. One of them removed his hat and held it over his chest, as if he was at a ceremony.

The lights flashed and then dimmed, and the audience cooed and writhed like a tickled baby.

'Here we go,' Terry whispered.

Martial brass music strode from loudspeakers.

'Give me strength,' Shona muttered as a middle-aged man in a blue suit jogged up the steps onto the stage, whose curtains were now slowly opening, revealing a red podium and a row of Union Jacks. The man – trim, toned – waved, and the audience cheered. One bald man stood up and began a solo ovation. One of the policemen was clapping.

Gary Watson MP walked not to the podium, but to the side of the stage. He stood there, unmoving. The music came to a ringing crescendo, and a video began to play on the screen. The bald man sat down as a hush fell over the audience.

The video was a dream of green and blue. It showed Tyrdale, beautiful, shimmering under a summer sun. It looked like Eden, luminous trees beside the wide blue river. Beside it, in jeans and a gilet, strode Gary Watson, arm in arm with a severe-looking blonde woman. The voice of a Northern man, not Watson, was talking about heritage, history, community, enterprise, culture, a profound love of tradition. Shona was overwhelmed by the colours of it, the volume, the swelling orchestral music.

'Values, deep values, forged in centuries and renewed in a new promise and a reforged vow,' the voice rolled on. 'Heritage, tradition and the old ways made anew for a cleaner future.'

The video showed the land from high above – the hills, the deep cleft of the valley, the distant blue mountains, the spread of fields, the town with its ruined castle and the bend in the old river. The camera moved higher until the dale was a crease in the wider land, and then vanished beneath shreds of cloud, the sun shattering on sea and mountain, and then the view moved into orbit, and the blue world rotated beneath a rising sun.

'Watson: for honour, for history,' the voice continued, confident in its resounding depth, its polished grain, its relentless earnest fervour.

'Watson: for the right path, for that quiet, confident voice of the Pennines that says a loud and resounding yes to now, as much as to then, and tomorrow. Watson: for Tyrdale – and Britain. Watson Wins!'

The film ended. Watson moved to the podium, his hands in the air, as the audience rose to their feet, clapping.

'For fuck's sake,' Shona said.

'Is he running for Lord of the Universe?' Terry whispered.

Shona smiled and whispered back: 'Was that a wife?'

'I thought he was single.' Terry shrugged. 'Widowed. Maybe that's just an actress.'

Watson began to speak. Compared to the video, he was diminished. His voice was surprisingly flat, unimpressive.

As he spoke – a brief thanks to his staff, to the party, to the prime minister, to the hotel, to the 'ceaseless power of the Great Fosse' – Watson recited a series of boilerplate lines from his party's hymnbook of phrases.

Shona began to take notes, squinting to see her notepad in the dim lighting. But after a minute or two of Watson's speech, she stopped. She fished out her phone, looked about her and turned on the Dictaphone.

As Watson spoke, the audience seemed transfixed. But Shona sensed a change, somewhere nearby. She and Terry looked back at the entrance. The man with the buzz cut had his back to the room. He was half in the hall and half out, leaning into something.

There was a shout. People in the audience turned their heads. The shout cut through the air – ending the speech, ripping open the suspension and belief. It was a naked human shout. An old man's yell.

Shona froze. There was a sudden burst of movement. A pile of clothes fell into the room. There was a loud slap of human flesh on wood. There was grunting and gasping. The man with the buzz cut was on his side on the floor, his legs in the air, the pile atop him. The pile of clothes re-formed into an old, wild, yelling man. The audience began to shout, and some stood up. The hatless policeman stood on his toes, trying to see over the crowd.

The old man stood up. He had a shock of white hair and a beard. He was shaking, glaring at the stage. From his tattered overcoat, Old John pulled out something long and bulky.

'No!' someone yelled.

But it was a roll of paper.

'Now, now,' Watson hummed into his podium microphone, flushing. 'Who let the in-laws in, eh?' He ran a hand over his face.

There was some scattered laughter. The buzz-cut man rose to his knees. He seemed to be in pain.

'This is not a hustings, sir! We can debate my policies another time!' Watson said, to more laughter.

Old John unfurled the roll – it was a poster or a scroll. On it were phrases, written in large black letters.

'Sorley is here,' the old man shouted. 'Sorley is here!'

Shona could see the phrases on the scroll.

> THERE IS NO TIME
> TAKE THE RIGHT PATH
> SAY YES TO NO
> ODE ADA HEAD O
> 045 141 8514 0

Suddenly the hatless policeman was upon Old John. They tussled violently as the room murmured like a sea. The old man was swiftly overwhelmed and dragged to the door. His scroll dropped to the ground and rolled under a chair, snapping back into a tube. The room seemed to be frozen. Shona could hear Watson breathing heavily into the microphone on the stage. There were desperate gasps and strangled coughs from the huckled man. Another besuited man appeared, moving swiftly, grabbing the man's flailing legs, as the policeman gripped a fat arm across Old John's neck.

Terry was taking photographs, on the floor, on one knee.

The rapid click of her camera seemed to fill the room.

'You will be in the stones! You are heading to the rocks and stones!' Old John shouted as he was dragged outside. 'Sorley is here. You are all rocks and stones!'

Shona mumbled an 'excuse me' to a prim woman and grabbed the scroll, which was lying under her seat.

Watson whistled into the microphone and looked around the room. 'Available for birthdays, weddings, christenings up and down the dale – the wizard Merlin!'

The crowd burst into laughter. Watson's grin opened like a slashed sirloin.

Shona left the hall, and Terry followed. They were in the reception again, but there was no one around. No one was behind the desk. No police. No Old John.

Terry slid past her and stepped outside. 'They've gone,' she said on her return. 'They've probably gone to kick the shit out of him somewhere.'

'Tip him off the falls,' Shona murmured. 'Jesus.' She was looking at Old John's scroll, spreading it out on the reception desk. The paper smelled of damp and mildew. The smeared black words were written in charcoal or ash.

She looked at the numbers, which were linked to ODEADAHEADO by, she could see up close, tiny lines. O was a zero. The other numbers followed the letters' place in the alphabet.

'What does it say?' Terry said.

'Hang on,' Shona said. She tapped the numbers into her phone. She rang it. It went straight to a voicemail, beeping, anonymous. It closed and disconnected. Terry said something, but Shona shushed her and called Reculver. It went straight to his laconic voicemail. She pressed another number stored on her phone: Hector Stricken. She knew he'd answer.

Inside the meeting hall, Watson's voice was rising, and the audience were murmuring, laughing, clapping.

Stricken answered his phone.

Terry had moved to the double doors to peer into the hall. She glanced back at Shona and tapped her watch – the speech was winding up.

'Shona? What the hell–'

'Shut up – I need your help quick. What's an 0451 number?'

'Phone number? Where are you?'

'Yes, phone number. Do you know? 0451.'

'I think it's the number for MPs – I have a few in my book. Let me check.'

'I need it now,' she said.

'Keep your hair on. Yeah, it's the mobile code for the special phones the MPs get when they get into government. Why?'

'Nothing. Thanks, Hector.'

'Shona, I need to tell you–'

'Ta. Bye.' She hung up.

The hall was emptying now, the audience filing out, pink-faced and loud, jostling through the reception to the lounge bar, whose doors were opened by uniformed staff.

Shona's elbow was touched by someone, and she turned around to see a thickset man with pale grey eyes. He made a hooking shape with a finger at Terry, and she sloped over.

Shona recognised him. She had seen him buying chips in the town.

'I'm Knott,' he said. His mouth, a straight line of pink. No lips, like a shell.

'Knott what?' Terry said, with a smile.

'Hilarious. I thought you were a bloke,' he said to her, looking her up and down.

'Common mistake,' she said.

'Oh, I very much doubt it, love.'

He then explained that Mr Watson had ten minutes in his diary and the interview would be embargoed until the following week.

'Embargoed?' Shona said.

'Yes – strict embargo. Midnight next Monday: we have announcements planned every day for the next six weeks. This cannot cut across.'

Shona nodded, and they moved up the stairs. Terry's camera clunked against her bag, Shona's stick rapped on the wood, before their feet sank into thick carpet, and the hubbub of the party below receded. Soon, beyond stone walls and down a long silent corridor, they fell into a hush of quiet. Closed hotel doors paced past them.

All this began in a hotel, Shona thought. It will end in one. Transitory. Clean. Liminal.

'Sit here and wait,' Knott said, pointing to two padded chairs.

'Bit of a commotion, that, wasn't it?' Terry said to him.

He said nothing and stumped away.

Shona wrote down some questions on her pad. Terry checked her photos.

After some time, Knott came back, asking them to follow him, and they all moved deeper into the hotel.

A small man with red hair came towards them, padding on the carpet like a burglar. He had an ill-matched suit, trainers and a leather satchel.

'Mr Mickle, as I live and breathe,' Knott said in an approximation of warmth.

'All done, thanks very much,' Colin Mickle said. He glanced at Shona quickly and nodded.

'Thanks, Colin. See you at the do in Bishop,' Knott said.

'I'll be there,' Mickle said, suddenly noticing Terry and quickening his step. Terry glared at him, her face suddenly as mean as a hawk, but they walked on.

Knott reached a room at the end of the corridor and knocked lightly. He tilted his head gently and then opened the door.

'Ladies,' he said, ushering them in.

It was a large suite, filled with light, with large square

windows on two sides. Shona put her hand to her eyes. Through the windows she saw a tumbling hillside studded with boulders, a thin fringe of tall conifers and then, beyond the pines, the tumult of the Great Fosse. A white wall of water breaking from the wide river into a haze of mist below. Behind the falls, the moor top and the bare horizon. Shona looked at the falls, their constant tumult and stasis. They were silent beyond the glass.

It was only with the sound of a clearing throat that she saw, on the sofa, Gary Watson. He had removed his suit jacket and tie and rolled up his shirtsleeves. A tumbler of iced clear liquid sat on the table. He smiled and stood up, clapping his hands. His arms were hairless, as if waxed.

He looked to Knott.

'So, Bax, what do we have here? Another interview? I've given all my best lines to little Colin there.'

Knott looked momentarily confused and then went on. 'This is Sandy Shonason from a . . . news agency and Terry, her photographer. They have ten minutes with you, Mr Watson.'

Shona said hello. Terry sat in the corner, her camera on her lap. She said she would take a couple of portraits after the interview.

'I'll just be here, Mr Watson. I'll keep an eye on the time, and, just to let you know, Alyce is waiting downstairs,' Knott said in a low voice.

Watson turned his head. 'Alyce? Downstairs?'

'In the lobby.'

'Is Bax around?'

'No.'

Watson blinked rapidly for a moment.

Shona sat down and put her phone, its Dictaphone application ready, on the table. She felt her stomach turn over. She leaned her stick on the table.

'How do,' Watson said, turning to Shona, composed again. 'That was a good show downstairs, wasn't it? Did you enjoy it?

Colin said he'd never seen anything like it.'

He looked to Terry, checking her camera, and clapped his hands together.

'Lovely! A threesome, is it?' he said and laughed a short, dry laugh. 'I'd rather start with the blonde over there. This one looks like hard work.'

Terry was impassive, Knott as still as a dolmen.

Shona carried on.

'Nice to meet you, Mr Watson, and thanks for your time. So, the start of your re-election campaign . . .' She pulled her pen from the rings of the notepad.

'Day one,' Watson said. 'And onwards to victory.'

'Did you know that old man who interrupted you?'

'No.' He shook his head and pursed his lips. 'But there's always a headbanger or two around. Mentally defective. It didn't really mean anything. I thought it was funny. Hopefully, the police have taken care of him. As I said to Colin, hopefully they've given the silly old coot a quick bath. That's what I would have done.'

'He said something about someone called Sorley – do you know who that is?'

Nothing in his eyes moved. Then he smiled. 'Sorley? Surely you're mistaken! No, didn't hear what he said. Anyway, fire away, my good man here says we have ten minutes. Don't waste it.'

He took a bottle of water from the table and twisted off its cap. His suit was blue-grey, well-cut. Bespoke.

He pointed at Shona. 'What kind of reporter are you? I'm not familiar with your byline.'

'Crime, mainly,' Shona said.

'You can't catch many criminals with that bad wheel, eh? Guess you don't chase them very far.'

Watson slumped back in the sofa. He took a swig of water.

Shona glanced at the window. The waterfall fell slowly,

silently into its constant destruction. 'I only write about criminals, Mr Watson. I leave catching them to others.'

'Quite so, quite so,' he said, making a winding motion with his hand. 'Let's get on with this, shall we?'

'I'm interested in your election plans,' she said. 'Do you think you're going to win here in Tyrdale again?'

Watson turned up his hands, his palms facing the ceiling. 'Well, one should never count the votes before they're cast, of course. That's basic common sense. But we as a team are very confident that we have the right path for this dale, this county – this country. Are you from Glasgow?'

'Yes, the Southside.'

'I was up in Scotland recently, you know. Beautiful – it should be called North Britain again, don't you think? Such a resonant phrase. I love both those words: north, Britain. Magnificent. It reeks of ancient splendour.'

Shona looked at her notebook. Terry checked her camera. Knott stood by the door, like a bouncer. Shona leaned forward.

'Tell me a little bit about growing up here, Mr Watson. You're unusual in being an MP actually from the area you represent.'

'It is unusual, Sheena, as you say. I am a rare breed. It's a shame, isn't it, that the root and the blood and the soil of the constituency are not reflected in their MPs any more? It's like accents. Everyone has the same accents these days, don't they? It's all much of a muchness. On the telly, on the radio. In the streets of the south. It's the influence of America, of hip-hop, of TV comedies. Don't watch them myself. But I'm a proud Northerner. I've never hidden my accent. It's authentic, and, forgive my French, I think it's a no-bullshit accent. Anglo-Saxon. But, yes, to answer your question in the spirit it was intended: yes, I grew up here – I am Tyrdale born and bred. That's me. Very proud of the area and the stock of the people who live here. It's all about good, hard common sense around here. I was lucky enough to be educated here, and my father had a bob or two – good for him – so I didn't want for anything, and I think that made me really appreciate hard graft, the dignity of the shift and the value of money. Nowt wrong with that.'

'And you went to Ullathorne Comprehensive?'

'I did, that. Grand school – I'm on the board of governors now. Very proud to have guided it towards independent status and back to being a proper grammar school. The problem with what they called comprehensive education was it was trying to be *too* comprehensive, and that's not actually a meaningful education, is it, Sheena? Why did I, as a young man, have to learn home economics? Waste of time. But, yes, great school, all that being said.'

Shona clicked her pen, tapped it on her notebook. The phone carried on recording, silently. 'In the sixth form, you lived through a bit of a tragic time.'

Watson frowned. He drank some more water. 'Tragic? I had a lot of fun and got four As at A-level. What's tragic about that? I don't follow.'

'You were in a very small sixth form, and you were friends with Andrew Banks. He went missing. He's never been found. That must have been a tough time.'

His face was blank, but his voice became reedy and thin, as it had in the meeting hall. 'That was many years ago,' he said. 'And what a shame that was. But you know, Sharon, I didn't really know Andrew. I didn't really go around with that crowd – he was more into books and theatre and poetry and all that. I was more into the sports side of things. Cricket team, the football. But, of course, it was a big story at the time, and I have nothing but sorrow for his poor family. I do know the police did a thorough job looking for him. Combed the valley. A terrible thing, but we all moved on. I didn't lose a friend.'

'You didn't know him? There were only a few of you in that sixth form. And you were with him the night he died.'

Watson put the cap back on the bottle of water and screwed it tight. His eyes flicked to Knott, who was standing by the door.

Shona looked around briefly. Knott's pale eyes were fixed on Watson. Terry was standing now, looking out of the window at the waterfall. Spots of rain were gathering on the sheets of glass.

'Andrew was into football, wasn't he? He loved Newcastle United,' Shona said.

Watson shrugged and crossed his legs. His trousers rode up his leg – his skin was smooth, hairless. He spoke quickly. 'Aye, maybe so. Well, like I said, I knew of him. But we weren't friends. As I say, a tragic thing. Feel very sorry for his family. And you say the night he *died* – we don't know he died.'

'You were one of the last to see him – Alison told me.'

'Alison?' His eyes were screwed up now. Arms crossed, legs crossed.

'Alison Harmire, your sixth-form classmate. Part of your gang back then.'

'This is all a long time ago. Ancient history. Before her dad passed. Look, if this is all you're going to ask me about, I'm afraid I don't have much to say. I'm here to talk about my campaign and the election. My future – not the past.'

Knott was beside Shona now. He tapped the back of her chair. 'Time's up, love,' he said. His voice was all edges.

Watson held up a hand. 'No, man, no – it's fine. I'm entertained. I want to see where this is going, with this little crippled hotshot reporter. Next question?'

Shona smiled. Knott walked away. He moved to the window, beside Terry, who was looking through her camera at the waterfall.

'Your wife's death, that must have been hard for you,' she said.

'It was, it was. But I've spoken about that before, too. It's all in the public domain. I don't think I have anything more to say on that. Sarah was driving on the wrong side of the road, for some reason. Straight into a truck. But that's all ancient history.'

Shona made marks in her notebook. She looked up. 'Would you say that you're to the right of the party?'

'People say I am. All I know is that I am always right! Little joke there. Look, I think the road we're on, it's taking the right path. I am fully supportive of the prime minister and his mission to bring back civilisation to this country.'

'So, you'd say you've taken the right path.'

'Oh, yes. And I think the results of this general election will prove it. An empire of opportunity lies ahead of us if we have the gumption to seize it.'

Shona moved on swiftly. 'Another one of your other school friends, Robert Stang, was found dead yesterday. Did you know that?'

Watson's face and body momentarily froze, as if he had been paused on a screen by a higher hand. He then un-paused. He carried on. 'That's news to me. Oh, now that is a shame. I remember Bobby. Great soldier, great veteran – great man. I believe he worked in one of our factories. I think the issue of PTSD really needs to be looked at. In fact, if I have any influence in the new parliament–'

'No, he was found stabbed to death, in Deepdale. That's what the police are saying. I have a press release here if you'd like to see it.'

He blinked repeatedly, but his voice rolled on smoothly, like a teleprompter. 'Well, that is terrible. Youth crime – that's another thing. In our cities–'

'And last week, another school friend of yours, Daniel Merrygill, killed himself.'

His face was a slab of flesh, his mouth agape.

'I didn't know that. Again, a shame. But that's all I can say. I need to go, I'm afraid. That's me done. I have about two minutes.'

Knott cut in: 'One minute.'

Watson reached for his suit jacket, which slithered into his hand.

Shona looked down at her pad. 'I was wondering why, Mr Watson – and my colleagues have looked this up – you keep repeating the same phrases in your interviews, in your opinion pieces for the papers, live and recorded on TV and radio?'

Watson pulled a silk tie from the inside pocket of his jacket. 'Oh, aye? What phrases are they, love? "Vote for me"? I guess that might scare the likes of you.'

She tapped her notebook, as if they were written there. But she knew them by heart. '"Take the Right Path", "There Is No Time" and "Say Yes to No".'

Not a flicker on his face.

'Just turns of phrase, Sheena. Have you heard this, Knott? Have you heard this nonsense?'

'Shona,' she said, 'my name's Shona.'

'Whatever, love.'

He stood up, pulled on his jacket and sat down again, on the arm of the sofa. He was higher than her now, looking down at her. He shot his cuffs.

'Why do you use those phrases?' she asked, staring up at him. 'Over and over?'

'We've strayed off the beaten track here, Shona, have we not? I was more than happy to talk about our independent economy, about the safety of our borders, about–'

'No, Mr Watson. I want to talk about the Ouija board sessions you and Alison, you and Beverley, you and Bobby and Andrew Banks took part in as teenagers.'

He closed his eyes. His put his hands up. 'Okay, okay. That's enough. Game's a bogie. No more of this.' He stood and swiftly moved to the door.

Knott looked towards her. Terry, ignored by the men, took photos from waist height, clicking quietly.

'Time for you two to go,' Knott said.

Watson brushed out imaginary creases from his shirt and looked at his large silver watch.

'Yeah, get the poisoned dwarf and the dolly bird out of here.'

Shona gripped her stick.

'Mr Watson, I just want to ask–'

'There's no more time for that, love. You shot your bolt,' Watson said.

Knott came closer to Shona, his hands up.

'Don't touch her, you prick,' Terry said suddenly, angrily.

Knott stopped abruptly, as if shot.

Shona stood up and moved away from the table, away from Knott. She cleared her throat and addressed Watson directly: 'You were the last person to see Andrew Banks alive, weren't you?'

Watson looked to the door. 'This is ridiculous, just ridiculous.' He shot a furious look at Knott. 'Where's Bax? Where is he?'

Shona carried on: 'Alison and Beverley, I've interviewed them. I would appreciate a comment from you.'

'You do that, love – you do that. See who gives a fuck,' Watson said. He laughed.

The door opened suddenly. A tall woman stood there, dressed in a dark blue trouser suit. Her face was a mask of sheer planes. Her eyes were dark. Her hair, scraped back hard into a ponytail, was blonde.

'Alyce?' Watson said, surprised.

'Hello, everyone,' the woman said in a deep velvet voice. 'Hello, Gary.'

'Alyce,' Knott said.

Watson smiled at her. His eyes glistened. He turned back to Shona. 'You going to write about Daniel?' he spat. 'You do that. Hadn't seen him in decades. Always a bit weak, he was. A soft lad, if I remember. I'd forgotten him until now.'

Alyce nodded at Shona and Knott. 'Is this an interview?' she said.

'It's all right, Alyce – it's over,' Watson said.

Knott grunted an assent.

'I was at the wedding,' Shona carried on.

'What wedding?' Knott said.

'On his body, on Daniel's body, was this number,' Shona said, pressing a saved number on her phone: *Odeadaheado*.

A moment later, a buzz fizzed in Watson's jacket.

'That's your number, isn't it? Why would Daniel Merrygill have that? Did he get it from the Ouija boards?' she said, doubt in her mind but not in her voice. 'Somehow?'

'I don't know what the fuck you're on about.' Watson shook his head. 'How have you got my phone number? That's a security matter, you know. Knott?'

Shona took out a folded piece of A4 paper from inside her jacket and held it out.

Watson was standing stiffly now, his back against the wall. Alyce was staring at him. Knott stood, impassive.

'This is a photo of an old Newcastle United shirt found in Deepdale woods,' she said. 'Just last week.'

'Whose is that?' Alyce said.

Watson leaned forward to stare at the picture.

Shona raised her voice. 'This is Andrew's shirt, isn't it? He wore it the night he died – the night you were with him, in the woods, taking drugs in Deepdale? 1992?'

Knott ripped the picture from her hand. 'Fucking give me that, you silly bitch,' he grunted.

Shona flinched at his force. Terry jolted forward, her jaw clenched, her eyes flashing.

'It's fine,' Shona said to her quickly.

Watson gestured to Alyce, who was leaning, languid, against the doorframe. 'I'm out of this pantomime,' he said. 'Alyce? Knott?'

Alyce smiled at Shona and nodded at Terry. Knott grunted and threw the screwed-up picture to the floor. The three moved to the door, and Knott and Alyce left quickly, vanishing into the corridor beyond.

Shona looked to Terry, who was wide-eyed.

Then, suddenly, her eyeline tipped, and a pinching pain stung her. Something hard and forceful had grabbed Shona. It was Watson. He was suddenly there, grasping the collar of her shirt, twisting. She dropped her stick. His lips were moving. She could smell his sweet cologne. It barely masked the seeping sweat of his body and something else, something chemical and noxious.

'Write one word about all this, and you'll never write another,' he hissed. 'I can find you, wherever and whatever you are, bitch. I'll fucking fuck you to death.'

His fingers were around her throat.

From somewhere hidden, somewhere deep and hard, she found the strength to respond. 'Fuck *you*,' Shona said, pushing her voice past his hand. 'I'll write what I fucking want. You can't stop me.'

Terry took photographs of the two. The flash snapped like lightning.

Watson's fingers loosened.

Knott was now at the door, eyes wide, mouth open. Watson let Shona go with a sudden violent shrug. She rocked backwards and fell.

'Right enough,' he said. He wiped his face.

Shona slumped on the soft carpeted floor, her heart pounding.

'Right enough,' Watson repeated quietly. He turned on his polished heels and strode out of the room. Knott, eyes closed, shut the door behind him.

Terry was beside her. She put a hand on Shona's shoulder and looked into her eyes. 'My God,' Terry said. Her eyes were wild. 'Oh, my fucking God.'

'Don't worry. I'm absolutely fine,' Shona said firmly. She reached for her phone, which she had dropped. It had been recording, unnoticed.

'Got it all on tape,' she said. 'Twat.'

'Got what?' Terry's eyes were bright with angry tears.

'Got the fucking story, didn't we?'

You will resign and withdraw tomorrow.
I have informed PM.

It was dark, but not silent. The waterfall thundered nearby, behind the trees, behind the wall of night.

That had been the message from Raymond. He'd read it, and it had disappeared.

Watson was alone. Knott had gone – after the interview debrief, he had resigned on the spot and returned to London. Alyce, shaking her head, not touching him or looking at him, had also resigned. And Bax had not yet come back. Not a word from him, not a sign of him. As if he had never existed.

The campaign event in Bishop Auckland had been cancelled. The diary had been cleared. Knott, before he had left, had told the campaign team to knock off and go home. The phone had not yet rung: the London press office had been informed of the incident, but the reporter had not yet called for comment. But she had enough to run a story. He had attacked her. In front of the photographer. That was enough. No need for reactive lines. No need for briefing. No use for balancing quotes. The police had not yet been in touch. But they would be, he knew. His father and John Harmire were no longer around to make things go away.

He was still in the hotel room. Bare-chested, wearing only his suit trousers.

'Fuck them,' he said out loud, to no one. He held in his hand a heavy square glass. Whisky filled it to the brim. 'Fuck it.'

He had lain on the bed, the empty glass on his chest. But it had not moved. He had called, he had pleaded, but it had not moved. Sorley had not come. He had taken a break, had a drink – had a few – and tried again. But it had not moved.

He had taken paper and written it all out, laid it down on the table, waiting, patiently, conventionally, for the glass to move. Nothing. Sorley had not come. Sorley was not there. Sorley, dead, was dead. The dead had died and only the living were left.

How had the reporter got his government number? He did not know. Sorley had asked for it once. But it wasn't from Sorley – that reporter wouldn't have known a thing about it. She must have found it another way.

The football shirt was another thing entirely.

He looked out to the woods. The Great Fosse thundering, somewhere, beyond. The road outside lit by the hotel light. A string of puddles glinted alongside the path to the falls. The endless darkness.

He reached inside his suit jacket for the plastic bag of cocaine. A toot of the white stuff. He tipped it out on the table and scraped it to and fro with his credit card. He looked at the tiny landscape of powder on the glass. Crumbs cast thin shadows.

Nothing to fuck tonight – apart from himself, he thought. He snorted it all up, then swallowed some pills.

His hands were shaking. They were dark, wet with his blood. Sliced finely by edges of the penknife. Slippery with strands of cum. His soaked jeans, covered in mud, splattered with blood. His necklace, ripped and broken, a string around his neck, beads scattered like tiny eyes in the muddy earth. In the dark woods. In the hot summer night.

No. He shook his head.

No. His hands were fine. His clothes were fine. That was not there. His hands were clean, pink, slightly swollen. A forty-nine-year-old's hands. Clean, almost. Clean, for years. Nothing on them. Nothing to see. Nothing was ever there.

His head was heavy now, swimming. Down by the path,

there was a shape. There was a distant figure. Was it Alyce? Tall, elegant, a white shirt with – was that a dark skirt or dark trousers? The woman was on her phone, her face turned away, partially lit. A ghost on the edge of the forest. He banged the window. She did not look up. He picked up his phone and called Knott – nothing. He called Bax – again, nothing. He called Alyce – it was engaged.

He pulled on a shirt, fastened a couple of buttons and left the hotel room, padding down the corridors. He recoiled from the cold as he left the lobby. He noticed his campaign posters were still up. They would be gone in the morning.

He walked uneasily across the car park in the frigid air. There, at the roadside, was the glow, which turned and moved into the woods, along the path to the falls.

He could hear the Great Fosse, the constant roar and boom of it. The path was dark but for the light from the mobile phone, like a blue candle.

He paused to look back at the hotel. He looked up, but the moon was obscured by cloud. The sky was empty; there were no stars. He looked back, once more, and then he plunged into the trees.

The light had gone, but the path was long and winding, doubling back on itself, climbing up and up as it moved towards the Great Fosse. The roar was louder now, as he moved along the path, using his phone as a light. Its torchlight flashed on bark, and board, on fencepost and into the blackened tangle of undergrowth. He peered along the path to where the woman could be, but he could not see her. It was cold. He shivered.

There was a rope-lined bridge over a sudden black crevasse, and he crossed it slowly. On reaching the other side, he stopped.

Maybe the woman had not been there at all. He had been drinking. He was wired and buzzing. He looked at his phone. He called Bax: there was nothing. Just a quick sequence of bleeps. Not even a voice message. The same for Knott.

'Cunts,' he said and spat.

He stood for a moment in the dark, out of sight of the waterfall, but hearing its thunder. The rocks around him were high and jagged. In the flickering light of his phone, they cast sharp shadows, coiled into odd shapes. He moved the beam about, and a rock became a face – a bearded man with coins on his eyes. He flashed it again – a building crowned with battlements, grinning mouths and blinded eyes multiplied and magnified in the sharp beam. A tongue, lolling from a fat mouth in a green face full of leaves and vines.

And in the dark beyond the precipice, he saw another shape – the shadowy bulk of a vast tree. It was monstrous, a giant. It was dark, even against the darkness. It rose to a height above the others, set back in its own glade, in an aura of lightless space. Its trunk was more than one body, it was multiform, its branches high and wide, tangled at their tips, and it had a rent in its side, like a tear in a curtain. Watson stared into it and saw nothing. The light from his phone could not reach it. The light within it was extinguished.

He knew the hollow tree, the great Coine Tree. But it was not here. It was deeper down the dale. It could not be here. Trees don't move. Hollow trees don't walk.

Then, in a blur of movement to the side of his eyes, there was a flicker. He saw, again, in the corner of his sight, a shimmer of light on the trees up ahead. A definite glow. A radius of light and movement, like someone walking with an open phone, a lantern, a candle.

'Hello?' he called out, although his voice melted into the noise of the falls.

He walked on, his feet slipping now on the wet boardwalk, and as he turned a corner, the volume of the waterfall increased suddenly.

There in the darkness was the Great Fosse, where the Tyr, fresh from the moors and emboldened by tributaries slicing down steep ravines, fell smooth-faced to a constant hammering demolition of foam and cloud.

He could see the viewing platform, a row of telescopes on metal posts and a steep path down to the edge of the rushing water.

There was no one here. He was alone. There was no Alyce. The spray from the falls settled on his hair and smooth face.

He sat down on a bench, and with water soaking into his clothes, he stared into the darkness until he saw a figure again, below on the narrow path. A face, pale, lit by the light of a mobile phone. In amongst the rocks, a billowing white shirt. It could be Alyce. But it could be a man.

Something in the bearing of the shoulders. Something in the limbs, the head. It seemed familiar.

'Alyce?' he called into the tumult. 'Bax?'

He moved as if in a dream now, as if frictionless, in one movement to the steep rock steps. He flashed his phone torch again, and its brightness slapped on the descending stair of wet rock. He could hear nothing now but the roar of the falls and the timpani roll of their violent resolution on the jagged rocks, far below.

'Bax? Knott?' he called again. 'Alyce?'

Down there, by the riverside, the light glowed. A definite glow. Iridescence. She was down there.

And if it wasn't her, it was someone. Someone was down there. Did someone call him? Was that a voice? The past, inside the present.

He moved to the tight line of stone steps and began his quick descent. It began to rain.

As he stumbled down the wet steps, his mind began to detonate with light.

33

Shona was waiting for the train north.

They had driven from Tyrdale to Darlington in silence. The rise out of the valley and onto the main road had been in faltering sun and a darkening sky. As they left, Shona had glanced back at the valley of the Tyr. She knew she would not see it again. Its silent beauty, its wordless perpetuity, stood, and would always stand, until there were no human eyes left to see it.

Terry had put some old disco music on, and Shona, after a time, had smiled. She didn't like it, but she didn't feel the need to complain any more. Shona had rung her father several times. She'd left messages. There was a tightening in her chest and around her heart.

Now they were in the cold echoing space of the Victorian station, suspended in waiting. They sat together in the grimly lit café, their cups empty. Terry was quietly skimming through the images of the events in Watson's hotel room.

Shona checked her phone again. Nothing.

'So,' Terry said, at last, 'I guess you'll be on your way.'

'Yep,' Shona said. She looked at Terry briefly and then up at the departures board high on the brick wall. A cool wind was blowing through the iron arches of the station. It was getting dark. An arm of dark clouds was moving slowly across the vast sky. She wondered what the clouds had seen on their journey over the land.

'You all right there?' Terry asked softly.

'Aye.' Shona nodded but put a hand to her throat. It was sore.

They had considered calling the police. But Shona wanted to hold off, for a time. She wanted the story to herself first – and Terry had the pictures. She wondered why Knott had not tried to seize the camera. She had seen that happen before. But Watson's entourage had just disappeared.

'I've had worse,' she said.

'Of course you have,' Terry said. 'But that was rough – are you sure you're all right?'

Shona nodded. She stared at the black square of her phone. She was exhausted.

'Right, well, I'm not one for emotional goodbyes,' Terry suddenly said and stood up.

Shona stood slowly, too. The darkening light cast a dusty drift of gloom over the photographer's fine features.

'Look, we'll talk about your pictures, the images, when I'm back, after I've written all this up,' Shona said. 'Ranald will want to see them. Package them up. Fuck knows how I'll piece all the words together.'

'You've got a hell of a story, you know that?'

'Yes, I have. I know that. I'm just not sure how to write it yet.'

'Just start at the end. Or the very beginning.'

'That's a very good place to start.' Shona nodded and smiled.

'You just need to begin with: why did Daniel Merrygill kill himself at the Scottish wedding, right?'

'I know. And we can only guess,' she said, as if pacing out the words she was soon going to type. 'But we know, now, he thought he was doing it for a reason. There was a method and a rationale. And it was, definitely, with no doubt, linked to the disappearance of Andrew Banks, all those years ago. He was pointing to it. In a strange and unusual way.'

'And his dad was strange.'

'His dad is a mad hermit who thinks when we die we go into the stones,' Shona agreed. 'Maybe Daniel believed him. We'll never know for sure – how could we? But we have enough. And we have enough to fuck Gary Watson, that's for sure.'

'Exactly. You've got it,' Terry said. 'You said you'd need to contact the police down here?'

'I'll have to. I'll go to the Durham police. I don't trust the Ullathorne lot. I have a contact in Police Scotland, who I know will be interested. Ranald will need it legalled. It'll be legalled to kingdom come. But I need to write it first.'

'Just start typing,' Terry said softly. 'It'll come. How many stories have you written? Thousands?'

Shona grinned, her stick loose in her hand. Terry's eyes glittered.

'Thank you, Theresa Green,' she said and moved towards Terry. Terry moved quicker, and they hugged. Terry smelled of light sweat and coffee. A faint perfume, and warmth.

They held each other for a while.

'I'm not quite sure what to say,' Shona said, resting her head on the photographer's shoulder.

'What cannot be said will be wept,' Terry said quietly.

Shona gave her a squeeze.

'Right,' Terry said, suddenly pulling back. 'Have a rest on the train. Don't get into any more fights. Hope your old man is all right – and let's talk next week about pictures.'

'That would be good,' Shona said, gripping her stick hard.

A train thundered through the station, its lights ablaze. It felt like a mountain was rolling through. Then it was gone. Shona looked closely at Terry's face as light moved across her cheeks and the soft glistening in her pale eyes.

'Do you still have pals in Edinburgh, from art school?' Shona said.

Terry blinked and tilted her head.

'Aye, a couple of reprobates. Wait, are you asking me if I ever visit Edinburgh?'

'I didn't, no,' Shona said. 'I asked . . .'

'You've got my number,' Terry said, grinning.

'I've got your number,' Shona said, looking down at her bag.

Her train arrived, pulling into the station with great noise and movement.

'All right, snapper – see you around,' Shona said. Terry nodded.

Shona took up her bag and stick and looked for her carriage. She stepped on board.

It was raining now, outside the station. A sheet of rain fell from the pitched roof. Shona watched as Terry stood, half turned. Then she waved, ran a hand through her hair, seemed to laugh and slowly walked away.

Shona found a seat. The train moved on and the grey roofs of Darlington faded away into the rain. She rubbed her damp eyes for a moment and then called her father again. No reply. She looked down at her trainers – they were spattered with mud from Tyrdale. Grains of sand from the riverbank. A tiny green curled leaf, plastered to the side.

Her phone buzzed. It was a text from Bernie: *Got your message. Can you come straight to the allotment as soon as you get back. Your father needs your help. B x*

Shona texted back: *I'll be there. Is everything OK? Have you called the doctor? I'm on the train. I'll be there in 2 hours.*

She shook her head. Outside, the passing fields were soaked with rain.

She called Ranald.

'Good afternoon, scoop,' he said cheerily. 'How's it going?'

'Heading back to Scotland – so, I think I may have something for you. Probably a news feature.'

'Marvellous. Can it make three to four thousand words? We can sell that. Should I approach the weekend magazines? Email me a synopsis and we'll take it from there.'

'Fuck, yeah. Three thousand won't be enough, though. How about thirty?'

'Jeez, Shona, what is this – Watergate?'

'Similar.'

'Tell me more.'

The train sped north. The sky looked clear ahead at the border.

'Well . . . it might be the big one,' she said.

By the time Shona arrived in Edinburgh, she had typed out the structure of her story and emailed it to Ranald. She included a rough transcript of her encounter with Watson. She was not yet sure how to weave in the new details of Daniel's life – his mother, his deranged father who believed the souls of the dead vanish into stones and rock – so she outlined it in a separate section.

She had ordered the story methodically and, unusually for her, used bullet points and bold lettering where it was required. She had hesitated momentarily before clicking the send button. Her finger hovered. Then she pressed it. It whooshed its way to Ranald. The story moved from the entirely secret to the nearly public in one tap.

It was overcast in Edinburgh, but the watchful old city was still resplendent, an opened pop-up book of elegance and shadow. Walkers moved like black dots on the tip of Arthur's Seat.

She took a deep breath. With a solid dread, with a sinking trepidation, she called Viv from the train. But there was no answer.

And then, as the train slowed to a halt under the glassy canopies of Waverley station, her phone buzzed. It was a text from Viv.

Don't ever contact me. I never want to speak to u again. Lose this number.

The train stopped and she sat as passengers moved out of the carriage and into the blaring station, its glasshouse of anxious noise and movement.

As she unsteadily left the train, Shona felt a heaviness move over her and through her. It was too much. She sat on a metal bench on the platform and put her hands to her face. Shona wept. Her shoulders shook. She took deep gasps, racking sobs. She felt a fine lattice of pain spread across her chest.

'Vivienne,' she said to herself – to no one.

The phone buzzed. It was Ranald.

He was shouting, but she couldn't make out the words.

She took a deep breath and wiped her eyes.

'Shona?'

'Hi,' she said, as firmly as she could.

'You okay?'

'Yeah, fine, what is it?'

'Your amazing story!' he yelled.

'Oh, thanks,' she said. She looked around. The platform was empty.

'You must be fucking exhausted. But it's a cracker, an absolute belter. I think I can sell it to one of the big Sundays – one of the London papers. I'm thinking the *Observer* or maybe even the BBC might take it. Run it online as a long-form . . . I take it you taped the interview with that prick?'

'Yes,' she said. 'Of course.'

'He fucking *attacked* you?'

'Yes,' she said.

'Great! I'll need that recording,' he bellowed. 'We'll need to move quickly. A sharp intro, a long lead and let the quotes run. I was thinking maybe do bullet points at the top like you have, get the big lines all spelled out, as it's complex. It's got all these layers, like a puzzle. I'll get someone here to do the background stuff on the missing guy and take in the investigation into the wedding suicide. Do you remember the name of the polis there?'

'Lorimer.'

'Fine, fine. I'll get him on it. Now, I think we need reaction from the Banks family. This shirt and so on. And what I think the right thing to do is inform the police and then get reaction from the family.'

'Yeah,' Shona said, 'I'm on it.'

'I'll get someone else to do that, don't worry. I know you're close to them, so probably not best for you to do that. Unless you think there's an "in" there?'

'No, I don't think there is,' she said.

'Right, okay, well, we can discuss that. Shona, this story's going to be huge. I've got to say – this could bring it all crashing down. On Watson. And there's so many follow-ups . . . There's all the occult stuff, which is probably a story on its own, and the weird stuff with Daniel's father . . .'

'Weird stuff,' she said.

'I'm thinking here . . . maybe we go to a tabloid first? They can sell it hard, make it the splash, and we get a bigger fee. They'll edit your stuff to within an inch of its life, but you'll be fine with that, right?'

'Ranald?'

'Yeah?'

'I need to go right now. Let's talk tomorrow. I need to see Dad.'

'Okay, fine, let's talk tomorrow. And great work, Shona. This is going to take off like a fucking rocket. This is Reporter of the Year stuff.'

'Great. Thanks,' she said and hung up. She began to shake. 'For fuck's sake,' she said, wiping her eyes with the back of her hand. Blowing out air. Pushing back her hair. Straightening up. Another wave of lonely sorrow suddenly broke, and her head dropped.

A passing train guard stopped beside her. 'You all right there, hen?' He looked down with large brown eyes.

'Sure,' she said. 'Sure I am.' Unsteady, she stood up, grabbing her bag and stick, which was spattered with dried mud.

'You need a hand?' he said.

'Thanks, pal. No. Never do,' she said and moved slowly along the platform and through the ticket barrier.

Her phone buzzed again as she walked to the taxi rank on Market Street, where the cabs gleamed like black beetles under the wide arches of North Bridge.

The message was from Bernie: *Come to the allotment as fast as you can.*

Shona swallowed hard and gulped. The train station blared around her. Passengers moved and the tannoy yelled and buzzed. She called Bernie, but again it went to voicemail.

'Fucking hell,' she yelled. No one could hear. People with no faces swilled around the space of metal and glass. The whole wretched world moved around her, uncaring and unhearing. People, intent on catching their train, pushed past her.

She called Stricken.

'Shona!' he yelled. 'Are you coming?'

'Hector.' She tipped her shoulder to let her bag slide onto the pavement. The sun suddenly appeared from behind a bank of clouds.

'Where are you?'

'I'm at Waverley – coming where? What the hell!'

'With everyone else. To your dad's–'

'Hector!'

'What?'

'What the fuck are you on about? Come to Dad's what? What the fuck is happening?'

'Everyone's here – to help your dad.'

'Where? Why does he–'

'At the allotment. To clear it up. Loads of folk are here. Bernie's rounded them all up.'

Shona found a taxi on Market Street. It sped across Princes Street and rattled its way down Leith Walk to the greener north of the city.

Her father's allotment stood in a field of them, huddled by an old railway line. Out of the cab in a hurry, Shona, lugging her bag, her stick rattling, picked her way through the neighbouring allotments to her father's patch of land. A group of people were gathering around the shed.

The allotment was in a state of disarray. The patch of land was overrun with weeds and grass, and canes had tumbled and broken. A container for compost, roughly made from wooden pallets, had collapsed, and the compost had slewed out in a landslide of black sludge. Beside the shed, whose roof was tattered and sagged, was a heap of rubbish: plastic-cased machinery, bulging and ripped green refuse bags and a soggy mound of dead leaves. Huge weeds towered.

As she got closer, she could see her father, in a warm coat with a hood, sitting on a foldable chair. Bernie was addressing the men and women as if she was a captain issuing orders. She was wearing waterproof trousers, her hands in large yellow gardening gloves.

As Shona moved closer, Bernie saw her and gave a quick wave. Her father raised a hand. He looked tired, but his beard was neatly trimmed, and someone had put a green tartan blanket on his knees.

Shona stopped walking. The sun emerged from behind the shuddering grey clouds and glistened on wet wood and soil, on plastic and painted sheds. Exhaustion pulled at her, and she dropped her bag and stick. The directions from Bernie had now been issued, and the crowd were dispersing with much talk and laughter.

'Welcome back, Shona,' Bernie said.

'Just in time!' someone yelled.

Bernie moved towards her, and Shona wondered what might happen. Bernie hugged her. Shona let her. Bernie was small and solid, bundled in layers of warm clothes. She smelled of fresh air. After a moment, she let Shona go.

Then Shona moved to her father and knelt beside him.

'My love,' he said, beaming.

She nodded, not knowing what to say, and what it was to see him alive, again, here in his garden.

'How lovely you're back with me,' he said. 'Look at this. Look what's happening.'

He pointed to the people who had begun to work: weeding, ripping up grass and dandelions and straggling nameless greenery and stuffing it into large refuse bags.

'Wonderful of them, isn't it?' he said.

He peered at her. 'You've been crying. What's happened?'

'Allergies,' she said.

'You don't have any bloody allergies. What's happened?'

'Nothing you need to know.' She stood up to watch the work on the allotment.

'Let me guess: I'll read about it.'

'You will.'

More people were coming down the path to the allotment, their wet raincoats gleaming in the new sun. They were carrying hoes and rakes, garden shears, spades and forks. Others were carrying bags and pushing wheelbarrows. They were moving down the slick duckboards like pilgrims. Bernie greeted them all with smiles and hugs, with handshakes and laughter.

Shona felt tears on her cheek and brushed them away. She felt lighter, even as her neck began to ache.

Hector Stricken, in his bright red anorak, emerged from a group of men fixing the compost heap. 'What a mess, Hugh,' he said, smiling at the old man. 'But nothing that can't be sorted. I think it can be done and dusted in a day or two.'

'I can't thank you enough,' Hugh said.

'Shona, you made it,' Hector said, wiping his hands on his anorak.

'Looks like it,' she said. 'Thanks, Hector. For coming.'

'Did you get your story?'

'Always do,' she said.

He grinned at her. He opened his mouth to ask something but stopped.

'Thanks again,' she said.

'Nae probs,' he said, looking back to the compost heap, where men were dismantling the sodden wooden walls. 'I best get back and help the lads.'

Bernie put the kettle on in the shambolic shed, which was now being emptied and cleared. Out of it came rusted shovels and clippers and two large spades. There were plastic pots and tubs, a broken chair, a strimmer with a frayed lead, broken packets of seeds, eaten by mice or rats, and long bamboo canes. Under the roof were slings of cobwebs, bobbled with egg nests: a woman with a head scarf and determined expression was pulling them away. The whole allotment was moving with people intent on work.

They worked the rest of the short day, and the allotment began to be cleared. Knotty weeds were pulled, and a whole pile of grass, an infestation of marigolds and a brown prickly outcrop of teasels were ripped from the ground. Dandelions were dug up and pulled, oozing white blood from their green veins.

Shona helped where she could, ferrying hot drinks and sandwiches for everyone from a café on Ferry Road, and she held her father and kissed his bald frail head, and the sun began to fade, and the garden was almost clear by the time the shadows of the trees were long and wide over the soil. Shona noticed tiny waxy green buds growing on their branches, glimmering in the falling light.

The last of the helpers were leaving now, but their work remained. It had saved the garden. As they left, some waved; others held single thumbs aloft. They were exhausted and dirty and happy. The men had nodded to Hugh or shaken his hand. Some women had kissed him on the cheek. Others had worked hard and gone without a word. Stricken had hung around for a while and asked Shona about her story – she had said he would have to wait, and he'd read it soon.

Now, Shona stood by the newly tidied shed, exhausted.

'What a wonderful scene. You know, it reminds me of a stained-glass window I saw once,' Bernie said, standing beside her, slipping her hand through Shona's arm. Shona had no energy or desire, any more, to shake it off. They admired the tidied allotment and waved to the last of the helpers, as they slunk off into the twilight.

'Oh, yes? Tell me more. In Edinburgh?' Shona said, looking deeply into the surrounding trees.

'No, love. In a small church, in the North of England. I stayed in this village for a while, after I left the convent. I had no friends. They were all locked away, in my former life. So, I'd go to church.'

'And it's in this church.'

'Yes. It's a beautiful picture. I used to sit and consider it and pray by it. It shows a garden and children and the saints, all in the garden, in the trees, the flowers. There are vines growing, and there's a mother with a baby, and it's all bathed in the most beautiful sunlight. There are gardeners with wide hats, working in the trees, and others are calling in the harvest. There are children – some looking up at the workers, others playing. One child is helping up another who's fallen. The people are working. But living. And loving. It's a beautiful thing. There's a scroll at their feet, with something written across it. Something I think of, often. Especially now, especially since I met your father.'

'And what does it say?'

'It says something religious. You wouldn't approve.'

Shona looked to Bernie, who was looking out at the allotments, their neatness, their messiness and humanity.

A light shower began to fall. The leaves shook in the new rain. The dug earth darkened, and tiny pools formed in the folds of the plastic refuse bags and the new tarpaulin that temporarily covered the roof of the shed.

Shona moved over to her father. He was sitting in his low chair, staring at his new, tidy garden, and she pulled up his hood.

He was still with her. Still alive with her. She looked across to Bernie, who was standing with hands folded, observing the daughter and her father.

'Tell me then, what did this window say?' Shona said.

'No, you wouldn't see anything in it,' Bernie said softly.

'Try me,' Shona said.

'Go on, love,' Hugh said to Bernie. 'Tell her.'

'It says, my love: *Of Such Work, Is the Kingdom of Heaven.*'

35

It was a new day. Karl needed a walk. He wanted to walk to the ends of the earth. He wanted to walk into the sunlight. He wanted to walk through a portal in the trees and step into new light.

Bev had left for work, in a flurry of exhortations and jangling keys.

He had been up half the night. She had slept like the dead, while he had spent hours on his computer, on social media, on the internet, searching. But there had been no stories about missing people or men in black with knives. There was nothing. No missing men. No swordsmen in the dale. If he didn't have the bruises on his hands, from the solid shock of the axe blade on a man's very real skull, he could have dreamed the entire killing.

He walked on, tramping down the track that led through his village and along to the river.

It was early yet. The farmers were up, he knew, but they rose as the sun rose. Spring was coming, the earth was tingling with it, but it had not yet arrived. The buds were closed on the branches, and although some eager daffodils were beginning to shake in the open spaces, and flowering weeds glimmered in the open meadow, the trees were still bare.

He reached the old river. He stopped at the shingle shoreline. The Tyr was wide and quiet here, the water brown, dark as beer, and deep, with drifting bubbles and lumps of yellow foam on the far side. The trees were tall and ancient, and their lower boughs hung heavy, skimming the water that slid by their still branches.

Karl wondered if now, as a murderer, as a slaughterer of men, he could live in this peace. Now, as a murderer, he thought he should run away, leave the hills, hide himself in a city. He could find a cold room above a shabby shop in a backstreet and live an anonymous life. He could change his name, walk the streets at night, watch his reflection shattered in the oily puddles pockmarking the scarred roads. Live in the stench of it all, his own sinful stink unnoticed.

But here, by this ancient river, under this sky, the idea of life in a city seemed unreal. Nothing was as real as what lay before him: the moving water, the growing wood, the earth alive.

This was the puzzle, Karl thought. The city does not care for you and can break you. It constantly changes, but there are comforts to be bought and attended to. The country does not care for you and cannot be changed, unless it is destroyed by men. But it can comfort you with its silence, with its beauty, with the peace of the seasons and the soft silent nights.

Karl walked on. After a time, he stopped and looked at his phone. Nothing from Beverley. The world turned on, with or without his presence. It didn't matter.

The sun was reflected on the slowly surging water, and the trees imperceptibly lifted their limbs to the heat. By the river there were small cliffs overhung with ferns and grass. White roots twisting from exposed slabs of rock. In the low hollows, in the wet mud still, there were hoof prints.

Karl wondered if he should keep walking downstream, away from his village, away from the buried man with the smashed face, into the depth of the valley. He trudged on. Birds were singing their mad songs. The woods deepened, and pools of shadow lay unmoving in the depths.

He decided to walk to the Coine Tree. It was a mile downstream, and from there he could walk to a nearby village and catch the bus home.

He came to an old black-and-white iron sign pointing

downstream to ULLATHORNE 7 MILES, or east to THE FAMED COINE TREE ½ MILE.

Karl was about to cut inland. Before he left the river behind, he stopped to look at it again. Below him, beneath an overhanging rock thick with moss, was a narrow beach. He and Bev had picnicked there many times, lit a fire, smoked and kissed. There were good, flat, skimming pebbles there. On a good day, with a whip of his arm, he could skim one and reach the other side. A swift white trail of skimming kisses across the water. It was a good beach.

He moved to the edge and looked down. Caught up on the flat exposed rocks near the river's edge was a white body. A slump of dead flesh, chewed and spat out by waterfall, rapids and river. The body was half naked. Things were amiss: one leg was bent cruelly back, folded against the back, its knee bulbous and grotesque. One of its arms was missing. Instead, there was the gape of an opened shoulder, dark red and purple sinews held loosely inside. It had a battered pulpy head like a large rotting apple and an open mouth smashed of its teeth. A single eye, red and open, stared.

Karl felt sick.

The sunlight shifted, dappling through the river's moving surface, bleeding a stream of light across the chest of the man. It illuminated the script inscribed on the twisted body, in a vivid black tattoo: the letters of the alphabet, numbers from 0 to 9, Yes, No, Hello, Goodbye, the sun and the moon.

Karl found himself on his knees. He waited until he was breathing steadily again, then he reached for his phone and called the police.

Days later, miles south of the River Tyr, in the never-ending purring hum of London, Alison Harmire lay in bed, pale under the tawny light of the city, her children asleep.

They lay on either side of her in their pyjamas, breathing heavily. She moved a damp lock of hair from her son's forehead, his closed eyes as smooth as shells. His tears had dried.

The house was empty now; Nigel had packed his cases and finally gone. She moved her daughter's head and arm from her chest and slid out of the bed. She padded across the room. The wardrobe was still open, with Nigel's rails cleared. She slid it shut.

She looked back briefly to her sleeping children as she moved through the dark of the hall to the stairs.

The lights in the white kitchen glowed from copper pans and neatly arranged pots, a bowl of luminous lemons and the clutched petals of flowers in vases. She moved past them all, into her study. She flicked on a lamp and sat at her desk. The blinds were drawn. The room flashed briefly with the yellow flare of a passing car.

She pulled the scroll of laminated plastic from under her desk. Printed neatly on one side were the letters of the alphabet, Yes, No, Hello, Goodbye, the sun and the moon, and the numbers 0 to 9.

Alison took the small shot glass. She had stolen it from the Lion thirty years ago. She placed it carefully in the centre of the board. She waited for it to answer, as it always had, all these years. Advice, confusion, shattered poetry and a psalter of repeated phrases. Mantras for life from the board of the dead.

But, this night, the glass did not move. It stood dead under her finger. Sorley was gone. From the land of the dead to nothingness. There would be no more. Alison sat back in her chair and rubbed her eyes.

She was alone, again.

East of Alison Harmire's house, in the shadow of the House of Commons, Knott was leaning on the stone parapet of a bridge. The Thames flowed thick and strong underneath. It had been a long day. He pulled his collar up. The streetlamp's fragile light was lengthened and torn by the moving waters below.

Knott's phone buzzed with a message. He walked along the bridge, and a black car pulled up by the Westminster security gate. He stepped into it.

A blonde woman sat on the back seat in a grey suit, neat as a pin. Next to her, a crumple-faced old man in smart country clothes. Raymond. Opposite them, Alyce sat, deep in a phone conversation.

'Mr Knott, good evening,' Raymond said.

'How do . . . Alyce.'

Alyce looked up, her violet eyes flashing in the city lights.

The car was gliding through the stuttering London traffic, past Westminster Abbey, wending its way to the airport for a brief journey north.

'You will know Sally,' Raymond said, opening a hand towards the woman with blonde hair.

The woman nodded to Knott.

'Of course,' Knott said. 'Seen her on the telly.'

The woman smiled and looked out of the window to the smear of light and darkness outside. The immensity of it all.

'The new candidate for Tyrdale, Mr Knott,' Raymond said, gently reproving.

'So I've seen,' Knott said.

'You know Alyce, of course. She'll be Sally's principal support. I'm assuming you've seen what has been reported about our former colleague,' Raymond said evenly.

Knott shrugged. 'Sad,' he said.

'Tragedy,' Alyce said.

'Most unfortunate,' Sally said.

'Indeed,' Raymond added, patting Sally's knee. 'Well, he can join his wife at last – which, I think we can agree, is some kind of justice. So, that is the end of that story. But not for us. We remain. And continue.'

Karl and Bev had lit the new fire pit in their back garden. Karl had laid paving stones and a heavy metal basin over the freshly turned soil. Now, the flames flickered and spat with green wood, dancing in the gathering twilight. Karl was strumming a guitar.

A recent newspaper, gently rippling in the evening breeze, lay beside Bev, its headline: *Gary Watson MP Found Dead in River Tyr*.

She took the front page from the paper, scrunched it into a loose ball and tossed it into the warming fire. She put her head on Karl's shoulder, and he stopped strumming and put his arm around her, and they watched the flames consume it all.

In the fire, Watson's face blackened and shrivelled and then collapsed, lost in a sudden flaring gout of green flame.

Karl took up his guitar again and picked out a new tune.

'I'm sorry, love,' she said, at last.

'Don't worry. It's nowt,' he said, over the chords. 'Don't worry.'

Bev gently hummed along to his sweet melancholy melody and looked past the dancing fire and out over the garden fence to the old moor. Her sight rested on the old stones on the high hills. They, at least, would remain.

Until all the days were no more.

In Ullathorne, Ashley was in her room, her face lit silver by the laptop screen. A cursor pulsed at the end of a sentence. She did not know what would come next.

She was trying to write, her mind drifting in and out of concentration. She wrote as best she could: her left hand fully in control, a single finger ready to type on her closed right hand. She had removed all distractions. She had turned her music off and switched off the router in the hall, but her mind was flitting and flyting.

Ashley sighed and slapped the laptop shut. Her mother had left her a list of chores, and she wanted them done by the time she got back. She was out, seeing to something that needed done, she said. Off to see the cops, she said, about the football jersey. Now that Alison had gone back down to London.

Ashley walked into the room where the Glaswegian reporter had stayed. It had not been cleaned. It was unkempt and lank with the sadness of abandonment. She began slowly stripping the bed. There were two used mugs on the sideboard, with cold coffee congealed in small pools. A single black-and-silver sock lay forgotten on the carpet.

There was a small, polished pebble on the side by the night light. Ashley picked it up. It was as smooth as an eye. It had a stripe of paler rock within. She put it in her pocket.

Then she noticed a note ripped from a pad which had been dropped under the bed. Its curled edge was in sight. She picked it up. It was scribbled in a mix of shorthand and longhand, in a pen that was low on ink.

Ashley could not understand the shorthand marks, a series of half-letters and swooshes, of dots and contractions. It seemed to be another language entirely. But at the bottom of the note, beside a large asterisk and a doodle of a heart, Shona had written a message to herself.

Call V.

Ashley took the note, crumpled it up, threw it in a bin bag and stood up with a sigh.

She stripped the bed, hoovered the carpet and wiped the surfaces. It now looked tidy and ready for another visitor: an empty room, waiting for another person to arrive, inhabit and depart.

Shona Sandison had left no mark. It was as if she had never been there at all.

Inspector Benedict Reculver's apartment was filled with light on a quiet Sunday morning.

The clear sunlight fell on the silver frames of the paintings in lancing gleams and lay warm on the sleek surfaces of his lean furniture. In the bathroom, a man was showering. He was singing a sad French song.

Reculver, in a loose green silk robe, elaborate dragons swimming about his limbs, rubbed his face and smiled. He was sitting on his sofa, reading the Sunday papers. They had been left on his doormat earlier, their many supplements slithering away from the paper in a glossy coiled pile.

He knew Gary Watson MP had been found dead in a river: it had led the BBC news for two days, and his colleagues in the North of England had been in touch.

He imagined journalists from all newspapers now descending on Tyrdale to cover the story, to dig out their own information, to interview the locals, to find new lines and fresh takes. But Shona Sandison had them all – that story was written. She had the whole story and, it seemed, all the follow-up tales, too. She had not named several sources. Some of Watson's school friends were quoted but left anonymous. Reculver raised an eyebrow: he wondered why.

One tabloid had given over its front page to her story, as well as several pages inside. Shona's fingers must be several millimetres shorter, Reculver mused. Her boss at the Buried Lede had clearly struck a good deal with the paper, even if all the subtleties and ambiguities of what Shona had discovered had been hacked and mauled into a brutal tabloid style. He read it again:

DEATH MP 'MURDER' LINK SHOCK
EXCLUSIVE: MYSTERY OF LOST BOY AND
DROWNED WATSON

GARY Watson, the controversial MP found dead this week, can be linked to the suspected murder of a former school friend thirty years ago, we can sensationally reveal.

The mutilated body of Watson, 49, found in the River Tyr, County Durham, the day after the launch of his re-election bid, has thrown the general election campaign into chaos.

Today we reveal a shocking hidden life which would have derailed Watson's career if he had not mysteriously fallen to his death.

An Exclusive Investigation by award-winning reporter SHONA SANDISON can reveal:

- *The* sinister links *between Watson and the tragic disappearance of school friend Andrews Banks in* 1992.
- New evidence *linked to vanished Banks has been* handed to cops *after being found in recent weeks.*
- *How the outspoken* populist MP attacked *our reporter after being confronted at his fiery campaign launch hours before his death.*
- *The* occult teenage gang *in which Watson was a key* member.
- *The* mysterious murder *of his ex-Army school friend.*
- *The* shocking suicide *at a Scottish wedding linked to* Watson's *bizarre obsession with* Ouija boards.

The story continued on pages two, three, four and five inside. In the magazine supplement, there was an illustrated profile of Watson and a brief colour piece on Tyrdale, also penned by Sandison.

Reculver looked up. His friend, a white towel tied tight around his slick torso, had brought him an espresso in a fine china cup. An amaretti biscuit had been placed on the saucer.

'*Merci beaucoup*,' Reculver said and returned to his reading. The colour piece was illustrated with luminous photography:

> At the heart of the valley of the River Tyr is an ancient giant. They call it the Coine Tree.
>
> Few people from outside the valley know of it. Tyrdale and its market town of Ullathorne are better known for their natural beauty, with tourists flocking to the pretty town to view its ruined castle and walk in the idyllic glades of woodland beside its famous river. But at the dark green centre of those ancient woods is that tree – said to be the oldest in England. Some say it is the biggest, too. The monstrous tree has been standing deep in the valley's native woodland for three thousand years. It stands as an ancient, silent witness.
>
> What has this wordless giant seen? A long, troubled span of human time. It has seen the people of Tyrdale emerge from the dark green prehistorical world, from the era of clans and tribes and pagan belief to the Roman Empire and the coming of Christianity. It has seen the people of the dale overcome the brutalities of Norman invasion and feudal rule, the ravages of plague and cholera, the devastating disruptions of the Industrial Revolution, the loss and sorrow of two world wars and the social and economic revolutions of the twentieth century.
>
> In all this time, it has gripped the same parcel of soil and stone not far from the ancient River Tyr. It has endured and grown imperceptibly while generations of humans have been born, lived and died. Both hollow and alive, the tree will stand long after the grim story of Gary Watson and his troubled school friends has been long forgotten.

Looking back on my days investigating this story in Ullathorne, it is tempting to see this deeply impressive, unmoving but living thing as a powerful symbol of all that has been discovered.

Like the branches and trunk and leaves of the ancient tree, parts of the story exist in the world of the visible: the disappearance of Banks in 1992, the rise of Watson to fame and success, and then the very public death of Daniel Merrygill.

But this tree also exists in the world of the unseen. Just as the Coine Tree's roots plunge unseen into the rock and soil of the ancient dale, so do the roots of this tragic story. So much is still unclear, and so much is subterranean. Banks's body has never been found. The reasons for his disappearance and likely death remain unknown. And the occult shadows that drove Merrygill to his untimely end, and which clearly engulfed that small group of Tyrdale teenagers in the early 1990s, remain largely unknowable – and may remain so for ever . . .

'Breakfast?' a voice called from Reculver's echoing kitchen.

Reculver bellowed an agreement and stood up, dropping the paper on his coffee table. He reached for his personal phone, which lay on the marble mantelpiece.

He looked down at the paper: the paper had wrung the story for all it was worth. Above the newspaper title, it boasted: LOST LEADER: WHICH MINISTRY WAS SET ASIDE FOR GARY WATSON? *Page 9 for insight* and another puff said: WHERE NOW FOR PM'S NORTHERN STRATEGY? *Comment section.*

His thumbs moved over the phone's black screen.

Bravo! he texted Shona.

He looked at his screen for a moment and then put it down. There was no reply, and he suspected there would not be one for several days.

In the kitchen, an egg was cracked onto a sizzling pan and moved from slick translucent liquid to the firm and the white and the edible.

goodbye

Shona Sandison took a long, slow walk in the gentle sunshine. Spring had finally arrived in Edinburgh, and a field of daffodils blazed beside her. She paused to sit on a bench in Victoria Park, a grassy acre of tree-lined pathways between the traffic burr of Ferry Road and the pretty harbour at Newhaven. She lay her stick beside her.

A small blue coffee van, smooth and neat like a beetle, was serving coffee to tired parents and dog walkers. In the playground, children in raincoats clambered over a large colourful climbing frame. In the unlikely warmth, some skinny teenagers were throwing around a basketball on the nearby fenced court.

The BBC had been leading on her story in the Sunday paper and was running news bulletins on the links between the death of Watson and the human wreckage of Tyrdale.

Ranald had already been asked by Durham police to hand over the audio file of Shona's interview with the late MP.

The prime minister was beginning to be asked questions about how well he knew Watson, what he knew and when he knew it. It was disrupting his election campaign. There was a chance that her story would begin to dominate the news cycle. Ranald told her that a young woman from Spennymoor in the North East of England had made a five-figure deal with a rival tabloid, claiming to be Watson's lover.

Terry's photographs were everywhere – expertly taken in the heat of the moment and pin-sharp. One of them showed the MP grasping Shona by her neck. Shona's face was blank, her eyes wide. Her stick was visible on the floor. Watson's grim shiny face was a tangled root of hatred. It was believed to be the last photo of him alive.

Reculver had texted her, but she was ignoring him, for now. It felt like work. Her phone buzzed again. It was a text from Stricken: *Your stuff is bloody everywhere! Beautiful job, pal!*

It's been emotional, she texted back. The sun flashed on her phone screen. A little brown dog with a face like an otter ran up to her feet, snuffled at her stick and sprinted off again.

More to come?

Not from me. I'm done.

Another text zipped to her phone. *What about that poor guy at the funeral?*

Despair, shit parents and guilt, she tapped back. She knew Daniel's death was more complicated than that. More than she could probably ever sensibly explain.

Why do you think Watson ended up in the river? Stricken texted.

Who knows? Cops found enough drugs in his body to kill a horse. But we might never know. Speak later.

The sky was vast above her. Her mind felt empty, her body washed out. She looked to the stones in the path and wondered what they contained. She looked up, to the canopy of reviving trees.

She leaned on her stick and watched a group of children swing back and forth on a large circular swing. Three boys and three girls giggled and laughed in their multicoloured clothes. One boy urged them all to stand up on the swing, to grip the chains. They stood up, and the boy huffed and puffed, his pale hair distraught, and pushed his friends forward. They slowly moved, a pendulum full of young souls, into the air before them, and with yelps of joy, they swung back. The boy pushed again, harder.

Shona smiled. Some adults walked slowly over to the swing, shaking their heads and wagging fingers. The aroma of coffee and hot chocolate steamed from the van. The sun glittered on grass and gravel, on stones and the sea of new leaves, the refreshed grass.

Shona reached into her bag. There was an envelope of photographs, retrieved from the chemists. Newly developed, but the pictures were old. Analogue, fuzzy, splodged with orange light. Several were darkened with the shadow of a thumb across the lens. Other pictures had been destroyed by time or had never been good in the first place – empty frames or hazy, formless.

The photographs had been taken by Daniel Merrygill, in the summer of 1992. The first few showed teenagers sitting in school playing fields, squinting into the sun, neat in their last-day uniforms.

She flipped through the rest. There was some lad with floppy blond hair giving the photographer the finger. A girl looking shyly from behind a curtain of black hair. Some boys in short sleeves, bending their elbows over a pool table in a dark, wood-lined pub.

She pulled one picture out. She had asked for a copy to be printed in a larger format. It showed all the friends sitting closely together on a grassy incline. The sky was blue above them, unsullied, framing their faces. They had big hair, bright eyes, ready smiles. Their last summer together, on the precipice of unforeseen loss and change.

Young Beverley was wearing a tie-dyed T-shirt, a garish rainbow of colours at odds with her blue school skirt. Peg was neat, holding a hand to her eyes. Resting his head on Peg's shoulder was a big lad with shaved hair and shiny new boots – Bobby. Next in line, sitting on a tree stump, was Alison, serious, her legs crossed, a cigarette unlit in her left hand. Beside her, beaming, was Andrew Banks. He was slim and handsome, with long hair down past his ears. His large, beautiful eyes were wide open, his eyebrows arching, as if he was surprised, as if he was delighted.

And close to him, his arms in the air, celebrating or signalling, knelt the young Gary Watson. His mouth was open, saying something now lost and unrecorded, his eyes squinting, his hair cropped and sharp. He wore white jeans, with a tucked-in white T-shirt. On his belt, there was a small leather sheath which held a folded penknife, and around his open neck, a necklace of white beads. And out of sight, the taker of the photograph – Daniel Merrygill. A young man, already broken.

Shona's phone buzzed again. It was probably Stricken again, or possibly Ranald, excited about some new legal development. It felt like her editor had been calling her hourly for days.

She put the phone to her ear without checking who it was. 'Aye, what now?'

There was a long silence. Shona looked down at the photograph in her hand. Young Andrew, beaming, with only days to live in his life.

'Hello?'

'Hello to you, too,' Viv said, at last.

'Vivienne,' Shona said.

'Who else would it be?'

Shona felt suspended in the air. Her body felt adrift from her mind.

'I've seen what you did,' Viv said. Shona nodded, as if Viv could see her. 'And what you've written. The cops called Mam last night. They had a long chat. Nice woman from the Durham cops. There's talk of digging up Deepdale – to see.'

'Okay, that's good,' Shona said.

'Mam's been asked to identify an item of clothing – the shirt you wrote about.'

'That makes sense,' Shona said. She said it as gently as she could.

'I think it's Andrew's,' Viv said. There was a short silence. 'I've been busy. Dan's funeral. They've released the body.'

'Ah, right.'

'It's a quiet one, at the crematorium,' Viv said.

'That's good you're doing it,' Shona said. 'That's kind of you.'

'Aye, well,' Viv said, 'I can invite his old man now, since you've found him. We've been trying to prise his mam out of that care home.'

Andrew's printed eyes in Shona's hands were gleaming. Daniel, poor, pale broken Daniel, was in her hands, too. He had made the pictures; he was the author of these memories. But he was unseen.

'So, can you meet me for a drink?' said Viv suddenly.

'All right. But only if you're paying,' Shona said. 'Tap into that wee windfall of yours.'

Viv didn't respond. Shona winced and bit her lip. She looked to the canopy of trees above her. Birds in formation leapt from the branches and skimmed to the empty sky.

'You've some cheek, Shona fucking Sandison,' Viv said softly.

'But isn't that why you love me?'

Viv seemed to suck her teeth. Then she gave a laugh. 'I guess so.'

'So, a drink, then?'

'Yes. Life's too short, Shona.'

'It is,' Shona Sandison said. 'Far too short.'

Acknowledgements

With much gratitude to my friends and early readers: Simon Stuart, Allan Donald, Freya Davison and Callum Smith. With great thanks to Alison Rae and Taz Urnov for their faith and trust, and to Robbie Guillory for his guidance. And with love to Hope: for everything.